Praise for the Novels of Anna Jeffrey

Lone Star Woman

"A story about a woman with brains and spirit, Lone Star Woman delivers a powerful punch.... a book overflowing with romance and sensuality."—*Kimberly, Coffee Time Romar*

Sweet Return

"...Great characters who worm there way into [illegible] love story - well worth a trip to the bookstore."—*Lisa Gardineer, All About Romance*

"Anna Jeffrey shows she is a master at writing a Texas tale that is not only enjoyable, but authentic as well. This one should not be missed." —Scarlet. www.romancejunkies.com

Salvation, Texas

"Anna Jeffrey continues to demonstrate her spectacular storytelling talents. ...A first-class romantic suspense tale." —*Affaire de Couer*

"[E]xciting...Readers will enjoy Anna Jeffrey's fine thriller." —*Midwest Book Reviews*

"A good solid read, with great characters and a fast-paced plot. Do yourself a favor and pick it up, and while you are at it, clear your plans for the evening!" —*Romance Reader at Heart*

Sweet Water

"Jeffrey mixes just the right amounts of soft, sweet, and funny, making Agua Dulce hard to resist." —*Detroit Free Press*

"Sweet Water"...is filled with wonderfully complex characters whose personalities are gradually revealed. There are no easy answers for any of them, but the ones they find are mostly happy and satisfyingly realistic. A pleasurable read!" —*Romantic Times*

"Sexy, tender...romantic doesn't begin to describe how wonderful this story is." —*Romance Junkies*

The Love of a Lawman

"Real characters come to life in this heart-wrenching tale littered with imperfect characters readers come to love and root for." —*Rendezvous*

"If you like well-written character-driven romances…with engaging characters and lots of internal conflict, I highly recommend *The Love of a Lawman*." —*Romance Reviews Today*

The Love of a Stranger

"Delicious…a riveting read." —*Publishers Weekly*

"Fun…a delightful solid novel." —*Midwest Book Reviews*

The Love of a Cowboy

"This book is on fire! Intense, romantic, and fiercely tender….An authentic and powerful love story."
—*Joan Johnston, New York Times* Bestselling Author

"Anna Jeffrey delivers a big, bold and passionate story of second chances and starting over. Curl up and enjoy!"
—*Susan Wiggs, New York Times* Bestselling Author

"Anna Jeffrey's…novel, *The Love of a Cowboy*, is a welcome rarity in contemporary because its hero and heroine are kept apart by real obstacles." —*Romantic Times*

"Anna Jeffrey has penned a passionate story of unconditional love and second chances. I highly recommend this book because I could not put it down." —*Romance Fiction Guide*

ALSO BY ANNA JEFFREY

Miranda's Chronicles
Desired

The Sons of Texas
The Cattleman
The Tycoon

The Strayhorns
Man of the West (w/a Sadie Callahan)
Lone Star Woman

The West Texas Books
Sweet Water
Salvation, Texas
Sweet Return

The Callister Books
The Love of a Lawman
The Love of a Stranger
The Love of a Cowboy

THE TYCOON

ANNA JEFFREY

Cover and book design by THE KILLION GROUP
www.thekilliongroupinc.com

ACKNOWLEDGEMENTS

I would never have finished this book had it not been for my friend and critique partner, Laura Renken, who writes historical romances as Melody Thomas. Thank you for your support and patience, Laura.

Chapter One

Bill Cody Arena, Amarillo, Texas
2005

DRAKE LOCKHART WAS freezing his ass off. February was not the ideal month to visit Amarillo, Texas, or to sit in a cold arena watching one cutting horse performance after another. His younger half-brother, Troy Rattigan, had asked him to come and the kid looked up to him. No way would Drake disappoint him by not being here. Troy had trained a horse that would be competing in the world cutting horse finals later in the year, so Drake had taken time out of a busy schedule to see him and his mare show their stuff.

In truth, Drake was in no mood for frivolous undertakings today, even something he enjoyed as much as cutting horse shows. He had come to Amarillo to parley. His mind was on money and leases for hundreds of electricity-producing wind turbines to be constructed on one of his family's cotton farms between Amarillo and Lubbock. Now and for years to come, the long-term leases would add much-needed cash to the coffers of the Double Bar L Cattle Company—better known in North Texas as the Double-Barrel Ranch. Negotiations had gone well and firm commitments from a large electricity supplier would be forthcoming.

The second reason for his visit hadn't gone so well. He had met with an engineering company, exploring the possibility of investing his family's money in the manufacture and construction of wind turbines. A deal could be worth millions to the Lockhart family and jobs for the local area. An issue that defied common sense had popped up and Drake had backed off, but he hadn't given up. With the scent of money in his nostrils, he wouldn't let one small setback kill a deal. Issues could be resolved. He was nothing if not determined.

While he waited for an announcement of Troy and his horse's names, he sat with one boot resting on the back of the seat in front of him, absorbing familiar pungent animal smells ever present in horse competitions. A pouty-mouthed blonde a few seats away gave him another come-hither smile. She had been sending signals ever since they had first made eye contact. She was something to look at. Tall as a tree and hair the color of honey. It fell like a golden waterfall all the way to her ass. Long legs encased by jeans that fit like a coat of paint were stuffed into the knee-high shafts of fancy boots. Above that, she wore a woolly vest over a bright pink sweater that all but advertised tits the size of melons. Any fool could see this babe's game was not horses.

Just then, Troy's name on the loud speaker caught Drake's ear and he turned his attention back to the activity in the arena. Troy and his mare, My Peppy Girl, entered and approached a herd of calves bunched in the arena's business end. Drake recognized when the calf was selected. He leaned forward, watching intently as the mare separated it from the herd, then wheeled right and left on powerful haunches, preventing its return.

A fine cutting horse in top form and a superior rider were a joy to behold. My Peppy Girl was a shiny bay, small for a quarter horse and agile as a cat. The kid sat deep in the saddle, looking as relaxed as if he were in a rocking chair. He and Troy his horse performed as if they were one unit. Troy should be good. He had been horseback since he was eight years old and he had an instinct about horses.

The nearly flawless performance ended with a high score and Troy and My Peppy Girl still in the finals. Drake's mood improved.

Drake left his seat and made his way to the stalls behind the arena. Finding Troy and the mare, he raised a palm for a high-five. "Good job, Little Brother."

"Hey, Drake." His coffee-brown eyes dancing, Troy slapped his hand enthusiastically. "Girl's in top shape. You saw us? I figured you'd be too busy to come."

Drake stuffed his hands into his jeans pockets and scrunched his shoulders against the cold. "I wouldn't miss my little brother's performance as a champion. Girl looks great, kid."

"We're going again tomorrow in the finals."

Drake gave him a thumbs up. "Good job."

"Listen Drake, I got an offer on Girl. Can we—"

"Oh, Troy." A hot little brunette in tight jeans, pink boots and a thick coat suddenly appeared. She grasped Troy's forearm with both hands and made a little bounce on the balls of her feet. "That was so amazing!" She looked up at him with huge and adoring brown eyes. "You're so wonderful."

She cupped his neck with manicured and be-ringed fingers, pulled his head down for a sloppy kiss and Troy openly melted. Drake grinned. Even at twenty-one, his little brother had a reputation with women that equaled his standing as a horse trainer. He also had a room at the Holiday Inn just minutes away. Without a doubt, the kid was in for a rollicking good time tonight. And why not? He was smart, able-bodied and hard-working. He had earned a good time.

"I'll catch you later, Troy," Drake told him. "I'm going home early tomorrow. I'll miss your ride in the finals, but I'll be pulling for you. When you get back to Drinkwell, we'll get together and talk about the offer on your horse." He liked that Troy valued his opinion.

"Right," Troy replied, now more interested in the girl hanging all over him than the potential sale of his mare.

Drake, too, had a room at the Holiday Inn and no one to share it with. Having no steady female companion at the moment, he hadn't indulged his primal urges in weeks. He beelined for the willowy blonde.

Minutes later, he knew for sure she was neither cowgirl nor horse owner or trainer. She barely knew one end of the animal from the other. Her name was Gretchen Something from somewhere in Sweden. While her politician father schmoozed in Washington, she had come to Texas to visit a friend who had brought her to the cutting horse show to meet "big, rich cowboys."

Drake met both of those criteria. A short time later, he had a bottle of Jack Daniel's in a brown paper sack and he and Gretchen were on the way to his room. She liked cutting to the chase. So did he. All of that let's-get-acquainted bullshit was a waste of time. And if there was anything Drake had not nearly enough of, it was time.

He had no sooner shut the hotel room door, locked it and bolted it before she backed him against the door. She unzipped his jeans, slid her long fingers inside his shorts and stroked him with her fingertips. "Oohh, I like you are big. Hmm."

His erection turned to blue steel. He gave a low groan.

"And you are very hot," she said breathily.

"You're not kidding." He pushed away from the door and yanked off his coat.

A few minutes later, he had rid her of her boots, jeans, that woolly vest and tight sweater, leaving her wearing only a pink lacy bra and a tiny pink thong.

While he unbuttoned his cuffs, she quickly disposed of the wisps of underwear. Without inhibition, she struck a pose and let him drink in her nearly perfect body. He almost drooled. She was tanned to golden all over and waxed in strategic places. Why women did that to themselves he didn't know. It had to hurt. "Awesome," he mumbled.

He hadn't finished unbuttoning his shirt before she was on him like a hungry tigress, pushing her tongue into his mouth. He urged her backward toward the king-size bed. Together they fell onto the mattress, landing with a bounce. She rose to her knees and straddled him, then licked and nipped her way south. Evidently she didn't intend to stop with his mouth.

Just then, his BlackBerry warbled from the bedside table. He turned his head and stared at it, as if a stern look could cause him to divine the caller's name. He had too much money at stake and too much going on both here and back in Fort Worth to ignore a call on his business cell phone. "Shit. I've got to get that."

He leaned to his side, propped himself on his elbow and reached for the phone. Caller ID said Kate. His baby sister. *Uh-oh.* Personal calls didn't usually come on his BlackBerry.

Gretchen Something crawled behind him and pressed her hot tits against his back. She reached around him and played with the happy trail on his belly.

He pulled himself together and tried to sound as if he hadn't been running a marathon. "Hey, baby," he said into the phone.

Breath-hitching sobs came at him from the other end of the line. His gut kinked, his erection shrank. He pushed Gretchen's hand away, swung his feet to the floor and sat up. "Kate. Baby, what wrong?"

She launched an effusive speech, but it was no more coherent than the Swedish that came out of Gretchen's mouth.

He leaned forward and braced his elbow on his thigh. "Calm down, sweetheart. And tell me what's wrong."

She gasped and sniffled until her words came more clearly. "It's Mama and Daddy, Drake. They had this big fight and Mama's moving out."

Drake frowned. "She's what?"

"She's moving. Away from the ranch."

Jee-zus Christ. His parents, the king and queen of melodrama, were no strangers to loud, cussing brawls. "Why now? It's not like she hasn't been pissed off at him before."

"But it's different this time. She went to town to get her hair done and she heard the women in the beauty shop talking about Daddy sleeping with Marilyn Bilberry. You know how much Mama hates her." Kate began to cry and her voice began to hitch again. "Mama says that's the...the last straw. She's through...with him."

"Calm down, sweetheart," Drake said again, closing his eyes and rubbing his forehead with his fingers. "I can't understand what you're saying when you're so upset."

Kate regained control of her voice. "She told Daddy she hopes he doesn't forget that she raised his bastard son, because it's the last thing she'll ever do for him. Oh, Drake, I'm just glad Troy wasn't here to hear her say such a mean thing about him."

Drake and his siblings never thought of Troy as a bastard, although that was, in fact, what he was. "She's just pissed off again, right? She doesn't mean it."

"Yes, she does, Drake. She's bought this big house in Oakwood in Fort Worth. Nobody even knew she'd done it. She's been sleep—sleep...Oh, Drake, she's been dating some real estate agent up there."

Drake's eyes popped wide. His mother sleeping with somebody? Dating? He couldn't imagine it. Not even with his dad, although they had three kids. Drake got to his feet, cradled the phone against his shoulder and yanked on his jeans. "Where's Dad now?"

"At his desk in his office. He's got a bottle of Wild Turkey and his forty-five. A moving van came and picked up most of our furniture and he shot half the tires. Then he threatened to shoot the driver and Mama both." She broke into sobs again. "Now—now he says he's go—going to shoot himself."

Drake had been refereeing his parents' upheavals since he was a teenager, had largely become immune to them. This one didn't sound much different from some of the others. He picked up his shirt and stuffed his arms into the sleeves. "He didn't hurt anybody, did he?"

"No. But he scared that poor van driver and his helper to death. And now their big truck's stuck in the driveway. Mama took them to town to get the sheriff and somebody to work on their truck. The driver wants Daddy arrested, Drake. He says his company will bring charges against him."

Drake wasn't worried about Bill Lockhart Junior being arrested in Treadway County, nor about charges being brought against him. The sheriff knew who had handed him his election to office. While an arrest might be unlikely, the thought of the possibility still brought a new knot to Drake's gut. He stuffed in his shirttail and zipped up. "Are you there all by yourself? I assume Pic's taken a powder."

Since Drake had moved to Fort Worth, conflict resolution had been left to Pic, Drake's younger brother who was a peace-loving guy. More often than not, he handled the various eruptions by getting into his truck, driving to town and staying at some girlfriend's house until the tempest passed.

"He's here." Kate sobbed again. "He's scared Daddy really might do something crazy....And Jordan's here."

Shit. Drake's jaw clenched. "Kate, stop crying. What's Jordan Palmer doing there?"

"I ca—called him...and he came down...from Fort Worth."

Jordan Palmer would slit his own mother's throat for a dollar. Drake had to get to the ranch. "Palmer has no business being there. This is a family matter."

"He's my fiancé, Drake. He practically *is* family."

Drake rolled his eyes. He had never figured out his little sister's attraction to a flakey tinhorn ten years older than she was. She had met him hanging out with the cutting horse crowd. Drake was surprised Pic or Dad hadn't already run his ass off. "Okay, okay, but—"

"You can come home, can't you? Mama always listens to you. And the sheriff will listen to you, too."

His siblings had always said he was their mother's pet. Indeed, his relationship with her was different from theirs. Being the oldest, he was also the reluctant family arbiter and he'd had conversations with the sheriff before. "I'm on my way, Kate. The weather's a mess, but I think we can still fly out of here. I'll have to find my pilot. I'll call you back if he says we can't."

He disconnected, dropped the phone on the bed and worked on his cuff buttons. His companion, posed on the bed with one knee cocked, looked up at him, no longer smiling. "You are leaving?"

He buckled his belt. "I've got to go."

Her cocked knee fell wide, showing her sex, pink and glistening with moisture.

Tension strained low in his belly, but Drake summoned his will. "I've really got to go, darlin'."

"You do not know what you miss." She slid her middle finger in and out of her mouth, then moved it down and began to stroke herself, her eyes all the while giving him a lazy-lidded invitation.

He shook his head and turned away, trying to clear his mind. He sat down on the bed and pulled on his boots. "Stay here if you want. The room's paid for. Checkout time's around noon tomorrow." He got to his feet, picked up his wallet and shoved it into his back pocket. The unopened bottle of Jack Daniel's sat on the bedside table, still in its brown sack. "And keep the whiskey," he added.

She flounced off the bed and stormed toward the bathroom. "Asshole! I do not like American whiskey." *Crash!* She slammed the bathroom door.

Drake puffed his cheeks and blew out a long breath. While disturbed by her being so angry, he didn't have time to deal with it. He picked up his phone, reattached it to his belt, picked his coat off the floor and pulled it on. He grabbed the duffel he had already packed in anticipation of tomorrow's early departure and hooked it over his shoulder.

He made one quick perusal of the room and let himself out, locking the door behind him. As much as he hated to leave the hot and gorgeous Gretchen, at the moment, nothing else was as important as quashing the latest crisis at the Double-Barrel Ranch in Drinkwell, Texas. No way would he leave his little sister to deal with it alone.

Chapter Two

Camden, Texas
Seven Years Later...

ON A FORTY-FOUR degree Monday morning after the long Thanksgiving weekend, Realtors Shannon Piper and Kelly Thompson stood outside Kelly's SUV staring at Shannon's greatest wish—a weedy 500 x 450-foot corner tract of land at the edge of the city limits of Camden, Texas. A huge FOR SALE sign towered in the middle of it, touting in bright red letters the name of a Dallas real estate company and a phone number.

"My God. It's finally for sale." Kelly's breath made little vapor puffs in the chilled air.

Shannon's excitement had vaulted the minute she had seen the sign. Bundled up to her earlobes by a heavy wool coat, she scarcely noticed the cold north wind that riffled tendrils of her hair and made her eyes tear. She had waited so long for this 5.17-acre tract, this diamond in a golden crown, to come on the market.

And why was this postage-stamp-size corner so desirable? Because adjoining it on two sides were three other parcels directly in the path of Camden's growth pattern, roughly thirty acres that she already owned outright or was buying. Kelly, as well as all three of Shannon's other teammates, and even the receptionist at Piper Real Estate Company, knew how desperately she needed to own this five acres. It would square up a thirty-five-acre parcel and amp up the value of the total package.

A crumbling vacant house almost hidden by huge old live oak trees hunkered in the far corner of the largest piece. A small farm many years back, this parcel had been the most expensive of the three properties. She'd had to use most of her business emergency fund as a down payment. At one point, she had considered fixing up the house to rent and offset the monthly mortgage payments, but the costs to make it livable rendered the rental option unfeasible. Thus, she had been making the payments out of the skimpy salary she paid herself.

"Should we walk over it?" Kelly asked.

Shannon would love to walk out onto the property as she had done many times and let her imagination bask in the delight of owning it and selling it to a Walmart or a Costco or a Target. But she and Kelly both had on high heels and the ground was wet from the past weekend's rain.

She shook her head. "No need. I've already walked over it a dozen times. Believe me, I know every little bump and swale."

"I wonder why they listed with a Dallas broker," Kelly complained. "Why wouldn't they have listed with us? We'd do a better job than an out-of-towner."

As the owner of Piper Real Estate Company, Shannon appreciated that Kelly wasn't a passive agent who sat at her desk and waited for the phone to ring.

"We aren't associated with a national chain," she replied. "And we aren't part of the big boys' club."

Kelly huffed a laugh. "What club is that? It sounds naughty."

"Commercial Realtors. They're a breed all their own. And they're worse than naughty. Most of the ones I've met are snobs. They look down their noses at us residential agents."

Busy pressing the information from the sign into her phone, Shannon's thoughts traveled to where they always did when she came to this five acres. If she could bring a major retailer to Camden, she would finally be a real player in the real estate game. The company she had started in a friend of her grandmother's abandoned store would become the real estate office to call in Camden, for both buyers and sellers. She and her agents would never again be beggars in a profession that ate its young.

"The owner lives in Dallas," she said. "He's a speculator. I tried to buy it from him before, but he wouldn't sell."

"You know him?"

"No, but I've talked to him on the phone a couple of times."

"Do you know how much he's asking?"

"He would never say. A lot, I suspect." Shannon couldn't keep her mouth from tipping into a huge grin. "But then, that's what negotiation is all about, isn't it?"

Kelly grinned, too. "You got it, boss. Does he know you own all the property around it?"

"If his agent is worth his salt, he's researched the neighboring properties. So it's my guess that he does."

When Shannon and Kelly had seen the new FOR SALE sign, they had been on their way to evaluate the potential of an upscale home Kelly wanted to list. Homes valued at a quarter-million and up were Piper Real Estate's specialty. Shannon and her team diligently cultivated such homeowners and homebuyers both. With Kelly being a newcomer in Camden and the newest member of the Piper Team,

Shannon took pains to assure her the value of her efforts to bring new business into the office. She turned her attention to her now.

"Do you think your house would wait until this afternoon? Of course we can go now if someone's expecting us."

"Oh, any time's okay," Kelly replied. "The owners aren't home. I've got their key. We can take care of this five acres first."

"Let's get back to the office then." Shannon turned and opened the SUV's passenger door. "We'll go look at your house after lunch."

"Right-O," Kelly said.

As Shannon latched her seat belt, she cast one last look at the corner and a comfortable future, not only for herself, but also for her elderly grandmother.

On the way back to the real estate office, her thoughts settled on her grandmother, Evelyn Piper, in whose home Shannon lived. With the elderly woman's only income being a small social security check, to help her as well as herself, Shannon had moved in. In exchange for a roof over her head, Shannon had assumed their living expenses. And plenty of living expenses existed in a Victorian house built in the nineteenth century. The heating and air-conditioning bill alone was a monthly gasp.

Still, Shannon was happy living there and felt fortunate to have her grandmother in her life. It was nice to go home at the end of the day to someone who genuinely cared about her, something she'd never had until now. Grammy Evelyn had given her a new start when no one else in the world gave two hoots that she was alive. Shannon would never forget it. She owed her.

Unfortunately, with the collapse of the mortgage business, home values plummeting and foreclosures popping up all over the county, home sales had slowed to a crawl. Once, more than a dozen agents had hung their licenses with Shannon and her small company teemed with enthusiasm and dynamism. It had been on its way to being the best. Now, most of the agents had left to take jobs with regular paychecks. Shannon's sales staff had shrunk to one team of herself and three other women.

The four of them were lean and mean, but they had to dig business from under every rock. No one of them could afford to be a slacker. The three others had husbands to fall back on, but when it came to keeping the bills paid, Shannon was on her own. Her commissions covered expenses and still allowed her an income, but a small one. If the market didn't pick up soon, she could be in big trouble. But all of those facts only reinforced her enthusiasm for buying the five-acre tract.

Kelly was as excited as Shannon. "Just think, Shannon, if you could get that corner, you could sell all four of those properties to a big box store for millions. This town needs more retail."

Kelly was quick, but Shannon was ahead of her. Maybe not millions with an *S*, but *one* million for sure. “I know. Thirty-five acres is big enough for most of the big box retailers. Or even a small mall.”

Without the corner on the other hand, the bordering thirty acres weren’t worth much more than Shannon had paid for them.

Shannon had sold a couple of homes for over a million dollars in her short career and that had been adrenaline-pumping enough, but the idea of so many zeroes in her own bank account and the financial security it represented boggled her mind.

Back at her office, Shannon immediately called the Dallas listing broker. He told her the owner of the five acres was out of the country through Christmas and difficult to reach, but any offer that came in would be presented as soon as possible. Shannon studied her calendar and bit down on her lower lip. Christmas was a month away. Any number of snafus could erupt between now and then. She hated having her bid hanging loose for weeks, but she could do nothing else.

Kelly’s head poked through her office doorway. “Well? Is it doable?”

“Owner’s out of town until after Christmas. You know what that means. There’s plenty of time for other bids to come in.”

“Maybe you’ll get lucky and there won’t be any.”

“Maybe,” Shannon said absently.

She had never relied on luck. For her, luck had been mostly bad or non-existent. Hard work, sacrifice and self-discipline, fueled by her grandmother’s faith in her, had gotten her to where she was now.

Chapter Three

The Double-Barrel Ranch
Drinkwell, Texas

DRAKE LOCKHART, FOUNDER and CEO of one of the Dallas/Fort Worth Metroplex's most successful real estate investment companies, spent the Monday after his thirty-fifth birthday riding fence. He had done this job as a kid when he lived at the Double-Barrel and cowboyed for his dad. The ranch owned numerous mechanized vehicles he could have used, but he liked reacquainting himself with the land from the back of a good horse.

Through acres of pasture destroyed by fire, Drake rode along a line of new barbed wire fence, checking for loose strands. He had been riding since daylight. He wore a down coat, a neckerchief and silk long johns under his jeans, but still, he was chilled. The temperature had been near freezing when he first left the barn and it hadn't risen much. An unseasonable early norther had blown in and twice brought rain the past week. With fog shrouding the landscape, a penetrating dampness hung in the air.

His mount, a stout quarterhorse named Mouse, obviously loved the brisk weather. He stepped out with purpose and showed high-energy, causing Drake to keep a tight rein. He liked a horse that constantly reminded him he was horseback.

Climbing a rise, he spotted a dark object the size of a small steer darting behind a low hill. *Hog!* Adrenaline surged. Drake refocused.

He clucked to Mouse and spurred him to the crest of the rise, at the same time yanking his rifle free of its scabbard. He reined to a halt, set the gun at his shoulder and scanned ninety degrees through the scope. Spotting the hog again, he set his boots firmly in the stirrups, leaned forward, aimed and fired. *Crack!*

Mouse shifted and whirled, but Drake controlled him and stayed aboard until he settled down. Then he sheathed his rifle and gave the horse reassuring pats on the neck. "Good boy, good boy. 'Sokay, boy."

Drake was proud of him for not going into a full-out buck and pitching his ass to the ground. Few ranch horses would tolerate a rider shooting from their backs. Silas had said Mouse would. He trotted the horse downhill toward where he had aimed. Where a hog carcass should be lying, he saw nothing. Not even a sign. He was a good shot, didn't usually miss.

"Shit," he mumbled.

He circled a small area, searching with his "hunter's eye," though it wasn't as sharp as it had once been, he had to admit. He was out of practice, for sure. He sat for a few minutes, watching and listening. Starting to shiver, he gave up on the hog, turned Mouse and walked him back up the rise, still scanning the landscape for more hogs. Feral hogs had become a scourge to ranchers and farmers all over rural Texas. They tore up fences, destroyed crops and attacked livestock. They were so prolific the state had declared open season on them.

He halted the horse on the brow of the hill and relaxed the reins. As the gelding lowered his head and began to munch on tufts of grass, Drake gazed out across a shallow valley. The fog and low clouds hid the far side, but he knew that in the distance on the other side of the basin, a miles-long blue mesa met the sky. It and everything between here and there made up a part of the Double-Barrel Ranch's many thousand acres.

His near view took in four sections, roughly twenty-five hundred acres, known on the ranch as the North Pasture. That is, what was left of it. Last spring, it had been lush with good grazing. Now, grass struggled to take hold on charred, arid ground and hazy blackened skeletons of scattered live oak trees and sagebrush showed through the fog like contorted skeletons. He couldn't keep from thinking of the years of work that had gone into making the North Pasture an example of what conscientious range management produced. Ranching was about more than raising good cattle and horses. It was also about responsible stewardship of the land and common sense.

Before Drake had first left the ranch to make his home in Fort Worth, the North Pasture had been a thick snarl of cedar and mesquite trees and a haven for rattlesnakes. Cattlemen hated mesquites and rattlesnakes. The snakes were a hazard to man and beast. The mesquites sucked water from the ground, depriving grass of needed moisture. Their razor-sharp thorns tore cattle's hides, inviting infection and blowflies. They had even been known to pierce a cow or calf's eye.

His younger brother, Pic, along with the ranch's brush removal crew, had spent Pic's summers home from college beating back the North Pasture's thorny growth, reclaiming grazing land and seeding with hybrid grass.

But Pic and the crew's efforts had been all for naught. The past few years, high temperatures and low humidity had dried grass to kindling that was ripe for rapacious fire. Drought had turned trees and desirable brush into fodder. Spring had ended with the Lockharts, like every other landowner in Texas, sitting on pins and needles, hoping no accident of man or nature, chose them.

They hadn't escaped. One hot, windy afternoon the past June, range fire had rolled over the land and consumed every living thing on the North Pasture's surface. In this pasture alone, a hundred head of cattle—mothers with calves—had been trapped, suffocated by smoke and roasted where they stood.

Some believed the Treadway County fire had been set. A half-assed arson investigation was ongoing, but Drake doubted anyone would ever know for sure.

Half the state of Texas had been on fire all of last spring and summer. Hundreds of homes had burned and more than a million acres. Besides the North Pasture, thousands more acres of the Double-Barrel's rangeland had gone up in flames. Drake had fought the fires himself. He and his two brothers, his dad and even his little sister had stood shoulder to shoulder with firefighters, national guardsmen and volunteers from all over the country.

The Lockhart reserves had taken a major hit. In an industry at the mercy of Mother Nature, disaster of one kind or another loomed ever-present, but in Drake's lifetime, he had never seen the Double-Barrel faced with so much calamity all at one time. Yet, the Lockharts were luckier than some. Oil and gas royalties and, thanks to Drake, wind turbine leases on the family's cotton farms in West Texas kept the ranch in cash.

After five months, memories of the fires and the aftermath no longer reduced him to weeping, but a knot of emotion had been in his throat all morning. This ranch had been his home from birth until he was twenty-five years old. He might not live here now, but he owned a part of it and felt an undying loyalty to it. He dabbed at his eyes with a corner of his neckerchief. He hadn't known much true grief in his life, but over the past summer, he had learned it had a way of overpowering even a will as strong as his.

The record-breaking drought continued. He gazed down at the dry and cracking soil with sadness. With only a little help from man, the grass could grow back thicker and richer on the burned ground, but it would take rain. A lot more rain than had been seen so far. And time. So much time. Perhaps more time than today's fast-paced business world would allow struggling ranchers.

Drake finally gripped his emotions and willed away his downbeat thoughts. He couldn't do what he had to every day if he allowed negativity to gain a foothold in his psyche.

He breathed in the earthy smells of the damp earth and relished the solitude that surrounded him, let himself be sucked into a silence so profound he could hear it. Lonesomeness had been born in his soul. No wonder people called him a loner.

He loved the land and being alone with the wide unfettered views, the quiet that came with being forty miles from the nearest population.

This was where he found his strength, where he refueled, where he regained his perspective after weeks of wrangling in the high stakes investment and commercial real estate world in Fort Worth and Dallas.

That environment was a rough-and-tumble landscape populated by big-moneyed cutthroat players, arrogant lawyers and slick accountants, self-important architects and temperamental designers. Daily, he dealt with self-righteous inspectors, tricky politicians, environmentalist wackos and greedy bankers.

Among that throng, he had found his niche. And he was at the top of his game. As much as he loved the ranch, he loved his business in the city. The rush that accompanied a multimillion dollar deal thrilled him. He delighted in the euphoria that followed triumph, perhaps even more than the financial reward. He didn't enjoy the deals that went sour—and in the ten years since he had put together his company, he'd had his share—but he didn't hate them either. Every one of them had taught him something. Money gave no man mercy, he had learned, but making it with his wits had brought Drake deep personal satisfaction.

His stomach rumbled and he checked his watch. Noon. He was famished. Breakfast had been light. He inhaled another helping of the cold fresh air, then drew Mouse up, urged him down the hill and reined him toward the ranch house and food. The Double-Barrel's sprawling barns and buildings came into sight and he nudged Mouse into a lope.

Silas Morgan, who had lived in the ranch's bunkhouse most of his adult life, met him at the horse barn. Silas had never been married as far as anyone knew and had no family. That was the way it was with several of the ranch hands. They rode for the brand, loyal to the bone. The Double-Barrel was their home, the Lockharts their family and the Lockharts respected that.

Drake swung out of the saddle, feeling a deep ache in muscles he hadn't used since he had been down from Fort Worth for the fall round-up.

"How you like ol' Mouse?" Silas asked, taking hold of the bridle.

Drake untied his rifle scabbard and set it against a stall. "Good horse. He got a little rattled when I took a shot at a hog, but he didn't toss me."

"The hell," Silas said, loosening the saddle cinch. "What happened with the hog?"

"Missed him." Drake patted the horse's neck and told him again what a good boy he was.

"That's not like you, Son."

Silas had always called him "Son." Indeed, Drake saw the old cowboy as sort of a second father. Years back, Drake had spent a year and a half living in the bunkhouse alongside the ranch hands. Silas had mentored him, taught him to be a real cowboy. And he had gone a long way toward teaching him to be a man. To this day, Drake lived by something Silas had told him: *Don't never give up 'til you just have to.*

And if it turns out you have to, pick your own place and do it on your own terms.

"I couldn't see that well through the fog," Drake said absently, now more interested in his mount. He no longer owned a horse, but there had been a time when a good horse had been a big part of his life. "You know something, Silas? I miss the horses." He dragged the saddle off Mouse's back.

"You were always good with 'em." Silas removed Mouse's bridle. "This been a good birthday for you?"

To Drake, his thirty-fifth birthday was special. A landmark. His business was ten years old and successful. He could claim his own fortune. He had put his childish inner battles behind him and grown up "The best," he answered, carrying the saddle into the tack room and placing it on its tree.

This year, the birthday had landed on the day after Thanksgiving Day. The annual holiday feast had included a cake and champagne. The whole family, including Drake's ninety-year-old paternal grandmother, who now lived in Drinkwell, and Pic's girlfriend, Mandy, had been present. Mom had come down from Fort Worth. Even some of the older ranch hands had been there. The gathering had been almost genial for a change. Mom hadn't nagged him about getting married and having kids. Dad had been sober and on his best behavior, so Mom hadn't picked a fight with him.

Drake removed his chinks and spurs and hung them on a peg, then returned to where Silas was brushing Mouse.

"Everybody but your mama's folks turned out, didn't they?" Silas said.

Drake had hoped his maternal grandparents might come for this particular birthday, but they had not. Evidently the thirty-fifth birthday wasn't as special to them as it was to him. His mom said they were in Indiana. As full-time RVers, they were rarely in Texas these days, thus, Drake and his siblings saw little of them.

"Yeah, they did," he said.

"With that big-deal horse show going on up in Fort Worth, I couldn't believe it when Kate and Troy showed up," Silas said.

The "big-deal-horse-show" *was* a big deal for those in the cutting horse business. The NCHA—or for the uninitiated, the National Cutting Horse Association—World Championship Futurity was the be-all, end-all cutting competition in the country. The three-week event started the last part of November every year. Both Drake's little sister and his half-brother participated as breeders and competitors and Troy as a trainer.

Drake chuckled. "Me either. I didn't think either one of them would be here."

"Just goes to show how much folks miss you around here," Silas said. "Think you'll ever come back to the ranch?"

"Nah. Not any time soon."

Drake could say that with confidence. This year, the family had celebrated more than his birthday. This year, at the family meeting conducted at the end of every year, Dad had announced the family had agreed to name the middle Lockhart son, Pickett, as General Manager of the ranching and farming operations. Pic had lived and worked on the ranch his entire life. He knew every cow and calf, every blade of grass. Still, Dad would spend the coming year grooming him in the nuances of managing a ranching empire. The move was a huge relief to Drake. Up to now, with no one named to replace Dad, the possibility had always existed that Drake would someday have to.

Just then, Drake's phone warbled. He plucked it off his belt and saw the name of one of the associates in his Fort Worth company. "Hey, Gabe, what's up?"

"Hey, Drake. How was Thanksgiving?"

Phone pressed to his ear, he mouthed to Silas, "I'm going to the house." He picked up his saddle scabbard, gave Silas a two-fingered salute and trudged toward the ranch house. "Good, Gabe, good. You have a good visit with your family?"

"Ate like a horse, as usual. Listen, sorry to bother you when you're on a holiday, but I didn't want to let this wait."

Gabe Mathison paid little attention to holidays and weekends. He was the youngest broker in Drake's organization of forty-five real estate brokers and was still more or less in training. He was also one of the most ambitious. When it came to sniffing out a good deal for the company or a customer or investor, Gabe turned over every stone. In some ways, he reminded Drake of himself.

"You know that corner piece of land on the Fort Worth Highway just out of Camden?" he continued. "The one with the big oak trees? It's across the highway from that new grocery store and strip mall Lincoln Properties built."

Drake traveled through Camden when he drove to the Double-Barrel. He had watched the small town's rapid growth with only distant interest. His playing field was the Metroplex. "Vaguely. What's up?"

"It's for sale. We got a flier from Emmet Hunt in Dallas."

Drake's interest stirred. Bare ground for sale in a hot growth area like Camden always had good potential. "How much land?"

"A little over five acres. Not a big chunk, but the ground all around it is unimproved except for one old house that looks like it might fall down. I'm going to do some research to see who owns it. Could be a deal for the right buyer. It's a perfect spot for a C-store. A RaceTrac maybe."

Drake involved himself in his agents' deals only peripherally. He often didn't even know the names of buyers and sellers. His primary concern was that his people performed ethically and legally. Mostly, he left them to their own creative ventures. "Do some work on it," he replied. "I'll be back up there tomorrow and we can go over it."

"Shouldn't we go ahead and make an offer?"

"I don't think anybody will snatch it out from under us before tomorrow. It's the holidays. And knowing Emmet, it's overpriced anyway."

Gabe laughed. "Gotcha. See ya tomorrow."

Chapter Four

DRAKE ENTERED THE Double-Barrel's tan native rock ranch house through the back door and the large utility room where long ago, game and beef had been butchered and packaged. The sprawling single-story house had been built in 1902 by the ranch's founder, a Scots immigrant. It had been added on to and remodeled more than once. In many ways, it remained outdated. Still, it had an elegance about it.

The aroma of lunch preparation set his taste buds to dancing. He laid his Stetson on the long stainless steel counter and hung his coat to the side of the door on a coat rack made of steer horns. A shudder passed over his shoulders as warmth seeped into his body.

He found his dad and brother in the den enjoying a fire blazing in the massive rock fireplace. Two artfully-welded horseshoe lamps flanked a long cowhide sofa and cast an amber light into the day's gloom. Heavy western-style furniture, a large TV, brown wood-paneled walls and a few hunting trophies made the room's ambience decidedly masculine.

Two eight-foot sliding doors opened out onto a large stone-paved patio and outdoor room. The roof that covered it never allowed bright light into the den, even on a sunny day. When Mom lived here, she had declared this room "a dark and depressing boar's nest." She had tried to change it by adding flowers and candles that the men in the family had barely tolerated. They liked the room as it was. Pic called it a man cave. Drake thought it one of the most relaxing places he had ever been.

"You've been out there a long time," Pic said, grinning from the end of one of the sofas. "Thought we were gonna have to send out a search party. You're gonna have a sore butt tomorrow, Brother."

Drake carried his gun scabbard to a built-in gun safe in a corner, pulled out his rifle and began to unload it.

Seated in a bulky leather recliner, his dad looked up from behind a newspaper. "How'd the new fence look?"

Drake closed his rifle into the safe. "No breaks. Saw a little bit of grass peeking through."

"We need more rain," his dad said, folding the newspaper. "I just hope this weather keeps on coming."

Weather. A never-ending grievance of a rancher in Texas.

His brother rose, walked over to the fireplace and stood in front of the blaze, his hands behind his back. "How many hogs did you shoot?"

"Missed one," Drake answered.

Pic shook his head, sighing. "We've hunted hell out of those hogs. Every hand's taking a rifle every time he goes out."

"I'll tell you this much," Dad groused. "We can't afford to lose one more calf to rustlers or hogs. Damn rustling is at an all-time high. And sheep raisers southwest of here? The paper says those bastard hogs are putting them clear out of business. Lambs are a hundred percent defenseless."

Drake and Pic traded knowing glances. Repeating conversation about the financial loss the ranch had taken and continued to take was unnecessary. Dad was endlessly vocal in his belief that the summer's fires and the hogs had cut the spring calf crop in half.

Just then, Johnnie Sue Struthers, the ranch's latest housekeeper, stuck her head through the doorway. "You boys come eat 'fore it gets cold."

Dad stood. "Let's go eat dinner. Johnnie Sue's fried up that mess of birds we shot."

Drake and his family were lifelong hunters. His father had taught him and his siblings gun care and shooting as children. They had grown up eating game meat. Bird hunting was one of Drake's favorite activities. On this visit, he, Pic, and his dad had hunted quail every morning. With him returning to Fort Worth tomorrow, today was the day for a quail feed.

The three of them filed into the kitchen and sat down at the round oak table. The rectangular table in the formal dining room seated twelve, but they rarely ate there. They liked the intimacy of dining in the breakfast room, an alcove off one end of the kitchen that overlooked the deep canyon carved into the earth by the Brazos River. There, they could observe nature's ever-changing tableau.

Johnnie Sue served them fried quail, mashed potatoes with cream gravy and homemade biscuits. After the meal, she cleared the table and they stayed at the table talking.

"You said you were going to Lubbock?" Dad said.

The Lockhart family owned fourteen thousand acres of cotton farms and grazing land between Lubbock and Amarillo. Seven years ago, Drake had negotiated leases on a third of the land with an energy provider. Completed wind turbines stood in neat rows on part of the cotton fields and some were still under construction.

During his week-long visit, Drake had held a year-end meeting with his whole family. With the Double-Bar L Cattle Company being a family corporation, the Lockharts gathered several times a year to discuss the state of the ranch and plan for the future. He had reported that the windmill construction was almost finished and he was in talks with TXE about leasing more land. If he continued to be successful, at some point, all of the Lockhart West Texas holdings would be under lease for windmill sites.

Despite that positive news, the meeting's atmosphere had remained grim, the memory of the past summer's range fires still prevalent in everybody's mind. Mother Nature had not been kind. Everybody had to tighten his belt in the coming year. Or years.

"I'm going to try to get out there before the end of the year," Drake replied.

"I've been thinking about what we talked about in the meeting," Dad said. "About getting involved in building those windmills. I'm dubious, Son. Lockharts have never been venture capitalists. Cattle, oil and cotton have always been our businesses. Agriculture and energy have done well for us. It's what we know. I don't think I need to tell you this isn't a good year for gambling."

His father spoke of Pennington Engineering, the company erecting wind turbines on the Lockhart cotton farms. Robert Pennington, the company's owner, had approached Drake years ago about partnering in a turbine engine manufacturing operation and was now bringing the plan to a head. Drake hadn't committed, but he hadn't said no either.

In recent years, the ranch had become more dependent on its investments outside the cattle business. Making that successful had fallen on Drake. Shepherding the family's wealth was different from risking his own. He juggled between it and the edgier business his own company engaged in. Ironically, at this point in the Lockharts' long history, it might well be Drake's business acumen and his honed negotiating skills that saved the ranch.

"I understand, Dad. I don't know all I need to yet. What I do know is that wind energy has support. And a manufacturing plant in that part of the state would mean a lot to the local people."

"So what?" Dad said. "You into social engineering now? Not a damn one of those green energy companies has come up with anything that'll get a Boeing 747 off the ground. And until they do, I'm not impressed. I want us to just keep pumping oil as long as long they'll let us."

"You don't have to worry," Drake said. "I'd never do anything that would sink the ship."

"I know that, Son. I'm just reminding you I don't like those damn windmills. Every time I turn on the news, I hear about another one of those companies going broke. Besides that, they're killing high-flying birds and I don't like that. A balls-out effort has been made for years to save the eagles and now they're getting killed flying into windmills." His brow raised and his direct look came at Drake. "But I do like those energy company leases."

"I say just keep leasing the land," Pic put in. "Let somebody else take the risk of building the windmill engines."

As a murmur of agreement came from their dad, Drake tamped down his impatience. Often these days, he found his vision of the future in conflict with that of his father and brother. He had confidence in his own judgment. He always had, even when he was younger. No matter what might be going on in the economy in general, he had never feared making the hard calls and had always had an expectation of success. Most of his gambles had been spot-on and profitable.

Though he hadn't seen much success or profit in large-scale green energy production so far, he wasn't opposed to it. As for the windmills, the jury was still out.

"Speaking of social engineering, I meant to show you something," Pic said, preventing the conversation from escalating into an argument. He left the table and returned with a newspaper folded in quarters. "You made the paper, Bro. The *Dallas Morning News* no less" He slid the paper across the table toward Drake.

"What's this?" Drake picked up the paper and scanned it. A grainy picture was set within an article on a feature page—a shot of himself and the blonde heiress he had been seeing for the past six months, Donna Stafford-Schoonover.

The picture had been made at the Adolphus Hotel in Dallas, where last week he had escorted her to a function held by one of the many organizations she supported. He hated seeing himself in the newspaper, but as the only daughter of one of the richest, most powerful men in Texas, Donna made the paper if she sneezed. He'd had to learn to live with that, but he hadn't learned to love it.

"She told the reporter that wrote this story that you and her are about to do the deed." To Drake's aggravation, his younger brother chortled. "She says you're out shopping for a ring."

"The hell," Drake said and continued to read. Sure enough, the quote from Donna was there. A fresh annoyance niggled at him. He had never proposed to her. He hadn't said he loved her. Except for Tammy McMillan, his fiancé of years ago when he was a dumb kid, he had never loved any woman, nor had he told one he did.

"You got some news you're not sharing, Son?" Dad asked. Now, he, too, was grinning. "Your mother says she's Don Stafford's daughter."

Mom. Drake swore mentally. His mother had heard about him and Donna on some golf course and had been practically wheezing for breath when she had quizzed him about it.

Everybody in Texas knew Don Stafford, either directly or indirectly. He had owned an oil company that he sold for a fortune but in which he continued to hold a major interest. Now, semi-retired, he sat on many boards. Among other things, he owned a Cadillac dealership and a part of the Texas Rangers baseball team. His investments were eclectic and varied and his influence had long tentacles.

Drake rarely discussed his social life with his family. "You're acquainted with Don Stafford?" he asked his dad.

"We've met."

"If I were planning on marrying into a prominent family, you'd be the first to know. You know that, don't you?"

"Mom's planning your wedding anyway," Pic put in, still laughing.

Mom again. Drake had ended his affair with Donna twice, most recently a month ago. Then, somehow, influenced by his own mother and Donna's father, he had let himself be dragged back into it. But he wasn't happy. Donna was spoiled, self-centered, petulant and aggressive. She drank too much and he suspected she engaged in other substance abuse when she wasn't with him. He also doubted her loyalty. That might disturb him if he really cared about her.

He had been growing ever more vexed with her drinking, her aimless lifestyle, her superficial friends he viewed as being equally aimless and her in general. He had difficulty relating to people who had nothing productive to do or who couldn't carry on a conversation about anything more interesting than what somebody wore to some party or who'd had the latest plastic surgery.

For weeks, he had been thinking he and Donna had reached a dead end, wasn't sure why he had stuck around this long. Six months was longer than his affairs ever lasted. He slid the newspaper back toward his little brother. "That's garbage. It should go in the trash."

He left his seat and walked over to the counter and the coffee maker for a refill, leaving Pic chuckling behind him. "I can't trash it yet," his little brother said. "I've got to show it to Mandy. She'll get a kick out of it."

Amanda Breckenridge had been Pic's girlfriend off and on since they were all in Drinkwell High School together. The fall after graduation, Pic had gone away to college, leaving her behind in Drinkwell. Then, during Pic's senior year, he had met his ex-wife and eloped.

Before Pic brought his bride back to the Double-Barrel to meet the family, Mandy moved away to live with an aunt in West Texas. The Treadway County grapevine had blabbed about how she had left town because her heart had been broken by Pic's choosing another girl. Drake didn't know if that was true.

Years later, after being married and divorced herself, she returned to help care for her widowed and dying father. At the same time, she went to work as a teacher and coach in the Drinkwell school system. By that time, Pic had been divorced several years.

Pic and Mandy had been dating again. They appeared to be in love, or at least something like it. Neither of them saw anyone else, yet Pic never mentioned marrying her.

That could be because Mom constantly ragged on him, telling him he could do better than Mandy. Drake had no idea what drove their mother's thinking. After Pic's disastrous marriage, why wouldn't a mother want her son to marry someone who cared about him as much as Mandy obviously cared about Pic?

Drake's history with the fairer sex was different. After being jilted by Tammy, he had kept tight control of his relationships. Unlike his brother, no woman had ever led him down the aisle. His various female acquaintances had called him a litany of colorful names—rogue, commitment-phobe, self-centered bastard and others. He let most of that roll off of him. He had trained himself not to worry about the opinions of people outside his family.

Yet, a small part of him envied what his little brother had going on with Mandy. Drake couldn't imagine what it would be like to have a woman who cared about him simply for the man he was. Most of the women he had known liked his local celebrity and his reputation as a business success. They liked the Lockhart money and his status as an heir in a wealthy old Texas family, but he had never been convinced that any of them liked *him* all that much. What most women liked, he had concluded, was money and the status they could gain from marriage to a powerful man.

At some point, he had chosen for marriage not to clutter his life and distract him from his goals. Maybe deep down, at the bottom of it all, he hung on with Donna for two reasons: One, she was unimpressed by someone else's money and power. Few men in Texas, not even the governor, could compete with her own father. And two, she was a wild woman in bed—when she wasn't drunk.

"You won't be back 'til Christmas, I take it?" his dad said.

"Not planning on it."

"You'll be bringing your mother with you, right?"

"If that's what she wants."

Seven years his parents had been separated, but they hadn't divorced. Drake still vividly remembered the afternoon Kate, in a weeping phone call, had caught him in Amarillo and told him Mom was moving away from the ranch. That she would do such a thing had been unbelievable, but sure enough, she had bought a Greek Revival mansion in a staid old Fort Worth subdivision and left the Double-Barrel, taking a moving van full of the ranch's household goods with her. She hadn't returned for more than short visits, but she always spent Christmas with the family.

"Humph," Pic grunted. "It'd probably stay a helluva lot quieter around here if she made up her mind to either come back for good or stay away altogether."

"Don't be disrespectful, Son," Dad said sternly. "She's your mother. And she's still my wife."

Pic got to his feet. "I told Smoky I'd ride with him to check on the windmill up on Windy Ridge. See ya tonight, Drake." He walked out.

For years now, Pic had been vocal about his anger at their mother. He and Kate both believed she was responsible for most of the chaos that existed around the Double-Barrel.

Looking after him, Dad shook his head slowly. "If she came back, I guess Pic would move out of the ranch house."

No doubt, Drake thought, but he kept that opinion to himself, along with the fact that their mother still had the male friend in Fort Worth she had been seeing since before she moved there. And their friendship was not platonic.

But Drake had never been one to knowingly contribute to the family discord. Enough of it thrived without any assistance from him. He confined his energy to trying to help the Double-Barrel financially. And right now, it needed a lot of help.

Shannon's week passed quietly. On Friday morning, she called the Dallas real estate broker and followed up on the bid she had made on the five-acre corner. He told her he was expecting another offer, probably by Monday. *Damn.* She had so hoped for no competition.

Chapter Five

Clack-clack-clack-clack-clack...

SHANNON QUICKSTEPPED TOWARD the Worthington Hotel in downtown Fort Worth, her shoes clicking like castanets against a wet sidewalk.

Like fairy fingers, a fine mist peppered her face and hair. A north wind gusted through the canyons of multistory buildings, bringing tears to her eyes and penetrating the thin skirt of her evening dress as if it weren't there. Her feet had become blocks of ice. Silver sling-backs were lousy winter footwear. She berated herself for parking two blocks away, rued that she had been too cheap to park in covered parking closer to her destination.

The hotel entrance loomed just up the block and across the street in an ocean of bright lights. She shoved her evening bag under her arm, clutched her jacket collar against her throat with one hand, lifted her flimsy skirt to her knees with the other and quickened her pace to a trot.

...Clack-clack-clack-clack-clack...

Between her and there, a traffic light showed red. She halted at the block's corner, breathing hard after a near jog and filling her lungs with cold air. Her teeth chattered. She shifted from foot to foot waiting for the light to turn green.

Across the street, women decked out in fur coats exited limos—warm, she was sure. No doubt they had the jewels to go with the fur. Apprehension tweaked her. Her "jewels" were a pair of small diamond earrings that belonged to her grandmother. The closest thing she had to fur was her jacket's narrow fox fur collar and cuffs. The thin vintage evening garment, before tonight, had also belonged to Grammy Evelyn.

What are you doing here? her alter ego screamed. That cranky voice had become a bold part of her life ever since she had decided to attend tonight's gala.

"Networking," she mumbled.

The party, a charity ball, was hosted by the Tarrant County Commercial Realtors Association, more commonly known to real estate professionals as the TCCRA. Tonight, she would be rubbing shoulders with the elite of the real estate industry and who knew who else? She would be meeting prominent people in the Metroplex business world, making connections that could be important to her future.

And she might run into Emmett Hunt, the Dallas real estate broker who had listed the five-acre corner in Camden. *Her* corner. When she had acquired the tickets to this event, she had never heard of Emmett Hunt. Now he had suddenly become consequential enough to make attending this party a necessity as much as a desire.

The light changed, she picked up her skirt again and trotted across the street. Unnoticed, she edged past the portico's bustle and skidded into the spacious lobby. Instantly, tension-relieving warmth began to spread through her, making her shudder. She paused and drew a deep breath, taking in her surroundings and orienting herself.

She had never been inside the Worthington Hotel, but she had seen pictures and heard of its elegance when she had lived in Fort Worth years back. From what she could see, what she had heard was no exaggeration.

Red and green and gold decorated the lobby, along with a giant lighted tree. Her gaze landed on an amazing glass sculpture hanging over the red-carpeted double staircase that stretched upward before her. A scene from *Gone with the Wind* darted through her mind as she visualized Rhett carrying Scarlett up those red-carpeted stairs. Shannon Piper would have to lose a few pounds before some hero hauled her up a flight of stairs.

She spent another minute adjusting and gathering herself. Then as if she owned the place, she lifted her chin and strode forward seeking the ladies' room.

~

Drake slowed his Aston Martin as he neared the entrance to the Worthington Hotel. He could think of nothing he wanted less than to be attending a formal party on a wet cold night. He would rather be at home dressed in sweats, reading a good book or watching a movie on TV. He would have blown this evening off, but he had promised to be here. And to break a promise, even a trivial one, just wasn't in him.

He and Donna Schoonover were headed for the annual Christmas ball and silent auction conducted by the TCCRA. The event had occurred the first weekend of December since long before Drake got into the real estate business.

As he braked at the curb, Donna fumbled for the door latch. "You should've gotten a limo. "I can't believe you drove us here in this damn shoebox. I can't even get out of it."

Having already dipped liberally into a gin bottle, Donna's speech slurred. Comment from Drake wouldn't change that. One thing he had learned over time was not to fall into confrontations with women over issues out of his control. So he kept his silence about her drinking.

They had already quarreled over her telling a Dallas reporter they were getting married.

As for the car, maybe he should have hired a roomier vehicle, but he loved driving his sexy sports car, loved the rumble of the awesome V-12 engine and feeling the power under his right foot. The Aston Martin Virage was the first car he had ever owned. He had driven a pickup truck his entire life. And he still drove a truck daily to his various projects.

"Darlin', this car sits in a locked cage in the parking garage at Lockhart Tower most of the time. I don't get a chance to drive it that often."

Drake rarely fantasized about anything, but this automobile had gripped him with an unyielding fist the minute he had seen it.

His dream and goal of owning a sports car had ignited when he was eighteen years old, after one had slipped through his grasp like quicksilver. A couple of years ago, after closing on the sale of the last condo in Lockhart Tower, his thirty-story contribution to downtown Fort Worth's revitalization, without a second thought, he had stepped up and paid more than $200,000 for the sports car. No luxury his wealthy family had provided had proved to be as gratifying as one he had paid for himself with his own money.

A valet opened his door and stood waiting for him to exit. As he scooted out, a cold mist pricked his cheeks. Up the street, the fog-veiled lights of First Fort Worth Bank's marquee showed the temperature to be thirty-four degrees.

Lights and hubbub surrounded him—headlights reflecting on the wet pavement, various lighted signs showing on businesses, downtown Fort Worth's buildings outlined in white lights heralding the season. The hotel's brightly-lit portico was alive with busy valets and revelers exiting cabs, luxury cars and limos.

Before the valet took control of the Virage, Drake pulled a money clip from his pocket, slapped the valet's shoulder with one hand and passed him a twenty with the other. "We'll be leaving early," he told him and he intended for that to be true.

He rounded the car's backend to where a different valet had helped Donna, literally, out of the low-slung vehicle onto the wet sidewalk. He handed the second valet another twenty as the Virage moved away with a deep mechanical hum and a showy cloud of exhaust.

"I hope you realize I practically sprained my ankle trying to get out." Donna wrapped her fur coat more tightly around herself. "My God, it's cold. Cabo has never sounded so good. "I really want to go down there, Drake."

Without comment, Drake placed his hand on her back and guided her toward the hotel entrance. Responding to that remark was unnecessary. She had heard him say enough times that he considered trips to resorts like Cabo san Lucas a waste of time. He hadn't been a partier or drinker in years, cared not a whit for lounging beside a swimming pool or attempting to play tennis. He liked game fishing, but not enough to interrupt his work schedule for a trip to Mexico or Florida.

When he did take time off, he usually went to the Double-Barrel for some real physical work and some hunting. Or sometimes he looked in on a horse show. On occasion, he golfed or attended a ballgame.

"I told you, I don't have time for a pleasure trip right now. I've got a lot going on."

"You're the only person I know who doesn't take a winter vacation. I don't know what you could be doing that can't wait."

Specifically, he had a five-hundred-unit luxury apartment complex under construction, using borrowed money. From the outset, Lone Star Commons had been plagued with problems that had called for his daily attention. It was useless to try to explain that to Donna, so what he said was, "You know I don't enjoy Cabo."

"Humph. That's the real reason you won't go. You just don't like it."

He leveled a look at her profile. *And what better reason is there?*

They reached the warmth of the hotel's gaily-decorated lobby and Drake's mood lifted. He dug the Christmas season—the lights, the decorations, the busy people everywhere. He even liked the shopping, though he had little time to do it.

As they walked to the elevator, Donna shook back her long blond hair and patted at her tanned cheeks with her flattened fingers. "Damn weather has probably ruined my makeup."

Drake reached inside his coat for a handkerchief and handed it to her. She used it to dab dampness from her face, then returned it and looked up at him with blue eyes made lazy-lidded by too much alcohol. Nothing turned Drake off a woman—or anybody—more quickly than consistent alcohol excess. He had dealt with his own father's fondness for booze and the results it produced for too many years.

"You look fine." He exhaled a long breath.

"I know," she snapped. "You don't have to say it. You think I shouldn't have had those last two martinis."

Challenging Donna after she had overindulged in gin could bring on pure havoc. He wanted to get through the evening without a scene. He punched the call button for an elevator car. "I didn't say that, babe, but since you brought it up, you're right. You've had a lot to drink."

"Oh, Drakey, don't be a mean ol' prude."

He hated when she put on that "little girl" act and whined. He closed his eyes and arched his brow.

"You sound like Daddy. This is a party."

And partying was something at which Donna was very good. She had practiced all over the world.

Drake was especially irritated at her tonight. Here, they would be circulating among his peers, commercial Realtors. He wasn't a political animal—far from it—but he maintained a level of decorum among fellow professionals and he expected a woman in his company to do likewise, regardless of who her father was. Added to that, as far as he was concerned, those who couldn't hold their liquor shouldn't drink.

In spite of all of that pecking at him, he managed to smile down at her.

The elevator car arrived and they stepped into the dimly lit cube, the only passengers. They rode to the second floor in silence, with Donna hanging onto his arm and his mind sorting out how he had let himself be manipulated into attending this shindig. It had started with Donna calling his mother, then he had let the two of them shame him into coming for the purpose of buying something in the silent auction.

This year, the chosen charity was Wounded Warriors. Texans, rich or poor, were nothing if not patriotic. The charity, to which Drake had given generously for several years, was the only reason he had consented to obligate himself to lay down a wad of dough for something he probably didn't want or need. He never forgot that Purple Hearts resided on his mother's side of his family. His grandfather, his mother's father, was a member of the greatest generation. He had been at Normandy. And his uncle, his mother's brother, had been a helicopter pilot who died in Iraq. He felt a tinge of guilt because after he left school, he had not even considered serving his country as anything other than a substantial taxpayer.

The elevator doors glided open and he and Donna exited into the second-floor Grand Ballroom's thickly carpeted foyer. She released his arm and started for the foyer bar, but he grabbed her elbow and stopped her. "Hey, c'mon, now. No more martinis for a while, okay?"

Her vivid pink lips pursed, but she stayed by his side. He drew her closer, tucking her hand into the crook of his elbow. He leaned down and said near her ear, "Darlin', you're a beautiful woman. Being drunk doesn't show you in your best light. You don't want your family and friends to see you making an ass of yourself, do you?"

"Well..." She paused. "Mama would probably nag."

He patted her hand that curved around his arm. "Good girl."

She looked up at him. "Do you really think I'm beautiful, Drakey?"

"Of course I do."

And he wasn't lying. Donna's appearance was a monument to plastic surgery. She had been undergoing procedures since her teenage years. A man had to be in awe of that for what it had cost in pain and dollars if for no other reason.

Donna benefitted from every material advantage wealth could buy—expensive clothing and jewelry, memberships at the best spas and clubs all over the world, the best cosmetologists and hairdressers, the best plastic surgeons. From the date of her birth, she had been pampered like a prize poodle. She had no filter when it came to the cost of things. Drake was not so insensitive that he didn't realize she couldn't help that. He knew her parents.

She had attended the best schools, all of which she had flunked out of or quit before finishing. "Why do I need an education?" she said often. "I'm never going to have to work at anything."

She was right. She had never done a lick of work a day in her life and would never be required to.

And she suffered more hang-ups than a teenager. Lately, Drake found himself longing for the company of a woman with whom he could have a grown-up after-sex conversation about a meaningful subject.

A makeshift cloakroom had been partitioned in the corner off to the left of the ballroom's wide entrance. They strolled toward it.

"You never tell me you think I'm pretty anymore," she said. "You mostly just tell me to stop drinking."

"I tell you you're pretty more often than you realize. You don't hear me."

Drake helped her out of her coat and handed it to the steward, removed his own overcoat and checked it, too. Then he guided Donna into the ballroom.

At least five or six hundred people were stuffed into the room. Not everyone was in the real estate business. This kind of event always attracted most of Fort Worth's elite—politicians, an assortment of doctors, lawyers, oilmen, businessmen, TV personalities and other miscellaneous professionals. Even a few from Dallas were here. Drinking and laughing, they hugged, brushed cheeks and kissed air, glad handed and back slapped as if they were all old friends.

The mayor and city council members clustered off to one side. With the exception of the mayor, most of that cadre wasn't rich. But what they lacked in coin, they made up for in power and influence. He knew all of them well on a professional level and from what he knew of them professionally, he had little desire to know them personally. He might call all of them acquaintances, but none of them friends.

A bottle-blond councilwoman gave him the eye. She was coming off a nasty divorce, had sent him signals and emails. Women often came on to him. He didn't kid himself for a minute that it was because he was exceptionally handsome or charming. The reasons had been written about any number of times in newspapers and magazines. He was rich, under forty and had never been married, which apparently was a brew as potent as any aphrodisiac. Men envied his lifestyle. Women desired it. They thought they could distract him from his fourteen-hour workdays and his frequent seven-day workweeks.

And besides that, almost everybody near and far knew that his mother wanted him married and fathering babies, a frustration that called for all of his patience.

He wasn't against marriage and kids. His own parents, as rotten as their marriage had been, were loved by their children and seemed to be fulfilled by that. Most of the men he knew had wives or ex-wives and children they spoke of. But since an engagement fifteen years back, he'd had no desire to open himself and trust any woman he had met. Nor had he taken the time.

He had drifted into affairs, his interest mostly in sex, the raunchier the better, then drifted out when the pairings became burdensome. A few years ago, he started to be bored with seduction. Sex was easier with a regular partner. But when words like "commitment" and "marriage" and "love" cropped up, he always started for the door. He never led a woman to believe she had a long-term future with Drake Lockhart.

Lately, he'd had some melancholy moments over the emptiness of his life. The idea of a caring permanent companion and a family had become more appealing. What was the point in piling up assets if you had no one with whom to share them?

And he did have assets. Besides his part ownership of the Double-Barrel Ranch, his company, Lockhart Concepts, owned stand-alone commercial buildings, strip malls and apartment complexes with high occupancy rates. Despite how the disastrous economy had affected the real estate market, he was coming to the end of an enormously successful year. His broker/agents had put together deals that had brought more commissions than ever into his company. Early in the year, he had purchased several assets out of bankruptcies—one being a fifty-story office and retail building in downtown Dallas. His personal worth had grown significantly.

All of that was good for his financial statement and pumping up his ego, but on a cold night, he couldn't have sex or cozy up for warmth with a skyscraper.

But letting his mother know he had those thoughts even occasionally would be like waving a red cape in front of a mad bull. From thin air, she would produce a parade of women who wanted to get married.

And thinking about his mother, there she was. Over the heads of the crowd, Drake spotted her with Barron Wilkes, her boyfriend. Even after seven years, that phrase still sent a fingernails-on-a-chalkboard shudder over Drake. He made a mental groan. If his mother had to have a boy-friend, why in hell couldn't it be somebody other than a retired Realtor and land developer notorious for his crooked streak.

Chapter Six

IN THE IVORY marble ladies' room, Shannon stripped off her wet shoes and stockings, then spent five minutes drying them under the blast of warm air from the hand dryer. Using wads of damp paper towels, she tried to remove spots and stains from her skirt where water had splashed up from the wet sidewalk.

Finally, she stared in horror at her reflection in the wide vanity mirror. The least bit of humidity affected the curse from her mother's side, her thick, naturally curly hair. At home, she had spent an hour straightening it into a smooth waterfall that fell past her shoulders. Now, after exposure to so much dampness, it had sprung into an aura of unruly red ringlets.

"Oh, hell," she muttered.

She did not want the wealthy and sophisticated guests she would meet this evening to see her as some wild creature with out-of-control hair.

You should just give up and go home, her cranky alter ego grumbled.

But she couldn't. She had waited three months for this. Had bought the dress, bought the shoes and finagled a free ticket, none of which was returnable for a refund.

She had no hairpins, no clip, no tools except a tiny hair pick. Mumbling a litany of cusswords, she dug the hair pick out of her clutch and went to work. After she finished, she had a saucy curly do with loose wisps and tendrils.

She moved on to her makeup, attempting to preserve it by gingerly patting her face with another sheet of paper toweling, then tried to touch up her blush and lipstick. *Hell. Just hell.* Half her makeup was gone. She was such a mess, she could be in the ladies' room all evening redressing herself and applying new makeup, in which case she would never make it to the party.

Giving up, she dropped onto a thickly upholstered love seat and pulled on the warm thigh-high stockings. At least the warm stockings were bringing sensation back to her feet. Her numb toes had started to sting.

Feeling more put together, she rose and directed her attention to her dress, tugging and straightening. In her mind, it had become *The Dress*. She had never owned anything so striking. The long-sleeved, floor-length swatch of dark green fabric was adorned with strategically placed mirror sequins that sparkled when the light struck them just right. The mesh knit clung to her figure in all the right places except for where it showed bare skin.

With the neckline cut in a deep V in front and an even deeper one in back, it had a sewn-in uplift bra. She lifted and molded her ample breasts until they felt comfortable in the cups. Without a real bra with hooks and straps, she felt naked, which was bad enough, but what was worse, half of a yellow rose tattoo on the slope of her left breast peeked out from the neckline's edge. On her pale skin, it stood out as if it were neon.

The image wasn't huge. The flower was roughly the size of a half dollar. Nor was it ugly. As tattoos went, the artistry was good. Though it was ten years old, the lines were still crisp and clear, the yellow petals and green leaves still clean and bright.

She hated it. Too often when she saw it, the recollection of the night she had gotten it and the guy she had let convince her it was a good idea came back.

Fairly certain that none of tonight's guests sported tattoos on their breasts, she adjusted and rearranged until the yellow rose was out of sight. Then, exhaling a great breath, she stuffed a basketball-size wad of paper towels into the trash, picked up her jacket and tramped toward the elevators.

On the ride to the second floor, her alter ego continued to peck at her: *I don't know why being here is such a good idea, why mingling with this crowd is so important.*

But before Shannon could join that argument, the elevator stopped, the doors glided open and she was only steps away from the Grand Ballroom's arched entrance.

She paused beneath the wide archway, looking out over the huge room packed like sardines. Above the din of many voices, a distant mellow saxophone blew "Merry Christmas." The party was well under way.

She had suspected this would be a fashion show and she had been right. The men wore tuxes, the women had on high-fashion frocks, probably by designer names Shannon had only read about or seen in Neiman Marcus. Names like Armani, Versace, Badgley Mischka. Now she was glad she had bought *The Dress*.

Though excitement hummed from the roots of her mind-of-its-own hair to the soles of her frozen feet, she hesitated.

You're here, the alter ego's rival told her. *You wanted to mix with these big shots, so go for it!*

Nearby, several well-dressed women with manicured fingers were taking the white and gold-embossed tickets and dropping them into a big fishbowl on a long white-clothed table. Thank God she had one, although she noticed that not every guest was asked to authenticate him or herself by showing one.

A steward approached and asked for her coat, pointing out a makeshift closet in the left front corner of the room. *Damn.* She had no cash. She'd had so many other things on her mind, she hadn't thought of tips. She handed over the black jacket, feeling guilty.

As the steward whisked her coat away, she opened her clutch and pulled out the ticket her colleague had given her. She hesitated, then passed it to a perfectly-coiffed middle-aged woman who wore a light-fracturing rock on her left ring finger. A chubby balding man stood at her shoulder, ogling Shannon's chest. Fearing her tattoo showed, Shannon pressed her silver clutch against her breast and sidled away from the table.

She squeezed into the crowd where throngs of the well-heeled and impeccably dressed schooled like glittering fish among tinsel and colored lights. She had attended some professional events over the course of her six-year real estate career—meetings, seminars, parties, even—but she had never been to anything quite like this.

Stewards in white coats rushed about carrying trays of colorful drinks. At one table, a multi-tiered ice sculpture lorded over platters of artfully arranged boiled shrimp. Other trays held a variety of sushi delights and a dozen different kinds of canapés.

On another table stood a tall flowing chocolate fountain that saturated the air around it with the decadent aroma of the rich dark brown sweet. Plates and plates of fruits and nuts and little cakes for dipping surrounded it. One huge tray held chocolate-dipped strawberries decorated to look like little tuxedos and lined up like soldiers. She wanted to take one home to Grammy Evelyn, but how? One wouldn't fit into her clutch without being squashed and making a big mess.

Never having witnessed or been a part of such blatant excess, Shannon was as awestruck as if she were at Disneyland.

All around her, the air teemed with a kinetic energy and the smell of money. She imagined passionate conversations about profits and deals that would make sweeping changes somewhere. Sheer fascination chased away her initial fears and she was happy she had come. She eased through the room, watching one person she recognized as a Fort Worth politician, listening to another well-known TV anchor woman whose voice she recognized without seeing her face.

An inexplicable emotion rose from deep within. Not envy. Something more like a weighty longing. For her whole rocky and uncertain existence as an adult, Shannon had wanted to someday, somehow, be a woman of substance, a person who had earned a place in a room like this. Now, for the first time in her life, that nebulous desire seemed like a possibility. She might have experienced a few detours on her journey to this point, might have behaved impulsively, might have made some errors in judgment, but her life was on track now. She had learned self-discipline and goal setting and these days, there was little that could deter her from her chosen path to success.

Letting herself be carried along by the crowd, she sought Jordan Palmer, the man who had provided her with entrée to this hoity-toity soiree. They didn't have a real date. She would never feel comfortable dating any man who had an air of a huckster about him. They had run into each other in a continuing education class a few months back. When he told her he had an extra ticket to this affair and no one to use it, she had offered to buy it from him. He had refused her money and given it to her for free.

Shannon might be a small town girl, but she hadn't just fallen off a turnip truck. He expected something in return. Most likely sex. She had no intention of sleeping with him, which was why she had told him she would meet him here rather than accompany him.

He had said to look for him near the stage. Inch by inch she made it to the center of the swarm. The din elevated to a roar, the sound of the saxophone grew louder, so she must be nearing the stage. A few more steps revealed a small tuxedoed orchestra on a platform. A parquet dance floor lay in front of it and a few couples moved around to the strains of "I'll Be Home for Christmas."

Draped with thick ropes of gold garland and twinkling with hundreds of white lights, a Christmas tree at the corner of the dance floor soared toward the high ceiling. Red balls the size of volleyballs hung from its branches.

While she stared up at it in amazement, from somewhere behind it, Jordan came toward her looking sleek and handsome in a *GQ* casual way. He might not be her kind of man, but she had to admit, with his black hair slicked back and wearing a tux and cummerbund, he was easy on a woman's eyes.

"Hey, you made it," he said. "After the weather moved in, I thought you might not risk the drive."

Shannon tucked her clutch under her arm and she and Jordan touched cheeks and kissed air. "After you gave me a ticket and I bought a dress, no way would I miss it." She gave a foolish laugh. God, she was almost giddy.

"And that is some dress, gal." He stood back, holding her fingertips with his, and gave a low whistle. His eyes moved up to her face. "And your hair. I've never seen your hair like that. You make the other women here look like frogs."

And hearing a compliment like that made Shannon feel like a red carpet celebrity. She struck a playful hand-on-hip pose. "Why, thank you, Jordan."

He led them away from the dance floor to a quieter part of the room. "Have any trouble on the road?"

"Not a bit. It's a little misty, but not quite cold enough for ice."

"It's not supposed to freeze. Just be cold and nasty."

A server strolled past carrying a tray of flutes of champagne. Jordan snagged two and handed her one. "So how's your Benbrook deal coming? Wrapped it up yet?"

He spoke of a fifty-year-old apartment complex, her first commercial sale. She had been coddling it for eight months, saying a silent prayer every day for it to close. That very sale was one of the accomplishments that made her believe she was qualified to mingle with this crowd. At least she had something to talk about. She accepted the glass of champagne. "Not yet, but soon."

"You've resolved all the problems, then?"

Through the professional grapevine, Jordan had heard about the sale's many snarls and snags and called her, offering to walk her through it. She had suspected a trap. Jordan had never done anything underhanded to her personally, but she had heard plenty about him from others in the business. She didn't believe for a minute he had offered to help her out of the goodness of his heart. He wanted part of the commission.

She angled a playful look at him. "Hah. If getting me into this fancy wingding and showering me with compliments is a tactic for horning in on my deal, you'd better try another approach."

Jordan slapped a palm against his chest, gasped and frowned. "You wound me, darlin'. Do you think I'm that clever?"

She chuckled, looking out over the crowd. "You're a total shark, Jordan. And I'm still saying I'm claiming that Benbrook payday all for myself. I need that whole commission and I *don't* need anyone's help."

And at that moment, glancing over the rim of her glass and across the room, as if the mob had parted just for her, a tall man some forty feet away caught Shannon's eye. He looked different from the others in the room, like a nineteenth century throwback who might walk outside, mount his horse and ride away.

He was wearing a Texas tux, as were many of the men in the room—starched and ironed jeans, Wranglers, perhaps, or possibly Cinch—with a black tuxedo coat. The well-tailored jacket stretched across wide shoulders and emphasized a narrow waist. No tie. Instead, he wore one of those old-fashioned-looking collarless shirts. And cowboy boots. If he weren't in Texas—and *Fort Worth, Texas*, at that—he would look glaringly out of place.

An odd quiver shimmied through her stomach and as if a magnet held her eyes, she couldn't keep from staring.

He was too far away to see his face clearly, but his hair was a rich shade of brown, slightly sun-streaked. He had one of those sexy haircuts. Neither short nor long and skillfully layered to appear unruly and orderly at the same time.

He seemed familiar, but Shannon came in contact with so many people, she often saw those who looked familiar but weren't. Celebrity sightings occurred frequently in North Texas. At this moment, the NCHA World Finals was happening, populated by a cutting horse crowd rife with big name celebrity horse owners. Was he someone rich and famous? Movie star? Rodeo or country music star? Professional athlete? Too young to be an oilman.

This is silly, her alter ego said. *You'll never know who he is*.

Engaged in what appeared to be a serious conversation with a shorter, animated man, one of his hands clasped the bowl of a champagne glass. The other was stuffed into his jeans pocket, pushing back his coattail. He looked to be as relaxed as if he were having a drink in his den at the ranch instead of a fancy hotel ballroom.

Among the many things Shannon had learned in real estate sales was that she had an uncanny knack for reading people. This guy was a total alpha male. He had it—that maxed-out testosterone level, that arcane male confidence that had always caused her brain to short circuit.

Underneath his clothing would be a well-structured mass of powerful masculine energy. He would be a hunter, a fisherman, a poker-player—one of the boys. His credo would be lead, follow or get out of my way. Indeed, he was a man who went after what he wanted and got it—including women. Oh, he was bad all right. Bad to the bone. And he would be good in bed. Instinctively, she knew it.

A warm tingle began to hum in her most secret regions and a warmth crawled up her neck. Lust. Raw and pure. Recognizing it, she fought it. She had to. She was a different woman now.

Though her good sense took control and determined the wisest thing was to give a man like him a wide berth, the part of her she had never quite been able to control when it came to bad boys, the part that had driven her into regrettable associations in the past, wouldn't let her to stop watching him.

Watch your step, her alter ego warned.

She argued back. *Looking in a candy store window does no harm, does it?*

Jordan's voice broke into her musing. "You look flushed. You okay?"

Stunned by the intense physical reaction, she tried to will her erratic pulse to calm. She gave a silly titter. "This crowd must be making me nervous." She nodded toward the man who had seized her attention. "Who is that?"

"Who, the tall guy in jeans or the other guy?"

"The tall one."

"You don't recognize one of *Texas Monthly's* most eligible bachelors?"

Shannon detected a sneer in Jordan's comment. She didn't subscribe to *Texas Monthly*. The only place she ever read it was in her dentist's office. "No, I don't."

"It was a feature they did two or three years ago. That's his highness, Drake Lockhart."

She suppressed a gasp. If one was a part of the real estate world, one would have to be deaf, dumb and blind not to know of the cosmic Drake Lockhart. Articles about him appeared often in newspapers and trade journals. Most eligible bachelor? If he was unmarried, she had no doubt he had been deemed *most eligible* by any woman who ever met him.

She cocked her head to the side, still not taking her eyes off him. "I've read about him."

Jordan swallowed a sip of champagne. "Well, that's him. In the flesh. But don't get too excited. He's not someone whose acquaintance you'd enjoy. He's a real asshole. A big feeler."

"You know him? Why do you call him that?"

"He's so damned full of himself. I'm surprised his ego fits in this room. And he's one slick sonofabitch, I'll tell you. He aced me out of a skyscraper deal in Dallas before I even knew what happened."

Shannon's opinion of one of the most successful young businessmen in the Metroplex was not negatively impacted by Jordan's remarks. If anything, she was more intrigued. And since Jordan's words sounded small-minded and catty, she chose not to respond to them. Instead, she said, "I know of the Lockhart family. They're big ranchers in Drinkwell."

"Drinkwell? Is that a town?" Jordan gave a condescending laugh Shannon often heard from city people when discussing small rural towns.

"You're such an urbanite, Jordan. It's thirty-five miles from where I live. When I was in high school, we played their sports teams. The Lockhart family owns the old Double-Barrel Ranch. And has forever. It takes up most of Treadway County."

Just then, a model-thin blonde joined the subject of the conversation and possessively slid her arm around his. Tanned, tall and svelte like him, they were a magazine layout couple. The flutter in Shannon's stomach died as she compared her own milky-white skin that never tanned, her disorderly hair and her more voluptuous shape. Not that she was overweight, but she wasn't pencil-thin like the woman who was now hanging onto his arm.

"Oh. He has a girlfriend," she said. "Or is that his wife?"

"She's not his wife yet," Jordan answered. "That's Donna Schoonover. Donna *Stafford*-Schoonover to be precise. You know Don Stafford, the oilman? The guy who owns a Cadillac dealership for a hobby? He's her daddy. Schoonover's the name she got from a Dutch soccer pro she was married to for a while. People are saying Drake's going to be her fourth husband." Jordan followed up with one of those knowing "men" laughs.

"Who in North Texas doesn't know of Don Stafford and his millions? Why do you laugh?"

"Because my money says she'll never land him. Too many have tried before her. Drake's a lone wolf. He's got his own fortune. Her family's bucks aren't a temptation to a high-roller like him. And if she hasn't figured that out, she's dumber than I think."

Lone wolf. High-roller. The words stuck in Shannon's brain as if they had been thumb-tacked. The guy was even more dangerous than she had first thought and that idea sent another potent surge through her. "How is it you know him so well?"

"I just do."

As Shannon puzzled over that non-answer, the beautiful couple and the short man were joined by a striking middle-aged woman with silver shoulder-length hair. She, too, was tall and slender and draped in silver lame that fell to the tops of silver cowboy boots. She wore chunky Southwest style jewelry. Boots and turquoise were not choices Shannon would have worn with that particular dress, but the look had a certain panache and screamed *I'm-from-Texas-and-proud-of-it.*

"And there's his mommy," Jordan said snidely. "Drake Lockhart's a mama's boy and everybody knows it."

Shannon gave Jordan a look. "You really don't like him, do you?"

"Like I said, he's an asshole."

The silver-haired woman and the blonde walked away together, but Drake continued in conversation with the shorter man, seemingly unaware that half the women in the room must surely be drooling over him. Then, he raised his head and for absolutely no reason, turned Shannon's way. Their gazes locked for the briefest moment and her heartbeat stuttered. It happened in a matter of seconds, but she felt as if she had been undressed and thoroughly examined. Her whole body grew hot and needy in way it hadn't in a very long time.

She turned quickly toward a server and exchanged her empty champagne glass for a full one.

&

Drake was taken aback. He couldn't stop staring at the red-haired woman. She was wearing one of those glittery dresses and in the room's special lighting, she looked like an exquisite emerald. The eyes of every hard-leg in the room had to be glued to that centerfold body. For sure, she had the attention of that bastard, Jordan Palmer, who practically had his tongue in her ear. An uncharacteristic pang of possessiveness dinged him, making him wonder about his own sanity.

But it was more than her looks or the momentary envy of a man Drake disliked immensely that captured him. Like chain lightning, something he couldn't define sizzled straight from her to him, clear across the room. His thoughts flew to how fine it would be to slowly remove that dress from such a delectable body.

He had come here with no interest or intention of anything other than doing his duty by making a purchase, getting through the evening and returning home. Alone. But suddenly the idea of this beautiful stranger's company was downright enticing. At the very least, he had to know who she was.

"Anson," he said to his friend. "See the redhead over there in the green dress?"

"Sure do," his friend said, looking toward her with an unabashed leer.

"Do you know her?"

Anson gave a lascivious chuckle. "No, but I'd like to."

Drake glared with resentment at the man's profile, then checked himself, lest he reveal his own wicked thoughts. He sipped from his champagne glass, plotting the best approach to meet her, given that he was with a date and Jordan Palmer didn't appear to be going away. But before he could devise a plan, Donna returned and dragged him off to the silent auction.

Chapter Seven

DRAKE LAGGED BEHIND as Donna weaved past multiple white-clothed tables of donated wares and services at auction. Nothing interested him, but he was expected to choose something. He wrote bids on a lunch with the mayor and tickets to premium seats at the Fort Worth Stock Show and Rodeo coming up in January. He was ambivalent about the lunch, but he bid enough on the rodeo tickets that he would probably win them.

Just ahead, Donna swayed and gripped the display tables' edges for balance. Her agreement to lay off the martinis had gone bye-bye fifteen minutes after they arrived. He couldn't guess how many she'd had, but he could see the situation had nowhere to go but downhill.

"You're staggering, babe. You're going to feel like hell tomorrow. Let's call it a night." He grasped her elbow and attempted to guide her toward the doorway.

Yanking her elbow away from him, she teetered and stepped backward to gain her balance. "Kiss my ass. I'm having a good time. I don't know why I put up with your old-maid attitude."

"I don't know why either. Look, I'm trying to do you a favor. Let me take you home."

He took her arm again and tried to urge her forward, but she refused to budge. One corner of her mouth tipped up into a silly grin. "Got another hot piece lined up, Drakey?"

"Donna, c'mon. Let's just go home."

"Don't think I don't notice what goes on behind my back," she slurred. "Every bitch in this room would like to fuck one of—

"Don't say it, Donna."

"Fuck you. I'll say what I goddamn well please." Her lips curled into a drunken sneer. "State's most eligible bachelor. Hah. I used to be just like them. I used to think I couldn't live without—"

"Donna. Let's. Go."

"I wanna dance." She started for the doorway, swaying her hips and trying to step to the rhythm of the music. All at once her foot caught on a table leg and she lurched forward. Drake grabbed for her, but couldn't keep her from landing on her knees in front of the table.

He dropped to a squat and began to check her for injury. "Jesus, Donna. Are you all right?"

"Some sonofabitch tripped me." Breaking into tears, she pushed herself to a sitting position. "Who tripped me?"

"You caught your toe on something." He slid an arm around her waist. "Let's get you up."

Her body was limp as cooked spaghetti and he struggled to lift her to her feet. Just as he succeeded, a mutual acquaintance strolled past, accompanied by a woman Drake didn't know. "Jimmy, you cocksucker!" Donna yelled at his back.

Adrenaline zoomed through Drake's system. His jaw clenched. The din surrounding them ceased and people stared. Jimmy stopped, turned to face them and opened both arms in a "who-me?" gesture.

Donna lunged toward him, but was unable to escape Drake's tightened his grip on her waist. "You tripped me, you little fucker," she shouted.

"Jesus Christ, Donna," Drake said *sotto voce*, using his strength to restrain her. "Shut your mouth. Just shut up."

"God, Donna, I wasn't anywhere near you," the accused said, a stupefied look on his face. The woman with him stood slack-jawed and wide-eyed.

"Sorry, Jimmy," Drake said. "She didn't mean it. Please excuse us. We're going home."

Donna's mouth twisted into a snarl. "Fuck both of you." She jerked free of Drake's hold. "The only place I'm going is to the bathroom. I gotta piss." She stumbled away from them.

Before Drake could grab her or follow her, Jimmy looked up at him. "I'm sorry, Drake. But I don't think I tripped her."

"No, no, you didn't," Drake said. "She caught her foot on something. It's all good, okay?" He gave Jimmy a reassuring pat on the shoulder. "Have a good night, okay? I'm going to go check on her." He headed toward the ladies' room, grabbling for his own composure.

Just then, like a heat-seeking missile, his mother came straight at him.

Great. Just what I need.

She halted in front of him, placing her hand on his arm and looking up at him. "Son, are you and Donna quarreling?"

Drake's brow crunched into frown so tight his temples ached. "I'm not quarreling." He looked across the room rather than at her, trying to keep Donna in sight. "Yet," he added.

"What does that mean?" his mother asked.

"Don't worry about it, Mom. It's no big deal."

"There's so much noise. Maybe no one important heard what she said."

Barron Wilkes came from somewhere, placed his left hand on Mom's waist and proffered his right hand to Drake. "Good evening, Drake. Haven't seen you in a while."

Drake accepted the handshake. "I've been around."

Wilkes angled a sly look at him and smiled. "Talk is you've got something going on with windmills and some West Texas boys. Find that more profitable than building shopping centers? Or drilling for shale gas?" He followed up with a low, knowing chuckle as if he and Drake were confidantes.

"Look, you're going to have to excuse me," Drake said, clapping Wilkes' shoulder with one hand. "I need to help Donna. She needs to go home."

"Oh, of course," his mother replied. "I'll talk to you later. Maybe we can do lunch next—"

Drake left her still talking and started across the room.

Shannon drifted from one group to another listening to snippets of conversation but offering little comment of her own. Sans the miniscule eye contact with the Lockhart star, she was reminded that many of the rich were boring. God knew she had escorted enough of them through houses and over vacant building lots to form that opinion.

She hadn't seen Jordan in a while. Once he realized he couldn't lure her into a sleepover, he had flitted like a butterfly from one elegantly dressed female to the next. He must have landed one and left. A huge relief.

She hadn't seen Drake Lockhart and Donna Schoonover either. Evidently, they had left, too. His fiancé was obviously drunk, but still, Shannon couldn't keep from imagining what might be going on between the most appealing man she had seen in years and one of the richest young women in Texas.

Also one of the rudest, if tonight's behavior was typical, Shannon's alter ego put in sourly.

Shannon couldn't disagree. Half the room had heard her shout obscenities.

Shannon's partying mood had deteriorated. For all its pomp and pageantry, this party didn't amount to much. She certainly hadn't gained enough from it to warrant depleting her bank account to buy clothing or risking her neck driving in bad weather.

She hadn't made the contacts she had hoped to. She hadn't run into the Dallas broker who had listed her five-acre corner. And as for gleaning a tidbit that might be helpful to her cause, she now realized that such a small tract of land in a small town like Camden held no significance for the people at this party. The ones who were interested in the real estate business chattered about multi-million dollar projects like huge shopping malls and multi-story office buildings and renovating old skyscrapers in downtown Fort Worth or Dallas.

She began to think of the forty-five mile drive back to Camden. Realizing she had drunk enough champagne to take her from buzz to being slightly drunk, she declined a server's offer of another glass of bubbly and made her way out of the ballroom to the foyer bar.

❧

Drake wasn't easily embarrassed, but tonight, Donna had succeeded. He left her plush townhouse at a clip, grateful to be escaping with his hide. Breaking up with her while she was drunk had been risky, but he had dared. He told her flatly that it was over between them. She threatened to sic her father on him and threw a vase at him, but he ducked in time. He had left her in the care of her personal maid.

Now, driving back toward downtown Fort Worth and the Worthington Hotel, he considered that it wasn't over with Donna yet. He would hear from her tomorrow after she sobered up. Around noon, most likely.

Hell, he might even hear from her father and that bothered him. He liked and respected Don Stafford, believed the feeling to be mutual. He bit down on the inside of his lower lip. Well, if Stafford chose to end a friendship over a break-up with his daughter, so be it.

Soon he saw the city's white-lighted silhouette showing like a wide tiara through a veil of heavy mist. He narrowed his focus to the redheaded woman. He only hoped she hadn't left the party.

❧

Sitting on a tall vinyl stool, Shannon sipped ice water, mulling over how long she should wait before starting the trip home. She had just decided she was okay to drive when a deep but soft male voice came from behind her. "What are you drinking?"

Her heart leaped. She knew. Just knew. She jerked her head toward the voice and less than an arm's length away, he was there.

And Donna Schoonover wasn't.

His tanned cheeks showed high color, as if he had rushed in from outside. Late day whiskers shadowed his square jaw. He was near enough for her to clearly see his eyes—an unusual brown, not like chocolate, more like whiskey. And eyelashes any girl would envy.

She regrouped and willed herself not to stammer. "It's ice water. I'm driving."

He moved to the bar. Standing beside her stool, he summoned the bartender. In a black overcoat, his shoulders seemed even wider than they had looked in the ballroom. "Responsible thinking. I'm impressed."

His scent surrounded her. Heavenly, like chilled night air and expensive cologne. She had always loved a woodsy masculine scent on a man. One more thing about Drake Lockhart—as if any more were needed—met her expectations.

He summoned the bartender. "Bring me what she's having."

She looked up at him, questioning with her eyes.

He leaned on his right elbow on the bar's black padded edge. His gaze moved down to her mouth. "Water's fine with me, ma'am. The last thing I want to be at this particular moment is under the influence."

Her heartbeat raced off on a wild tangent. She turned away and set her glass on the bar.

He braced his left boot on the rung of her stool, his thigh touching hers. Heat rushed up her spine. "Where, um, are you driving to?" he asked.

"Ca—" She stopped herself. Did she really want to tell him where she lived? "Home," she said.

The bartender reappeared and set another glass of ice water on the bar. Drake straightened, picked it up, sipped and set it down. "You were with someone earlier. Did he leave?"

Oh, hell! "Jordan Palmer? He, um…yes. We weren't really together. We're just friends."

The next thing she knew, this beautiful man had stepped to her side, placed his hand under her elbow and urged her off the stool. "Walk with me," he said.

Her heartbeat raced off on another wild tangent, but as if he were Pied Piper, she offered no resistance as he steered her away from the bar.

❧

"Just friends" was a too-casual phrase that had no real meaning in Drake's lexicon. Could he believe she wasn't Palmer's girlfriend? "Do you have a coat?" he asked.

"It's in that coatroom in the corner."

He guided her without obstacle or interruption through the thinning crowd toward the coat storage area. She was tall, but still inches shorter than he, even wearing high heels. Her scent wafted to him, something womanly and sexy.

"Most of this crowd is associated with the real estate business," he said. "You're what? Broker? Investor?...Wait, lemme guess. A politician."

"Um, no. None of those things. I, uh, just came here with Jordan."

But she had already said she *wasn't* with Palmer. Something wasn't right, but Drake couldn't quickly figure out what, wasn't sure he wanted to know about it if it conflicted with his greater purpose.

They reached the makeshift coat closet. She opened her purse, pulled out her chit and handed it to the steward who manned the coat check. He hurried away and soon returned carrying a short black jacket. Drake took it and held it while she turned her back and slipped her arms into it. It was fancy, but lightweight. "This doesn't look very warm."

She smiled up at him, showing perfect white teeth. "It isn't. It's strictly an evening wrap."

He pulled his money clip out of his pocket, peeled off a twenty and handed it to the steward. "It's pretty," he told her.

She smiled again. "Thank you. It's a vintage garment. My grandmother wore it years ago. It makes me feel glamorous in a nineteen forties kind of way."

An old fashioned girl? She didn't look the part, but the idea that she might be intrigued Drake all the more. He couldn't think of a single one of his female acquaintances he would call "an old fashioned girl."

He took her elbow again and guided her out of the foyer, into the spacious hallway. He gestured toward an alcove almost hidden by a tall vase holding a splashy floral arrangement. "Let's stop here for a minute."

She turned to face him, her back pressed against the wall, her hands behind her. Her jacket opened, showing deep cleavage. Spurred by the blatant body language, Drake placed a hand against the wall beside her head and forced his eyes up from her breasts.

Up close, she was even more striking than from a distance. Her face was as flawless as porcelain. Her eyes were green. But not just any green. They were the distinctive color of sage in springtime.

He settled his gaze on her plump heart-shaped lips, parted and inviting. All he could think of was taking that mouth in a deep kiss. Saliva swelled in his mouth. Blood rushed to his loins, so hot and potent it left him disoriented. *What the hell was this*?

He blinked away the feeling. This was no place for kissing, especially in the way he wanted to kiss her. "Drake Lockhart's my name," he said softly. "What's yours?"

"Sha—" She stopped, hesitated, then looked down. "Uh, Sharon. Sharon Phillips."

What's to stammer about? A distant warning pinged inside Drake's head, but he ignored it.

Her pulse fluttered in the hollow of her throat. His tongue itched to touch it, but he reined himself in and took his pleasure by letting his gaze again move over the slope of lush mammary flesh between her chin and her dress's neckline, visualized it peaked into rosy pebbles waiting for his mouth. Everything about her screamed sex.

"You don't look like a Sharon to me." He pushed away from the wall, stepped back and stuffed his hands into his coat pockets. "I'd peg you as Lisa or Diana."

"Diana?" She chuckled. "Wasn't she a Roman goddess? Of the hunt? Or something like that?"

He joined her laugh with one of his own. "Forgive me if my mythology is rusty. Didn't that lady have a touch of brutality about her? Am I in danger here?"

She didn't change her position. Even her smile stayed in place, teasing and flirty. "Depends on your point of view. I don't think I've harmed anyone lately. Are Lisa and Diana your favorite names?"

"I don't have any favorite names. But those two strike me as being especially female." He paused, holding her eyes with his. "And that's how *you* strike me."

Her head tilted and a slow wise smile played across her mouth. Oh, yeah. She knew how she was affecting him. And she knew what he wanted, but what wasn't quite evident yet was if she wanted the same thing.

"Tell you what," he said. "Let's escape this joint." He took her arm again and guided her toward the elevator.

"Perhaps you should tell me where we're escaping to. I might not want to go."

"Are you hungry?"

"Actually, I am. Except for those *hors d'oeuvres* in there, I haven't eaten since lunch. Are the restaurants around here still open?"

"I'm thinking of my place. I live only a few blocks from here. I'll order something delivered."

She stopped, lifted her arm from his hand and looked up at him. "You're inviting me to go home with you at this time of night?...To eat?"

"It's quiet there. We can—"

"But you have a fiancé. Jordan said—"

"Not true."

"And what if I said, Mr. Lockhart, as clichéd as it sounds, I'm not that kind of girl?"

"You're the kind of girl who eats supper, aren't you?" He gave her his best half smile. "Anything more than that is strictly up to you."

Chapter Eight

OUTSIDE, IN THE hotel's brightly lit portico, Drake summoned a valet. Shannon stood to the side shivering and clasping her jacket's silky fox fur collar under her chin, her thoughts spinning like a wheel within a wheel. His invitation to supper was nothing more than a poorly disguised seduction. She should have declined, especially after he said it was to be "take-out" at his home rather than at a restaurant. For all she knew, he might call in a pizza.

But as the truth gradually centered in her thoughts, she had to ask herself, were her own intentions any more righteous than his? That urge to take a chance, that daring to walk on the wild side that had dogged her in her twenties, was still a part of her makeup. And that part said, *Go with him. When will you ever meet such an interesting man again? When will you ever get another chance to do something this exciting?*

Her alter ego piped up. *You've already given him an alias. He doesn't have to know who you are.*

And among those disjointed musings, a reality question burned through: *How could this ever go anywhere?*

Drake's attention returned to her, disrupting the melee in her mind. "On a summer night, my place would be a nice walk from here, but it's too cold and messy tonight. My car will be here in a minute."

Thank God he hadn't opted for a stroll. She nodded, tightening her jaw to prevent her teeth chattering. He removed his overcoat, stepped behind her and placed it around her shoulders. It almost dragged the ground, but enveloped in heavy wool that had been warmed by his body and smelled of his cologne, she pulled it close around her and shuddered with relief. "Thank you."

His hands cupped her shoulders, his head bent and he whispered near her ear, "You're welcome."

Lord, he had a devastating voice. She couldn't keep from imagining hearing it across a pillow. Another shiver that had nothing to do with the temperature darted down her spine.

A sleek silver sports car stopped at the curb in front of them, a make Shannon didn't recognize. *Oh, my God. It's one of those really expensive ones.*

The valet scooted from behind the steering wheel, rounded the backend and opened the passenger door. She held Drake's coat closed with one hand, picked up her skirt with the other and crawled inside. The interior was already warm, thank God, and it smelled of leather and richness.

Seconds later, he ducked behind the steering wheel, adding his scent to the heady mix of smells. With his height and wide shoulders, along with the black interior and mist-shrouded windows, the car became as intimate as a cocoon.

"It's late for a heavy meal," he said in a hushed tone as he turned his head to the left and checked traffic behind them. "Something light okay with you?"

"Of course."

He pulled onto the street and they motored away from the brightly lit portico into the dark wet night.

As the truth of what she had agreed to crystallized, Shannon's pulse began to thud in her ears. That daring part of her spoke up again. *Just be calm. This isn't the first time you've fallen into a spur-of-the-moment tryst. Not the first time you've done something crazy. Not so many years ago, "impulsive" was your middle name. You survived, didn't you? Besides, would a prestigious magazine like Texas Monthly select an ax murderer as the year's most eligible bachelor?*

He pulled a cell phone from his jacket pocket with his right hand. "Any objection to shrimp or possibly lobster?"

"Either's fine."

He speed-dialed with his thumb. He had wonderful masculine hands with long agile fingers and short un-manicured nails. He wore no rings, but his hands bore scars, the hands of someone who had worked at physical labor. Though she had heard of him in the real estate business for years, did he spend time in Drinkwell working on his family's ranch?

Phone pressed to his ear, he listened for a minute, then placed a detailed order for fresh Gulf shrimp, a salad of field greens and a dessert. Though he spoke with a soft Texas drawl, she detected a ring of authority. *No one ever tells him no,* she mused.

The small space in the car and the split up the front of her skirt made covering her knees impossible. He slid his phone back into his pocket and placed his right palm on her exposed knee. Swallowing a catch in her breath, she stared at it, but made no attempt to move it. Or to move her knee. His hand moved up and cupped the inside of her thigh only inches below the top of her thigh-high stocking and gently squeezed.

Yikes! Her sex clenched and she swallowed another caught breath.

You should've known he'd be a fast mover, her cranky alter ego said, obviously peeved.

In a matter of minutes, they arrived at a remarkable thirty-story building rising from the heart of the city. It had been written about in all of the local newspapers and magazines. The words LOCKHART TOWER, spotlighted with dramatic architectural lighting spanned the space above the wide entrance. She stared out at it, awed that he had bought, re-designed and re-constructed every part of it.

You, my dear, are definitely not in Kansas anymore. That damn voice in her head just wouldn't shut up.

She swallowed a gulp.

She hung onto the seat as he turned sharply into an underground concrete parking garage, bleeped open a steel gate, then expertly wheeled the sports car on into a cage of steel bars and killed the engine. She looked at him across her shoulder. "Is this it?"

He smiled. "It is. Home sweet home."

She turned to the left, seeking the latch on her seat belt.

"Sharon," he said softly. She looked up. He leaned toward her and his mouth covered hers in a gentle kiss. Her heartbeat spiked.

"I wanted to do that back at the hotel," he said.

Before she could muster even a reaction, much less a reply, he unfolded out of the car with the agility of an athlete. He came around to her door, opened it and offered his hand. She placed her hand in his, looked into his face again and her heart climbed into her throat. She didn't have to be a mind reader to know what the dark look in his eyes said. Her whole body flushed with…what? Embarrassment? Or was it something more like anticipation?

An elevator whisked them up. They exited into a huge gleaming lobby. A uniformed man met them. Security guard or doorman? Shannon couldn't tell, but he and Drake exchanged greetings. He called Drake "Sir" and "Mr. Lockhart."

Oh, God, this really is fairyland. And I'm with the prince.

She glanced in every direction, trying to take in her surroundings, wanting to absorb as much as possible.

Above them, a mezzanine of retail stores surrounded the lobby, the display windows showing wares and radiating low light. Dramatic indirect lighting softly glowed against lustrous deep brown marble walls and spotlighted a glass-beaded waterfall that covered the back wall. Shiny polished brass accented everything.

Off to both her left and her right, behind steel accordion security doors, wide empty walkways, dimly lit by nightlights, led away to what appeared to be stores in a shopping mall.

Shannon didn't even try to hide her awe. "This is incredible."

He took her elbow and they crossed an expanse of polished white marble floor. "We're very proud of our retailers. You've shopped in the stores, haven't you?"

She had heard about and seen ads and pictures of the exclusive shops in Lockhart Tower. Unwilling to reveal that information, she said, "I don't live in Fort Worth."

Inside, she winced at the fib, but now that she had started the deception, how could she not keep it up? She couldn't let him know she knew who he was. "We? But your name's on the outside of this building. Don't you own it?"

"Only partly now. The condos are all sold. Nowadays, my company owns only the lower three floors and the condo where I live."

They passed through glass doors into a second lobby, smaller and more private. More marble walls, tan rather than brown. A tall white Christmas tree, its white-flocked branches laden with gold ornaments and ribbons stood in one corner. Its tiny white lights reflected like stars in the walls.

He guided her to the elevator, pressed the call button and they entered a cube of smoky gold-veined mirrors, dark wood floors and soft lighting. He pressed the lighted button that showed *28* and they lifted off on a hum and a whoosh. Still enveloped by his overcoat, she hung onto the lapels as she leaned against the back wall.

I thought this building had thirty floors, she almost said, but caught herself just in time. "Is twenty-eight the top floor?" she asked instead.

"The building has thirty floors. The top units are two-story, so they take up the twenty-ninth and thirtieth floors. They're the premium units."

"You don't live in one of them?"

He shook his head. "They're over five thousand square feet each. I live alone. I don't need that much space."

He turned and leaned a shoulder against the wall, his face only inches away, the front of his shirt close enough to skim her shoulder. "You had my attention all evening. I left the party, but I went back to find you."

His soft baritone only inches from her ear sent a thrill snaking through her. Her heartbeat began to swish in her ears. Feeling lightheaded, she clutched his coat lapels tighter and stared straight ahead. She had to get control of this situation. "That must have made your fiancé unhappy."

Instantly, she wished she could take back that quip. It sounded petty and snarky and unsophisticated. It had just popped out of her mouth and surprised even her.

"If you're speaking of the woman who was with me earlier—"

"I was told she's your fiancé. And you're soon to become her fourth husband."

"If you believe that and if it makes a difference, why did you come home with me?"

Why indeed? The answer to that question would require more time than this elevator ride afforded. She arched her brow and shrugged.

The car halted. As the doors glided open, he moved into the opening, stopped the door with his body and gestured her out "She's not my fiancé. Nor is she my girlfriend. And I'm not slated to become anybody's husband."

Shannon might be persuaded that he had no immediate plans to get married, but after what Jordan had said, she didn't believe Donna Schoonover wasn't his fiancé or his girlfriend or at the very least, his sex partner. Shannon couldn't quell her curiosity about where the two of them had gone after they disappeared from the party.

She had no right to question him or be jealous. She wasn't even a jealous-hearted person. But as if a green imp were sitting on her shoulder, she couldn't seem to prevent the emotion. "Really? From the way it looked to me, she doesn't know that."

Oh, hell. Petty and unsophisticated.

"She knows it now," he said.

Shannon jerked her head toward him and gave him a look. She dared not let herself think what she was thinking.

The elevator car came to a stop and he urged her out into yet another lobby of sorts—a cubicle of spotless thick glass walls and thick carpet. Two sets of glass doors opened in two directions, each outfitted with a security keypad. Obviously only the chosen ever traveled beyond this point. Could she escape if she decided to run?

He pressed numbers into the keypad. "Let's stop playing this game," he said sharply. "I took her home. And that's all that happened."

"I didn't ask. I know it's none—"

"You're right. It's none of your business." While the heavy glass door quietly glided open, he gave her a direct look. "But you'd like to know if we had sex."

She hadn't meant to be so obvious. Her cheeks heated with embarrassment, but she refused to back down. "My thoughts are what they are. I can't control them."

"But you can believe what I say."

And perhaps she did. After all, two women in one night? How much of a stud could he be? "Okay. No big deal. I believe you."

"I'm a lot of things, Sharon. A few people think I'm the devil himself. But I'm not a liar."

Sharon! Damn! She was the one who was the liar. She passed through the doorway in front of him. "I said I believe you."

"My place is around the corner at the end of this hall."

As they walked forward, the glass door glided shut behind them, closing her into his sanctum. Passing from one secure area to another, one elevator to another, she felt less safe than she ever had. Her heart kept up a tattoo as they traversed the hallway's thick carpet.

"So much security." Her voice came out with an unexpected quiver.

"It's one of the perks to living here. We've found that the owners appreciate it. So, you don't live in Fort Worth? Where *do* you live?"

"South," she answered. "Houston," she added. *Hell!* Now she had turned a fib into an outright lie. It had just fallen out of her mouth. The alcohol must be keeping her from thinking clearly.

Or maybe it wasn't that at all. Her former reckless persona seemed to have risen up and taken over her mind and body. Maybe tonight it had no desire to be hard-working Shannon Piper. Maybe tonight it wanted to be Sharon Phillips, caught up in a fantasy, free of the demands of a struggling small business, free of the tension and drive to succeed that kept her tied in knots, free of the worry of keeping the bills paid and taking care of an adult who was much like a child. She could return to all of that tomorrow. Tonight, couldn't she just have a good time? Couldn't she just spend time with a beautiful man who made her blood hot and her heart race?

"Ah. A big city girl," he said.

"Houston *is* a big city. It makes Fort Worth look like a small town." Shannon had never been to Houston, but she knew that much.

"True. And what brings you to Cowtown? Other than the party?...And Jordan Palmer?"

Why was he so preoccupied with Jordan? Did they have history? Trying not to think of the hole she continued to dig, she focused on a massive abstract mural on the hallway wall. "Does it matter?"

"No, ma'am. Not a bit."

They turned a corner and faced a solid black shiny door marked with a polished gold *28C* and another keypad. He punched in more numbers and she heard the snick of the lock. "I can't believe you have to remember so many numbers just to get home." She looked up at him and smiled.

He smiled, too, pushed the door open and stood back for her to pass through. "And here we are."

She stepped into a spacious entry with extra-high ceilings and an incredible chandelier that looked to be made of iron and crystal. The scent of lemon oil and leather met her nose. A few more steps away to her left was an expansive living room. One entire wall was covered by nut-colored floor-to-ceiling bookshelves flanking an entertainment center and a huge flat-screen TV. A fireplace filled a corner. A long tan L-shaped sofa—obviously leather—took up the opposite corner. Everything was tan and beige and leather and tapestry. Texas chic. Expensive.

Beyond that, floor to ceiling glass stretched all the way across the living room back wall and on into the open dining area. The outside looked black tonight, but she had seen pictures of the view in magazines.

"Would you like a drink?" he asked, lifting his overcoat from her shoulders and turning away to hang it in a nearby closet.

"No, thanks. I still have to drive home."

A massive oak entry table stood immediately to her right. An intricate bronze sculpture of a cowboy roping a steer hunkered in the center of it. Carved horses galloped around the tabletop's thick edge. She laid her clutch beside the sculpture and unbuttoned her jacket.

He turned back from the closet, his eyes capturing hers. He traced her jaw with his fingers "Driving home will be safer tomorrow, don't you think? The Fort Worth PD has a low tolerance for DWI."

He expected her to spend the night. Was she that much a foregone conclusion? Stilled by the heated look in his eyes, all she could think of was, "I'm not drunk." She turned away from his touch and started to remove her jacket.

"Let me," he said, stepped behind her and helped her out of it. A shiver passed over her shoulders. "If you're still cold, I can find something warm for you to wear."

"Really, I'm fine, now. Thanks for the use of your coat."

"What kind of a jerk would I be if I let a lady stand out in the cold and shiver?"

He hung her jacket in the coat closet next to his overcoat, then removed his own tuxedo coat and hung it in the closet, too, allowing her to admire the ripple of his muscled shoulders beneath a shirt of white soft-looking fabric. *Silk? Probably.*

God, he was beautiful!

"How about some coffee?" His hand grazed her shoulder as he walked behind her. She almost jumped. Somehow, being twenty-eight floors off the ground, secured inside walls and doors accessible only by multiple key pads with codes, his every touch seemed even more personal than his hand on the inside of her thigh in the car.

Her alter ego was not napping. *Dummy. In the car, at least you could have opened the door and jumped out.* That inner voice was determined to try to make her walk the straight and narrow.

"Coffee sounds good," she told him.

"Coming up." He tilted his head toward a dark hallway and switched on a light. "The guest facility is up the hall."

"Thanks."

She picked up her clutch from the entry table and found the cleanest bathroom she had ever seen and the cleanest scent she had ever smelled. She closed the door and leaned back against it for a few seconds, trying to calm her nerves.

Minutes later, after washing her hands, she stood at the sink in front of the wide vanity mirror adjusting her dress to re-hide her tattoo and retouching her makeup. As she checked the security of her grandmother's earrings, the elderly woman's words from a few hours earlier came to her: *Oh, my dear, I've never seen you look so lovely. I know you're going to have such a wonderful evening. I'm so happy you're going.*

Grammy Evelyn, who Shannon suspected had been a social butterfly in her day, now lived vicariously through Shannon. When she had spoken those words, she had been hovering in Shannon's bathroom in Camden, watching her flatiron her hair. A visual of her bird-like hands, her fingers interlocked under her chin, rushed into Shannon's mind and a powerful emotion overtook her.

Her grandmother had shown her respect when Shannon's own self-respect had been lower than low. She'd had faith in her that Shannon hadn't had in herself. She owed both Grammy Evelyn and herself better behavior than to be picked up for a one-night stand with a man she didn't know.

Worse yet, a playboy who's looking for a good time with one of the peasants, the cranky alter ego growled.

Biting down on her lower lip, Shannon stared at the image in the mirror for a few seconds. Then, on a deep breath, she picked up her clutch and returned her lipstick and compact to it. Her hands were shaking and she clenched them to stop it.

But she had to stop more than her trembling hands. She had to end this whole sham. But how? He had already ordered dinner.

But that doesn't mean you have to eat it, her alter ego said.

As she made one more adjustment to her hairdo, she began to work out an exit speech.

Chapter Nine

DRAKE HEARD HIS guest's footsteps on the hallway's hardwood floor. He had lit the gas logs in the living room's corner fireplace. The fire and a lamp at one end of his sofa bathed the room in a low golden light. The aroma of a good Columbian roast floated on the air and the sound of some of Willie Nelson's moodier music thrummed softly in the background.

He looked up as she came into the room. He had thought her pretty at the hotel, but here, with the firelight casting her classic features in shadow and bouncing tiny shards of light off that incredible dress that hugged her shape like a lover's arms, she almost took his breath. The anticipation that had been harrying in his groin since he first saw her heightened.

She glanced at the fire.

"To take the chill off," he said.

"Country music?" She interlocked her fingers in front of her stomach, a pose that pushed her breasts into ivory mounds.

He wanted to smooth his lips over that cushion of flesh, but like a gentleman should, he made himself avert his gaze. He opened his hands. "What can I say? I'm a country boy."

The corners of her lips curved up in a faint smile and she lifted her chin. "Ah."

"I'm naturally partial to country music. Until I left home for college, I'd heard little else."

"I see."

When telling her something personal resulted in so little response, he turned back to the entertainment center and opened one of the doors, exposing his music system. "But if you don't like it, I'll change it."

She put out a hand and stopped him. "No, please leave it on. "It's fine. I'm just surprised is all. You don't seem like the country music type."

No plastic fingernails. Not even nail polish. He smiled. "And in Texas, what's the country music type? All of my family and more than half the people I know are country music fans." He closed the entertainment center's door. "I'm a little corny, but I'm tame. Cultured even. I sometimes go to plays. Or concerts. I've got season tickets to the symphony. Even give them money. You don't have to worry."

"I'm not worried."

"I grew up on a ranch in a rural part of the state. I believe it's a mistake for a man to stray too far from his roots. If he tries, people come to think he's a phony."

Why he continued to recite an autobiography, he didn't know. Something was keeping him blabbing.

A wry expression played over her face. "Among the many thoughts I have about you, Mr. Lockhart, that isn't one of them."

And what *were* her thoughts? Then it dawned on him. She might be teasing him. He smiled. "You know what? I can't think of a time when someone standing in my living room at midnight called me *Mister* Lockhart."

She shrugged. "It's just something to say. I mean, we don't know each other and—"

"Please. Call me Drake."

She shrugged again and smiled. "Okay."

Indeed, they didn't know each other, which reminded him of a question that had nagged him back at the hotel. "Tell me something. How well do you know Jordan Palmer?...And why did he leave a woman like you alone at that party?"

"You keep mentioning him. Do you know him?"

Drake more than knew Palmer. The bastard had caused considerable strife in the Lockhart family. Several years ago, after his little sister had handed Palmer his hat, he had stalked her, made her life miserable and kept her in tears for months. Finally, Drake had personally kicked his ass out of Kate's house and told him never to return.

"I've run across him here and there," he answered.

"He didn't leave me alone. I said before, we weren't really together."

Ping! The coffeemaker sounded from the kitchen. A conversation about Jordan Palmer could wait. "There's that coffee."

Drake started toward the kitchen. She followed him, her high heels making a soft clack on the hardwood floor. "Will the food be long?"

"Shouldn't be. In a hurry?"

"It's getting late. I need to get home."

Well, shit. Had she really come home with him only to eat? He hadn't thought so back at the hotel. She had raised barely a question when he invited her. In the car, he'd had his hand almost to her crotch and she hadn't objected. Had he misread her? She did seem more distant compared to the way she had been earlier. Could she be nervous? Maybe so. Hell, he was nervous, too, and a little unsteady, an uncharacteristic state for him in this situation. *Weird.*

In the kitchen, she turned in a circle, looking around. "Wow. This is some kitchen."

He, too, looked around at the state-of-the-art room with its high tray ceiling, abundant cherrywood cabinetry, tan natural slab granite counters he had personally selected and top brand stainless steel appliances. Everyone who had seen the kitchen was impressed, but to him, it looked like every kitchen his company had ever constructed.

"Thanks. I tried to dress up the kitchens and baths. I want the Lockhart Tower homeowners to feel they're getting their money's worth."

"You designed it yourself?"

"I have a professional designer. But she tolerates my input. I'm the marketer. I think I know what customers want to buy. And I'm the one with risk on the line. Those two things make me a hands-on guy. If I get stumped on something, I call on my mom for her two-cents worth. She knows her way around a kitchen."

He opened cupboard doors and dragged two mugs off a shelf, poured the coffee and handed a mug to her. "Cream? Sugar?"

"Black's fine." She took the mug and carried it over to the floor-to-ceiling window wall.

He hung back, letting his eyes linger on her hourglass shape. The back of her dress plunged in a V past her small waist. The fabric clung to her heart-shaped ass in a way that enabled him to discern the sexy little indentation where her butt muscles joined her spine. The dragon in his drawers stirred and his hands longed to caress those firm cheeks. Willing the hungry animal to settle down, he joined her and they stood side by side.

"Phooey," she said. "I wish I could see the view."

All they could see were their own hazy reflections and the rivulets of rain trailing down the thick glass. Mist and clouds and the blackest of black nights shrouded the outside. "It's too bad we can't. It's spectacular. We're facing east. On a clear day, you can see the Dallas Cowboys stadium, among other things."

"Ah. Something tells me you're a football fan."

"I wouldn't be a Texan if I didn't love football."

"You look athletic. Did you ever play?"

"In high school. I gave it a shot for a couple of years in college. Mostly warmed the bench."

Why in hell had he confessed that to *her*? He never declared his failings to someone who didn't know him. To this day, he regretted not being a better football player.

She looked up at him, smiling. "I'm surprised."

He chuckled. "Thanks, but compared to SMU's scholarship athletes, I'm a pretender. I don't know why they even let me on the team. Do you like the game?"

She returned her gaze to the nothingness outside and sipped from her mug. "Um, I don't mind it. I've heard about the stadium. Have you been in it?"

"You bet. It's quite a showplace. Jerry Jones has every reason to be proud."

"Next, you're going to tell me you have one of those fancy skyboxes."

Was she clairvoyant? He did have a skybox, but no one ever asked him about it. "Do you have some thoughts about that?"

"Not really. But I've heard someone say that those boxes are the height of decadence."

When the stadium had first opened, the VIP boxes and their $100,000 to $500,000 annual cost had caused a weeklong flurry in the media. Even as far south as Houston. Much had been made of their amenities and luxurious décor.

He chuckled. "Height of decadence? I haven't heard that one."

She looked up at him. "So you do have a skybox. You aren't upset over being put in the decadent category?"

"I'm not. But years back, it was a different story. That remark would've bothered me."

"You've changed?"

"Had to. You see, in the small town where I grew up, everybody gossips about my family. But it's small town talk that's mostly harmless. Up here, it's different. Up here, everything is political. The gossip has fangs and sometimes it shows up in print. I used to waste a lot of time coming up with schemes to counter the negative stuff people wrote about me."

"Big ego, huh?"

Ego? He would never deny personal pride in his accomplishments. He hesitated, studying her while he figured out a comeback to that remark. Finally, he said, "I was too naïve to realize that if you're out there doing something groundbreaking, some faction is going to pass judgment no matter what."

She looked down into her mug. "I know what you mean. People can be nasty."

"I got past worrying about it. I decided that if I allow other people's opinions to dictate my activities, I'll never get anything done. I get a steady dose of criticism for this or that, but now I mostly ignore it."

"People have said good things about you, too. You were *Texas Monthly's* most eligible bachelor."

Her knowing about that charade caught him off guard. "That was over two years ago. You saw the article?"

"Oh, uh, just the pictures. I didn't read it."

"What would you say if I told you that spread was an advertising campaign, bought and paid for by me?"

She looked up at him again, humor glinting in her eyes. "I'd say wow. You really *were* worried about what people thought of you.'"

"A Dallas PR firm was responsible for it. They thought it would improve my image."

She laughed, an easy good-natured laugh. "And did it?"

He still didn't know. It had brought marriage-minded women out of the woodwork. "I'm not sure it accomplished what it was supposed to. It had some unintended consequences."

"Well that title got my attention. I thought it was a real contest." Her incredible green eyes still sparkled with mirth.

Other than his little brother and his ornery little sister, few people laughed with him or at him. He liked her. He hadn't figured her out yet, but he liked her. And what could be better than hot sex with a smokin' hot woman he liked? "Ma'am, something tells me you're yanking my chain."

"Well...maybe a little. You seem so serious. You have that deep crease here." She touched between her own brows. "But I really am impressed that you have one of those boxes at the football stadium. I've never met anyone who has one."

Typically, he didn't discuss how he spent his money, especially with a woman he had known only a couple of hours. But he couldn't seem to steer the conversation off the extremely personal path. She had a genuineness about her that loosened his tongue.

"My company owns it. It's an investment. I and my associates use it to entertain customers and clients. My friends and family use it if they want to. But besides that, the Cowboys' owner is a friend of mine. A mentor even. I naturally support him as well as the team."

"Naturally. Birds of a feather, right?"

"Jerry Jones and I are hardly birds of a feather. He's a whole lot smarter than I am."

Just then, a blast of wind slapped sheets of rain against the windows. She caught a quick breath and stepped back, her palm flattened against her chest. Then she laughed. "Oh, wow, I've never been this high off the ground during a storm."

A powerful urge to protect her gripped him. "You okay? Afraid?" He placed a reassuring hand at the base of her neck. She stiffened, but he didn't remove his hand.

"I don't know if it's fear. I feel like I'm suspended in space. In my mind, I have this struggle going on, like I need my feet to touch the ground. I get the same anxiety from flying. I'm not sure I could live up high like this."

"You'd get used to it. On a clear day where you could see out, you'd feel more anchored." He gently squeezed her neck, stroked her silky skin with his thumb. "Want to know one of the best parts of living here?"

"Besides luxury and privacy, what?"

"On wintery days, I get the sunshine on my breakfast table."

"Oh," she said, blinking. "That would be nice."

"And I enjoy it even more if a beautiful woman shares it with me."

She sidled away from his hand. "Yes, well, if you recall, I came for supper, not breakfast. And you're making me nervous."

Damn! Embarrassment softened his burgeoning erection. He quickly shoved his hand into his pocket and redirected his eyes to the dark window. They stood in an uncomfortable silence, sipping coffee, staring out into the blackness for what seemed like forever. He had never felt so ill-at-ease with a woman.

She broke the awkwardness. "You know something? I knew your place would be at the top of the building. Even if it's only on the twenty-eighth floor."

"How would you know that?"

"The Discovery channel. I watch a show with my grandmother. I forget the name of it. To live on the highest pinnacle is a survival instinct that goes back to primitive humans. In most modern-day people, it's deeply buried. But in some people, it's still strong and unrepressed."

She looked up at him again. "If you have it, you might not recognize it, but it subconsciously affects everything you do. You know what I mean, I'm sure. It's having the confidence to do *anything*, no matter how hard it might be or how impossible it might seem. A big ego is part of the same instinct."

Drake was a private man, kept most of his thoughts and emotions to himself. He had no friends with whom he shared secrets. No stranger had ever delved quite so deeply into him. She was making him as tense as she said he was making her. He stared into her eyes. "And you think all of that applies to me?"

"I'm just saying. You live on a high pinnacle and you have a big ego."

He chuckled, trying to relieve the tension stretching between them. "God almighty, ma'am. I hope that doesn't mean I'm coming across as a Neanderthal. I'm trying like hell not to."

Her head cocked to the side and she gave him another one of those assessing, narrow-lidded looks. He had a dumb urge to squirm, which made him even more uptight. In a one-on-one, he wasn't usually the one who squirmed.

"You can't possibly care what I think of you. A man like you? I'm sure you have a long list of women in your life who have nothing but good opinions of you."

"But none of them are as interesting as you've turned out to be. Being a straight, red-blooded male, I always care about the opinion of a woman who intrigues me."

Her eyes told him nothing, but he had this insane notion that if he didn't claim her he would be losing out forever on something important. He wasn't ready to give up. She had come home with him for a reason. He just had to learn what it was.

He held her gaze. “You can’t blame me for wanting you in my bed. Any man would.”

Chapter Ten

THERE IT WAS. What he wanted, plainly stated. But then, Shannon had known from the beginning what he wanted. Sex was what most of the men she had known wanted. And in the past, too many times, she had been willing. For lack of a clever reply that wasn't too revealing of her history—and didn't make her sound like a hopeless cynic—she said nothing.

"You've got to know you're beautiful," he went on. "I'm sure you've heard it many times."

But so what? Her appearance had never gotten her anywhere. Hard work. Sacrifice. Self-discipline. Those traits were what had enabled her to own her own business and be halfway successful.

She shrugged. "Thanks, but beautiful is one of those blank words. It can describe almost anything. It's in the eye of the beholder I think they say. Dr. Frankenstein probably thought his monster was beautiful."

He sighed and returned to gazing out the window. "Point taken. I'm not doing very well here, am I? How's this? There's more to you than just a pretty face. I think the outdated word is moxie."

Moxie?...Oh, hell. She didn't know what that word meant. She only hoped it was complimentary. She was *so* out of her depth in this conversation. But she forced a cool demeanor, as if hearing flattery from a man like him was commonplace. "My goodness, Mr. Lockhart, you can tell that by looking?"

"Sizing up people is what I do. And I'm good at it. Even from a distance."

"Hm. Something tells me you're good at most things."

"And something tells me you aren't here to steal the silver. So if spending the night in my bed isn't on your agenda, what is?"

She scrambled for an answer. She had to stop digging this hole lest it become so deep she couldn't escape it. "You invited me to supper. Now I'm thinking accepting was a mistake. You didn't say the words, but it was clear you had more in mind than a meal."

"Busted. But that doesn't clear up what *you've* got in mind."

"Food. I really am hungry."

Just then, a buzz sounded from the direction of the front door. He grinned in that cute little boy way she had noticed sometimes sneaked across his face. "Well, then, fair lady. There's supper."

Saved by the buzzer!

As he walked away, Shannon closed her eyes and let herself deflate. Her muscles un-tensed and she slowly let out a great breath. She was a wreck.

Drake's words filtered through her mind: *...you didn't come home with me to steal the silver....that doesn't clear up what you've got in mind....*

Sex...sex...sex... That was what had been on her mind back in the hotel, what had lured her here. It was still on her mind. Just like the bad old days when she had been devil-may-care and found no reason to resist a romp with a sexy guy.

She was only human. Drake was an enormously attractive man and she hadn't had sex in more than two years. She hadn't had *good* sex since long before that. And she had *never* had sex with the likes of Drake Lockhart.

But something had changed between the hotel and now. When he first walked up behind her at the hotel's foyer bar, if he had invited her to a room upstairs, she might have raced him to it, stripping off her clothes as she went.

Now that she had spent some time with him, now that she *liked* him, doubt and frustration swarmed within her. Doubt that she should do this; frustration because she wanted to. A truth she hadn't counted on had surfaced. For her entire life she had wanted to belong to a man like him. He wasn't just an idle playboy. He was smart. Well-educated and successful. He exuded confidence and strength. If a dragon roared out of the kitchen, he would slay it.

She wanted his respect, wanted him *no*t to see her as a slut, wanted him to think of her as more than just another notch on his bedpost. Sleeping with him tonight could hurt her in myriad ways and most of them had little to do with a one-night-stand or sex or anything that simple. He was exactly the kind of man she could fall giddy, silly, head-over-heels in love with and he wouldn't, couldn't love her back. What he *could* do was break her heart, scar her soul and undo all the good she had done for herself.

That bone-deep realization affected her more acutely than guilt for doing something that would damage her self-respect or disappoint her grandmother.

From the entertainment center, Willie Nelson sang about an angel flying too close to the ground. Shannon stood rooted in front of the windows, listening to the lyrics she had heard a thousand times. And waiting. How long would he be gone? He had just left her, a stranger, alone in his home. He evidently really did trust her not to steal the silver.

You could just walk out, her alter ego said. *Just go. You don't owe him an explanation.*

But how could I escape? she countered.

She would have to go inside his closet for her coat, which she was loathe to do. Doors with coded locks stood between her and the outside world. Her SUV was blocks away. She would have to either walk back to it or call for a cab. Fort Worth wasn't a city where she could just walk out onto the street and find transportation. And last, she would, without a doubt, meet him in the hallway.

Dither, dither, dither. Why couldn't she make a decision? She made decisions every day.

Just then, he returned carrying a large aromatic bag with a REATA logo. *Good Grief!* When he had called in the order for food, she hadn't known he had contacted one of Fort Worth's best eateries. Reata made home deliveries? Maybe it didn't for anyone but him.

She followed him tentatively as he carried the sack into the kitchen. He set it on the granite island, opened drawers and pulled out placemats and cloth napkins, picked silverware from a different drawer. He pushed all of it across the island toward her. "Want to take these to the dining table?"

She hesitated, then picked up the utensils. He opened the sack of food and lifted out two heavy crockery ramekins. When he uncovered them, a bouquet of vanilla and butter bloomed into the room. *Oh, God. Crème Brûlée*. She had ordered it every time she had eaten at Reata.

But she had made up her mind. She couldn't let a sexy man who fulfilled her fantasies or even food she loved distract her. Regret nagged at her, but she cleared her throat and plunged. "I hate to say this, but I really do need to get home. I don't expect you to take me back to my car. I'll call a cab and—"

"You want to leave *now*?" His thick brown brows shot up his forehead.

Her alter ego cringed. *Jeez! Thank God he doesn't have a gun.*

Shannon winced inside. When he didn't speak or move, she looked away, a tight grip on napkins and placemats in one hand and silverware in the other. "Yes. I need to leave now."

"All right," he said sharply. "Not a problem."

"I told you back at the hotel I only wanted to eat. You even said the choice beyond that was mine to make."

"You're right. I did say that." He drew himself up, inhaled and exhaled audibly. "Well, then. Since food's what you came for and it's been delivered, maybe you've got a few more minutes to spare?"

She dithered again. How should she be rude after he had ordered supper? Delivered from Reata, it had to be expensive. And Crème Brûlée was so tempting.

She glanced at the digital clock above the oven door. 11:36. With the rain and fog outside, if she left now and ran into no problems, she could arrive back in Camden before 2:00 a.m. So, as he said, maybe she could take a few extra minutes to at least enjoy the dessert.

Dither, dither, dither....

"I can have dessert and coffee. If we hurry."

She carried the silverware and placements to the long rustic dining table that seated ten. *Ten? Did he have dinner parties?*

Centered overhead a chandelier similar to the one in the entry gave off a soft golden light. She hastily set places on opposite sides at one end. He brought the ramekins of Crème Brûlée. The air crackled with tension as he set them on the placemats.

He pulled back her chair, but before she could sit, he cupped her shoulder with one hand and turned her to face him. His mesmerizing eyes captured hers and she couldn't turn away. Her heartbeat stumbled.

"Don't go," he murmured.

The softness of his voice hung in the air and his scent filled her nostrils, as delicious as the dessert on the table.

Sexual energy radiated from him. A warm ache throbbed between her thighs. She wanted him. As much as she had ever wanted anything, she wanted him. Her will power made a dangerous slide downhill.

His head bent, angled to the left and his lips brushed hers. Delicately. Like a humming bird's wing. She closed her eyes and grabbed the chair back. While his lips melded with hers, she stood as still as her wobbling knees allowed. The kiss ended with a gentle, lingering bite at her bottom lip. Sexy. Primal. She opened her eyes, found him staring at her mouth. Involuntarily, her lips formed a silent *Oh*.

His hand slid along her shoulder and up until he caressed the side of her neck, his touch against her bare skin flooding her with more warmth. His head angled in the opposite direction and his lips brushed again—her eye, her cheek, the corner of her mouth. A shiver of pleasure passed across her shoulders and she tilted her head back, giving him her throat. *Here. Kiss here. You missed this spot.*

As if he had read her mind, his warm lips moved down her neck, his tongue flicked her sensitive places—where her neck joined her shoulder, the pulsebeat between her collarbones. *Oh, dear God....*

Finally, his mouth moved back up and settled squarely on hers. His tongue pushed inside and stroked hers in a gentle, lush glide. Nothing like the marauder she had expected him to be. When he stopped, she gazed up into his face. His amber eyes held her in place as if she were chained. His breath touched her lips. His thumb stroked her cheek.

"I don't expect a woman to do something she doesn't want to," he said softly, "I don't make promises I can't keep, but I'll say this. I'm not selfish in bed. If you stay, I'll do my damndest to see that you're not sorry."

She didn't disbelieve a single word. Her mouth had gone dry. She swallowed and managed to stammer out, "We—we...I don't want to be—I don't want either of us to be sorry."

His head slowly shook. "We were drawn to each other from the first. We both sensed it. It's one of those elemental things."

She couldn't deny it. His head angled again and his mouth covered hers. Oh, he was delicious, like good coffee and a dozen other concoctions that were less easily identified. The only logical place for her arms was around his hard shoulders, so that was where she put them.

His hands moved around to the small of her back, warming her bare skin. As he pulled her in closer, a hard ridge pressed against her stomach and a visual of him naked, his erection rearing, flashed through her mind's eye. A craving, dark and thick as molasses, oozed through her unmentionable places.

His tongue skillfully explored, thrust and withdrew in a slow, sensuous rhythm. Edgy. Confident. He was an excellent kisser and he knew it. Without a doubt, he'd had a lot of practice.

His mouth traveled to the other side of her neck, his hands coasted down and clutched her bottom. He moved her pelvis against his erection and she felt more than heard him groan. They kissed open mouthed for the longest time, his tongue finding new places to tease and the heat of him passing through their layers of clothing into her stomach. She took her own pleasure, licking into his mouth, her tongue dueling with his. The room spun and she felt she might lose her balance if she weren't hanging onto his shoulders.

Without warning, he tore his mouth away and stared down at her, his breathing shuddery.

"What?" she said, startled by the abrupt move.

His eyes had taken on a different look. Instead of being golden brown, his irises had turned a shade so deep they appeared to be black. He drew a hiss of a breath between his teeth and clasped her head between his hands, his strong fingers curving around her skull, his eyes boring into hers. "Have you got any idea…"

She had ceased dithering, ceased over-thinking. Every moment since she had first seen him in the hotel ballroom had shrunk into a taut ball pressuring low in her belly. She wanted his mouth all over her, wanted him on top of her, wanted him inside her.

"Yes," she said, returning his gaze. She rose to her tiptoes and kissed him.

Instantly, everything became more urgent. A gruff sound rumbled up from his throat. His embrace became a tight clench and they kissed savagely.

His lips still clinging to hers, he put space between their bodies. His hand moved between them. His belt buckle clinked. She heard the quick slide of his zipper. The scent of aroused male filled the space between them, dove straight to her core and her sex convulsed.

He grasped her hand and pressed it against him. He was big. And rock hard. And hot as a stovetop. Her vaginal muscles contracted so forcefully her moisture released in a gush, wetting her panties and making her thighs slick.

"Hold on to me," he said raggedly, his mouth hovering above hers. She gripped him hard and his hand closed over hers. "Thassit," he hissed. His mouth dragged down her neck to the slope of her breasts. "It's all yours," he breathed. "Any way you want it....Hard, fast. Slow and easy....All night long if that's what it takes."

All of it. I want all of it. A sound she didn't recognize escaped her own throat.

His hand came to her shoulder. Her dress sleeve slid down her arm, baring her left breast. Her nipples had already stiffened, her breasts had already grown heavy.

He cupped one with his palm. "A yellow rose," he mumbled, brushing the rosy nub with his thumb. He plucked at it with his fingers and they both watched it become unbelievably long and taut. Sensation echoed in every nerve ending deep inside her sex and her fist tightened on his erection.

Rolling her hardened nipple between his thumb and finger, he whispered, "Will this make you come?"

Just don't stop. "I don't know," she whimpered.

The Dress's long sleeve had her arm trapped. "Just a minute," she said. She let go of his erection and quickly pushed the sleeve completely off her arm, giving him better access.

Her alter ego gasped.

It's the practical thing to do, she argued, *to keep it from being torn.*

His head bent and he drew the sensitized bud into his mouth. *Wet! Hot!* Her sex clenched again and she made a silly sound she didn't recognize. He pinched with his thumb and finger and at the same time, tugged firmly with his teeth. *Pain! And incredible pleasure.* "Oh!" she gasped, stunned by the intense sensation that zinged to her clitoris. She grabbed a handful of his silky hair.

He drew the whole tip of her breast into his mouth and sucked her hard. Muscles buried so deeply inside her she had forgotten she had them convulsed wildly and her knees went weak. A sob broke from deep in her throat, but before it ended, his tongue was in her mouth again, absorbing the sound. She sucked at his tongue until the last spasms of her orgasm died.

He tore his mouth away on a growl and went for the other shoulder of her dress.

Her heart was thrashing in her ears. Her knees were quaking like an Aspen forest in a breeze. She needed to lie down, she needed to *sit* down, something. "Wait, you'll tear it," she said shakily.

She took the task of removing *The Dress's* sleeve from him and slid it off. With nothing to anchor it, the top fell loosely around her waist and she didn't even care. She had to have more.

He stepped back. Like a starving man at a banquet, his eyes roved over her torso. "Just look at you," he said reverently. "Jesus, you're exquisite."

She had never been proud of her breasts—too large, her skin too white, her nipples too large and too rosy. But at this moment, with them firm and distended and even a little sore from his attention, they felt golden. He looked up at her, a plea in his eyes. "You're staying?"

After he had taken her to an orgasm by doing nothing more than playing with her nipples, how could he doubt it? She only stared back at him, poised after two desolate years, to surrender her self-imposed celibacy.

"You're staying," he said.

He crushed her against him, length to length. She looped her arms around his shoulders and relished the feel of her nakedness against the hard wall of his chest. The fingers of one hand buried in her hair, holding her head captive while he kissed her ravenously. She ran her hands all over his muscular back, pulled at his shirt until she freed it from his waistband, allowing her to touch his hot silky skin.

Then his hand was under her skirt, sliding roughly up her thighs, cupping and caressing her nearly-bare bottom. He pulled away from their kiss, his breath shallow and quick. He pressed his forehead against hers as his hand moved around between them and his fingers rubbed her sex through her panties. "Move your leg a little. Let me in…"

Without hesitation, she obeyed. His finger easily slid into her and her vaginal muscles grabbed it. Her eyes closed as a shiver slithered through her and a tiny mew crawled out of her mouth.

"Good?"

"Yesss," she hissed. "I'm—I'm so wet."

"That's good….Just be still now. Let me play with your pussy."

On a muffled gasp she grabbed the back of the chair, bent her knees and shamelessly parted her legs. Anything to make it easier for him to continue. His finger moved inside her. He added another finger, pushed deeper, opening her. Their heavy breaths co-mingled as he rubbed steadily inside her. She felt feverish. Her sex felt over-hot and heavy, ready to receive the marble hard organ she'd held in her hand. Her greedy clitoris tingled and strained for attention. She was almost crazy with the need to come again. "Please," she pleaded.

He pushed his fingers deep, swirled his thumb around the desperate little core of her sex. Tension knotted in her belly, but release eluded her. "Oh, God….I—I can't…"

His deep voice came to her as a sexy whisper. "Don't try so hard. Just let it happen…"

"I want to, but…"

He stopped and withdrew his fingers. Her breath caught. "Oh, no, don't…"

"This isn't working." He gripped her bottom with both hands and lifted her. "Hang on to me."

Unable to do otherwise, she wrapped her arms around his shoulders. He turned and half carried, half stumbled with her until they reached the cooking island. He set her on her feet, quickly pushed her panties past her hips and they fell around her ankles. He gathered her skirt up her legs, gripped her buttocks again, lifted her and perched her on the island's cold granite.

The sack of food still sat on the counter inches away. With a sweep of his arm, it hit the floor with a *thwack!*

He quickly relieved her of her shoes, yanked her panties from around her ankles and tossed them aside. Then he nudged her knees apart and stepped between them. His erection, dark red and huge, jutted from his open fly and it was right there, only inches from entrance to the empty sanctum that wept for him. She couldn't take her eyes off of it. She reached for it, but he caught her hand and stopped her. "Not yet."

He leaned into her and his mouth devoured hers again. "Lift your knees," he ordered between heated kisses. She obeyed and planted her heels on the counter top, combed her fingers into his hair and they kept kissing and kissing.

His mouth left hers and he urged her backward. She caught herself on one elbow as his mouth moved down to her breast. He blew on her nipple, closed his mouth around it, tugged with his teeth. Electricity arched to the core of her sex. He sucked, his tongue swirled and at the same time his finger slid inside her again. Shamelessly, she let her thighs fall wide open.

"That's it, that's it, baby…"

His finger circled rhythmically inside her, stroking her vaginal walls relentlessly while he licked and sucked at her breasts. The tension in her belly began to coil again and she hung there, suspended between release and desperation. Then his finger found a place so sensitive that a shot of incredible pleasure curled her toes. A sudden spasm started somewhere deep in her belly and rolled through her like violent storm. She cried out. Her hips hitched. Her deep muscles contracted around his finger, shrieking for the empty channel to be filled. "Please," she panted, shaky and writhing. "You have to—"

"What?...Tell me what you want…"

"You….Not your fingers. I want *you* inside me."

"We'll get there," he mumbled against her breasts.

His heated mouth slid down her body, nipping and sucking bites of her as he went. Her skirt had wadded around her waist. He pushed it up and dipped his tongue into her navel and teased. She helplessly watched him trail kisses over her belly and suck little bites of her into his mouth, the dual sensations of seeing and feeling making her so hot she thought she might ignite. She squirmed and little grunts burst out of her throat.

In one quick motion, he peeled off one stocking, then the other. "Lie back," he ordered. She fell back supine on the cold granite, squeezing her eyes shut against the overhead light. He grasped her calves, his hands slid up the backs of her thighs and pushed her knees high and wide.

She struggled up and braced herself on her elbows. "Drake, no. You shouldn't…"

"Shhh. I want you to come again before I fuck you."

She fell back, so desperate she wasn't even put off by his dirty words. He nuzzled into her sex, his late day stubble rasping her tender flesh. His tongue made firm sweeps up her center, rimmed her labia, laved the deeper sensitive layers of her sex, but failed to touch the greedy little bud where she wanted it most. "Drake, now…now…oh, please…"

He urged her knees higher, all the way to her shoulders. His tongue circled her opening, then slid inside her. A spume of new sensation burst through her system. Frantic, she clawed at the countertop. He suckled relentlessly, his agile tongue spearing in an out in rhythmic thrusts. Reason deserted her. Her head thrashed left and right. Sounds she had never heard herself make burst out. Her clitoris had become a throbbing ball of fire. It strained forward, pleading to be quenched.

She reached between her thighs, grabbed his head, clutched fistfuls of his silky hair, tried to move his mouth to where she needed it. "Drake…Drake…I have to come…Please, I have to come…"

Finally, finally, his mouth moved up and he drew the greedy little knot of nerves full into his mouth and an explosion tore through her.... *Agony!* Sweet beyond belief. She sobbed and panted. Her hips tried to hitch, but he held her firmly pinned, tenderly sucking and swirling his tongue while she came and came and came. When she could stand no more, she struggled up and slapped at his head, fighting him away.

He caught her hands and drew her up and into his arms, enveloping her, holding her head against his neck. "It's okay, okay…You're okay now."

She was shaking and whimpering, in tears. "No…'Snot okay….'Snever happened to me before."

He stroked her hair away from her face, kissed her lips. "What, sweetheart? You can tell me."

"Over and over like that. No one's ever—"

"That's a shame…. Shh-shh. Don't cry now."

"I'm not," she whimpered.

"My God. You're sweeter than ripe fruit." And as if to prove it, he rubbed his fingers over her lower lip, pressed them into her mouth. "Taste yourself," he whispered. "See how sweet you are."

Robotically, she closed her mouth over his fingers and gently sucked the salty-sweet moisture of her passion.

"You're amazing." He removed his fingers from her mouth and replaced them with a long, slow tongue kiss.

But the shallow penetration of his tongue hadn't been enough. Now, she could think of nothing else but the hot hard thing she had held in her hand filling her, all the way to her womb. Surely, he didn't intend to leave her with this emptiness. She pulled back and looked into his face. "I need—I want to—"

"I know, sweetheart." He caressed her cheek with trembling fingers. "I know. I want the same thing….You on the pill?"

She shook her head.

"'Sokay. No problem."

He slid his hands under her bottom. "Can you put your legs around me?"

"Uh-huh." Clinging to his shoulders, she locked her ankles behind his back, pressed her wet sex against his bare belly and buried her face in his neck.

"That's it, baby. Just hang on now. Sweet, sweet baby. I've got you. I'll take care of you." He lifted her, carried her out of the kitchen and up a hallway.

Then they were in a huge bedroom beside a huge bed. It looked even bigger than king-size, but it probably wasn't. Low light shone from a table lamp beside the bed and the covers were turned back, revealing pale blue sheets. For a fleeting second, she wondered when he had come into this room and done that.

He gently laid her back. Her eyes fluttered closed. She didn't know how many times she had already come, yet all she could think of was doing it again with his hard thickness inside her. Sensing him move away, panic darted through her. "Drake?"

"Shh-shh," he whispered. "I'll be right back."

She lay there, her sex swollen and hot and drenched, her palms open beside her head, her legs parted in brazen invitation. He had drained her of strength, driven her mad, but all she could think of was his hard penis inside her.

A drawer opened, pocket change and a belt buckle jangled. Something rustled. Then he was back, crawling onto the bed and kneeling between her knees, hovering over her, sans his shirt. Braced on his hands, his arms bracketed her. The roughness of his starched jeans brushed the inside of her thighs.

He's still got his pants on, her alter ego screamed.

Shannon opened her eyes. His face loomed only inches above hers, his eyes dark and serious, the set of his mouth grim. A thick vein throbbed on the side of his neck. She ran her hands across his shoulders, down his muscular arms. "Please."

His gaze locked on hers, he reached between them and found her opening with his fingers, moved them in and out, circled and stroked, making her shudder. "I love that you're so wet," he said softly. "Lift your knees, sweetheart."

She complied and the plush smooth crown of his erection pressed at her opening. *Wide!. Hot! Like a burning coal!* She couldn't remember ever wanting anything as much as she wanted it inside her, but after so long without sex, she expected pain. Her body involuntarily stiffened.

"Relax, baby. Just a little…"

"It's…it's been a long time…."

"I'll be easy….If I hurt you, I'll stop."

The head of him slid past her tight muscle with an imaginary pop and instead of pain, her whole world stopped on an exquisite note of bliss. Her deprived muscles grabbed on to him as if they wanted to never let him go. "Oohh," she breathed.

A throaty grunt came from him. He withdrew and ducked his head, watching himself pull out and push into her again, then again, stretching her an inch at a time, taking a lifetime, until at last his thick shaft was all the way up inside her, filling every inch of her, as if their bodies had been molded for each other.

He gave another deep groan and a shudder passed over his shoulders. He held himself still, looking down at her with a quirky half-smile tipping one corner of his mouth. "Okay now?"

She was more than okay. She had left the earth and was floating in ecstasy. She smiled up at him. "Wow. It fits."

"Did you think it wouldn't?"

"You felt so big in the kitchen." She flexed her vaginal muscles against him, gripped his sinewy shoulders with her hands, lifted her head and kissed him. "Make me come again."

"Greedy girl," he mumbled roughly.

Greedy wasn't the word. She was beside herself. If he didn't start moving, she might surely expire from want. His head lowered and his lips brushed hers as he began a smooth slide in and out. The easy rhythm only added to the maddening pressure already building low in her belly again.

"I'm close," he ground out, his jaw clenched. "Hard too long…"

He lowered his weight onto her, braced himself on his elbows and began to rock. His rhythm was steady and quick. She found it as if she had always known it, burying her face against his neck, hugging his hips with her thighs, hooking her heels beneath his jeans pockets.

He picked up the pace. *...In. And in. And in...* Glorious friction seared her vaginal wall. Their breaths soughed in unison. Every rational thought left her head. Soon he was pounding and the root of him was pressing and rasping there where she needed it. "Don't stop," she murmured.

He hooked an arm behind her left knee, pushed it high and slid deeper, still driving hard, fast and steadily. She soared up and up and up until she shattered, her deep muscles convulsing and pulling at him in quick contractions. Her neck arched and her mouth fell open in a silent scream.

He thrust hard, once…twice…three times….She eagerly absorbed each thrust, clung to him, held him through his rapture. Then, with one gruff grunt, his body went rigid and he was done. Seconds later, he fell to her side, gasping for breath.

They lay in the afterglow, both sweating and breathing hard.

Finally, he turned onto his back, reached and found her hand, took it to his mouth and kissed her palm. "What did you mean, it's been a long time?"

Oh, damn. Why had she said that? She hesitated. "What? Nothing. Just…that."

"How long?"

No way would she answer that. "Just…a while."

A few beats passed. He turned on his side and faced her. "Is that why it wasn't that easy for you?...That second time back in the kitchen?"

Now she was embarrassed. She had no idea why she hadn't been able to come more easily. "I—I don't know….Nervous, maybe…" She gave a foolish laugh. "But it was worth the wait."

He smiled. "I knew we'd be good together. The minute I saw you, I knew. Getting inside you was all I could think about."

"I knew, too." And that was the truth. But all that had gone on and was continuing within her was too much to absorb. Somehow, she needed to lighten the moment. She clasped a handful of his jeans. "But you didn't even take all your clothes off."

"I'm going to though. Because, ma'am, we are not finished."

She frowned. "You're still calling me ma'am?"

He sat up, his eyes roaming over her body. She loved having him look at her.

"You're a real redhead." He clasped her knee and pulled it toward him. "I want to see you."

For some reason, she wasn't reluctant. She let her opposite knee fall wide, opening her sex to his eyes. He stared intently between her legs, sending an erotic thrill all the way to her toes.

"You're beautiful everywhere," he muttered.

"I like having you look at me," she said softly.

"You turn me on. Your body….how it feels inside you…how you taste…." He leaned down, buried his nose in her wet curls and inhaled deeply. "How you smell. Everything about you."

Her sex almost purred. She gloried in his adoration. Reaching down, she combed her hand through his hair. "You're wicked, the way you tormented me. You nearly drove me crazy."

He gave her mound a chaste kiss, then looked up at her and grinned like a self-satisfied little boy, his mouth shiny from her moisture. "Like you said, I've got a big ego. How could I face myself in the mirror if I couldn't make you come….More than once….And I wanted you to enjoy it."

He was a skillful lover. He had probably never met a woman he couldn't take to climax. "Hmm. And I'm sure you could tell just how much I enjoyed it."

"I could tell. I don't believe you were faking it." He gave her another mischievous grin. "Fortunately, the walls are more or less soundproof."

She gave his thick glossy hair a tiny yank. "Now you're embarrassing me."

He chuckled and traced her rose tattoo with his fingertip. "A yellow rose of Texas. Sexy."

He gave her mouth a quick hard kiss, then rolled to the edge of the bed, sat up and pulled her to a sitting position. "Do you need the bathroom?"

"Not now."

He pried off a boot. She gave a huff. "You had your boots on, too?"

Grinning at her across his shoulder, he pried off the second boot. "You've heard that old Texas saying, darlin'. A man who can't fuck with his boots on ain't much of a man."

"Get outta here. There's no such old saying."

He laughed. "Take that dress off and get under the covers. When I come back, we'll start over. I've still got a few tricks up my sleeve." He stood and yanked his pants and shorts up over his taut white buttocks. "I'll be right back," he said.

"And you'll be naked, right?"

Still grinning, he looked down at her. "What do *you* think?"

Chapter Eleven

SHANNON LAY THERE, spent, stunned and staring at the ceiling. *Good grief!* Had sex ever been like this? Would it ever be again?

The toilet flushed. Minutes later, Drake appeared in the bathroom doorway. Until now, she hadn't been able to see him unclothed from head to toe. She stared at his body. It was just as she had imagined—lean and tanned to bronze, his long bones padded with defined muscle.

A pelt of brown hair covered his chest and a tempting happy trail whorled down his belly. He had abs. Not sharply cut like a bodybuilder, but still, a flat belly without an ounce of fat. He had those thick ridges of muscle that started at his waist and veed down until it framed the delta of his groin as if his penis were a trophy. It was still deeply colored and extended from a thick nest of dark curls. Her gaze lingered on it. It was as yummy to look at as it had felt inside her.

She held the covers open and looked up at him. "You caught me staring."

He snapped off the bathroom light and crossed the room to the bed. "Like what you see?"

"You look like Superman."

"Just don't call me Clark." He chuckled and crawled between the covers. He scooped her into his brawny arms, tangled his hairy legs with hers and propped himself on his elbow. "I still want to know how long."

Aargh! She wished he hadn't remembered that. "What? … Why?"

You could ask him the same question, her cranky alter-ego said.

His agile fingers pushed a tendril of hair away from her face. "It's logical that I'd want to know. You're a beautiful woman. It defies common sense that you haven't had opportunities."

Anything she said would lead to a conversation she didn't want to have. "I don't want to talk about it. Can't we just leave it at that?"

He leaned and kissed her, a gentle joining of their lips. "It's never been this good. That's why I want to know."

His words had a solemnity to them, as if they might be true. But should she believe him? "Hah. Why do I think you say that to all the girls?"

"One thing you should know about me. Unless I'm joking, I never say things I don't mean."

Shannon suspected that at least that much was a fact. Not just in the bedroom, but in all parts of his life. "It was good for me, too."

He caressed her cheek with his palm and kissed her again. "I want to fuck you again," he whispered against her lips.

She had never heard any man use such frank sex words. Hearing them from him was like throwing kerosene on a smoldering fire. The kissing continued and desire began to build again. Soon they were stroking and caressing and turning on the huge bed, their bare bodies rubbing together sensuously, his soft baritone voice coaxing with naughty words and erotic promises. Shannon forgot everything—the weather, the urgency to get home, the fibs she had told him. The world outside his bedroom and his bed, ceased to exist.

At one point, she pleasured him with her mouth, but he only allowed it for seconds. Instead, he was attentive to *her* every desire, *her* every need. His mouth thrilled her with succulent kisses, his wicked tongue licked and titillated, his deft fingers teased. When he had pushed her to the edge again, he knew it at once, buried himself inside her and took her to yet another and another shattering orgasm. She had never known a more unselfish lover.

Afterward, he arranged her sated, languid, body against his, her head on his shoulder, her thigh across his belly. She draped her arm over his chest, breathing in the sexy scent of heated male, enjoying the feel of his soft warm skin against her cheek. Enveloped by thick covers on the cold night, she was so comfortable, she could easily drift to sleep, but she couldn't let herself.

"Let's talk," he said.

"About what?"

He yawned. "Oh, I don't know. You said something earlier about some TV show you liked."

She frowned and placed a kiss on his furry chest. "You want to talk about the Discovery Channel?"

"That was a joke. It's *you* I want to talk about."

Few men Shannon had known wanted to talk about *her*. She longed to tell him about herself—her real name, where she lived, her phone number. But she dared not. Talk might reveal too much and destroy this dream.

She gave a silly titter. "There isn't much to say. I'm not inclined to blab on and on about a subject I find a little boring."

He clasped her jaw and turned her face to his. "You're not boring." He kissed her thoroughly and sweetly, then resettled, holding her tightly against him. "Tomorrow. We talk tomorrow over breakfast. Deal?"

She squeezed her eyes shut, but said nothing.

"I like how you feel against me," he said softly, his fingers making circles on her shoulder. "Like you fit."

"Hmm. I think we already had that conversation."

"We did, didn't we? We fit that way, too. It's just about perfect." He yawned again.

"You're sleepy?"

"Hmm....Got up early....Had a lot to do today."

"Like what? Tell me what someone like you does on a wintery Saturday."

"Checked a construction site...early this morning....Couldn't get there yester—"

His speech had slurred, then stopped altogether. She waited for him to say more. Then she noticed that his breathing had become deep and even. "Drake?"

When he didn't answer, she pushed herself up onto her elbow and looked into his face. He was asleep! His thick dark brown lashes lay against his cheek. His facial muscles had relaxed, but the vertical crease between his brows was still evident. Even with whisker shadow, he looked young and innocent.

Yet, there was nothing innocent about the way he had made love to her, nothing sissy about the way he looked, especially not his square jaw. He was such a handsome man in a rugged way.

She lightly stroked the arch of his brown brow with her fingertip. "Lord, you're special," she whispered. "So special." He didn't stir.

The clock on the bedside table showed. 2:36 a.m. She still had time to get into her own bed before daylight. For a few seconds, she pondered if she could grab this brass ring and hang on to it. But she could think of no way. The fairy tale evening had ended. She had to go home.

She eased from between the covers, picked up her dress from the floor beside the bed, then continued toward the bedroom door, shivering as she went. Earlier, inflamed with passion, she hadn't noticed the chilliness of the bedroom.

She had to pass through the dining room to reach the kitchen where he had stripped off her clothing. Willie Nelson still sang and played from the entertainment center. She recognized "Georgia." She had heard him sing that song about a thousand times.

The two dishes of Crème Brûlée sat on the dining table where they had left them. Unable to resist, she stopped, picked up a spoon, dipped out a couple of bites and savored each one. Even cold, it was as delicious as she remembered.

The view through the window wall showed the weather granting no reprieve. Dense fog hugged the windows like a black drape, erasing the city lights. All she could see were water droplets marring the glass. Lord, she wouldn't be able to see her hand in front of her once she got outside. Well, at least ice wasn't peppering the windows.

She found her stockings near the cooking island and her panties and shoes on the floor three feet away beside a puddle made by the bag of food he had ordered. For a few seconds she looked at it, deploring the waste.

She returned to the dining table and scooped out one more bite of the dessert. On her way to the guest bathroom, she picked up her clutch from the table in the entry. Should she take a cab or walk to the parking lot where she had left her SUV?

Idiot, her alter ego snapped. *It's a six-block hike in high heels on wet sidewalks. Not to mention traipsing through cold fog and rain at 3:00 a.m., wearing an evening wrap. Call a cab, chica.*

Indeed. And she needed to do it now so it would be waiting for her at the curb as soon as she reached the bottom floor. Inside the bathroom, she pulled her cell phone from her purse and in a low voice, ordered a ride.

Next, she checked her ear lobes to be sure her grandmother's diamond earrings were still in place. After that, she hurriedly washed herself, then examined *The Dress* for tears, found every seam intact. She put it on and after carefully viewing her reflection, believed no one would be able to tell it had been lying on the floor in a heap for two hours.

She applied a new layer of powder over the tender whisker burns around her mouth and on her chin, then fiddled with her hair until it looked presentable.

She left the bathroom carrying her shoes, taking no chances that her heels would sound against the tile and wooden floors. She placed them and her clutch on the table in the entry.

When she had been in the kitchen gathering her clothing a few minutes earlier, she had noticed the coffee carafe half-full. She returned to the kitchen and quietly searched the cupboards, hoping to find a mug with a lid. She found a thermal one of stainless steel. She poured it full of coffee, loaded it with two heaping teaspoons of sugar, then switched off the coffeemaker.

For a moment, she considered going back to the bedroom to glimpse Drake one last time, but rejected the idea. What if she awakened him? The last thing she did was pad to the dining table and swallow a few more bites of the Crème Brûlée.

In the entry closet, her jacket hung among other coats. She was tempted to take one, but thought better of it. She was already taking—no, borrowing—one of his coffee mugs she hoped he wouldn't miss. Rather than have him think her a thief, she would make do with her own jacket. She slipped into it, then inventoried everything—shoes, car keys, phone, purse, coffee mug—and opened the condo's front door.

Easing into the silent hallway, she prayed not to meet anyone. Ahead of her and around the corner she would run into the glass doors with their security keypad. *Damn!* Would she be able to pass through the sliding door from the inside without keying in a number?

Why would it be locked from the inside? her cranky alter ego asked.

Shannon chewed on her bottom lip. For a few seconds, she considered going back into the condo and climbing back into bed with Drake.

Forget it, her alter ego told her.

She slipped her feet into her shoes, drew a deep breath and pulled Drake's front door closed. The lock clicked behind her. She had nowhere to go but forward.

Several dozen steps later, she approached the glass door separating her from the elevator. It glided open automatically and silently. *Yes!*

Mere minutes after that, she stood in the elevator's open doorway on the bottom floor, looking at the uniformed man at his desk. She lifted her chin, squared her shoulders and walked through the lobby with bravado.

As she neared the doorman's desk, he rose from his chair and greeted her with a "good morning."

"Good morning," she said cheerily.

"Can I help you, ma'am?"

"No, thank you."

She boldly strode past his desk, toward the front door and kept walking without looking back, praying that he didn't wonder why she was leaving this exclusive place alone at 3:00 a.m. and decide to call Drake. Or worse, the police. Outside, the cab she had summoned was parked at the curb. *Thank you, God.* In minutes, it delivered her to her SUV.

Driving through dense fog and cold misting rain, she reached the Fort Worth city limits and the open road to Camden. She could barely make out the white line that divided the four-lane highway. She set her cruise control at forty, gripped the steering wheel at ten and two and motored into the dense fog.

At exactly 4:30 a.m., she pulled into the detached garage at her grandmother's house. She'd had an hour and a half of driving time to reflect on tonight's events. She had made many mistakes with men in the past, but tonight?...She had enjoyed it too much to call it a mistake. But she had to put it behind her as if had never happened.

The warble of Drake's cell phone on the bedside table startled him from a deep sleep. Without opening his eyes, he fumbled for it. "Mmph," he said into it.

"Good morning, Son, did I wake you?"

Mom. Shit. He blinked himself awake. "What's up?"

He glanced at the opposite side of the bed. Empty.

"I just had a long conversation with Donna," his mother said. "You broke up with her?"

"Yeah," Drake answered absently. He listened for sounds in the bathroom. Hearing none, he threw off the covers and sat up.

"Why did you do that, Drake? She's very upset. She says she'll do anything to make up with you."

Where the hell is Sharon? "Do we have to have this conversation now?"

"But, Son—"

"Mom. I don't want to talk about it."

He got to his feet and padded to the toilet, freezing his ass off. He kept the temperature in his bedroom below seventy.

"You should call her, Drake. She says she knows she was too loud last night. She says she drank too much and doesn't—"

"Mom. Why are you butting into this?"

"When one of your women friends calls me and asks me to speak for her, what am I supposed to do?"

Finished at the toilet, he strode to the closet. "Leave it alone, okay?"

He shrugged into a robe and returned to the bedroom, annoyance just short of anger pricking at him. "Mom, I've got to go."

He opened the pleated shades on the window wall. Outside, the sky was still a dull gray, the weather still wet and messy.

His mother gasped. "Drake! Stop and think about what you're doing. I don't know how you could do any better than Donna. I know she's a little spoiled, but she's from a very important family. Her daddy—"

"Mom. It doesn't matter who her daddy is. She's got a screw loose and she drinks too much."

He walked up the hallway that led to the dining room, pausing to reset the thermostat. From the dining room, he glimpsed the kitchen. He had stripped Sharon's panties, stockings and shoes off her last night at the cooking island. They were nowhere to be seen. The bag of food from Reata lay on the floor with a puddle under it. The coffee maker had been switched off. The two dishes of dessert still sat on the dining table, one partly eaten. Willie Nelson still sang from the music system.

"Well you don't have to bite my head off. I've never heard you be so un-chivalrous."

For a minute, in his distraction, Drake had forgotten he was talking to his mother. "Sorry, Mom. I'm just tired of dealing with the drinking and a lot of other stuff. Last night, you heard her yourself....Look, you got me up. I'll call you back after a bit, okay?"

He disconnected before she could say anything else and stalked through the rest of the condo's four rooms. Sharon was nowhere.

Throwing open the door to the entry closet, he saw an empty hanger where he had hung her black jacket. Turning around, he shot a look at the entry table where he had last seen her purse. But for an original bronze sculpture and a lamp, the table was bare. *Shit.*

Back in the kitchen, the clock on the oven showed 10:30. The concierge on duty last night would be off work now, but a log was kept of non-residents who came and went in the late hours. Drake called downstairs. The daytime gatekeeper reported that the night man had written in the log that a red-haired woman in a black jacket left alone at 3:15 a.m. in a cab.

Drake hung up, stunned. *Good God!* She had fucked his brains out, given him half a blow job, then crawled out of his bed and disappeared? Never had anything like that happened to him.

Oh, Jesus. What had she taken with her? Other than original western art, he wasn't a collector, so he had few valuables in the condo that could be easily picked up and carried out. He quick-stepped back to his bedroom and checked his wallet. His cash and credit cards were as he had left them. His Rolex lay on the bedside table. He trekked through the condo again and checked each room, found nothing missing.

Baffled, he returned to the kitchen, cleaned the coffee pot and put a new batch of coffee on to brew. His cell phone bleated. He checked caller ID. *Donna. Shit.* He had hoped to have a reprieve from this phone call until noon. He hesitated a few beats trying to decide how to handle what was coming. Finally, he keyed into the call.

She began talking before he could say a word. "Hi, sweetikins, it's me. Drakey, I am so sorry. I should have stopped drinking gin when you wanted me to. It will never happen again."

"Donna, I—"

"I'm quitting gin. It does something crazy to me."

"Donna, listen—"

"Oh, I know. I don't blame you for being mad. But I know you didn't mean what you said last night.

"Donna, I did mean it."

"I just hung up from talking to Daddy about the cabin in Aspen. My friend Mitzi—you remember Mitzi—said the skiing up there is just fantastic right now. The snow is fabulous. Perfect. And a lot of the crowd is there. Kay and Jerry, Judy and Cal, to name a few.

Her friends, not his. Most of the people he called friends didn't have so much idle time on their hands.

"The weather's supposed to clear up later today and we could fly. I've already talked to Daddy about using the plane."

This was how Donna dealt with what didn't go her way. To try to steer a derailed train back onto the track, she used offers most reasonable people couldn't refuse.

"Donna, I can't do this anymore and you shouldn't want to either. It's not good for either one of us."

"Aww, I know you don't mean that, sweetie. We need some time. If we can just be alone, I know we can work everything out. I can't think of a better place to do that than Daddy's cabin." Her tone changed from whiney to seductive. "You know how good I can be. Don't you remember when we went up there a few months ago? That amazing romantic week we had?"

In fact, he didn't remember the romantic part of that trip that well. What he did recall was that he had gone trout fishing in a mountain stream and had gotten skunked.

"Hmm. I can see us in the hot tub, sipping wine, watching the stars. Doesn't that sound marvelous?"

Amazing. Fabulous. Marvelous. Fantastic. Donna's vocabulary was rife with words like that. But what the hell did they mean? He closed his eyes and pinched the bridge of his nose between his thumb and finger. "It's no good, Donna. It's not going anywhere with us. And you need help I can't provide."

"Drake," she said petulantly. "You are not going to tell me you can't go to Aspen after I've already talked to Daddy and gotten the plane and everything."

This, too, was how she dealt with setbacks. She simply passed over them. She was so used to having people kowtow to her every whim, she never heard the word "no." His patience collapsed. "Go to Aspen. Without me. As you say, a lot of your friends are up there."

And he didn't doubt that if one of them happened to be male and without a companion, after a few drinks, Donna would find him. He had never believed her to be a one-man-woman.

"Dammit, I've already told Mitzi and Conrad we'd be there. I warn you, Drake, if you embarrass me by not going—"

"Don't threaten me, Donna. I'm not going to Aspen. Period. I've had it."

He disconnected, threw the phone on the bed and stalked to the shower. He had intended to wait until next week to make the planned trip to Lubbock, but with the weather clearing, now suddenly seemed like a great time to go.

And as soon as he returned, he would find out who the hell Sharon Phillips really was. That probably wasn't her real name. And she probably wasn't from Houston, either.

Chapter Twelve

SHANNON AWOKE SLOWLY. Visions of sugarplums were not what danced in her head. What filled her mind was sex. And why wouldn't it? She'd had animal sex with one of the hottest men she had ever met and had happily let herself be thoroughly debauched. He had touched, kissed and observed every intimate body part and she had done likewise.

She envisioned him walking naked from the bathroom to the bed in all of his masculine beauty. The dark and naughty side of her wished she had stayed the night and awakened beside his warm body between his silky sheets. As much stamina as he had, she was certain this morning would have brought a reprise of the night.

Though her shades were drawn, a dull light stole into her bedroom. Last night's storm was on the wane, but everything was dripping wet. Today would be a good day to put on sweats and cuddle under an afghan in front of TV and wallow in the erotic memories of last night.

Before her thoughts took her further, light raps sounded on her door and a small feminine voice said, "Are you awake, dear?"

Grammy Evelyn. Shannon forced herself fully awake. "Come in, Grammy."

The wizened face poked through the doorway. Then she walked in wearing a fashionable navy blue suit with white trim and she smelled like lavender. As she came closer, Shannon saw that she also wore makeup.

Uh-oh. She was either going to or coming from church. Shannon usually took her to church herself on Sunday mornings. Last night's excursion into fantasyland had thrown her off track. She turned to her back, gathering the covers under her chin. She was naked and the room was chilly. "Oh, my gosh, Grammy. You've been to church already? What time is it?"

Her grandmother took a seat on the foot of the bed, crossed her thin hands on her lap and showered her with a patient smile, meant to gently punish. Shannon loved her dearly, but she had lived with her long enough to know the clever little woman could be a manipulative, though sweet, imp.

"It's a little after noon, dear. I called Colleen and she and Gavin picked me up."

Oh, hell. Colleen was Shannon's uptight older sister. No doubt she'd had plenty to say to Grammy Evelyn about Shannon sleeping in.

"I didn't want to miss the Christmas program," Grammy Evelyn continued. "It was so lovely."

Earlier in the week, Shannon and her grandmother had discussed going to the Methodist church's Christmas program together. Immersed in all that had gone on last night, Shannon had forgotten.

"I'm sorry Grammy. You should've gotten me up."

She stretched and yawned, then rubbed her eyelids with her fingertips. Her eyes felt like sandpaper. She smelled like sex. She had fallen into bed without showering or washing off her makeup. Could her grandmother detect the telltale smell?

"That's all right, dear. I knew you needed to sleep. I took canned goods for the Camden Mission boxes. Gavin donated two big turkeys."

Gavin Flynn, Colleen's husband, was a big turkey himself. He was a lawyer of mediocre talent. He made a substantial living handling divorces and minor lawsuits. No small amount of friction existed between Shannon and her sister and thereby her sister's husband.

"And how are Colleen and Gavin today?" she asked.

"They're just fine. Gavin is thinking about running for the legislature in Austin, so it looks like they'll be going to church more often."

"Grammy, you wicked thing. I can't believe you said that."

"Good heavens, you know how important it is for a politician in Camden to be seen as a God-fearing man."

"He must have decided which party he wants to belong to."

"I don't know if he's gone that far yet."

Membership in any of them would make him nothing other than a hypocrite. Still, Shannon laughed. A sense of humor helped when dealing with her sister and brother-in-law. "It's nice he has ideals he's true to."

"Now, now," her grandmother admonished. "We must be open-minded toward Gavin. He's family and we know he means well. Sometimes he's just confused."

And living with Colleen was enough to confuse anyone. "Humph," Shannon said.

"You must have come home very late, dear."

"Later than I intended."

"I thought so. I had to get up a little after midnight to let Arthur into the house and you still weren't home."

A shiver passed through Shannon as more memories assailed her. Around midnight, she had been naked and wantonly posed on Drake

Lockhart's kitchen island in a position that would challenge a gymnast, begging him for more.

Arthur was her grandmother's tomcat. Grasping the opportunity to change the subject, Shannon said, "Didn't Christa come by and try to get Arthur back in the house?"

Christa Johnson was Shannon's best friend. They had gone all through school together. Since Shannon's return to Camden, they had become fast friends again. Christa often came over and looked in on Grammy Evelyn if Shannon couldn't be at home in the evening. Christa didn't expect a favor in return and she wouldn't accept pay, so Shannon gave her and her boys every ticket she came by to various events around town and in Fort Worth and she sprung for a video game occasionally.

"Oh, yes. She and her boys came, but they couldn't find him."

Shannon frowned. "I thought Arthur didn't like cold weather. Why was he outside so late?"

"Oh, you know Arthur. He probably got interested in some little female somewhere and forgot the time." Her grandmother looked down at *The Dress* that lay on the floor beside the bed. "Oh, my. Your pretty dress." She bent forward and picked it up.

Shannon hid a catch in her breath. *The Dress* looked a little less glittery today and Shannon had no idea if it, too, smelled like sex. She wanted to grab it away from Grammy Evelyn, but she didn't want to throw off the covers and bare herself. Lord, she might have hickeys all over. "It's okay, Grammy. Just leave it. I'm getting up in a minute. I'll take care of it."

Her grandmother stood, spread the dress across the foot of the bed and smoothed out the fabric with her hands. "I made potato soup for supper last night and a loaf of yogurt bread. I was thinking of soup and toast for lunch. Would you like some?"

Shannon was eager for her grandmother to leave the room so she could get out of bed. "That sounds good. I'm starved."

"I'll heat it up," Grammy Evelyn said, still smiling. "It'll take me just a few minutes." She left the room, rocking from side to side in her little-old-lady gait.

Shannon sat up. She felt like hell. Her head throbbed. Every muscle was sore. A tenderness smarted between her legs. Sex with Drake had been an athletic event. Then, she had followed up with a tense drive in the soupy weather with her jaws and shoulders taut as a tightrope all the way from Fort Worth. She got to her feet and made her way to the bathroom.

Since the Piper mansion had been built in 1870, the bathroom adjoining her bedroom was one end of a porch that had been closed in thirty or forty years back. A metal medicine cabinet with a mirrored door hung above an antique porcelain pedestal sink. Shannon stood in front of it and stared at her reflection, able to see only her upper torso.

Her hair was a fright. She had raccoon eyes. She looked even worse than she felt.

And she did indeed have a purple hickey the size of a golf ball just below her navel. On her pale skin, the color competed with her tattoo. *Damn.* The thing could be weeks going away. She covered it with her hand and closed her eyes remembering the exact moment *Texas Monthly's* Most Eligible Bachelor had put it there. At that point, she had been so lost in ecstasy, she hadn't cared if he gave her a dozen hickeys.

The bathtub was an old claw-foot with an overhead shower and a plastic curtain hanging on an oval-shaped metal pipe. A clumsy and inconvenient set-up, but it gave total privacy. And that was what she wanted this morning while she bathed and further examined her body.

After shampooing her hair and washing herself, she found two more hickeys on the insides of her thighs, one in such an awkward spot, she could barely twist her leg far enough to see it. That one had occurred on the kitchen counter, no doubt, when he'd had her pinned with her feet in the air and his mouth had had free range of her most intimate parts. It was a wonder she wasn't suffering a back strain.

The breath-stealing orgasms Drake had taken her to rushed into her memory. Sex with Justin Turnbow, or any man she had known, had never been like it was last night with Drake. Just thinking about how his erection had felt inside her set a tingle buzzing in the tiny core of her sex. How had he driven her to climax over and over and made her want him again even after she thought she couldn't come again? He might even have found her G-spot that she had never been sure she had.

Experience, her cranky alter ego said. *The guy's had lots of experience. He knows too much about women.*"

Shannon couldn't argue the point.

God, she had been so needy. Embarrassingly so. She had given herself completely. Drake Lockhart could have done anything he wanted to her and she would have enjoyed it. Maybe celibacy wasn't such a good idea for someone who liked sex as much as she used to before she gave it up. She put her hand between her legs and cupped herself with her palm and gently rubbed her vulva with her fingers. With only a little help from her own fingers, she could come again right this minute.

She dried and straightened her hair, then wrapped herself in a heavy flannel robe and returned to the bedroom. She picked up *The Dress* from the bed and held it to her nose, testing. The only odor she detected was Pleasures, the Estee Lauder fragrance she wore most of the time nowadays. Not too many years ago, any Estee Lauder product would have been out of her reach.

She carried the dress closer to the window and inspected it for damage. It appeared to be none the worse for wear. None of the mirror sequins looked to be missing. As she carefully hung it on its padded hanger and placed it in its own plastic storage bag with its Neiman

Marcus logo, a flashback came to her of the day she and Christa had shopped for it and the whispery debate they'd had in the dressing room:

"Oh, my God, that is so you, Shannon," Christa had said. "It's sexy as all get out."

But Shannon's focus had been on the price tag. "It costs too much."

"Hah. If I found a dress that made me look that good, I wouldn't care what it cost. Buy it for yourself for a Christmas present. You've earned it. You've worked like a dog this year. C'mon. Go out and look at yourself in the three-way mirror. You look gorgeous."

When Shannon had stepped out of the dressing room to peruse herself, the clerk gasped. "Honey, that designer had your hair and your fair skin in mind."

That had been pure malarkey, of course. Shannon had worked in retail stores for years, knew the sales clerks at Neiman's were paid commissions. She recognized puffery when she heard it. Still, the barrage of flattery had been too much to resist. She had bought *The Dress*.

Sighing, she hung it in the back of her closet. Would she ever wear it again? Was there any point in spending the money to have it cleaned?

As she debated, the moment she and Drake had first seen each other at the party came back to her. No man had ever looked at her the way he had. And just like that, *The Dress* became worth every penny she had paid for it.

Finally, she ambled to the kitchen. She found her grandmother lifting the lid on a steaming pan on one of the stove burners and releasing a homey aroma into the small room. No microwave for Grammy Evelyn.

She poured herself a cup of coffee and walked to the refrigerator for cream. A dozen magnets her grandmother had collected were plastered on the refrigerator door. The one at eye-level said: BEHIND EVERY SUCCESSFUL MAN IS AN ASTONISHED WOMAN. Shannon had always wondered about Grammy Evelyn's sarcasm toward men.

"I thought potato soup sounded so good in this weather." Her grandmother ladled creamy soup into thick crockery bowls. "That television weatherman said this storm is supposed to go away later today, but I don't trust his forecasts. I have more faith in that woman forecaster. Did you have any trouble on the road, dear?"

"It was foggy and wet, so I drove slow. That's why I got home so late."

"Christa has already called. She's eager to hear about your evening. As am I."

"I'll call her later." Shannon sat down to eat at the small round oak table in the frilly Victorian breakfast room. Ivory crocheted lace shadowed the windows from the outside light. Mauve and blue floral-patterned chintz covered the chairs. A round blue antique rug lay on the floor under the round table. The room, like the house, was a step back in time, which, for some reason, made Shannon feel secure.

Grammy Evelyn brought a china teapot and two delicate china cups and saucers to the table. Shannon had always thought having tea in china cups with her elderly grandmother in this era-gone-by setting was fun. A fantasy, like *Alice in Wonderland.*

As that thought crossed her mind, she thought again of last night. The entire evening had been one big fantasy. But it was more like a porn movie."

Through the meal, Shannon described the party to Grammy Evelyn—the hotel's lavish decorations, the extravagant clothing and jewelry, the people she met, the luxury baubles in the silent auction and the outrageous prices the guests had paid for them. Her grandmother was enthralled.

Afterwards, Shannon called Christa.

"Come over," her pal said.

"I thought I might just hole up for today and—"

"You will not! I couldn't sleep last night for thinking about you all dressed up in that green dress at that party. I want to hear all about it. You aren't about to keep me waiting."

Christa was the only person with whom Shannon shared any part of her personal life. "Okay, okay," she said, laughing. "There's plenty to tell. I'll see you later this afternoon. I have to go to my office and do a few chores, then I'll be over."

Piper Real Estate Company was located in a forties vintage house Shannon had bought and had remodeled and on which she was making mortgage payments. It wasn't on the main street, but was just around a corner from the state highway that ran through the middle of town. It was open on Sundays only if Shannon or one of her team had a customer.

Usually, after taking Grammy Evelyn to church, she went into the office and spent the quiet afternoon updating her files and catching up on what she had put off through the previous week. Today, even in the silence and privacy of the empty office, she couldn't concentrate. Instead of working, she sat at her desk, her eyes closed, her cheeks resting in her palms while she replayed the previous evening, the hour or so in bed with a prince of Texas and the sexy words he had murmured to her.

She could make neither heads nor tails of her emotions. On the one hand, what she felt was akin to grief over blowing an opportunity with a man who could be the man of her—or any woman's—dreams.

On the other hand, her experiences with men had been so negative she didn't want a man—even one like Drake Lockhart—interfering with her life. For the first time ever, she was her own person, not relying on or worrying about what some guy was doing or thinking and she liked that feeling, had no plan to ever do anything that would obstruct it. Independence. She had never known it before and she liked it.

And she had no sooner had that thought than she returned to thinking about Drake and wondering how he had reacted when he awoke today and found her missing.

Despite having a hard time concentrating, she disciplined herself to finish her tasks, then headed for Christa's small house in one of Camden's older neighborhoods near town.

Christa had never left Camden. After high school graduation, she had played at going to a junior college until she married her first husband. She had gone to work for Vista Title Company as a clerk and researcher. Now, twelve years later, she was a closing officer. When Shannon decided to open her own real estate company, Christa was who she had talked to first, the one who had convinced her she had what it took to run her own company.

By late afternoon, Shannon was sitting at her best friend's kitchen table, drinking hot chocolate. Surrounded by the noise and commotion of Christa's sons playing a video game and the spicy aroma of chili simmering in the Crockpot, Shannon made a full confession. She didn't have to explain to Christa who Drake Lockhart was. Anyone in the real estate profession or any of its satellites knew.

The blond friend leaned across the table, her big brown eyes alive and warm. "This is so exciting. What's he like, really? I mean the things people have written about him—"

"Oh, Lord, Christa, he's hard to describe. He's charismatic. And intense." A visual flitted by of Drake's sleeping countenance. Shannon touched her forehead between her brows. "He's got this deep line here. It makes him look like he's frowning. It never goes away. Even when he's sleeping."

"Serious-minded, huh?"

"I suppose so. And he's aggressive. A real no-holds-barred kind of guy. And he's so...he's just so..." She looked down, embarrassed. "I was so torn about sleeping with him. But I couldn't tell him no. He's... persuasive."

"Oh, my God. Did he force you?"

"No, no." Shannon quickly shook her head. The look in Drake's eyes at the moment she consented flashed in her memory. "It was me. I could've left any time I wanted to. But I guess I didn't really want to."

"He's so good-looking in his pictures," Christa said.

Shannon nodded, thinking back again about seeing him fully dressed in a Texas tux in the hotel ballroom, then naked crossing the room from the bathroom to the bed and how she hadn't been able to stop staring at him in either place. "Trust me, he looks better in person."

"I hope he's as good in the sack as he looks like he'd be."

His words echoed through her memory: *I'm going to make you come again before I fuck you….Getting inside you was all I could think about…I want to fuck you again….*Even now, sitting at Christa's table, recalling those blunt words seduced her and caused a clench in her sex. She gave a little huff. Even if she were able to relate how good Drake was "in the sack," she wouldn't. Some kind of magic had happened between them and it was hers alone.

"I can't believe this," Christa said. "When you got that invitation from that other Realtor, who would've ever thought?"

"I know, right?"

"Do you think he'll try to find you?"

"God, no, Christa. I'm just a chick he picked up in the bar. He probably does that all the time."

But even as Shannon said that, she remembered the high voltage that had arced between her and Drake clear across the room. Would he be able to forget that?

"But why would a man like him just pick up women like that?" Christa asked. "Why would he have to?"

Both good questions for which Shannon had no answers. She shook her head. "I have no idea."

Christa heaved a sigh. "My God, Shannon. This is like a story. You know, a look across a crowded room, yada, yada, yada. It's like Cinderella. Why did you lie to him about who you are?"

Why, indeed? She frowned. "I don't know. I was so flattered and shocked that he even looked at me. And so nervous. I guess I was intimidated by the surroundings and the people. I've never been anywhere that was like that party. There was enough money in that room to buy Dallas. I wasn't thinking clearly and I'd had a lot of champagne. Everything got out of my control."

"Well it's easy to fix. You just call him up."

"And say what? 'Hey, remember me? The pick-up from Saturday night. I sure remember you.'"

"Tell him what you just told me. The way I see it, you wouldn't be any worse off than you are now."

Shannon gave that some thought. Christa knew more about men than anyone she knew. Drake's business phone number must be in the Fort Worth phone book. But then, Shannon hadn't heard him say the name of his company. The information would be easy enough to find, but she wasn't convinced that calling him was the right move. "I don't know, Christa. You know my rotten history with guys." She shook her head. "No, I think I'm better off to put it behind me."

"*Pfft.*" Christa waved away her concerns. "Before you do that, you should think about it some more."

The video game ended and the kids trouped into the kitchen for water and food. Christa invited Shannon to stay for supper, but she declined and left for home.

She drove slowly, considering options. Maybe she would look up Drake's company and call him tomorrow. An imaginary conversation sifted through her mind: *Hi, guess who?...Sorry I left in the middle of the night. Had to get home, you know. Don't worry, I didn't steal anything but a coffee mug.*

She shut down those thoughts. No way could she call him. She would never find the right words. Why cause herself pain on top of embarrassment?

Hell. Just hell.

Chapter Thirteen

SUNDAY EVENING, AFTER spending Saturday night with Barron Wilkes, Betty Lockhart withheld an invitation for him to sleep at her house and sent him home. She didn't mind sleeping at *his* house, which she had done last night, but she didn't want him spending the night at hers. She didn't want her stuffy neighbors seeing his car parked in her driveway in the early morning and she never knew when her estranged husband might drop by.

Tonight she had thought Barron would never leave. She was dying to know what had happened between Drake and Donna Schoonover. Reluctant to have so personal a conversation with her son in Barron's presence, she had sneaked a call to him this morning while Barron was in the shower, but she hadn't had an opportunity to call him since.

She worried over Drake quarreling with the daughter of Don and Karen Stafford. The Staffords were revered, not only in Texas, but everywhere. Don Stafford was friends with Saudi princes and had been influential with four or five Presidents. Karen Stafford was a member of every important organization for good causes in the state and had even written a children's book. And they had so much lovely money from God knew how many sources.

She wasn't well-acquainted with Donna. Nor did she know much about Drake's relationship with her. But obviously someone like her would be a good catch for any man. Betty did wonder what kind of mother Donna would make. For all of the heiress's plusses, Drake could be right about her drinking. She had a drink in her hand every time Betty saw her. And though she and Drake were near the same age, she was rumored to have been married three times.

But Betty refused to let herself get bogged down with minuses that conflicted with her wishes.

Now she paced in front of the marble fireplace in her family room. How should she approach her son? He hadn't appreciated her advice in years about his girlfriends and marriage.

Well, her children could brush off her opinions all they liked. Both of her boys were past thirty now and her daughter, Kate, was nearing the thirty mark. It was high time all of them settled down—time Drake spent less time making money, time Pic spent less time tending cows and time Kate chased after something other than wild cowboys and horse shows.

Then there was poor Troy, her stepson who had moved to the Double-Barrel when he was eight years old. With him having his trashy mother's genes, Betty doubted he would ever settle down and be loyal to one woman. Having lived in a family of animal breeders, Betty had learned a thing or two about genes.

All four of them had a bad taste for marriage. But why? Pic had a wife years back, though the girl never was a helpmate. She had hated the ranch and hated living in Drinkwell and after a while, she had behaved as if she hated Pic. An ugly divorce and settlement had cost Pic as well as the family a lot of money. Because of it, friction bubbled beneath the surface among Pic and his siblings to this day. And sometimes it erupted.

Betty walked to the kitchen and poured herself a fresh cup of coffee, continuing to think about her children and when they were small, when she'd had some control of what they did and said. She had loved those years. She loved kids. She wanted nothing more at this stage of her life than grandchildren.

But as she again tried to envision Donna Schoonover as a mother, that cruel bastard Reality punched her right between the eyes. While she might like seeing Drake married into one of the wealthiest and most influential families in Texas, she had no wish for him to bring her longed-for extended family into a world of messy parenting and an unstable home life. She had lived that story. Knew its heartache. One of the reasons she had stuck it out with Bill Junior for years had been for the sake of preserving a two-parent environment for their children, even at great cost to her own self-respect and happiness.

Or at least, that's what she had told herself many times. With Bill Junior, there were other factors to consider, to be sure.

She carried her coffee back to the family room. A shiver passed over her and she moved closer to the fire. These cold dreary days were so trying. She couldn't work in her flowerbeds, couldn't play golf and didn't like leaving the warmth of her home to go play Bridge or even go shopping. If she had some grandchildren, she could bring them here and bake cookies for them, read to them, play games with them. They would pay attention to her, as her own children had done only when they were small.

And as those thoughts tumbled through her mind, her landline rang. Only her family called her this late in the evening. She hurried to the phone in the kitchen and picked up.

"Hi, Mom," Drake said. "Look, I know we talked about lunch, but I'm—"

"Drake. I'm so glad you called. Did you and Donna sort everything out?"

"I didn't call to talk about Donna. I just watched the weather report. It's supposed to clear tonight so I can fly tomorrow. I need to go back to Lubbock to finish what I started a couple of weeks ago."

"Oh, drat. I wanted us to have lunch this week."

"That's why I called. How about breakfast? If you can come downtown tomorrow morning, we'll eat at Rusty's Campfire downstairs. Make it early and I'll still have enough time to get to Lubbock before evening."

"I'll be there," she said. "I have something to discuss with you."

Betty was up early the next morning. When Drake said "early," that was what he meant. She planned to be at the popular bistro on the bottom floor of Lockhart Tower no later than eight o'clock.

Though the weeklong storm had moved on and the sun shone brightly, the temperature was still cold. She dressed in a winter pants suit, its royal blue color flattering to her skin and hair.

When she reached the café, she spotted her son already present and reading the newspaper at a table in the corner of the room. He looked up as she approached, laid his paper aside, rose and rounded the table. "Morning, Mom."

The frown line that always showed between his dark brows looked deeper than usual this morning. Was he troubled by what had happened with Donna? They touched cheeks. "Good morning yourself," she said.

He pulled out a chair for her, then returned to his seat on the opposite side of the table. He was dressed as usual—jeans, a long-sleeved tan button-down shirt and boots. Just like his father dressed. He was built like Bill Junior—wide-shouldered and slim-hipped. He had always been a cowboy. She supposed he always would be. Just like his father. Both of them were such lovely men to look at.

"Did you sleep well?"

The waiter hurried over and poured her coffee cup full.

"Like a rock," he said. He looked up at the waiter and told him they needed menus. The waiter hurried away. "So what do you want to talk about?"

Drake wasn't one to waste breath on small talk. If he was so abrupt with the women he dated, no wonder he had never married.

"Well..." She draped her napkin over her lap, cleared her throat and steeled herself for her son's reaction when she dropped her bomb. "I'm thinking I won't go to the ranch for Christmas this year."

There. I said it. Let the chips fall where they may.

His pointed look came at her like a spear. He certainly had her eyes, she noted for the umpteenth time. He was the only one of her children who did. Whiskey-colored eyes you could drown in his father had always said. But given Bill Junior's fondness for drinking and partying, Betty hadn't found the description particularly romantic or flattering. Her other son and daughter had lake-blue eyes like Bill Junior's. Those were the eyes you could drown in.

And Troy, well his eyes were so dark she could hardly distinguish the pupil. They were probably like his trashy mother's.

Just then, the waiter returned. She ordered oatmeal with cream. She never cooked oatmeal at home. Too messy to clean up after. Drake chose a he-man breakfast—two eggs over easy, sausage patties and biscuits with honey, the breakfast he had favored as a teenage athlete.

"Why aren't you going?" he asked when the waiter left again. "I thought you and Dad made up when y'all went to Nashville."

Back in October, she had accompanied her husband to Nashville to take in the Grand Ole Opry. "Something's happened since then. Your father has a…is sleeping with someone in Drinkwell. I wasn't going to tell you, but maybe you've already heard it."

His eyes settled on hers. "No, Mom, I haven't heard that," he said gently. He was the only one of her children who knew, or cared, that gossip like this hurt her. "But you know you can't believe everything you hear. Who told you?"

"One of my old…acquaintances from down there called me a few days ago."

She had almost said "friends" instead of "acquaintances," but she no longer had friends in Drinkwell. "I don't think I'd be comfortable going anywhere near Drinkwell now," she went on. "I might never go down there again."

"Come on, Mom. What difference does it make, really? Even if it's true? You've been gone what, seven years? And you're sleeping with somebody in Fort Worth."

"Drake!" She looked around to see if anyone she knew was close enough to hear him.

"Well, aren't you? Although considering Wilkes' age, I'd believe you if you said no."

Her spine stiffened. "That is uncharitable for you to say."

She had to defend her choice in a companion, though she knew what Drake meant. Barron was fifteen years older than her fifty-two and Viagra or no, he hadn't exactly proven himself to be a stallion in the bedroom. More than once she had entertained the notion of finding a younger man more physically able to satisfy her carnal needs. And just what would her self-righteous oldest son think of that?

The waiter brought their meals. "I'm kidding," Drake said, tucking into his food, "but Wilkes must be seventy."

"What are you implying?"

"Sorry, Mom. It was just a smart-aleck remark. We don't need to get into geriatric biology over breakfast."

She gasped. "Drake, I swear. You can be so crude. Barron and I are very good friends. In fact, he's invited me to spend Christmas with him in Santa Fe."

Drake gave her an are-you-out-of-your-mind glower. "So that's what this meeting is really about. That's what you're planning instead of going to the Double-Barrel."

Silent gasp. Drake was prickly as a cactus. And he never hesitated to level criticism at her. Growing a thick skin to mask the hurt her children sometimes inflicted had taken as many years as learning to deal with Bill Junior's antics.

She lifted her chin. "Yes. I think I just might. He's also talking about a cruise in January. You know how much I've always wanted to go on a cruise and your father would never agree to it."

"Mom, give him a break. He can't swim. He's afraid of large bodies of water."

"Son, I have known Bill Lockhart Junior since I was six years old. I have never known him to be afraid of anything, not even when we were little kids. That's just an excuse."

"Jee-sus Christ." Drake set down his coffee cup with a *clack*. "I know he's got his flaws, but—"

"Son, I do not appreciate your tone. Why can't you understand? Life's too short to let myself be continually humiliated by your father."

"Mom, forgodsake." Scowling, Drake shook his head. "What do you expect him to do? You moved out. You two are separated. You're up here in Fort Worth flitting around like a damn debutant and he's alone down there in that nothing town that's turning into more of nothing every day. He gets lonesome. He wants companionship just like everybody else."

She waggled her finger like a pendulum. "Do not scold me, Drake. I endured ill treatment from that man for years. He's always found plenty of companionship in that nothing town."

Indeed, she had shed uncountable tears, most of them unseen by the outside world, while living as William Drake Lockhart, Jr.'s wife for nearly thirty years.

Drake reached across the table and picked up her left hand on which she still wore a multi-carat diamond cocktail ring Bill Junior had given her. A diamond tennis bracelet, a gift from him many Christmases ago, glinted in the bright café lights. "You also endured a pretty damn nice life."

She yanked her hand away from his and made sure her right hand on which she wore her 5-carat diamond wedding ring remained in her lap.

Drake returned to his breakfast. "You lived like a queen, Mom. You still do. He never kept you from doing anything. Nor did he fail to give you everything he could afford."

She set her jaw and turned her head toward the next table, not enjoying being reminded of the tradeoffs she had made.

"Has it occurred to you, Mother, that he could divorce you for bailing like you did? If that happened, I guess ol' Barron would have to pick up your expenses, which Pic tells me are considerable these days."

Inside, Betty flinched. Drake's frankness cut like a knife, but she would not let it show, would not be one of those whining mothers. She would never allow her children to see her as anything other than a strong, independent woman. Never mind that all she really wanted was to have a normal family life and receive as much love and affection from her offspring as she had for them.

But her affection hadn't mattered. When they were growing up, she had been forced to be the disciplinarian. Bill Junior had behaved more like their pal than their father, showering them with money, new cars and good times. Competing against him had been an unwinnable contest.

And she didn't need to be reminded that her husband and her second son, through the Double-Barrel's accountant, vicariously controlled her purse strings. She was quite aware that what Pickett knew, Drake knew. She resented her children having knowledge of her personal expenses.

"Pic has no business discussing what I do," she snapped. "If you weren't a grown man, I'd tan your hide for speaking to me like this. As for Christmas, if you need a hostess for the overblown family dinner, perhaps your father can drag the woman he's seeing out of the bar and dress her up suitably."

"Mom, wouldn't you like to spend Christmas with the family? With Dad?"

Her children refused to acknowledge that their father was a philanderer and a carouser. Her second son and her daughter had taken his side as children and that hadn't changed much now that they were adults. They blamed her for her and Bill Junior's marital problems. The only one who *didn't* blame her was her stepson, Troy. He was also the only one who dropped in on her to visit.

"They know where I live in Fort Worth," she said. "If they wish to visit me, they're welcome any time. But I'll tell you right now, I'm very close to giving up on those two."

"Suit yourself, I guess." Drake puffed out his jaws and blew out a long breath, an indication he considered the discussion closed.

He hadn't finished his breakfast, but he wadded his napkin and threw it on the table. "I've got to go. The pilot will have the plane ready by now." He got to his feet and picked up his hat.

Betty couldn't let him leave angry at her. She placed her hand on his arm and stopped him. "Are you spending Christmas at the ranch?"

"Sure am. Just like always."

"Lunch before I leave for Santa Fe?"

"I don't know. Maybe."

"I have Christmas presents for all of you. I could give them to you at lunch and you can take them down to Drinkwell when you go." She gave him a pleading smile. "Please?"

He sighed, a sign he was annoyed. "Sure, Mom. Look, I'll call you when I get back from Lubbock and we'll get together."

"Drake, you will call Donna, won't you? Surely you'll have time to—"

"Gotta go, Mom."

Her eldest child kissed her cheek and glided away, setting his hat on as he passed through the restaurant doorway. Betty released a sigh of her own. Every encounter with him always ended the same. With him rushing off to somewhere as if he couldn't wait to get away from her.

She sat there a few minutes, her oatmeal growing cold as she mulled over their conversation.

...Has it occurred to you, Mother, that he could divorce you for bailing like you did?...

She had left the ranch to save her sanity. Bill Junior hadn't wanted her to leave, but she had seen no other choice. He had battered her pride and self-respect to the ground.

He wouldn't divorce her. If he had wanted to, in the seven years that had passed since she moved away from the ranch, he could have. Instead, every time they met, he begged her to return.

She didn't want a divorce either. In spite of everything, she still loved Bill Junior, damn rascal that he was. For the first time in her and Bill Junior's long stormy history together, she had the upper hand. But back when she thought she did want him and the Double-Barrel Ranch out of her life for good, a lawyer had convinced her that with the ranch's ownership being legally and tightly protected for generations past and future, divorcing Bill Junior would be complicated beyond belief and he would make no guarantee what she would end up with.

She was just as well off with things as they were, with an accountant who knew more about money matters than she did paying her basic bills and doling out a generous monthly allowance.

Now she was in such a foul mood she couldn't decide if she even wanted to go to Santa Fe. Waking up every morning beside Barron Wilkes wasn't one of her favorite thoughts.

A sudden flash of heat cloaked her. *Oh, hell.* Another damn hot flash. After quarreling with Drake, she was in no mood for a hot flash.

She dabbed perspiration from her upper lip with her napkin, left her chair and made her way to the ladies' room. She sat down on a burgundy velvet-upholstered sofa in the lounge, leaned back, closed her eyes and let her mind drift back to September, when she had accompanied her husband to Nashville.

The memory was worth recalling. Bill Junior had rented a luxury suite at Leow's and they had behaved like honeymooners. At fifty-four, he could still send her over the moon. Fantastic sex was something she missed about life with her husband. He could still do it more than once in a night sometimes and she believed he took no drugs to enable him.

He simply knew all the right buttons to push. They had gotten married when she was seventeen and he was eighteen. They had learned about sex together, had tried everything. The memories made her blush. They had been so sexually in tune with each other, if it hadn't been for the pill, they might have twelve kids instead of only three.

The warble of her cell phone halted her stroll down memory lane. She dug it out of her purse and glanced at the tiny screen. *Oh, hell, Barron.* He wanted an answer about Santa Fe. She keyed into the call. "Hello, darling."

"Good morning, poopsie."

"I was just thinking about Santa Fe, Barron. It's a great idea. A holiday away from my kids sounds wonderful."

"You've just made me a happy man. I'll call the property manager tomorrow and make sure the house is ready....What are you doing?"

"Right now? I'm downtown. I just had breakfast with Drake."

"Care to have a little dessert?" He chuckled roguishly. "I just got out of the shower and I'm not dressed yet. I've got a bottle of champagne. We could follow up breakfast with a mimosa or two. In bed." He chuckled again.

Betty lowered her voice and tittered into the phone. "Barron. You are so naughty. Should you be drinking when you're taking that, um, drug?

"My doc says it's no problem."

She tittered again. "Well, then. I'll be there in about half an hour."

She disconnected on a sigh, resigned to the fact that when it came to men, a fifty-three-year-old woman couldn't have everything.

Drake left Rusty's Campfire relieved to escape his mother. A discussion of her romance set his teeth to grinding. He was her son, forgodsake, not some damn confidante.

Dad would settle down and behave like an adult if Mom would simply return to the Double-Barrel. Drake was sure of it. But hell, now she was planning on twisting off to Santa Fe at Christmas with Barron Wilkes. He could imagine what that would cause at the Double-Barrel and it wouldn't be pretty.

Meeting with her had temporarily taken his mind off the weekend and the phantom woman who had stolen from his condo like a thief in the night. His ego still smarted. Would he ever know her real identity?

At least his trip to Lubbock would take his mind off of her. Nothing would be better for clearing his head than the Texas Panhandle's cold clear air.

As he neared the airport exit, his thoughts veered to Christmas again and the Double-Barrel. He plucked his cell phone off his belt and called his brother. "What's Dad up to?"

"He's got a meeting with the vet today," Pic answered. "Why?"

"I just heard he's fucking around with somebody in town. Who is it?"

"Hell, I don't know. I don't keep up."

Drake didn't believe for a minute that his brother didn't know what their father was doing. The two of them lived in the same house and were close. And Drinkwell was a town where very little that a Lockhart did went without being widely blabbed about. But Pic was a peace-loving, closed-mouthed man who saw no point in making waves.

"He needs to get up to Fort Worth and talk to Mom," Drake said. "Otherwise, Christmas is going to be all fucked up."

Chapter Fourteen

AFTER TOSSING AND turning and stewing half the night over whether to call Drake Lockhart at his office and rehearsing what she might say to him if she did, Shannon dragged herself out of bed, pulled herself together and arrived at her office at the usual time. Why had she let calling some damn guy keep her awake all night? Deep down, she had never intended to do it anyway. She hadn't even bothered to search for the name of his company in the phone book. Saturday night was firmly fixed in her rearview mirror and she intended to forget it.

The one important call she had to make today was to the Dallas broker who held her secure future in his hands. She forced herself to wait until nearly noon.

Emmet Hunt's story was the same as it had been on Friday. He still expected to receive an offer from another buyer, but try as she would, Shannon couldn't cajole the name out of him. She was an amateur trying to play a professional wheeler-dealer's game. Emmett was probably secretly laughing at her. Her stomach churned. She reached into her middle drawer and found a roll of TUMS.

Drake's plane landed in Amarillo mid-afternoon. He called Pennington Engineering to let Robert Pennington know he had arrived. Pennington's daughter, Heather, answered the phone and invited him for a Christmas cocktail.

When he and Heather had first met a few years back, after a few drinks, they had ended up at her house having a sexy good time. For a while, every trip he made to Amarillo became a follow-up with Heather and for Drake, a growing discomfort. Casual sex with the daughter of the man with whom he was discussing a business partnership was tabu, a violation of his own rule of never mixing sex and business.

Heather had wanted, and still wanted, more than a recreational relationship, but the spark wasn't there for Drake. She was smart and good-looking, but she had tried to manipulate him and he recognized a willful streak that made him uncomfortable. Today's meeting with her amounted to nothing more than a drink and a Merry Christmas wish.

The week progressed better than expected. His primary purpose for his trip—securing more leases on Lockhart land—was successful and a relief. Now more than ever, his family needed the cash stream those leases provided.

His meeting with Robert Pennington went well, but nothing was concluded. Drake couldn't ignore his dad's admonishment about investing Lockhart money in Pennington's company. Drake would never play with the family's money without his father's approval.

Beyond that, drilling activity in West Texas was flourishing again. Even with the frosty temps, a smattering of snow on the ground and the distraction of the holidays, he was able to get a seismograph crew out to do tests on investment land he had bought some years back. So far, the government hadn't stopped private property owners from drilling on their own land, although some group constantly opposed it—just as with cattle grazing and real estate development. He had grown accustomed to dealing with the never-ending conflict with government and various organizations with idealistic agendas.

On Friday morning, he flew back to Fort Worth in a good mood. Four days of feverish business activity had pushed the foolish incident after the TCCRA party to the back of his mind where it belonged. He might never know who that Saturday night mystery woman in his bed really was, but that was okay. He had moved on.

Halfway to downtown, his phone jangled with his brother's personal ringtone. He pressed the phone into the dash cradle, put it on SPEAKER and keyed into the call. "Yo, Brother."

Pic didn't even say hello. "Where are you, Drake?"

"Nearly home. Listen, Pic, things in Lubbock are looking pretty good. The wind—"

"Drake, we've got a problem. Kate's barn burned down last night. Can you come down here?"

Drake's stomach lurched. "Jesus, what happened?"

"Don't know yet."

As adrenaline kicked up his heartbeat, a visual of his little sister's large state-of-the-art horse barn zipped through Drake's mind. He had been the general contractor on its construction. It was a two-story ultramodern horse facility that had cost as much to build as an upscale home. "You said burned *down*?"

"Pile of ashes," Pic said.

"Christ, was anyone hurt? Is Kate okay?"

"She's upset. Suffering from smoke inhalation and got a few burns, but she's okay. She lost some horses, though. Proud Mary's no longer with us. Damn shame. Kate just had one of her colts at the futurity up in Fort Worth."

Proud Mary was a seven-year-old award-winning mare Kate had raised from birth. "Oh, my God."

Drake's mind reeled. His sister did love her horses. Drake had affection for horses himself. Just then, a loud horn blared and an SUV charged past him with only inches between them. The news about Kate's barn had so totally grabbed his attention, he forgot he was driving. He jerked the steering wheel, veering his truck back into the right lane. "Where's Kate now?"

"The EMTs took her to the hospital. She's still there."

"I thought you said she's okay."

"She is, she is. They admitted her as a precaution. I was at the hospital earlier myself, but with Dad gone, I had to come home and take care of some stuff around here. They'll probably release her tomorrow. Or maybe even later today."

"Who's with her?"

"Will. He said she was in the barn trying to get the horses out and he dragged her out just before the roof fell in. God, Drake, it sounds like he saved her life. If he hadn't been there, we could be having a different conversation."

Will Harrington, Kate's neighbor. The Lockharts considered him a friend. "Where's Dad?"

"Who the hell knows? I haven't seen him since Monday and he's not answering his cell. He called and talked to Johnnie Sue a couple of times, but I was out of the house both times. He didn't tell her where he was."

Just ahead, Drake's exit loomed and he slowed. "So what caused the fire? Electrical—"

"They haven't said."

"But someone's looking into it?"

"The sheriff's over there. And the fire chief. I've called Kate's insurance man up in Camden. He should be there by now. They'll probably have something to say later today."

Drake had little faith in the Treadway County Sheriff who was more a politician than a cop. He doubted the man knew any more about investigating fires than he did about capturing criminals.

He had more confidence in the fire chief who had earned the whole family's respect during the range fires back in the summer. The guy managed an all-volunteer fire department and was a volunteer himself, but he was a dedicated firefighter who even had some advanced training, something unusual for Treadway County's officials.

"I'm just hitting my exit. Let me go." Drake glanced at his dash clock. "I need to stop by my condo for a few minutes. I'm going to drive down. I should get there early this afternoon."

"I'll be waiting for you at the ranch."

"And Pic?...Tell Kate to hang in there."

"I will. Just don't drag your feet getting here. Somebody's gonna have to make some decisions."

And if Dad wasn't around, Drake knew that somebody most likely would be him.

As he navigated the city traffic toward Lockhart Tower, he was troubled—grief-stricken even. In the world of agriculture, nothing was much worse than a barn burning, especially if it housed live animals. Many farmers and ranchers cherished their barns more than their homes.

He was also puzzled. Multiple safety features had been built into the barn, including a sophisticated automatic sprinkling system.

At his condo, still rattled by the latest family catastrophe, he threw some clean clothes into his duffel and informed his assistant and his housekeeper of his plans. When he checked his voice mail messages, he listened through half a dozen from Donna. The slur in her voice told him she was drinking heavily. She had gone to Aspen without him. Fine. That chapter had ended.

Soon he was on the road to the Double-Barrel, ninety miles away, girding himself for the chaos that thrived there. Where was Dad? It wasn't unusual for him to go on a bender and be gone several days, but still...

At the halfway point, he approached the town of Camden, forty miles from Drinkwell. Camden was larger and more scenic than the town where he had grown up. Because it had both a drive-in and an indoor movie theater, as well as a huge freshwater lake, it had been a date destination during his teenage years. When he was a boy, Camden had been closer to the size of Drinkwell, but now, due to the real estate boom in the nineties and the development of sub-divisions on lakefront lots, it was several times the size of his small hometown.

Nearing a railroad crossing on the outskirts of the town, he slowed, prepared to stop if necessary. At the same time, as he always did, he glanced up at the billboard standing on the right side of the highway. From a white background, a life-size shapely red-haired woman, arms crossed over the chest of a sleek black business suit, smiled down at the passers-by. Drake nearly ran off the road. He slammed on the brakes. Tires squealed behind him, horns blared.

Shit! It was her! Sharon Phillips!

He knew it as surely as he knew his own name. Like a whirlpool, a torrent of mixed emotions swirled through him.

He drove across the railroad tracks, turned around and drove back toward Fort Worth. He turned around again, re-approached the billboard and eased off the pavement onto the shoulder. He stared up at the sign, trying to remember what was on the billboard when he had last paid attention to it. If the good-looking woman had been there, he surely would have noticed.

FOR YOUR REAL ESTATE NEEDS IN CAMDEN
CALL AN EXPERIENCED PROFESSIONAL
PIPER REAL ESTATE COMPANY
SHANNON PIPER, OWNER/BROKER

A phone number followed.

He chewed on his lower lip. Man, oh, man. If he had time, he would drop in on the *professional* Miz Piper, just to see the expression on her face. No doubt she thought she had pulled off a clever ruse and would never see him face-to-face again.

He found a notepad in his briefcase and jotted down the *professional* Miz Piper's information, then studied the billboard image a few more minutes convincing himself he was right about the identity. He picked his phone off his belt, called his assistant in Fort Worth and asked her to find out everything she could about Shannon Piper and Piper Real Estate Company.

Driving slowly along the highway through Camden, he looked for Piper Real Estate signs on buildings, but didn't spot one. He was soon all the way through the town and on his way southwest toward the Double-Barrel. He didn't have time to turn around and search for Piper Real Estate, but the image of Sharon Phillips' womanly body in a glittery green dress compared to Shannon Piper in a smart black business suit filled his head. He thought he had put that woman out of his mind, but now she was back.

Before he reached the ranch, Debra called him back. In a brief search she had learned that Shannon Piper had owned her own real estate brokerage for four of the six years she had been in the real estate business. Her company specialized in high-end homes. She was a multimillion dollar producer and a respected professional. Had even won some awards.

That information came as no surprise. Saturday night in his condo, Drake had seen she was no dummy, though she was apparently a liar.

He had learned something else about the professional Miz Piper Saturday night, something that might surprise her peers. The dominant fact that wouldn't leave Drake's mind was that Sharon Phillips/Shannon Piper, or whatever her name was, was hell in bed. Not only were her face and body a vision to see, she liked sex raw and dirty. Every man's fantasy. She had ignited a flame in his loins like he hadn't experienced in a long time and he wanted more. Just thinking about her caused pressure to build behind his fly. And today wasn't the first time.

Forty-five minutes later, he rumbled across the iron pipe cattle guard entrance that took him into a different world—the Double-Barrel Ranch. He set thoughts of Shannon Piper aside.

Pic and his two border collies, Frissy and Fancy, met him in the driveway. He never saw his brother's dogs without thinking of when they were boys and their mother had refused to allow male dogs in the house or on the porch. To this day, Pic kept only female dogs. Drake scooted out of his truck. He and his brother man-hugged and back-slapped. The energetic dogs danced around them. Pic whistled and ordered them to calm down.

Drake bent over and scruffed the dogs' ears. "Is Kate still at the hospital?"

"I just talked to her. They're gonna release her later today. Will's gonna bring her home."

"Let's get over to her place. I want to see it for myself." Drake climbed back into his truck.

"Let me get a coat." Pic trotted back into the house. He returned wearing a brown barn coat and a bill cap. He ordered the dogs to stay, then climbed onto the passenger seat. "I warn you, it's bad. You'd better get prepared."

Soon, they were passing through the gate to Kate's small horse ranch, Blue Horizons. Usually, the barn—a structure much larger than the vintage frame house where Kate lived—was the first building visible on approaching. Today, Drake saw nothing familiar. Columns of smoke rose into the chilly air and floated into nothingness. He drove directly to the barn site the length of a football field away from the house.

He was stunned to silence. "Bad" didn't begin to cover the scene before him.

A tall and wide heap of black rubble lay over a large area where the barn had been. A blackened skeleton of one partial wall still stood, reminding Drake of giant black toothpicks. Drake swallowed a lump in his throat. The barn had been grand. As barns went, it had been an architectural work of art.

A burned-out truck chassis and the warped frame of a long trailer were parked to one side and partially covered with smoking rubble. "Is that the Cimarron Kate just bought?"

"What's left of it," Pic replied.

Without warning, moisture flooded Drake's eyes. "My God," he mumbled. "How could this happen?" As he struggled to wrap his mind around the destruction, he said a silent prayer of thanks that their little sister hadn't been killed.

Several other vehicles had parked haphazardly around the site. Half a dozen people engaged in a flurry of activity.

Pic scooted out of the truck, but Drake stalled. He dug his handkerchief from his back pocket and dabbed at his eyes before exiting.

As soon as he opened the door and stepped out, the smell of smoke and ash and the stench of charred flesh met him. The thought of horses burning alive sickened him. His chest felt as if a rock filled it. His stomach roiled and he swallowed bile. "My God," he said again, stuffing his handkerchief back into his pocket. "You didn't say how many of her horses."

"Four. Will said she had a dozen in the barn, but she got eight of 'em out."

Drake scanned the landscape. Horses grazed on the hillside in the distance. "I thought she had a groom or somebody who stayed in the barn apartment."

"Mexican kid. Miguel Lara. Loves the horses. He wasn't here last night. The futurity's been going on up in Fort Worth, you know. She's still got some horses up at the coliseum and Miguel's staying with them."

The Treadway County Sheriff, Tom Gilmore, came toward them, accompanied by a man wearing earmuffs and gloves and carrying a clipboard. Drake didn't recognize him. The sheriff offered Drake his right hand. "Haven't seen you around here in a long time, Drake."

"How's it going, Tom?" Drake shook hands. "I don't get down here as much as I used to."

"I thought your dad might come over and—"

"He's out of town," Pic quickly replied.

"We're about to wrap up for today," the sheriff said. "Soon be too dark to see."

Drake nodded, cursing the short days of winter.

The man with the sheriff shoved the clipboard under his arm, snapped the glove off his right hand and offered a handshake. "George Mayfield. Farmers Casualty up in Camden. My company holds the policies on all of Miss Lockhart's property."

"Adjustor?" Drake asked, shaking the newcomer's hand, too.

"Yessir. And you are?"

"Drake Lockhart. I'm Kate's brother. I built this barn."

"Oh, yes, Mr. Lockhart. I've heard of you. Sheriff Gilmore says the barn's about six years old. That about right?

"Yeah. Six."

He wrote something on his clipboard. "You wouldn't happen to have a blueprint, would you?"

"In my office in Fort Worth. I'll ask my assistant to overnight it down here."

As Drake reached under the bottom of his jacket for his cell phone, Mayfield handed over a card. "Please ask her to send it to my office in Camden."

After Drake made the arrangement with Debra, he returned his phone to his belt, planted his hands on his hips and looked the adjustor in the eye. "So what do we know about this?"

"Too soon for conclusions." Mayfield looked toward the rubble and began speaking and gesturing with gloved hands. "It appears to me that the fire started inside the barn, perhaps over there in the hay storage area. Spontaneous combustion is a possibility, but it's been awfully cold and wet for that. I've requested someone more knowledgeable than I am to come from our regional office and look things over."

Drake stuffed his chilled hands into his coat pockets "Where's your regional office?"

"Austin."

"That's not the other side of the world from here. This fire took place eighteen hours ago. Why isn't somebody already here?"

Mayfield's face took on a hurt expression. "*I'm* here, Mr. Lockhart. We do the best we can. We do have a procedure that we follow. A team will be up tomorrow."

A team? Arson investigators? Drake was only slightly mollified. "The sooner the better."

"We think the fire started in the wee hours, Drake," the sheriff put in. "It must've got so hot so fast it was already too late by the time Kate got here from the house."

"This barn had a sprinkler system," Drake said. "It didn't work?"

"We've been talking about that," the sheriff answered. "But nobody's figured it out yet. Maybe it was broke."

Drake refused to believe Kate wouldn't have kept the sprinkler system in working order. She cared so much about her horses, she had been known to sleep in the barn nights in a row when a mare was due to foal.

Drake knew how laid back and even bungling small-town officials could be. Giving the sheriff's comment no credence, he looked across his shoulder at Pic. "Did you hear Kate say anything about the sprinkler system not working?"

"Nope."

Drake turned to Mayfield again. "I assume you'll be handling the claim all the way through the process. I don't know what she had this facility insured for, but—"

"We'll have to separate the destroyed property from what's left before we assess value," Mayfield said.

An idiot could see that *nothing* was left. Drake's hackles rose. Being in the construction business, he had tangled any number of times with insurance people, had developed a strong distrust of insurance companies and had little respect for their procedures. And he had short patience when he sensed somebody was about to try to baffle him with bullshit. "As I started to say—George, is it?—I know what this barn cost to build. And I know the value of the lost horses."

"Ah, yes, the horses," Mayfield said. "Would your sister have some bills of sale or—"

"Of course she would if she'd bought 'em," Pic said testily. "But not all of her horses are bought. Some of them, she breeds herself."

Drake could tell that even his easygoing little brother was annoyed.

Mayfield frowned and stroked his chin. "Well, that could be a problem. It's hard to put a value on something that wasn't bought and paid for."

"Our sister turned down a quarter million for Proud Mary just last year. That should tell you what they're…what they were worth," Pic said.

"Not entirely, Mr. Lockhart. That's speculation. And we have no way of knowing for sure which horses were destroyed. But I understand what you're saying."

"Kate knows which—"

Just then someone called to the sheriff and he excused himself. Obviously relieved for the opportunity to escape the Lockhart brothers, the insurance adjustor, too, excused himself and followed the sheriff. Drake added George Mayfield's name to his list of people who strained his patience. He could already see trouble.

He and Pic walked the perimeter of the rubble. Nothing had been removed, including the burned carcasses of what had once been talented, beautiful athletes. Drake's stomach rolled, but he held himself in check. "This makes me sick," he mumbled.

"Me, too," Pic said grimly. "I threw up when I first came over here this morning."

Troy darted into Drake's mind. He and Kate weren't a partnership, but they worked closely together. At the same time, he remembered that the NCHA Futurity finals were going on. With Troy being well-known in the cutting horse world, of course he had horses competing. "Does Troy know about this?"

"Not yet. He's still up in Fort Worth. He trained a mare that's probably gonna win it. He's riding her in the finals."

"Whose horse is it?"

"Guy from Kansas. Pretty Kitty is her name."

"Ah. I watched him ride her in the pre-lims. I figured they might make the finals."

"Well, they did. Good purse this year, too. Around four million. None of Kate's horses made it though. That's why she was here when the barn caught fire. She was upset and came home. I haven't called Troy and told him what happened yet. I didn't want to distract him when one of his clients is depending on him. I'm gonna try to catch him closer to the end of the show, before he heads for Dallas."

"Dallas?"

"He's got a girlfriend up there now. He stays at her house for days at a time."

"That sounds serious. Who is she?"

"Some gal Jordon Palmer introduced him to. I told him he ought to keep away from that lowlife and any of his friends, but he and Jordan have been halfway buddies ever since Kate's engagement to the asshole."

"That's not good news," Drake said.

They stayed at the fire site until dusk began to cast the landscape in shadow and the temperature grew colder.

"Let's get on back to the house," Pic said. "I'm freezing my ass off and I'm hungry. We can't do anything here anyway."

"Yeah, you're right. Let's go."

They climbed into the truck again and Drake slowly drove away, continuing to look across his shoulder at the rubble. Pic unclipped his phone from his belt and keyed in a number. "I'm gonna call Will at the hospital and tell him not to bring Kate back to her house. I don't want her to see this. At least, not yet. He should take her to the Double-Barrel."

"Good idea," Drake said. He listened to Pic's conversation with Kate's neighbor. They rode another short distance in silence before Drake said, "Have you called Mom?"

"I figured *you* would. You're the one who gets along with her the best."

Drake hadn't talked to their mother since their breakfast on Monday. On a sigh, he reached for his phone, speed-dialed her number and reported Kate's tragedy. Betty Lockhart gasped and exclaimed and broke into tears. She planned to drive to Blue Horizons immediately, but Drake persuaded her to wait until tomorrow morning.

"Tomorrow, huh?" Pic said, after Drake disconnected. "That's good maybe. But it could also be bad."

"What's that supposed to mean? This is still Mom's home, you know."

"Bullshit. This stopped being her home when she moved to Fort Worth. Besides, you know how Kate feels about her."

"Kate needs to get off her high horse. She doesn't know that much about all that's gone on between Mom and Dad. There's no reason for her to be so judgmental. Mom hasn't done her any harm. And right now, Kate needs her support. Doesn't look like she can rely on Dad."

"She doesn't need either one of them, Brother," Pic said. "She's got you."

Chapter Fifteen

BACK AT THE Double-Barrel, the aroma of searing meat and spices floated through the house, but Johnnie Sue reported that supper was still forty-five minutes from being ready.

"I don't know about you, Brother, but I could use a drink," Pic said.

Pic was a moderate drinker. After his divorce, he had been a hard partier for a while, but once he started seeing Mandy again, he had found peace in his soul. Drake, too, had consumed his share of liquor after Tammy had dumped him, but he got past that phase. Fundamentally, growing up with their father had made Drake resistant to irresponsible overindulgence, but this evening, something to dull reality's sharp edges was welcome. He followed his brother into the den.

A fire burned in the fireplace, forging a cozy ambience. Pic walked over to paneled doors beside the fireplace. "God, what a day." He opened the folding doors and exposed a small bar. "I've been up since three o'clock this morning. I thought you'd never get down here." He lifted two heavy crystal tumblers off a glass shelf. "What's your poison these days, Brother?"

Drake sank wearily to the seat of a massive leather recliner. "Whatever you've got."

"Whatever Dad's drinking is what we've got," Pic said, scanning the contents of a wall cupboard. He pulled out a full bottle of whiskey and read the label. "Looks like his latest preference is Jim Beam."

For the first time in hours, Drake thought of their father and the fact that Pic claimed not to know where he was. "Pic, we need to try to find Dad. He needs to know about this. And you know damn well Mom will expect to see him."

Pic brought a glass with an inch of whiskey in it over to Drake, but made no comment.

Drake took the drink, shaking his head, thinking again of the senseless dichotomy of their father's behavior—whining about his wife not returning, yet chasing after a string of other women. But this wasn't something Drake wanted to even think about, much less have a conversation about at the moment. For once, he refused to allow his parents problems to overshadow the horror of the day and the magnitude of Kate's tragedy. Their feuding had already divided the family.

He sipped at the whiskey, grimacing as it burned his gullet going down. "You said Kate got a quarter-million dollar offer on Proud Mary? She never mentioned that to me."

Pic took a seat on the sofa to the right of Drake's chair and set his glass on the coffee table. "Probably because she never even considered taking it. If you recall, from the time that horse was a filly, Kate had her pegged as a winner. She always figured she would collect more than two-fifty in cutting competitions and breeding fees. And she did."

"Who made the offer?"

"Some syndicate. You know how it is in Texas these days. If you've got a little money and a wild hair to be a cowboy, you invest in a cutting horse."

Being horse lovers, Drake and his family disliked the syndicates that had evolved as a result of cutting horse values skyrocketing. Those who were afraid of the risk of owning a horse, or couldn't afford one, often put together a group with the intention of sharing winnings. Or losses. One crippling incident or fatal illness had its obvious tax benefits.

Most syndicate members knew or cared little about the horses or the sport and skill of cutting. Cutting horse ownership gave them access to an exclusive club. If the animal turned out to be a champion, which was rare, the windfall might be small, given that it was divided among so many investors, but the bragging rights on the cocktail circuit got heftier.

"Several Fort Worth bankers, I think it was," Pic said. "You know bankers. Cheap fuckers when they're on the buying end."

Speculative investing in a living animal had a capriciousness to it detestable to Drake. Too often he had seen the money become more important than the animal. As an investment, he preferred the solidity and permanence of land.

Pic leaned forward, his forearms propped on his thighs, his big hands wrapped around his glass. "Want to know what I'm thinking?

"Shoot," Drake said, leaning back in his chair and propping an ankle on the opposite knee. "Maybe what you're thinking makes more sense than what's going through my head."

"I'm thinking about what that insurance man said. Or didn't say."

Drake hadn't devoted all of his thoughts to George Mayfield, but insurance had been in the back of his mind ever since he had first seen Kate's damage. "And?"

"I'm betting they won't pay fuck-all for those dead horses. The minute Mayfield started blabbing that crap about bills of sale and so on, all I could think was this'll be like that little bunch of our cows that got run over by that fuckin' semi a few years ago. We couldn't prove their value because we bred 'em. Registered mother cows got turned into hamburger and the insurance company paid us by the pound. Like they were culls."

"I remember," Drake said.

"Four purebred cutting horses with bloodlines long as my leg? They could be worth a million, if not more. Proud Mary went all the way back to a King Ranch horse. Her foals were worth a hundred thousand the minute they hit the ground."

Drake sat forward, too, cradling his glass between his hands. "The insurance company will investigate this before they pay out a dime for anything. We might as well suck it up and swallow it. I'm assuming that the Austin people Mayfield referred to are arson investigators."

Pic's eyes widened. "You think it was arson?"

Drake wasn't ready to give voice to his suspicion. "I'm not saying that. I just know insurance companies. Kate's barn cost roughly three-hundred thousand when we built it six years ago. Replacement at today's prices will be higher. Even without considering the value of the horses, there's equipment, a new dually truck and a fancy horse trailer. Easily a million-dollar loss. They won't process a claim that large without a thorough investigation."

"That figures," Pic groused.

Mentally, Drake chastised himself for not being more involved in the business end of his little sister's horse operation. Especially after he had built the high-tech barn for her and knew the kind of money she was earning and spending on horses. "What do we know about Kate's insurance? I've never seen her policy, have you?"

"Nope. She bought it through Jordan Palmer. If you think back, you might recall that when Kate was engaged to that flake, he was in the insurance business. Hell, at one time, he carried the insurance on most of the stuff on this ranch."

Before he switched to the real estate business, Drake thought and again, Shannon Piper drifted through his mind.

"Shit," he said. "No telling what kind of policy she's got." He sighed. "How long have we been tied to Jordan Palmer?"

"Long enough. Kate was about twenty when she got engaged to him that time. About twenty-one when she finally saw the light and got rid of him. She's twenty-eight now, so that would be seven years he's been hanging out with Troy off and on and moving in and out of our lives."

Drake huffed a bitter laugh. "All I know is I'm suddenly seeing and hearing way more of that sonofabitch than I want to. Sometimes I wonder if it's some kind of karma."

"You don't believe in that crap any more than I do," Pic said. "What it adds up to was damn poor judgment on Kate's part back when she was just a kid. But nobody could tell her anything. The whole time that mess was going on, I kept reminding her what Grandma always says."

"Which is?"

"You lay down with dogs, you get up with fleas. Now I find myself trying to tell Troy the same thing."

Just then, Johnnie Sue called them to supper and Drake and Pic sat down to beef fajitas and all of the trimmings. They didn't talk much. Drake had been so sobered by what he had seen at Kate's place he was out of words.

Half way through the meal, a truck engine sounded from outside. "That's Will's rig," Pic said. "Kate's here."

They met their little sister at the front door. She looked haggard and bedraggled. Both of her arms were swathed in burn wrap. Her lips were cracked and dry, as if she had suffered a severe sunburn. They glistened from something greasy. But what was more painful to see was her blond beauty masked by a look of defeat. An urge to pound something with his fist flew through Drake. When they were younger, he had been his little sister's avid protector. That instinct came back in spades.

He carefully drew her into his arms and held her. "Kate, baby. I'm so, so sorry."

"They wanted her to stay," Will said, coming up behind her. "I tried to get her to, but she wouldn't."

Her face buried against Drake's shoulder, she began to weep. "Oh, Drake, it's so awful. I lost Proud Mary. And—and Peppy's Pretty Boy and Blue Diamond and her colt, Baby Blue."

Drake had heard all of those names of horses Kate had bred and raised. He stroked her back. "Shh-shh. We'll fix it, darlin'."

"Not even you can fix it, Drake. You can't bring them back. They needed me and I wasn't there. They were penned up and I couldn't get to them." She broke into sobs. "I can still hear them crying for me. I'll never forgive myself."

Seeing his little sister's broken heart pierced Drake's own. He stroked her hair and clasped her head to his chest. "Shh, darlin'. It wasn't your fault."

"I don't know what happened, Drake. I've thought and thought, but I can't figure it out."

"Let's don't talk about it tonight. You hungry? Want to eat something?"

She sniffled and shook her head.

Over Kate's head, Drake caught Will Harrington's eye. The neighbor shook his head and said, "I think they've given her enough drugs to put down a horse. She ought to drop any minute."

Drake held her away and looked into her face, saw an unusual glitter in her sky blue eyes. "Then it's time for you to get to bed and get some rest. We'll tackle all of this tomorrow. Remember what I've always said? Even the worst things look better in the daylight."

Johnnie Sue spoke up from behind them. "The bed's all made up in your old room, Miss Kate."

"Let Johnnie Sue help you to bed." Drake hugged her again and urged her toward the housekeeper. "We'll get together tomorrow after you're rested."

After the housekeeper escorted Kate from the room, Will said, "God, y'all, this is just about the worst thing I've ever seen."

"What do you think happened?" Drake asked him.

"No idea, Drake. By the time I got there, the barn was already collapsing onto itself. The truck and trailer were gone and the horses were already done for. I had to drag Kate away to keep her from getting hurt bad."

Drake, along with Pic and Will, stood there, silent and grim-faced for a few beats, the pall of the tragedy cloaking all of them.

Finally, Will said, "Well, I need to get going. I've still got stock to take care of."

"I saw horses grazing in the pasture," Drake said. "I presume they were Kate's. Do you have a place they can stay for tonight?"

"I was planning on rounding them up and putting them in my barn. I've got room."

"Thanks, Will," Pic said. "If you need help, I can send—"

"That's okay, Pic. I got it."

"We won't forget what you've done for our sister," Drake said.

"Don't worry about it," Will said. "Kate's my neighbor. But more than that, she's my friend."

The next morning, Drake arose before daylight. He and Pic met in the kitchen at the coffeepot. After finishing breakfast, they climbed into Pic's truck and rode the ten miles to Blue Horizons. As they came to a stop, Drake saw several vehicles already there and parked at odd angles. Jose Avalo who owned a small construction company in town was sitting on his backhoe, the engine idling.

Drake spotted Sheriff Tom Gilmore, several other people he didn't know and George Mayfield, still wearing earmuffs. Also in the group was Blake Rafferty, the Texas Ranger assigned to major crime investigation in Treadway County. The Lockharts had known the Ranger for years. They often hunted together. His presence confirmed Drake's suspicion of arson.

"Shit, there's Rafferty," Pic said, yanking on the door latch. "That means they think this is a crime."

They scooted out of the truck. The stench of the fire still hung in the chilled air. "Sickening smell," Pic said and walked over to Avalo.

As Drake approached the investigative group, the Texas Ranger broke away and met him. "Mornin', Drake." The Ranger put out his right hand.

Drake shook hands. "Blake. How's it going?"

George Mayfield walked up and took charge immediately, called one of the other men over and introduced him as Carl Barlow, an experienced arson investigator. He also explained that the people combing through the debris were part of his team, along with a forensics team from the Department of Public Safety's lab in Austin.

The fact that arson was out of the closet for all to know suited Drake fine. "So where are we?" he asked.

"Too soon to tell," Blake answered.

Pic walked back from Avalo's backhoe. "Any reason we can't move these horse carcasses out of here?"

The Ranger and Carl Barlow exchanged looks. "Give us an hour," Barlow said.

"Where's Miss Kate?" the Ranger asked.

"Back at the Double-Barrel recuperating. Yesterday was a horror for her. We didn't wake her before we came over. We figured she needed the rest."

"We'll have to talk to her," Blake said. He paused, then added with a no-nonsense tone. "Pretty soon."

Drake nodded, accepting that their old friend had to do his job. "No problem, Blake. Any blatant clues what happened here?"

The Ranger shook his head. "Not yet. We're sure it was set, but that's about all so far."

"Can you think of anyone who'd benefit from this fire?" Carl Barlow asked. "Other than your sister?"

"Don't go there, buddy" Drake said firmly. "Kate's broken-hearted. Money won't replace what she's lost. She would've died last night if her neighbor hadn't dragged her out."

"It's a question that has to be asked," Barlow said.

"You better not ask our little sister," Pic said. "She might claw your eyes out. Those horses were just about as close to kids as she's ever had."

Just then the bleat of his cell caught Drake's attention. He grabbed it and checked the screen, saw their mother's number. He keyed into the call. She informed him she was in Camden, headed for the Double-Barrel.

Drake's jaw tightened. If she went to the ranch and learned that Dad was nowhere to be found and had been gone for a week, she would be royally pissed off. If she came here to Kate's house, Kate would be pissed. Drake made a quick decision similar to those he had made in the past when it came to dealing with his family. A pissed-off Kate was easier to handle than a pissed-off Betty Lockhart, so he said to his mother, "Why don't you come on out to Kate's place? That's where we are right now."

"Mom, huh?" Pic said after Drake disconnected.

"She's on her way. And she'll want to know why Dad isn't with us."

"We'll just tell her he had to go up to Fort Worth for some reason. Let Dad explain to her why he isn't here."

Their mother soon arrived. She alit from her Cadillac SUV wrapped in a gray cape that nearly touched the ground. She broke into tears when she saw the devastation. "Who are all these people?" she asked tearfully, looking around. "Where's my Kathryn?"

"Asleep at the Double-Barrel," Drake answered, offering her his handkerchief. "She hasn't seen this in the daylight and Pic and I don't want her to come over here yet."

Mom took the handkerchief, removed her black leather gloves and wiped her eyes. "My God, it's cold. Where's your father?"

Pic spoke up. "Dad had to go up to Fort Worth. Nobody's been able to reach him. You know how he is about his cell. It's probably turned off or not charged.

Their mother glared at him, brow arched. Her breath emitted little puffs of vapor. *Like steam*, Drake thought. She wasn't fooled for a minute.

"If he's with some floozy, I'll kill him," she said. "He should be here. Someone needs to keep all of these people in line. This is a horrible situation. Someone needs to take control."

"Mom, we've got this," Drake told her.

He refrained from speaking his thoughts. Dad taking control might or might not be a joke. Even if he were here, for a brawl to erupt between him and Mom and take precedence over the "horrible situation" wouldn't be unusual.

The Ranger approached again and lifted off his hat. "Mrs. Lockhart. Nice to see you. How are you this chilly morning?"

"Not well, Blake. Not well at all." She sniffled and wiped her eyes with her fingers."

"I understand, ma'am."

"How did this happen, Blake?"

"We're all doing our best to find out."

"I'm sure you are. I'm sure you are. Thank God for friends like you."

The Ranger turned to Pic. "How soon do you think we can talk to Miss Kate?"

Drake caught Pic's gaze. Pic glanced at his watch. "I guess we can call and see if she's awake."

Drake said to Blake, "She just came home from the hospital last night. She was pretty shaken. We want to spare her seeing this until we can get the horses out of here and buried. Instead of having her come here, maybe you could go over to the Double-Barrel."

"I'll see if that's okay with Carl," the Ranger said and walked away.

Before he returned, another truck wended up the caliche driveway. "Oh, hell," Pic said. "That's Will's truck. And there's two people in it."

Drake made a mental groan. He started forward to intercept them, but before he reached the truck, it came to a stop and Kate clambered down from the passenger side. She headed for the fire site.

Drake stepped in front of her. "Kate, wait—"

"Get out of my way, Drake."

Mom quick-stepped around him and enveloped Kate in a smothering hug. Kate pushed her away and looked at her. "What are you doing here, Mama?

Mom hung onto Kate's arms, looking into her face and not letting her move. "I'm here to help you, darling. This is horrible. You need support from those of us who love you."

To Drake, his sister looked somehow smaller. She looked up at Pic, her eyes accusing and glistening with fresh tears. "Where's Daddy, Pic?"

"Fort Worth," Pic answered quickly.

Before he had to say more, the Ranger and the arson investigator approached Kate. "Miss Kate," Blake said, lifting his hat.

"Hi, Blake," she said.

"I'm sorry to disturb you when you're so upset, but we do need to ask you some questions."

She nodded, looking down. Will looped a supportive arm around her shoulders and pulled her close. Blake and the arson investigator questioned her about when she first knew of the fire and what she did thereafter.

Between bouts of tears, she told that the groom who usually slept in the small apartment attached to the barn had stayed in Fort Worth with the horses that had competed in the futurity. She had been asleep, but was awakened by the commotion in the barn and the smell of smoke. By the time she reached the barn, it was already on the verge of collapse. She was able to save eight horses, but couldn't save all of them. At that, she broke down and sobbed. Mom closed her into an embrace and Kate gave no resistance.

The two investigators apologized and backed away, but not before asking her not to go near the fire site and not to leave town.

"Have you eaten, sweetheart?" Mom asked. "Can I make you some coffee? Or tea?"

Kate shook her head. "No, I—"

"That's a good idea, Kate," Drake said. "Go in the house with Mom and let us finish up out here."

Chapter Sixteen

AS SOON AS Kate and their mother disappeared into Kate's house, Drake turned to his brother. "Dammit, Pic, you must know somebody in Drinkwell who knows where Dad is. Mom's right. He needs to be here."

Pic bristled. "He doesn't discuss his social activities with me. And I know damn well he wouldn't like me nosing into them. He's not a kid, forcrissake. He's fifty-three years old."

"Then he needs to stop acting like he's seventeen," Drake said. "Get on the horn and see if you can find him."

"You know, if you had to deal with some of his and Mom's crap yourself—"

"I hear plenty of it from Mom's end. This is no time for a debate. Let's just find out where he is."

"Goddammit," Pic mumbled, shaking his head. But he unhooked his cell phone from his belt. "I'll make some calls."

Drake watched the activity around the fire site while Pic made calls, which seemed to go on forever. Finally, Pic hooked his phone back on his belt. "Maybe I found him. Perry Jenkins said Mona Luck's been calling around. She wants somebody to come get him out of her house."

Perry Jenkins owned the only bar in Drinkwell. Drake vaguely remembered the breakfast the past Monday when Mom had told him her friend has reported his dad sleeping with a woman in Drinkwell. Was Mona Luck the woman? Drake thought Mona was married. Releasing a great sigh, he clapped a hand against Pic's shoulder. "Come on, Little Brother. Let's go see what our daddy's been up to."

"I'm against this," Pic groused, stalking toward his truck. "It's been a long time since you've enjoyed one of these episodes, Drake. You've forgot just how damned unpleasant it is."

Drake didn't react to his brother's criticism. He knew Pic's real thorn was that Drake still held sway in ranch decisions though he hadn't lived here for years. Pic climbed behind the steering wheel and fired the engine. Drake took the passenger seat. Then, leaving a rooster tail of caliche dust behind them, they were barreling toward the road that would take them to Drinkwell.

At the state highway, Pic made a quick right turn and sped toward town, thirty-eight miles away. Once inside the city limits, he drove unerringly to one of Drinkwell's few organized neighborhoods. He crept along the narrow streets until he arrived at a redbrick single-story house, its lawn turned beige by winter. The windows were trimmed in white and Christmas lights were strung along white gutters.

The place was so shuttered, it appeared no one was at home, but their father's work truck was parked in the driveway.

"You found this place pretty easy," Drake said. "I take it you've been here before."

"I picked him up here a couple of other times."

"How long did they say he's been here?"

"They didn't. He doesn't leave his itinerary with anybody, you know. Sometimes he goes to town for something and just doesn't come back. Like on Monday. This bullshit is Mom's fault. She called him Monday afternoon, he yelled into the phone, then he hung up and left."

Inwardly Drake groaned, again remembering his breakfast with their mother. Had she told Dad she planned on going to Santa Fe for the Christmas holiday? If so, that could have been enough to send him off on a toot, especially if she had told him she was going with a man.

They sat in front of the squatty house in silence for a couple more minutes. Finally, Pic said, "You going in with me or are you waiting out here?"

Drake sighed. "I'll go."

They scooted out of the SUV and walked to the front door together. Pic pressed the doorbell. After a few beats, the door flung open and they were face to face with a disheveled blonde who could have been forty or sixty. She wore bright red lips and a flimsy yellow robe. A cigarette was propped between two manicured fingers of one hand.

"Hi, Miz Luck," Pic said.

"I hope to hell you've come to pick up your ol' man." she snapped. "It's about damn time you got here." She stepped back and allowed them inside the house that was dark as a cave. Little daylight found its way through the closed drapes and blinds. "Five days of this shit is enough. I can't stand him when he gets so goddamn drunk."

"Yes, ma'am," Pic mumbled.

"Where is he?" Drake asked.

"In bed."

She led them down a dark narrow hallway, the stench of stale alcohol and unwashed bodies filling the space around them. Drake silently vowed this was the last time he would ever do this.

They reached a small bedroom where Bill Lockhart, Junior, who was Drake's height and as bulky as Pic, filled a double bed, his body and head hidden by a thick comforter. Rhythmic loud snores rumbled from beneath it. Like a heavy tapestry, the odor of sweat and alcohol hung even more pronounced in the tiny bedroom.

"Jesus Christ," Drake muttered.

"Goddammit," Pic growled. He walked over to the bed, bent down and shook their father's shoulder. "Dad?...Dad, wake up. It's me, Pic."

Their father snorted and grumbled, but didn't awaken.

Standing in the doorway, Mona leaned a shoulder against the jamb, her arms crossed under her breasts. "You ain't gonna wake him up. He's out cold. You're gonna have to carry his ass outta here."

Drake shot her a look. "He's been like this for five days?"

"He's only been out of it for a couple."

"What's he been doing the other three?"

A lurid grin curved up one corner of the woman's mouth and Drake instantly wished he hadn't asked the question.

"Well...when he ain't too drunk, he can be a lot of fun, if you know what I mean. For an old fart, he can—"

"That's enough!" Drake had no interest in hearing what his dad did for fun and he didn't consider him an old fart. Fighting anger, he glanced to where Pic had somehow gotten him dressed and sitting up on the edge of the bed. Time to get him out of here.

He turned back to Mona. "Where's his coat?

She left the room and soon returned with a brown barn coat. Together, Drake and Pic wrestled their dad into it. Then Pic leaned his shoulder into the older man's midsection, gripped his dangling arm and hoisted him over his back as if he were a sack of oats. He jostled and settled the load into a fireman's carry. "Okay, I got him. Glad he's lost a little weight." He staggered up the hall toward the front door.

"Where's his stuff?" Drake asked Mona.

"What stuff?"

"His truck keys and wallet. His hat. His boots and belt. Including the buckle."

If Dad wasn't working at the ranch, he wore custom-made boots for which he paid thousands. No doubt, even worn, they would fetch a pretty penny on eBay. He also wore a hand-tooled belt with a sterling silver buckle on which a solid gold longhorn's head was mounted inside a circle of emeralds. In happier times, their mother had had it made as a present.

Mona's bloodshot eyes shot daggers for a few seconds, then she stamped to the corner at the end of the dresser, jerked the boots up and slammed them on top of the dresser with a loud *thunk*. She grabbed his wallet off the dresser and stuffed it into one of the boot shafts.

"The belt and buckle," Drake reminded her.

She yanked open a top dresser drawer, produced the two items and shoved them, too, into a boot shaft.

"Thanks," Drake said, pulling the wallet out of the boot shaft and thumbing through it. No cash. Surprise, surprise. The credit card slots were full, but Drake didn't know how many credit cards his dad usually carried. "I suppose his wallet was empty when he got here."

Mona's lips curled into a sneer. "Eat shit, pretty boy."

Spearing her with a don't-mess-with-me glower, Drake stuffed the wallet back into the boot shaft.

"What the hell did you expect?" she snapped. "He ate everything in the fuckin' kitchen. Drunk my whiskey, too. I'm entitled to—"

Drake stopped her with a finger pointed at her nose. "If you kept a credit card, don't make the mistake of trying to use it. I'll have your ass arrested and be assured, I'll prosecute."

"Oh, yeah? Well, I know Tom Gilmore better than you do, hot shot. Your ol' man ain't the only one who likes what I got."

Before Drake could retort, Pic called from up the hall. "Hey, Drake, come on. He's heavy."

"Where's his truck keys?" Drake asked Mona.

Mona stomped up the hallway. Drake followed her, carrying the boots and belt and pausing to open the front door for Pic to pass through with his load.

Inside the kitchen, soiled dishes and scraps of food littered the counters, including a cardboard pizza box and the remains of a pizza. A pile of dirty dishes filled the sink. Mona clawed through the clutter on the counter, found the keys and thrust them at Drake. "Here, pretty boy."

Drake took the keys. "Don't forget what I said about that credit card." He reached back for his own wallet, pulled out a couple of C-notes and dropped them on the counter. "For your trouble," he said, then walked out of the kitchen.

"Don't you ever come to my house again, you big-shot bastard," Mona shouted behind him. "And tell your sonofabitchin' ol' man not to come back here, either. If there's anything I can't stand, it's some ol' fucker that can't hold his liquor and can't keep it up. Money don't cure either one of those problems."

Jaw clenched, Drake walked outside where Pic struggled to open the back door of his crew cab with one hand. Drake quickstepped to the truck, opened the back door and Pic unfolded their father onto the backseat.

They started back toward the Double-Barrel, with Drake following in Dad's truck. At the ranch house, they tussled him out of the backseat and walked him into the house, ignoring his snorts and rumbles. Inside his bedroom, they undressed him and helped him into his bed.

After they had him settled, Pic said, "He won't come around 'til tomorrow."

"With any luck, Mom won't come to visit before he sobers up," Drake said. "It's a wonder we got his boots and belt buckle back." He paused a few seconds, staring down at their father. "I don't miss this crap, I'll tell you."

They left the bedroom, both of them peeling off their coats. "I'd like the chance not to miss it myself," Pic said as they reached the back porch and hung their coats on the steer horns by the back door. They headed for the kitchen and the coffee pot. "But unless he can talk Mom into coming back, I don't see it getting any better. He says nothing's worthwhile without her."

"Does he think this kind of stuff is going to get her to come back?"

Pic dragged mugs out of the cupboard and poured coffee. "I wish he'd throw in the towel on Mom. She waltzes him around, Drake. She leads him on, telling him she'll come back, then not doing it. She tells him she loves him, but she keeps living up there in Fort Worth and hanging out with her friends."

"Jesus," Drake said again.

"I'll be damned if a woman will ever do anything like that to me again," Pic said. "I had my turn, but at least I had enough sense to get out of it and stay out of it."

Pic had caught his ex-wife and a lover in a motel in Fort Worth. A nasty divorce had followed. Another day, Drake might have gouged his brother with how much it had cost for Pic to "get out of it." But today, Drake kept his silence.

"Oh, well." Pic shrugged. "Maybe they can get it worked out over Christmas, right? How many times have we said that now?"

Drake shook his head, unhappy to be delivering news Pic didn't want to hear. "She's not coming down here for Christmas."

Pic's pointed look came at him. "Something tells me you didn't finish that story. What's she doing instead?"

"She's going to Santa Fe with a friend," Drake said.

"A friend," Pic said, his expression flat. "You mean that boyfriend. Shit." He lifted his free arm and dropped it. "Well there goes Christmas. With Kate's barn burning and her hurt and Mom not coming down, I just don't know what the point is." He set down his mug with a *thunk*, turned and stamped out of the room.

Uncomfortable and unnerved by all that had happened as well as his brother's display of attitude, Drake no longer had a yen for coffee himself. He left his mug on the counter and retired to his own bedroom. Seeing the father he loved and admired in such a degrading state depressed him. He needed some quiet time to regroup.

He made some phone calls and caught up with what was going on in his office in Fort Worth. Soon Johnnie Sue called him to supper. Only he and Pic were present to eat. Conversation, stilted and strained, was about the fire and Kate and the latest bomb Mom had dropped into the family circle.

Drake went to bed early. He slept miserably, with images of flames and screaming horses filling his half-sleep. And threading through all of it were moments awake and multiple images he couldn't erase of a flame-haired woman in a glittering dress.

The next morning, Pic had already eaten breakfast when Drake reached the kitchen. Saying he had chores to do, Pic shrugged into his coat and clapped on a bill cap. Clearly, his attitude hadn't improved overnight. Drake chose not to push him.

"I'm going to call Troy today," Drake said.

"Wait 'til later in the day, okay?" Pic said. "He called and left a message that he's in the final go-round today. Don't fuck up his chances at winning."

"Fine. You call him then. I'm going to Kate's. When you finish up, see if you can help Dad get well, will you?"

"I'll see what I can do. If Jose's still working over at Kate's, tell him to send us a bill for his work."

Drake spent the day dealing with the fire investigation and avoiding his mother as much as possible. He didn't even go into Kate's house to eat lunch. Instead, he joined Blake Rafferty and his Ranger partner when they drove to town for burgers. He learned nothing new about the investigation.

By the end of the afternoon, the arson investigator had wrapped up, the horses were buried and everyone official had left. To Mom's credit, she had managed to keep Kate sequestered inside the house through it all. Drake dropped in and told them he was returning to the Double-Barrel.

As he walked out of Kate's house, his mother followed him outside. "I cannot believe your father hasn't come over here to look at this and comfort Kathryn."

"He just got back from Fort Worth. He isn't feeling well," Drake said.

"You mean he's drunk. Or hung over." Mom glowered for a full thirty seconds. "And you and your brother are covering for him. I should've known. If he were sober, he'd be over here consoling his daughter."

"Mom, please, can't we—"

"You know something, Son? You're right. Why should I worry about what he does? I'm going to be here a couple more days helping Kathryn, then I'm going back to Fort Worth. I have to pack for my trip to Santa Fe."

"Good plan, Mom. You do that."

She stood there shaking from the cold and blinking at him for a few beats. "I'm freezing," she said. She turned sharply and stalked back into Kate's house.

On the way back to the Double-Barrel, Drake decided he had been here long enough. At the ranch house, he found Pic and their father in the den. Dad looked like hell, but he was dressed and sitting upright in his favorite chair drinking a Coke.

"I've been telling him all about Kate's barn and what's happened," Pic said. "But I talked him into waiting 'til you got back before going over there."

"There's no point," Drake said wearily. "The horses are buried, the investigators are finished. I'm sure Blake will have something to tell us in a day or two."

"Troy called," Pic said. "I told him about the fire. He can't get back down here 'til tomorrow. He and his horse lost by two points."

"Who won?" Drake asked, thinking that he wished he had been able to see his little brother ride in the finals.

"An Oklahoma stallion. Nobody ever heard of him."

"Your mother's over at Katie's house?" Dad asked.

Drake nodded. "She's planning on going back to Fort Worth in a couple of days."

"Is she coming by here before she goes?"

Drake gave his dad a look, bewildered anew by the screwed-up union between his parents. "I don't know, Dad. If you want to see her, you might have to go to Kate's. But I recommend you wait until you're cleaned up and shaved and completely sober."

Their father turned his head and stared out the sliding glass door. Drake didn't try to construe exactly what that meant. At this point, he only wanted to escape what he couldn't control.

Chapter Seventeen

TUESDAY. THE SCENT of cranberry and cinnamon filled Grammy Evelyn's house. Over the weekend, Shannon had bought new Christmas candles, new lights and red and gold garland. She had given the whole weekend to making the holiday as warm and wonderful as possible for the sake of her aged grandmother. Grammy Evelyn was healthy and in good shape for eighty-four, who knew what could happen?

Shannon had hauled the six-foot artificial Christmas tree they used every year down from the attic and set it up in the parlor in front of the wide bay window. While munching Grammy's homemade cookies and sipping hot apple cider, they had decorated the tall green tree with the new lights and garland and ornaments Grammy had collected over the years. With garland to spare, Shannon had hung it around the room.

The parlor, with its tall mullioned bay window, its ivory crocheted lace curtains and burgundy velvet furniture, looked formal and elegant every day, but decorated for Christmas, it could be a picture right off a Victorian Christmas card. Grammy Evelyn had reveled in every minute of the decorating and told stories of Christmases past. Just knowing how much the time had meant to her gave Shannon deep satisfaction and a happiness of her own.

Presents had already mysteriously appeared under the tree. Shannon suspected her grandmother was giving away some of her personal treasures that Colleen so coveted.

Now, ready to leave home for the Camden Multiple Listing Service breakfast, she stopped and studied calendar on the kitchen wall. Twelve days until Christmas. Time was fleeting. She had to finish work on a business plan for the coming year. Only God knew what was going to happen to real estate in the near future, but no matter what the market brought, she had to have a plan. She had to donate food to some of the local charities and deliver Christmas gifts to her friends and business associates.

Eight days had passed since she had talked to the Dallas broker, Emmett Hunt, about the five-acre purchase. To pester him with another phone call or not? That was the question.

The calendar sent another memory through her mind. Ten days had passed since the insanity that had followed the TCCRA gala. She had endured a gamut of emotions, swinging between guilt and depression and embarrassment and regret. Straying memories still skulked the perimeters of her contentment, but through sheer will, she had put that evening in its proper place. Drake Lockhart was nothing more than a figment of her imagination. She would never see him again.

The Multiple Listing Service meeting usually ended by nine, but ran late with holiday business and announcements and discussion of the local Realtors' Christmas party.

The Camden Realtors Association party, scheduled for the coming Saturday, would be small potatoes compared to the TCCRA extravaganza in Fort Worth, but still, it would be a dress-up event. Did she dare put on that green dress and wear it? She should, if for no other reasons, because it was so beautiful and to get her money's worth from it. The idea made her smile. If she showed up in something Jennifer Lopez would wear with ease, Camdenites would think she had lost her mind.

She arrived in her office a little after ten and found her assistant Chelsea alone. The girl was bubbling over. "You're wound up today," Shannon said, slipping out of her long wool coat. "What's happening? Wait, don't tell me. Jason gave you a ring."

Jason was Chelsea's steady boyfriend and the receptionist made no secret of how much she wanted to receive a ring from him for Christmas.

"Nothing like that," Chelsea said, not even appearing to be disappointed. "I hope you don't mind, but I set up a showing for you. I couldn't find Kelly or Terry."

Shannon hooked her coat on the oak coat tree in the reception room, picked up her hobo bag and walked toward her office at the end of the hall. Chelsea followed, still talking. "This guy called on the ad on Jim King's house. He said he's from out of town. He sounded legit, like he was familiar with the market. He said he's a cash buyer. He didn't seem put off by the price."

In the month of December of any year, a cash buyer for a home that had started out at three-quarters of a million dollars was something to celebrate, but in the current market, it was like manna from heaven. Homebuilder Jim King had stuck his neck out, built the luxury home on speculation on an expensive lakefront lot and gotten caught in the market crash like everyone else in real estate. Shannon gave Chelsea her full attention.

"He said he doesn't have much time," she went on. "He wants to look at empty houses 'cause he doesn't want to hassle with a long closing and waiting for someone to move out. He wants to take possession by the end of the month.

December had been the leanest of a year of lean months for Piper Real Estate. The dropping home values were the worst setback Shannon had experienced since opening for business. Ending the year with a solid cash sale and a nice commission would be sweet. Shannon sank to her chair and began unloading items she would need for the day from her purse. "Chelsea, you are worth your weight in gold. You set it up for when?"

The receptionist beamed at the compliment. "Late this afternoon. I told him you'd meet him there at four."

"Great. What's his name?"

"Oh, gosh. I don't think he said. He got another call and put me on hold for a few minutes. I was so excited about someone looking at Jim's house, I just—"

"That's okay." Shannon was unperturbed. She had shown homes and land to any number of nameless customers.

At 3:30 p.m., she popped into the bathroom, touched up her makeup and straightened her clothing—a brown tweed skirt and tunic over a white turtleneck sweater. Not the most attractive outfit she owned, but the warmest. Since she might have to spend time outdoors at the King house, she was glad she had worn it, along with her knee-high boots. The temperature had hovered in the low forties all day and now, the sinking sun was already losing heat.

Back in the reception room, she unhooked her coat from the coat tree and pulled it on.

"Good luck," Chelsea said.

"Amen. Baby needs a new pair of shoes." Shannon hung her bag on her shoulder, plucked a key off the key holder behind the receptionist's desk and slid it into her coat pocket.

"And Chelsea needs a Christmas bonus, hint, hint." A big grin spread over the receptionist's face.

Picking up her brief case, Shannon grinned back at her. "You don't have to worry, my girl. Deal or no deal on Jim's house, Santa will not overlook you."

Shannon made a point of treating her assistant well. A good one was hard to find and she remembered the days when she had been an assistant herself.

Her destination was located twelve miles out of town. As she drove, she mentally practiced her pitch, visualizing the house Jim King had built, reacquainting herself with its extra features. The sprawling one-story cut limestone sat on two acres. It rambled over the lot, with huge windows in almost every room taking advantage of a breathtaking view of Camden Lake. Jim had built it to appeal to well-heeled retirees who didn't like stairs.

She arrived a few minutes before four, expecting to be there first. But to her surprise, a late-model crew cab pickup was already parked on the concrete driveway. A King Ranch luxury model was not a cheap vehicle, so the customer must truly have some spare change in his pocket. Always good news when someone was looking at an expensive home.

She saw no one. Every prospect who had looked at this house had headed for the backyard first to take in the view of the lake. She scooted out of her Sorento. An icy breeze blew off the lake, so she buttoned and tied her coat, then grabbed her bag and briefcase and started across the muddy yard for the back of the house. She had taken only a few steps when a man emerged from around the corner.

Her heart went *ka-thunk!* She halted in her tracks.

"Good afternoon," Drake Lockhart called, walking toward her with that macho male grace that had hooked her the first time she had seen him.

It happened again—that awareness of his masculinity setting off chaos low in her belly. The same odd pull had rendered her stupid at the TCCRA party. Lust, pure and simple. She recognized it, knew only too well where it could lead. Her face heated as her heart began a tattoo.

He appeared to be even bigger than he had in the hotel ballroom. He looked like a damn cowboy—a red gimmee cap with some kind of logo on it, a short quilted down coat like many of the cowboy types wore, starched and creased butt-hugging Wranglers, the hems stacked just right over his boot tops.

He came nearer and she steadied herself. *Do not stutter, do not stutter, do not stutter.*

"Good—good afternoon," she said, straining to show she was not stunned all the way to her boot soles. She was, after all, an experienced salesman, able to think on her feet, wasn't she? She even managed to dredge up her best real-estate-agent smile as she readjusted her bag on her shoulder.

He stopped a few feet in front of her, the deep crease between his brows still there. His keen whiskey-colored eyes drilled into her. They watered from the cold and his cheeks were rosy, just like that night at the foyer bar in the Worthington Hotel. One corner of his mouth tipped up, but she wasn't sure if that was a smirk or a smile.

"Shannon Piper, right?"

His tone sounded even, leaving her unable to perceive anything good or bad. Skipping over every intimate detail they knew about each other, she said, "Yes. I don't believe you told me you were looking to buy property in Camden."

"I don't believe you told me you had property to sell. Or for that matter, your real name.... Sharon."

A long-winded attempt at an explanation was not happening. She looked past him and expelled a breath, spewing a tiny cloud of vapor from her lips.

When she didn't reply, he turned away, shoving his hands into his coat pockets. "So what've we got here? Looks like a nice place." He made a hundred-eighty-degree scan of the area. "Awesome location."

"Well, you know what they say in the real estate business. Location, location, location."

He gave her an arch look across his shoulder.

"Something tells me you don't really want to see this home," she said.

"Why not? Especially if it's warm inside."

She hesitated. Did she really want to go inside a vacant house with him and let herself in for God knew what? From his demeanor, she couldn't guess his state of mind. She couldn't even define her own.

Resigned to whatever came next, she finally said, "The builder leaves the thermostat on low. I guess we could go inside."

She led the way and unlocked the front door. After the cold outdoors, the house's interior felt too warm. She untied and unbuttoned her coat and started for the thermostat, but as if he had installed it himself, he walked toward it and reached it before she did.

"It's set on sixty-five," he said. "Tropical."

He unzipped his coat, then switched on the lights and turned around. He had on a yellow button-down shirt with a tiny white pinstripe. A perfect color for his tanned complexion and brown hair color. Damn him for being so good-looking and looking so freshly ironed.

A blue embroidered logo on his shirt struck him at about nipple-level. A tingle passed through her. She had licked and kissed his nipples and the tiny mole beside one of them.

Determined to be professional, she cleared her throat and began her pitch. "As you can see, the living room has a panoramic view of the lake." She strode toward the kitchen, wanting to get this over with ASAP. "The builder was careful to make sure the lake can be seen from both the dining room and the kitchen." Her voice sounded too high and quivery, but she carried on.

She circled the kitchen, her boot heels clicking against the wooden floor and led him up the hallway toward the master bedroom end of the house. "It has a split bedroom floor plan. The master is—"

But before she could get more words out, he took the lead, switching on lights as he walked up the hallway. *Hell. Just hell.* He probably knew more about new houses than she did.

Hands tucked into his coat pockets, he strolled through the master suite, looking around, taking in the lake view and all of the extra features Jim King had added to the sleeping area and master bath. She followed him, saying nothing. She couldn't keep her eyes off his butt in the tight-fitting Wranglers, flaunted by his short coat. She well knew that a taut bottom hid inside those jeans.

They changed directions, moving back toward the living area. Tension stretched tighter in her rib cage. Sooner or later, he was bound to get around to what he really wanted to say.

He stopped in a wide archway leading from the dining room to the kitchen and looked up. At the construction, she presumed. "Nice" he said. "Local builder?"

Pleased for a question she could answer with confidence, she pasted on a smile, slipping into her professional persona again. She still doubted he was interested in this house, but perhaps she was wrong. "Absolutely. Hometown boy. He's been building homes like this one for years."

He walked back into the kitchen. He stopped at the gray slab-granite cooking island and turned to face her so abruptly, she nearly collided with him.

"Oh! Excuse me!" She stepped back.

He planted a palm on the cooking island, a fist on the opposite hip and gave her a piercing look. "So why the charade?"

Seeing him standing beside the cooking island set off another erotic memory and her heart began pounding so loudly, the entire county, the world, the universe must hear it. She might forget many things, but sex on that cooking island in his condo would not be one of them.

She gathered herself. "How did you find me?"

"Babe, if you're hiding out, you probably shouldn't have your larger-than-life-size picture plastered on billboards on a major highway."

She bristled. No one called her babe. "What are you doing in Camden? Somehow, I can't believe you're planning on settling down in this quaint little community. From what I saw, it doesn't fit your lifestyle."

"Ahh, *fit*. I like that word. I think I've heard you use it before."

...Wow. It fits....

Oh, hell. A blood rush heated her face. Speech failed her. She closed her eyes and drew a deep breath.

"You're right," he said. "I'm not interested, though it does have some charm."

She opened her eyes in time to see him smooth his hand over the cooking island's glossy surface. "I like the cooking island." He looked up at her and grinned in that devilish-little-boy way she had found so charming at first.

"Okay," she said shakily. "I get it. I *get* it. You came here to rub my nose in it."

"Now, darlin', your nose is too pretty to risk harming it. But you know what? Your reaction tells me you've got a fondness for the cooking island yourself."

She rolled her eyes. "Oh, please."

"Honey, that's exactly what you said the other night. And more than once, as I recall. I did my best to oblige. I'm even willing to do it again, just in case I didn't get it right the first time."

She drew in a controlled breath. "I do not appreciate your calling me babe and honey and silly meaningless names. It's insulting."

He continued to grin. "I haven't gotten used to your real name yet. Shannon." He chuckled, obviously amused by her distress. "But to answer your question, I'm passing through. I've been down with the family in Drinkwell for a few days. A blind man couldn't miss your billboards. And I couldn't control my curiosity."

"Oh, really? Should I be flattered?"

His expression changed from smirky to earnest. "I don't know. Are you?"

For a fleeting second, she saw in his eyes the steely resolve she had seen before. More memories of that Saturday night flooded her mind:

...It's never been this good.

Why do I think you say that to all the girls?

I don't say things I don't mean....

A profound yearning wrenched her insides. A deep ache throbbed between her thighs. *Oh, dear God.* She had to get control of herself and the situation. "You've seen the house. You said you aren't interested. We should go now."

"Let's go to dinner," he said. "Talk a little bit. We were talking the last time I saw you." His accusing eyes bored into her again. "Before I fell asleep and you skipped out."

Was he angry? Why should he be? He had gotten what he wanted from her. "Wrong word choice, Mr. Lockhart. I didn't skip out. I merely left. I told you I had to go home."

She tried to walk past him, but he clasped her arm, his touch like an electrical shock to her system. "Don't get so excited. There must be a good place to eat in Camden."

She stepped away from his grasp. "I don't have time to go out to dinner. Someone's expecting me."

"Call 'em up. Tell 'em an old friend dropped in. Believe me, sugar, I won't take no for an answer."

He was angry, all right. She had no idea what he might do if she didn't agree to eat with him. She was worse off than a bug caught in a spider web. The smartest plan would be to walk away from him and never look back. But the easiest was to just go to dinner and be done with it.

And then there was that lustful, out-of-control part of her that wanted to just be with him. *Oh, dear God. Get thee behind me, Satan. Please.*

Her mind whizzed through Camden's limited list of restaurants as she tried to think of one that would get them in and out quickly and afford the least privacy. She was sure he would not go for McDonald's. "Do you like Mexican food?"

"This is Texas. Who doesn't like Mexican food?"

"There's a café in the shopping center. *Casa Familia.* We can go there. It's on your way out of town."

His brow arched. "Shopping center?"

She gave him a flat look. "This is a small town."

"Okay then, shopping center it is." He held out his arm, gesturing toward the front door. "After you, sugar."

She swished past him, giving him a defiant glower. "You can follow me. *Sugar.*"

His laugh sounded behind her. *Damn him.*

Once she got in her SUV, her shoulders sagged and she let out a breath she felt as if she had been holding thirty minutes. She should just speed away, but since he seemed to be determined to torment her, he would probably chase her down.

As she drove toward Camden's only shopping center, she called Grammy Evelyn and told her she would be late. Her heart kept up a drumbeat in her ears. Such a huge spike of adrenaline had flooded her system she might never calm down.

Reaching the strip mall, she eased behind *Casa Familia* and parked in the darkest corner of the employees' parking lot lit only by a single mercury-vapor light. She had expected him to park out front with the other customers, but he followed her and brought his pickup to a stop beside her SUV.

He walked over and opened her door. "Are you sure it's dark enough back here? Maybe we could park in the alley."

She scooted out, ignoring his smart mouth and pulling her hobo bag behind her. They walked toward the front door with her hyperaware of his close proximity.

"Why are you parking in the employees' parking lot?" he asked.

"Because I want to. And I know the owners. Their daughter and I were friends in high school. Why do you ask?"

"It's pretty dark is all I'm saying."

"You're concerned for my safety?"

Before the conversation could become more confrontational, they reached the entrance.

She had suggested Casa Familia for a reason. It was a popular, colorful haunt that held happy hour at this time of day. A loud crowd was always present.

They stepped inside to a roar of conversation and earsplitting *Tejano* music, just what she had hoped for. The place was brightly decorated for Christmas and the crowd was larger than usual. Drake asked the hostess for a table for two, his voice almost a yell.

Inwardly, Shannon smiled.

"Right this way," the hostess shouted. She led them to a booth at the back of the dining room a few steps from the bar's wide entrance. They were surrounded by noise and bodies passing in and out of the bar. The din of many voices combined with the blaring music made conversation impossible.

"Do you have a quieter spot?" Drake asked the hostess in an elevated voice.

"Nossir," she yelled back. "Somebody just left or we wouldn't even have this."

Shannon looked over the crowd, still smiling inside. Though she couldn't see Drake's face, she heard him grunt. He probably never got this kind of treatment in a restaurant.

Serves him right, her alter ego said firmly.

"This is fine," Shannon told the hostess who was obviously busy and eager to escape them.

Shannon shrugged out of her coat and claimed the side of the booth that would allow her to watch the front entrance. She hardly ever went to any restaurant in Camden that she didn't run into mutual acquaintances. Almost anyone might see her and call her tomorrow asking about her escort. Who knew? Someone might even recognize Drake.

Drake, too, shed his coat and cap and scooted into the booth. He ran a hand through his perfectly-layered hair, but it still looked mussed and sexy, just like that night at the Worthington. Shannon cautioned herself again about letting her focus be diverted and looked for the cocktail waitress over the heads of the crowd. A strong shot of alcohol was what she needed to settle her nerves.

Seconds later, a young woman appeared. "I'll have a margarita with a splash of Grand Marnier," Shannon said.

"Make that top shelf," Drake told the waitress, then ordered a Dos Equis for himself.

Knowing the price of top shelf liquor, Shannon started to protest, but stopped herself. She suspected that if Drake was buying, he always asked for the best. The waitress had no sooner left before a waiter came, presented them with menus and hurried away. Shannon studied the menu, not wanting to look at him.

"It's too loud to talk," Drake shouted.

Thank God for that. "It's a popular place."

The waitress brought their drinks. Shannon called on all of her will power to keep from gulping hers and at the same time, tried to recall if she had ever had a margarita made with the best tequila on the shelf. The waiter followed the waitress, ready to take their orders. Shannon pointed to taco salad on the menu and Drake ordered beef enchiladas. When their food came, Shannon ate lightly and hurriedly and mostly in silence since yelling was the only option for talking. But soon the crowd had dwindled and the din had diminished to a purr.

"Decent food," Drake said in a normal tone. "Is it always this loud?"

"It's happy hour."

She signaled the waitress and ordered another margarita. Drake declined a second beer.

He pushed his plate aside and rested his forearms on the table. "So tell me about your business."

She couldn't believe he had any real interest in her brokerage. "Nothing to tell. A small town sales office. Just me and my team. Nothing like what you do."

He leaned forward. "Not typical. I had my assistant look you up. You're a multimillion dollar producer, even in this small population. That's no mean feat."

Her ego trilled. She wanted him to know she was good and was flattered to hear him say it. But that didn't mean that she wasn't wary.

As the waitress came again and placed another frosty margarita in front of her, Shannon gave him a quizzical look. "Why would you do that? Look me up, I mean."

"Why wouldn't I? We got along. We had a good time."

Hah. And "a good time" was all that Saturday night had meant to him. Sex with someone besides his regular partner. By now, he had probably made up with Donna Schoonover, if they had ever really broken up in the first place. Shannon drained her drink.

"How else was I going to find you?" Drake continued. "Or find out about you? You weren't exactly forthcoming with information."

"What difference does it make? We both know why you invited me to your condo at eleven o'clock at night. And for that matter, why I went. I'm not pinning on any self-righteous airs here."

A busboy came and cleared off the table, interrupting their conversation. She asked him to send the cocktail waitress. Two drinks were her limit, but so far, tequila hadn't done much toward calming her, though she was beginning to feel a buzz. "After this drink, I have to go home," she said.

"I also know you specialize in high-end homes," Drake said, as if she hadn't just declared she needed to leave. "I assume that house we just left is an example of your listings?"

"I list all of that builder's homes. He and his wife and I went to high school together."

The waitress came with a fresh margarita. Shannon thanked her and sipped. "He knows I work hard and I'm honest."

Drake leaned closer, holding her in place with his eyes. "Does he now? Then he's one up on me."

Was that an insult? It had to be. Lord, his eyes were almost hypnotic. A flashback of those eyes dark with lust almost undid her determination to be strong and tough.

She sat back against the booth's tall back, putting distance between them. "Why are you doing this? What is there to discuss? If you're afraid I might become a pest in your life, you don't have to worry. Until you showed up today, I'd almost forgotten that…that what happened …happened. Actually, I've put a lot of effort into forgetting it."

"I hate hearing that, darlin'. My impression was that you didn't think it was that bad."

"What I thought isn't the issue. You and I live in two different worlds. And for the sake of my well-being, it should stay that way."

"That's why you cut out in the middle of the night? For your well-being?"

She shook her head impatiently. "I told you. I had to go home. I live with my elderly grandmother. I couldn't let her wake up on Sunday morning and find my bed empty. With the bad weather, she would've been frantic with worry."

As she reached for her drink, across Drake's shoulder she spotted an acquaintance headed in their direction. Hal Grayson, Camden's divorced city manager. *Oh. Hell.*

Hal had asked her out a few times, but she had only met him for drinks twice. He had made it plain he would like to see more of her, but she kept him at arm's length. He was an attractive man, but not her type. She didn't know what her type was these days, but a guy with a whiny voice and fewer muscles than she had definitely wasn't it. In terms of being attractive, he was far from being competition for Drake. She held her breath, hoping he didn't stop. His eyes locked on hers, but he neither stopped nor spoke.

Even more stressed by the appearance of a local that she knew, she signaled the waitress again, then reached over and picked up her bag. "I'm going to the ladies' room. When the waitress comes, if you don't mind, order another margarita for me."

Drake gave her that little-boy grin. "There's not a window or a back door in that restroom, is there?"

"Oh, just stop it."

When she came out of the ladies' room, Hal sat perched on a tall stool at the end of the bar, as if he were waiting for her. She couldn't avoid him. His hand reached out and clamped around her arm and he pulled her near. He placed his opposite hand on her waist. "How have you been?"

She had never allowed him to touch her in a proprietary way. He must have had more than one drink. She tried to back away. "I'm good, Hal."

"Where have you been keeping yourself? I've called a couple of times." His hand moved down to her hip.

She gasped. He had to be drunk. She pulled her arm from his grip. "Look, Hal, I need to go. I'm with someone."

"I saw. Is he from Camden? I think I've seen him before, but I can't place him."

A tiny panic zipped through her. If he recognized Drake, she might just faint dead away. For that matter, Hal Grayson might faint at being in the same room with a celebrity millionaire of Drake's repute. A vision came to her of the whole room gathering around him and asking for his autograph or something equally bizarre. "Um, no. He's from out of town."

"The Realtors' party is coming up this weekend. You'll be there, won't you?"

"Wouldn't miss it. I really do have to go, Hal." She finally was able to back away.

Chapter Eighteen

DRAKE HAD SEEN Shannon when she reappeared in the bar. The dude she had traded looks with a few minutes earlier—she thought she had hidden that little exchange—had reached out, caught her arm and drawn her over to where he sat. His hand had landed on her hip and she had made no attempt to move it.

An odd annoyance coursed through Drake, out of his control, pushing him to an uncharacteristic reaction. The closest word he could think of to define it was "possessiveness." Or jealousy?

He was stunned. He had never been jealous of a woman, had always felt sorry for poor bastards who were so whipped they let a woman control their peace of mind. Men like his dad who let Mom flip him inside out and turn him into a fool.

The bar's lighting cast Shannon's crown in a flaming halo, her face in dramatic contrasts. She had a movie-star profile. He recalled her standing in the firelight that Saturday night in his living room and how delectable she had looked. Tonight, even with an uptight hairdo and covered from neck to toe in a plain brown dress and boots, she still looked sexy and elegant. Visualizing her hair loose and free and the perfect woman's body that was under all of that clothing, he felt a tightening behind his fly.

But she was a different person from the woman in the hotel ballroom and in his bed. Christ, she was behaving as if he had never seen her naked, never had his tongue inside her most intimate place, never taken her to multiple screaming orgasms and never heard her beg him for satisfaction.

Was she fucking that dude at the bar? She could be. Hell, the guy might even be an ex of some kind. To his frustration, Drake knew almost nothing about her.

Trouble and turmoil. She was both. A threat to his orderly life. Didn't his family generate enough tumult without him asking for more from an outsider? Perhaps it had been a bad idea to even have looked her up. Maybe he should have been content to just discover who she was, then leave her alone.

But he was confused by his own desires. Hot sex was one thing, but as juvenile as it sounded, what he wanted from her most was for her to look at him with genuine awe and admiration, the same way she had looked at him in that hotel ballroom.

Just then, the waitress appeared and he ordered Cokes for himself and Shannon both. She'd had three margaritas, which was enough. He didn't want her snockered and driving drunk. He shouldn't care, but he felt responsible for her.

Seconds later, his very own mystery woman was reclaiming her seat across from him in the booth. She must have applied new lipstick. Her lips looked full and wet and inviting in the indirect lighting, which sent another sensation beyond his belt buckle.

Frowning, she gave an evil eye to the spot where a small glass of Coke and ice had replaced her margarita glass. "What's this?"

"Coca-Cola. You're driving, remember?"

Her eyes narrowed. "What?"

In spite of warning himself not to be a damn fool, he asked, "So who's the dude with his hand on your ass?"

Her green eyes roasted him, a tiny frown coming and going between her brows. "What?...No one had his hand on my—"

"Boyfriend?"

"I told you before, I do not have any boyfriends. But it's none of your business if I have five."

The idea that she might still be lying to him shot an inexplicable white-hot anger through him. "That guy would like to be."

"He would not. He's the city manager. I have to deal with him sometimes. I don't date people I have to work with."

"He touched you in a possessive way."

"Were you spying on me or something?"

"I didn't have to spy. You were in my line of sight."

She blinked a few times, then opened her palms and shook her head, a gesture of annoyance and frustration. "Well this is just insane." She looked around, avoiding looking at him. "Where is that damn waitress?"

Drake leaned forward and said in a low tone. "I still say his hand was on your ass."

She released a great sigh and leaned against the booth's back. "Look, I don't know what this is about, but let's stop it. Just because we…we…"

Her words trailed off. He was already on his way to being a jackass. He was so angry and confused as to why, he couldn't stop himself from morphing into an unrecoverable one. "Fucked is the word you're looking for, sweetheart. Fucked."

She ducked her chin. "Let's just call that Christmas party a mistake and go our separate ways. That's the civilized thing to do."

"Look at me," he said, and she looked up, her eyes wide, her lips parted. He wanted to grab her and kiss her silly. "Darlin', there was nothing civilized about what went on in my condo. I had my mouth in some real private places. Now, you're right. That doesn't brand you for life, but the way I remember it, you did return the favor."

She flinched and leaned forward, fixing their faces inches apart. "Shut up," she stage-whispered. "People will hear you."

Apparently she didn't like being reminded of her enthusiastic participation. "I'm trying not to believe you were trolling the Worthington for a score with a guy with a fat checkbook. So why don't you clear that up for me?"

"You're being a bastard." She got to her feet, snatched up her coat and bag and stamped toward the front door, wrestling on her coat, her heels clicking on the tile floor and her perfect nose high in the air.

Christ, she shouldn't get behind the wheel. He sprang to his feet, jerked his wallet out of his pocket and dropped a C-note on the table. He grabbed his coat and cap and strode after her. She had almost reached her SUV's door when he caught up with her. "Shannon."

She stopped, but continued to dig inside her bag. For her keys, he hoped. Hell, she was so unpredictable, she might be carrying.

"This is nonsense," she said, still digging. "I never fight like this with anyone."

He moved closer, within a foot of her. "I'm not trying to fight with you. I'm trying to tell you how I feel."

She looked up at him, but he couldn't make out her features in the dark. "And how is that?"

"Seeing that sonofabitch grab you like he had a right to made me want to crunch nails with my teeth and—"

"What?"

"You heard me."

"You and I don't even know each other. We spent a few hours together and we didn't even…didn't—"

"I'm trying to change that."

She shook her head, dismissing him. She returned to digging in her purse. "I've got a busy day tomorrow. I need to get home."

He refused to let her brush him off. "I wish you wouldn't.

She looked up at him again, one hand still in her bag. "Wouldn't what? Go home?"

"Let me take you. You shouldn't be driving. You've had too much to drink."

She said nothing and he couldn't see her face clearly enough to read her expression. Then, "Damn you," she whispered, a shudder in her breath confirming that she wanted him as much as he wanted her. "I don't need this in my life." She shook her head fiercely. "I do not want it, do you hear me? You'll ruin my life."

All he could think was she was about to leave him. "Take me home with you," he said roughly. "You know you won't be sorry."

"I can't. I live with my grandmother."

But she wanted to. She had said she *couldn't*, not that she didn't want to. "There's a motel across the highway. I'll get a room and—"

"If I did that, half this town would know it before daylight."

"Dammit, Shannon—" He couldn't help himself. He was about to burst his zipper and he remembered the taste of her lips. Hooking one arm around her neck and the other around her body, he kissed her.

She didn't return his kiss, but she didn't push him away either. She let his mouth work at her succulent lips and he drank of their sweetness. The longer their lips remained joined, the more she relaxed into him and kissed him back.

And the more he wanted her.

When he finally lifted his mouth from hers, she whacked his hip with her purse. "You're an arrogant jerk. Let me go," she said weakly, but he felt no effort on her part to move away.

"After you kissed me like that?" She stepped back and started to turn away, but he stopped her with a hand on her shoulder. "Don't you get it? This is it, Shannon. The bottom line. I've been trying to figure it out. It's what the whole damn thing was about at that party and in my condo, what it's been about all evening. Chemistry. It's why my cock gets hard as a rail spike when I'm near you. All I have to do is think about you and I'm close to embarrassing myself. This picking on each other, driving each other crazy is an extension of it. And I think you know it as well as I do."

"I don't know what you're talking about. It doesn't matter anyway."

"You're wrong, baby. You're so wrong." He gingerly cupped her jaw with his palm. "It matters to me," he said softly. Then, he bent his head and covered her mouth with his again and kissed her as gently as he knew how. To his astonishment, her hand came around his neck and her lips parted. She sucked his tongue into her mouth and he was lost.

It was all the encouragement he needed. He delved deeply, pulled out and bit at her lips. The kiss turned hotter. Hungrier. He caged her against the side of the SUV with his arms and pressed his erection against her belly. She lifted herself to it. An image of the thick red curls that covered what she pressed against him passed through his head and his dick turned even harder.

He had to touch bare skin. He slid his hands under her coat, over her body, her butt, her breasts, everywhere, fondling and kneading through her layers of clothing, looking for an entrance. "What in the hell are you wearing?" he ground out, finally discovering a way beneath her top.

He tugged her sweater from her skirt's waistband, felt warm flesh. She didn't resist. They kissed again in a lush melding of mouths. He wedged his fingers beneath her bra and filled his hand with her warm breast, felt her nipple erect. He brushed with his thumb and a tiny sound came from her throat. He gently fondled until the nub was rigid while she made little grunts that only added to his ardor.

He tore his mouth away from hers and shoved her clothing up and out of the way, buried his face against her breasts. They were orbs of fire against his lips. He hunted for her firm nipple with his mouth. Finding it, he sucked hard, worked it against his tongue. She clutched his hair and clasped his head tightly, making soft little whimpers.

Every sound she made sent a new rush of hot blood straight to his groin. He was shaking, close to passing the point of no return and she was on the edge, too.

He lifted his mouth from her breast, moved his hand down and caught the hem of her skirt, yanked it up and worked his hand beneath it. "Baby, let me get us a room—"

"No." She kept kissing him and teasing him with hot bites and tongue flicks.

She was wearing those thigh-high stockings and those tiny panties, just like before. *Thank you, Jesus.* He moved his hand again and slipped his fingers between her legs. She was hot as a furnace, the crotch of her panties damp. His cock screamed for the paradise his fingers had claimed. He hooked his fingers into her panties' waistband and jerked them down, combed through her woman's hair, dipped between her slick petals. She was so ready.

She made a strangled sound. "Drake, stop," she panted. We're…we're…we have to…"

"Not yet," he said hoarsely, continuing to stroke. Her breath caught and she wilted against him. God, she was so hot, he almost couldn't bear it. "You don't really want me to stop," he whispered hoarsely.

"No….Don't…stop…"

They stood there, forehead to forehead, while she hung onto him and he played with her and listened to her shallow breathing and little sounds that nearly drove him crazy. "You like that, baby?"

"Uh-huh."

"This?...Like this?..."

"Uh-huh."

"More?..."

"Yesss…"

He managed to push two fingers into her and searched for her sweet spot with his thumb. "Is this the right place?"

She gasped and her vaginal muscles grabbed his fingers. She buried her forehead into his shoulder, her grunts muffled by his coat as her muscles rhythmically milked his finger. A few seconds. That's all it took. He continued to stroke until he was sure she had finished.

She went limp against him. He smoothed her hair with his free hand, clasped her neck. "Aw, baby, baby…that was good, wasn't it?…Wasn't it good?"

"What about you?" she said in a tiny voice. "It isn't fair—"

"Rain check," he choked out. Knowing his screaming erection wasn't going to find a home in that tight sheath tonight nearly had him in tears, but he murmured against her ear, "That was for you."

She pushed him away. "No. It's not fair. Just a minute."

She went at his fly with both hands, unbuckling his belt, undoing his pants and lifting his rigid penis out of his shorts. He was so hot and hard the cold temperature didn't even soften him. "Oh, Jesus, Shannon, what are—"

"Do me," she said frantically, wrapping her hand around his penis.

He needed no second invitation. He shoved her skirt higher, above her ass. She arched to him. He lifted her thigh with one hand and squatted while she pulled the crotch of her panties to the side and guided him to her, but her panties were still in the way.

"Tear it," she said. "Hurry."

He yanked, the flimsy fabric ripped and the tip of him was at her hot entrance. He lifted her bottom, thrust upward and plunged into her, pinning her against the SUV. She let out a little yelp. Her hands gripped his shoulders and she hugged his hips with her thighs. "Oohh...Oohh, Drake..."

Those same powerful muscles that had contracted around his fingers clutched his cock, working him, taking him ever more deeply.

He held his breath, clenched his teeth. Every coherent thought left his mind. His hips pumped. He rooted up into her again and again, animal sounds chuffing from deep in his chest.

Her head lolled backward. "OhGodohGod..."

"Hold on, baby..." He bit into her neck, worked his fingers between her slick lips, found her clit, swollen and firm. He gently plucked at it with his fingers, soothed it with his thumb. She cried out, but he caught her mouth with his and kissed her while she made muffled grunts and sobs and milked him with quick pulls.

He had been so hard for so long, tension had coiled tight as a spring in his belly. He could stand no more and he couldn't move from where he stood. He lost control and his own orgasm burned through him like a flame thrower. He spurted into her, again and again until he was empty, not even caring that his semen filled her with no barrier. All he could think of was marking her as his. And in a flash of rationality, he knew he might never get enough of her.

"Christ," he said, his voice breaking. "Jesus, Shannon. I can't believe..." He gave up trying to talk. He was too weak. Neither of them moved. Finally, he began to feel the cold. "You okay?"

She made an incoherent noise. Gripping her bottom, he lifted her and eased out of her, his essence draining onto her thighs.

"Oh, my God," she said weakly, her head falling onto his shoulder.

"God, Shannon....I'm going to get us a room....Do this right....It shouldn't be—"

"You aren't wearing a condom," she said in a tiny voice. She clasped his wet penis, which hadn't yet gone completely flaccid. "You came...inside me."

His own lungs still bellowed. "Hunh?" he barely uttered.

"You came inside me....Without...without—"

Oh, Christ! "You didn't say anything. I thought—"

"I have to go home." He let her push him backward. She began to fumble with her clothing. He grabbed the bottom of her skirt, helping her pull it down over her butt. "You're on the pill, aren't you?"

She slapped his hands away. "I don't need to be. I haven't had sex in over two years."

As she pulled and twisted at her top, their brief conversation from that Saturday night zoomed into his memory:

...What did you mean, it's been a long time?...

Nothing. Just...that....

How long?...

Just...a while....

What the hell did all of that mean? *Two years?*

She tightened her coat belt and began looking around. For her purse, he presumed. He saw it on the ground, picked it up and handed it to her. "Nobody goes two years without sex."

"I do." She began digging inside her purse again, came up with keys. She bleeped the SUV's door open and scrambled inside, slammed the door and fired the engine. The dash lights lit her face. He motioned for her to lower the window.

When she did, he leaned in and kissed her. She kissed him back. "Don't worry," he told her. "If anything happens, we'll take care of it."

"Easy for *you* to say." She looked at him a few seconds, a glimmer of moisture in her eyes. "I have to go," she said softly.

"Are you sure you're okay to drive?"

"I live less than two blocks from here. I could walk if I had to."

He stepped back, she buzzed up the window, backed up and left him standing alone in the dark parking lot with his pants undone.

Chapter Nineteen

MORNING. SHANNON STOOD at her bedroom window staring out at Camden's Victorian era square. There, the city and the Camden Historical Society devoted much time, energy and money to preserving the look of 1880, right down to the narrow streets paved with red bricks. Grammy Evelyn's rambling vintage home on its large lot stood less than a block away.

A century-old courthouse in all of its four-storied, white limestone glory rose from the center of the square. Giant, old deciduous trees surrounded it. Tiny white Christmas lights wove through their bare branches. In the silvery light of the dawning day, they looked like stars come to earth.

Shannon had been awake most of the night. A dull ache throbbed behind her eyes. Last night's margaritas. She should have known better.

The memory of *Casa Familia's* employee parking lot lashed her. She would like to blame tequila for that, too, but how could she? Three margaritas had rendered her stupid, not unconscious. Just as champagne hadn't been the most persuasive influence at the TCCRA party. Something else was at play. Something she didn't understand. Something about Drake turned her into a sex-crazed fool. In only two meetings, he had become another of Shannon's Follies.

God knew she had been anything but a good girl in the past, but unprotected sex in a parking lot in freezing temperatures? That was the ultimate thoughtless behavior. Her brow crunched into an uncomfortable frown and she bit down on her lower lip. *Dear God.*

Her alter ego piped up. *See there? A few quick minutes of careless sex could wipe out everything you've spent six years building.*

She didn't need to be reminded.

...If anything happens, we'll take care of it...

What had he meant by that? If she got pregnant, would he expect her to have an abortion?

She had been pregnant once. She remembered it only vaguely now, but she clearly recalled what followed. Having no clue what to do, she and her baby's father, her steady boyfriend, Kevin Barton, had gotten married in a quickie wedding. With teenage naiveté, she thought she was in love. But no one could have been more unprepared for marriage and parenthood than she and Kevin. Those days had been one of the more miserable periods of her existence.

She miscarried at six weeks, but getting out of what turned out to be an abusive marriage had taken much longer and was one of the hardest undertakings she had ever tackled in her short twenty-one years. Even now, though her ex lived in Fort Worth, he wasn't out of her life and he might never be. She still heard from him occasionally when he needed money. He had been the first of Shannon's Follies.

Well, at least this morning, she didn't have to worry about being pregnant. On arriving home last night, she had checked her calendar first thing. Her period should start any day. The little Lockhart soldiers had missed their window of opportunity.

She blamed herself for what happened. Drake might have kissed her and teased her to an orgasm, but if she had kept her hands to herself, he would have stopped there. She closed her eyes and arched her brow. Most of her wretched history with men had resulted from bad judgment on her part. The past few years, she had been able to look back and see that. She thought she had finally gotten to know herself. Was she wrong?

Well, this craziness wouldn't happen again with him. After she drove away and left him standing in the parking lot, she doubted she would hear any more from him. His pride would be hurt. And if any man she had ever met had more than his fair share of pride, Drake did. He would be too angry to ever contact her again.

Something good thing had come out of the evening, though. He now knew who she was. She no longer had to worry that someday he might find her when she least expected it. It was time to stop thinking about it and get on with her life.

She directed her thoughts to what the day would bring. The Christmas week's weather forecast was for sunshine and temperatures in the sixties. Texas weather. One extreme to another. People would be out shopping and bustling, readying for the holiday. She and her team would decide if they would hold a holiday open house during the week for their customers and peers. She might even go shopping herself.

But despite her best effort, intruding into every one of those plans was the memory of last night and something Drake had said: *...This is it, Shannon. The bottom line. I've been trying to figure it out. It's what the whole damn thing was about at that party and in my condo, what it's been about all evening. Chemistry. It's why my cock gets hard as a rail spike when I'm near you. All I have to do is think about you and I'm close to embarrassing myself. This picking on each other, driving each other crazy is just an extension of it. And I think you know it as well as I do....*

Did all of it mean he felt something? Was she wrong in assuming his only interest was another good time? What did he mean by "The

Bottom Line?" What did he mean by "It?" What were her own feelings, truly? Now that she was removed from the out-of-her-world settings in the Worthington Hotel and his condo, did she feel something other than lust?

Lust wasn't the right word for the explosion of emotions and sensations he aroused in her. It didn't explain why just seeing him turned her into a senseless person she didn't recognize. Did that happen because of his larger-than-life persona or who he was as a man? If he were plain Joe Blow who had an ordinary job with an average income, would her reaction to him be the same?

The stew going on within her and the events suddenly evolving around her were scary, like carrying a bomb in her purse.

The warble of her cell phone in the quiet room jolted her. No one ever called her so early in the morning. She checked Caller ID and saw *Unknown Number.*

Drake!

Her stomach dipped. His name might not be there and he had never called her before, but she knew. He had picked up her business card in Jim King's house and all of her phone numbers were on it. She bit down on her bottom lip, tempted to let the call go to voice mail, but she couldn't make herself do it. She had to admit it. Hearing from him thrilled her.

After a few more seconds, she answered with a soft hello.

"Hey, it's me," he said equally softly. "Don't hang up," he added quickly.

Her self-doubt fled. She loved the sound of his hushed tone that implied intimacy. She even liked that he worried she would hang up when she heard his voice. "I'm not going to."

"Are you at work?"

"It isn't even daylight. You?"

"Soon. I always go in early. I like the quiet time....Shannon, I've been awake all night, trying to wrap my mind around what happened. Are you okay?"

"In what way?"

"Do you think...well...you know."

"That I'm pregnant?"

"Well...yeah."

"You don't have to worry. I checked as soon as I got home. It's the wrong time of the month."

"You sure?"

His tone sounded almost as if he were disappointed. Silence followed it. Well, her mind had to be playing tricks on her. No way could he want her to be pregnant. That kind of irrational thinking came from too many margaritas, having no sleep and being stressed to the max.

Then he said, "You don't have to worry about diseases. You probably won't believe it, but I'm careful."

STDs! Oh, hell. She hadn't yet allowed herself to consider that possibility.

Her cranky alter ego piped up again. *You know what they say, girlie. When you have unprotected sex, you're having sex with everyone he's ever been with.*

Oh, God. A mild panic zipped through her mid-section. How many women had shared Drake Lockhart's bed? Dozens? Hundreds?

Finally, she cleared her throat and spoke. "Listen, this isn't doing either of us any good. Last night was off the chart crazy. We're too old to be so irresponsible. We should call a halt to whatever this is."

"I don't agree. Look, I—"

"I'm struggling to build my real estate business, Drake. It's only a few years old. That's where I need to put my time and energy. Selling real estate is an all-consuming job. I'm sure I don't have to tell you that. I've invested everything I own, every dime I've made in the last few years. I've avoided involvement with anyone because I know myself. If a guy's hanging around in my life, I can't keep from being distracted."

There. She had made that speech without stammer or pause. And every bit of it was true.

"You think I'm a distraction?" He sounded almost joyful.

"Absolutely. We just met and my life's been upside down ever since."

"Don't say that. Look, I've got some things to say, but not on the phone. And I don't want to try to talk in the middle of a screaming happy hour in a cantina."

"Drake, please. Really, I—"

"This evening. I'll drive down to your office and—"

"No," she blurted. "I don't want you coming to my office. Someone might see you. Then I'd have to explain who you are. This town would never stop talking. Please. Don't come to my office."

"I was about to suggest we could go to dinner. Somewhere besides that Mexican cafe."

"There aren't any restaurants in Camden like you're used to. Besides, I don't go out. Honestly. I try not to call attention to myself. People in town know me. Not only is my business here, I have family here. I'm doing my best to present myself as a professional businesswoman and not cause anyone embarrassment, most of all me."

"Don't professional businesswomen eat? If anyone asks, you can say I'm a customer. After all, I did call you about a house."

She rolled her eyes to the ceiling. Telling him no was so hard. "I can't, Drake. I just can't.

"Then you come up to Fort Worth. If you don't want me to pick you up, I'll send a car for you."

Was he begging her? "I meant what I said last night. I don't want a relationship interfering in my life. I'd rather just...well, I just can't do it."

She pressed the OFF button with more firmness than necessary.

Drake stood at his kitchen counter a few seconds listening to dead air. Had she hung up on him? Or had the call been dropped? He picked up her business card from the counter and started to re-key her number, but stopped himself. *Hold it, hoss. What she said couldn't be clearer. She hung up on you.*

To his annoyance, he understood her conflict. If anyone knew the anguish of making a choice between accepting responsibility and following his urges, he did. He had faced it many times. But he refused to believe she didn't want to see him again. Her words didn't match her actions.

Before he called her, he had steeled himself, prepared to hear her say she feared she might be pregnant. He had spent the whole night keyed up, thinking about the consequences if she said she was worried. Now that she had said just the opposite. he felt an odd letdown. *Got to be adrenaline,* he told himself.

He sighed. He had no time to dwell on it and try to figure it out today. He had big problems at Lone Star Commons. Resolving them during the holidays was hard. In addition to that, he hadn't heard from the insurance adjustor about Kate's barn fire. He had to try to talk to him before Christmas.

For the moment, he had to be content with knowing he had done his duty toward Shannon by calling her.

Soon after daylight, Betty Lockhart sat at her bathroom vanity studying her hair. The front of her silver-gray hair had turned white. White as snow. A nice beige-blond would go well with her eyes and complexion and perhaps make her look younger. She was considering the pros and cons of that possibility when her doorbell chimed. She glimpsed her clock. 8:30.

Normally on Wednesday, she would already be getting dressed to go to an early meeting with her book club, but because of the holidays, today's meeting had been canceled. Only a delivery service of some kind could be ringing her doorbell so early in the morning. She tightened the belt of her robe, walked to the front door and peered through the peephole.

Her estranged husband stood on her front porch. She bit back a swear. Yesterday, after spending the weekend at Kathryn's house, she had stopped by the Double-Barrel on her way back to Fort Worth. She and Bill Junior had had an unpleasant parting.

Well, in truth, it had been more than unpleasant. An outside observer might have thought it downright hair-raising, although it was typical. He'd had one of his tantrums over her going away for Christmas.

In no mood for another scene, she opened the door a few inches, but didn't unhook the chain lock.

"Got a cup of coffee?" he asked.

She thought she heard sheepishness in his voice. No doubt he had come to apologize for having been a such an ass yesterday. She knew him well. "What are you doing here?"

"Looking for coffee. I came to see my wife who makes the best coffee I know of. You gonna let me in?"

"You're full of it, Bill Junior." She unhooked the chain and stepped back.

He came through the doorway, lifted off his Stetson and looked her up and down. She was only too aware that she had nothing on under her silky robe. Knowing Bill Junior, he was aware of it, too. A shiver passed through her.

The scent he had worn forever, Lagerfeld, filled the space around her and zoomed straight to her most primitive place. Her heartbeat began to thump in her ears. She didn't trust herself any more than she trusted him. Good grief, would she ever get past his affecting her this way? "I repeat, what are you doing her, Bill Junior?"

"Couldn't get you off my mind, sweetheart. That argument yesterday upset me."

That was as close to "I'm sorry" as he would ever get. He had never been able to say those two words easily. He had too much ego.

He started toward her kitchen, unzipping his down coat as he went. Of course he knew the way to the kitchen because in the seven years that had passed since she bought this house and moved into it, he had been here many times.

She followed him cautiously, re-tightening the belt of her robe. "How's Kathryn this morning?"

"Haven't seen her today."

Betty shook her head in sadness, still affected by their daughter's grief. "I feel so bad for her. She loved those horses so much"

"She's a Lockhart. She'll get over it. It's not like there's a shortage of horses."

"I know, but she thinks hers are special. As much as they cost, I suppose they are. And she has so much to deal with."

"Her family will take care of her. Drake will handle the insurance company. Pic and Troy have already got people lined up to get the place cleaned up for her. And she can come to me or you for money or advice any time she wants to."

"I doubt she'll be asking me for advice. You're the one she listens to."

They reached the galley-style kitchen that had a breakfast nook on one end. He set his hat on the distressed maple breakfast table, peeled off his coat and hung it on the back of a chair.

Wearing starched and creased jeans and a white-and-blue check button-down shirt, he looked ten years younger than his age. He could be a model in any Western clothing magazine. He had never needed anyone to put together his clothing. She had never met another man she thought more handsome than her husband. Even at fifty-three, he still had a head of thick caramel-colored hair only slightly streaked with silver.

"I started to call you, but I wanted to talk to you in person," he said, "so I just got out of bed and drove on up here." He found a mug in the cabinet and helped himself to coffee, then turned around and leaned his backside against the counter as he sipped.

She mimicked his pose against the counter opposite him, her arms crossed over her breasts, inhibiting what he might see through her robe. "Have you had breakfast?"

Why she asked, she didn't know because she had no desire to cook it. On the other hand, if he answered with a "no," she might drop everything and do just that. She was that dumb where he was concerned and she always had been.

"Stopped at Waffle House," he answered.

"Ah." She lifted her chin. "They weren't serving coffee this morning?"

"It doesn't taste like yours."

Silence passed while he sipped and butterflies danced in her stomach. "You must have left home before daylight. I don't believe you came by for coffee, so what brings you here, really?" To her own ears, her voice sounded reedy and feeble.

"I'm trying to save Christmas. What the hell will it look like to the family if you're not at the ranch? What will I tell my mama?"

A flicker of regret at her decision passed through Betty. She had sincere affection for her ninety-year-old mother-in-law. They had much in common from living as Lockhart wives. Betty disliked the thought of hurting her.

He set down his mug, stepped across the room and tugged on the belt of her robe. Damn him. She grasped his hand, preventing him untying the bow. "Keep your hands to yourself, Bill Junior."

He chuckled, low and sexy, but didn't move his hand. "I figured you were naked under that robe. And you just told me so."

She angled a look up at him. His eyes had gone from blue to violet, an unmistakable leer. He was horny all right.

"You smell all soapy," he said huskily. "You just get out of the shower?"

"I have an appointment," she lied, knowing exactly where this visit was headed if she didn't stop him.

As if she hadn't said a word, he gently removed her hand from the knot in her belt and pulled on the bow, untying it with nimble fingers. "It'll keep, don't you think?"

Her robe listed open, partially exposing her nakedness. He eased the garment's panels apart, exposing her skin to the room's coolness and she shivered. His gaze roamed over her body. She knew that dark look too well. Excitement began to stir deep in her sex, but she drew a deep breath, still determined not to give in to him as she usually did.

She clutched at the panels of the robe, pulled them tight around her again and re-tied the belt. "Stop it, Bill."

"Stop what, darlin'? Admiring your body? I've always appreciated your body."

Betty's cheeks warmed. She had worked at maintaining a toned and tanned body for years, all for Bill Junior. She still worked at it, although she wasn't sure nowadays if she did it for him or for herself. Fearful of hurrying the arrival of wrinkles, she no longer tanned like she used to and her Yoga sessions three days a week at Bally's were mostly a habit.

She pushed away from the counter edge, crossed to the coffee maker and took a mug from the cabinet. "My body's getting old. It isn't the same as your teeny-bopper girlfriends'"

"Teeny-bopper? Godalmighty, woman, what would I do with a teeny-bopper?"

"I wonder," she said.

As she poured coffee, he stepped behind her, his size making her feel small and feminine and his body heat radiating against her back. She wanted desperately to lean back against him, but didn't dare. His thick arms came around her waist and his warm lips brushed a sensitive spot on her neck. She stiffened. Now her heart was galloping.

"I don't care if we're a hundred years old, Mrs. Lockhart," he said softly. "You'll always be beautiful to me."

"Hah. Me and how many others?" She moved her neck away from his mouth. "You're wasting your time coming here, Bill. We settled the Christmas issue yesterday." She willed her hands not to shake as she measured three teaspoons of half-and-half into her coffee.

"That cream will make you fat," he murmured.

His lips moved to the other side of her neck. At the same time, he easily loosened her belt again. His big hand slid beneath the robe's front panel and closed over one of her breasts. She let out a sigh and her eyelids drifted shut. Her breasts fit into his hands as if that were their purpose. Many times they had joked about it. She stood deathly still, hating herself for loving his touch so much. She had never been able to resist him, the reason she had gotten pregnant with their oldest son while they were both still in high school.

"Hmm-hmm," he said softly, carefully lifting, slowly caressing. His other hand moved down between her thighs and he cupped her, his fingers teasing. "I want to fuck you, Betty," he whispered, his warm breath against her neck giving her gooseflesh.

God help her, she wanted it, too. *Wanted* it. *Lusted* for it. But she should order him out of her house.

His finger slid between the lips of her sex. "Right now, I can't think of anything I want more than to lay you down and kiss you all over."

And he would, too. He had done so many times. She squeezed her eyes shut, fighting her own weakness.

He continued to stroke and gently penetrate. "Remember how it was in Nashville? Like when we were kids? We can have that again if we want to. We can make it come back for good. Right down at the Double-Barrel, in our own bed."

She shouldn't have gone to Nashville with him, shouldn't have let herself or him believe their marriage could be reconciled.

His hand moved back up. His calloused fingers began to gently pluck at her nipples. A contraction clenched deep in her sex. *Oh, God.* "Bill, please don't..."

He eased the robe off her shoulders. It slid noiselessly to the floor leaving her wearing nothing but gooseflesh and heady desire. Fool that she was, she raised no protest.

He began to kiss her shoulders and neck, kept stroking her breasts and nipples. She was already wet. Her deep vaginal muscles were already contracting, readying to receive him and she wouldn't tell him no. That was the problem. When it came to sex, she had rarely ever refused him.

"Just look at those little puppies' noses," he murmured against her ear, continuing to tease. "They're perked right up there. I know just what that means. Your pussy's wet and begging for my hard cock."

He made a deep soft chuckle and nipped her ear lobe. "'Member when you were having trouble dropping that stubborn Pickett? How that little devil didn't want to come out? I wanted to get a calf-puller, but the doc sent us home and told me to play with your nipples. 'Member that?"

She hated when he used terms related to livestock when they made love, but she smiled at the memory. Thirty-three years ago. She was nineteen, big as a barrel with her second child and two weeks overdue. Bill Junior was a twenty-year-old college student. Both of them had thought that doctor was crazy, but they had followed his orders dutifully and she had soon gone into labor. Even now, she didn't know if it had been the result of the nipple stimulation or if it would have happened anyway.

Bill Junior turned her then and kissed her, his hands moving down to her bottom and pressing her against him with his strong arms. In spite of herself, she slid her arms around his middle and pushed closer, his starched shirt rasping her bare breasts. He was hard. Visualizing him naked, she wanted him more.

His tongue thrust deeply into her mouth with a sexual rhythm. It was a devastating kiss. Tender, as he had always been, but firm and controlling and arousing.

When he lifted his mouth, he looked into her eyes. "I love you, Betty. I've never stopped."

Then why do you cheat on me? a part of her wanted to ask, but a greedier part didn't want to lose the moment. He hadn't often said the words, "I love you," but she believed he did have those feelings, which made up for many of his flaws and together they had begotten three wonderful children.

"I think you still love me," he went on. "I don't blame you for what's happened. I know most of it's been my fault."

He was right on both counts. She still loved him, perhaps in a different way, but loved him nonetheless.

"Let's go to bed," he said huskily. He scooped her into his arms and she didn't object. At this point, what harm would it do? After all, they were still married and they had explored nearly every avenue of sex. And besides that, she loved making love with him.

He carried her toward her bedroom. He knew the way to that part of the house, too, because he had been there as many times as he had been to the kitchen.

And that was another problem, dammit. She had left him, tried to divorce him, but she still wanted him and she couldn't deny him anything.

Chapter Twenty

DRAKE SAT AT the drafting table in the workroom that adjoined his office, trying to study a blueprint of the construction project that had been giving him fits for weeks. Usually, architects and engineers resolved the types of problems that faced him, but they had been wrong on so many issues, he no longer trusted their recommendations or even their suggestions.

With Lockhart Tower and the old Sears building re-models, he had established a reputation for high quality and cutting edge innovation. He refused to allow pedestrian ideas on one apartment complex in a bedroom community to detract from that, so he had personally taken on the review of the plans for Lone Star Commons. For his next project, he would hire a different architect.

He'd had so little sleep his eyes burned. He had even resorted to the glasses he was supposed to wear, but seldom did. He couldn't concentrate. The parking lot episode in Camden wouldn't leave him alone, especially the end. The conversation tumbled through his mind: *...You're on the pill, aren't you?*

I don't need to be. I haven't had sex in over two years....

Nobody goes two years without sex....

I do....

The front door opened. He checked his watch. Debra, his middle-aged personal assistant of several years and his right hand. She kept up with his bank accounts and credit cards, paid his bills, knew most of the ins and outs of his business and quite a bit about his personal life. He trusted her more than he trusted his mother.

When she came into the workroom, he looked up and said, "Good morning."

"Same back. What time did you come in?"

"Six."

Removing her coat, she gave him a cautious look. "You look a little peaked, bossman. Are you sick?"

He braced his elbows on the drafting table and rubbed his eyes. "Stayed out too late with some friends."

"I can tell." She carried her coat into the supply room where a coat tree stood. "Did you make the coffee?" she called back to him.

"Yeah. Drank a lot of it, too."

She came out and picked up his empty mug, carried it over to the coffeepot, refilled it and returned it to him.

His cell phone bleated with his brother's ring. He yanked the phone off his belt and keyed in to the call. "Hey. You're up early."

"When am I not up early? I wanted to call you before I leave the house 'cause I won't be back in 'til noon. I heard from Blake. They got a lab report back on Kate's fire. The accelerant was charcoal lighter fluid."

Drake frowned. "Barbecue stuff?"

He left his stool, walked into his office and wilted into the chair behind his desk, relieved to escape the drafting table's tall backless stool.

"That's what they said. They figure it started in that little pile of hay flakes at the end of the stalls."

"Do they have a suspect?"

"Nope. Nada. Dead end for now."

"Shit, they'll never be able to trace lighter fluid to one person. It's for sale everywhere."

"Common as a loaf of bread. You heard anything from the insurance company?"

"I don't expect to until they finish their investigation. You know how it goes during the holidays. Nothing has any urgency. But after Christmas, they won't have any excuses."

"Kate told me she thought she had the barn and equipment insured for a million dollars," Pic said. "That sounds about right, but I know she doesn't have a good head for things like that. Is that the amount the insurance company told you?"

"It's a million-dollar policy all right, but they're balking on the value of those horses. I was planning on asking Kate for any written records she might have related to them. You know, bloodlines, registration docs, receipts for breeding fees. That kind of stuff. We need to try to establish the value of Proud Mary. If we can do that, we can put a value on her colt and maybe the other two, too."

"Fuckers. Didn't I tell you that's the way it's gonna be? How would they feel if it was their horses?"

"It's how the game's played, Pic. Can you help Kate get that information together?"

"Yeah, if I can ever cross paths with her," Pic answered. "When you coming down?"

"Next Wednesday."

"How long you planning on staying?"

"About a week. I'll need to get back up here before the thirty-first."

"Good. We can get in some bird hunting. My trigger finger's getting itchy. Listen Drake, I thought I'd invite Mandy out for Christmas dinner. Since her dad passed on, she doesn't have anybody in town anymore."

"You don't have to explain. Just bring her on out."

"Okay, I will. Well, I gotta get going. Got a lot to do. See you next Wednesday."

The minute he disconnected from his brother's call, his thoughts swung back to Shannon and it dawned on him she didn't have his number. By design, the calls he made from his private cell left no callback number. He used his Blackberry for business, but only his family and special friends were able to reach him on his private cell phone.

He walked out to his assistant's desk. "What's a good present to give to someone you just met and things went a little off the rails? If you want to make her like you?"

She looked at him across the rim of her half-glasses, blinking. He didn't doubt she was surprised. He could count on his fingers the number of times he had bought presents for women, other than the obligatory ones, like birthdays and Christmas. And usually, Debra had been the one to choose them.

"Flowers can be fairly safe."

"Roses?"

"Sure. Why not? Not red ones, though. Red ones might, you know, send the wrong message. But peach or pink, maybe. Sweet, but noncommittal."

He gave a low laugh. "Well, I'm not sweet, but maybe it's time I got committal."

"Lordy me, I can't believe I just heard that. She must be some chick."

He laughed again. Debra knew him better than most of the women he had dated. And she knew his screwed-up history in the social part of his life.

He chewed on his lower lip a moment, trying to decide, then returned to the storeroom for his coat. As he passed Debra's desk, he said, "I'm going to that flower shop up the block. I'll be back after a bit."

As he walked through the doorway, he heard her mutter, "Will wonders never cease?"

Slow to pull herself together, Shannon arrived at her office midmorning. She looked as if she had been hit by a truck. She had barely gotten through her grandmother's questioning and fussing over her and now her team members and Chelsea looked at her with curious expressions. She offered no explanation.

Several tasks awaited her. She closed her office door and eased into her desk chair. She had no time to think about Drake, but she couldn't keep from it. Last night, she had convinced herself he would be mad and she would never see him again. Today, after his early morning call, she had a haunting feeling that she hadn't seen the last of him.

What had been a dull headache had turned into a bass drum behind her eyes. Her stomach burned from the citrus in last night's margaritas. She survived the rest of the morning on ibuprophen, doughnuts Kelly had brought in and TUMS.

At noon, she went home for lunch with Grammy Evelyn. They sat at the small round table in the dining room and munched on non-spicy chicken salad sandwiches and sipped soothing hot tea. Her grandmother was an expert at comfort food.

When she arrived back in her office, she no sooner stepped into the reception room than Chelsea was in front of her, her eyes alive with excitement. "Shannon. Look on your desk."

Shannon gave the receptionist a look, then walked to her office and peeked in. In the middle of the desk blotter, framed by the vivid green of fern fronds and the white of dainty baby's breath, stood a bouquet of yellow, not-quite-open rosebuds.

Ker-plunk! A rock dropped in Shannon's stomach. Instantly, a memory of the evening in Drake's bed in Fort Worth flew into her mind....*A real redhead....With a yellow rose of Texas tattoo.*

"Wow," she said, schooling herself to react normally. She walked into the office, bent over the bouquet and sniffed a rosebud.

"A florist from Fort Worth delivered them," Chelsea said, her heightened energy almost stirring the drape on the window. "There's a card."

Kelly and Terry rushed in and skidded to a halt in front of her desk. "Open the card, open the card," Kelly said.

"We started to peek at it ourselves," Terry chimed in, laughing, "But it's sealed. You must have made some client extremely happy."

"Or maybe you've got an admirer you're not telling us about?" Kelly added, elevating the end of the sentence into a question.

Hoping she was succeeding in hiding her own excitement, Shannon found the small sealed envelope pinned to a stem and opened it.

CAN WE START OVER? PICK UP WHERE WE LEFT OFF IN FORT WORTH? BEFORE I WENT TO SLEEP? CALL ME.... PLEASE....D.

A phone number followed. Shannon stared at it. Was this the *Unknown Number* from which he had called her before daylight? That phone call now seemed as if it had occurred days ago. Her heart tapping in a full-fledged pitty-pat, she quickly slid the small note back into its envelope and dropped it into her purse.

"Well?" Kelly demanded. "Who sent them?"

Kelly was just naturally nosy. "Oh, they're from the guy I showed property to yesterday. No big deal. He's just saying he appreciates my making the effort this close to the holiday."

It was only a partial fib of convenience.

"Now that's what I'm talking about," Terry said. "Yellow roses this time of year? That had to cost him extra. And that vase looks like real cut crystal, too. A hundred bucks easy."

"Yeah," Kelly agreed. "I should pick up such a customer."

Shannon hid a smile as she gingerly touched a bud. To Drake, a hundred dollars was coffee money. "Well, he must have more money than sense."

She ran a finger along the vase's smooth edge. To steer her associates off the trail, she added, "Let's just hope he's got enough to buy Jim King's house."

The chatter and jokes continued, but Shannon tuned them out. The last thing she wanted was to discuss her sudden new romance with her sales team.

All of them departed for home early, leaving her alone. She pulled the note out of her purse and studied Drake's writing—bold, forward-slanted strokes, all capital letters. She would love to be a handwriting analyst, able to learn his hidden traits from the note she held in her hand.

She placed the bouquet on an end table beside a small wicker sofa, where she could see it from her desk, then propped her chin on her palm and sat looking at it. Flowers from *Texas Monthly*'s Most Eligible Bachelor and an invitation for another meeting. How many women would like to be her at this moment? Legions, no doubt.

She had never seen more beautiful roses. And Kelly was right about the quality of the vase. Neither the roses nor the vase had been picked up at a discount store. Not to thank him would be rude. She should call him. But once she said thank you, then what? He would bring up getting together again and she had already proved she wasn't strong enough to resist him.

Finally, the person she did call was Christa. "Want to go somewhere quiet for a drink?"

"Uh-oh. This sounds serious. Red Rover's Lounge in the Traveler's Hotel is quiet. I'm wrapping up here. Meet you there in half an hour."

Happy hour was underway at Red Rover's with dramatic lighting and Christmas carols serenading in the background. The buffet offered a plentiful assortment of treats, including hot Armadillo Eggs and cold shrimp. Shannon and Christa filled small plates and carried them to a secluded table. Over cold beer, she told Christa about Drake finding her and the gift of roses.

"Oh, my God. He's hot for you," Christa said.

"I don't think that's why he sent the flowers," Shannon replied, reluctant to look Christa in the eye. Then, she summoned her nerve, drew a deep breath and confessed to her best friend the erotic parking lot encounter.

Christa shrieked and nearly choked on an Armadillo Egg. She gulped quick drinks of beer to recover. "Oh, my God! I can't believe you did it in a parking lot! In December! You bitch!" She giggled with glee.

"Christa, stop laughing. People are staring."

"He's sooo hot for you. Don't you see? He wanted you to show an interest in him and he got upset when you weren't glad to see him."

"Holy cow, how could I be glad? I was in shock. I honestly thought he'd never find me."

"Have you given a thought to the idea that he might have looked for you? That he might be in love with you?"

Shannon shook her head, her brow tugging into a deep frown. "No, Christa, no. He was mad. He isn't in love with me. I've only seen him twice. And he's had a different personality both times. I'm wondering if he's got a screw loose."

"It wasn't you he was mad at, Shannon. He was mad at himself. That's classic. I'm telling you, the guy could be in love with you. And he doesn't know what to do about it. Or maybe he hasn't even figured it out yet. So he acts like a dumb jerk."

"That's impossible. I don't believe in love at first sight. And I doubt if he does either."

"How old did you say he is? Thirty-five? Stop and think about it. A thirty-five-year-old single guy like Drake Lockhart has been around the block more than once. He's had a chance at any and every single woman in Texas and even some married ones. Obviously he hasn't found the one he wants. Trust me, girlfriend. He knows what he wants. But that doesn't mean he knows how to handle it when it lands in his lap."

Shannon finally laughed and shook her head. "I just can't believe that, Christa. What could he possibly see in me that he hasn't seen in all of those others he's had a chance at?"

Christa studied her plate for a few seconds. "Okay, consider this. I'll tell you what I saw in you before we got to be friends again. I saw a woman who's a survivor. Someone with a brain. Street smart, with a boatload of common sense. Someone not judgmental, who's good company and easy to be around. I saw someone who doesn't ask for handouts, either emotionally or otherwise.

"You've always taken your lumps and risen above the fray. But most of all, Shannon, you're someone who's capable of being a friend. Someone I could share a secret with. I know you'd split your last dollar with me. You can't *have* a friend if you can't *be* a friend. Just a lot of people don't know that. It's my guess that most of that is what he sees in you."

Tears welled in Shannon's eyes. "My Lord, Christa. I didn't know you thought all of that about me."

"Oh, hell, let's don't get mushy. We're not talking about me and what *I* think. We're talking about this Texas prince." She took a bite from an Armadillo egg and chewed thoughtfully. "These are so good. Why aren't you eating yours?"

"My stomach's been unsettled all day. I don't know why I chose something made of jalapeno peppers. I had too many margaritas last night."

"And what happened last night brings us to the next question related to this guy. What about you, dear friend? What do *you* want? Other than the obvious."

"What's the obvious?"

Christa's eyes grew round. "Money and sex. What else? The money speaks for itself, but the sex is another matter. It has to be good sex. Having a lot of money doesn't make up for bad sex. Faking it over the long haul would be hard. Nights would get real long. And let's face it. You can get just as pregnant from bad sex as good."

Shannon felt a flush crawling up her neck just thinking about the time she had spent with Drake. "I don't think I'd ever have to fake it."

"Oh, that's good. Very good. Because you know how men are. The sex comes before anything else. My second ex? He told me men think about sex one out of every ten waking minutes and even dream about it at night."

Shannon had no trouble believing that about Drake. And since meeting him, she had spent a fair amount of time thinking about sex herself. "I don't want to deal with any of it, Christa. I'm trying to make a living and build my business. Getting involved with him, or anyone, would cause me all sorts of problems."

Closing her eyes, Christa shook her head. "Shannon, Shannon, Shannon. You are fibbing to your friend. What's your definition of involvement? You've done it with him twice when you don't even know him. You've even done it without protection and risked getting pregnant or catching something really bad. How much more involved could you get? So tell me the truth. What's really bothering you? Why are we having this meeting?"

Shannon rested her elbows on the table, clasping her cheeks with her palms. "I'm scared, Christa. I don't understand what he could possibly see in me."

"Don't think about that. I say grab that wild horse and ride that sucker all the way to the buzzer. How many women ever get a chance at a young, good-looking millionaire? Most rich guys are old and fat with a bunch of spoiled kids and baggage. If it doesn't work out, it doesn't work out, but meanwhile, just look at the fun you can have."

Dark flashbacks battered Shannon. The hookups she'd had with men who obviously had no futures, including two years of clandestine trysts with the married Justin Turnbow, with whom she had once thought she was in love. She had never had difficulty attracting men.

Finding one worth having or who hadn't lied, cheated or used her had been harder.

Over the years, she had armored herself with a perverse wisdom learned from experience: Get over one lost lover by hooking up with another one. When the new had worn off one, she had simply drifted on until she bumped into another one.

"You just described my attitude from a few years ago," she said. "Before I came back to Camden, my life was a colossal mess and I was miserable. I'm much happier now without a man around at all."

"But you live like a nun. I hear talk from all quarters, you know. I know of a dozen guys who'd like to date you, but they're afraid to ask you. The Ice Princess, they call you."

"I don't care what they call me. For the first time ever, I'm in control and I'm going to stay that way. My God, if I let myself, I could go completely bonkers over Drake Lockhart. What sane woman wouldn't? He could hurt me in a big way. That common sense you just mentioned? It tells me to stop it now." She squeezed her eyes shut and shook her head. "But I'm afraid of that, too. I'm scared that if I don't give this a chance, I'll regret it for the rest of my life."

"Exactly," Christa said.

"Tell me what you think of this. What if I call him back and thank him for the flowers and sort of feel him out, see what's on his mind? If he still wants to play around, I'm thinking I could tell him okay, but I want to have just sex. No emotions. That way, when he drops me, it won't hurt so much."

Christa barked a laugh and nearly choked again on a drink of beer. "Good luck with that."

"That should make him happy. Don't men want sex with no strings attached?"

"Not if they've fallen for someone, Shanny," Christa said softly. "Emotional sex is different from sex for fun."

A huff burst from Shannon's chest. "You'd think I'd know that, wouldn't you? But to be honest, except for Justin, I don't know if I've ever been involved with a guy where there was a sincere emotional attachment. I mean, I'm thirty-three years old and the only lips I've ever heard say those three little words belonged to a man who was married to someone else. How can I not think getting involved with Drake Lockhart will turn out like all of the other jerks I've known?"

"All I can say is relationships are hard. And I've had plenty of experience. As for love?"—she flipped her hand—"Pfft. It's whatever people think it is. Everyone, male or female, gambles and hopes. They make plans, buy presents, take trips, go through all kinds of gyrations. No one ever really knows what's going to happen, but they still take the chance."

Shannon grabbed her napkin and dabbed more moisture from the corner of her eye. Ever since she met Drake, she had been on the brink of something she couldn't quite grasp. "Hope. That's the key word, isn't it? If only I could get over fearing his motives. Or that I might wake up beside him some morning and he'll have three heads. Or God knows what else."

"You're crossing bridges before you get to them, Shannon. You do that all the time. The jury's still out on this guy. Do yourself a favor and do not tie a can to his tail....Yet."

Chapter Twenty-One

SHANNON AWOKE ON Thursday morning reenergized and without a hangover. Her stomach had calmed and she no longer had a headache. She had made a decision how to deal with Drake and her attraction to him.

When she reached Piper Real Estate, the fragrance of roses permeated the air even in the reception room. In her office, the rosebuds had opened into baseball-sized, lemon-colored blooms.

If softening her attitude toward him by sending exquisite flowers had been Drake's plan, it had worked. She felt peculiarly appreciative, thus, vulnerable.

After being shored up by last evening's talk with Christa, she had gone to bed with what she would say to him firmly fixed in her mind. But she had awakened this morning with a new speech. Then there was the option of not calling him at all. She believed in fair play and not calling him wasn't fair, even if she was nervous about talking to him. So she sat dithering.

Finally, taunted by the flowers, at midmorning, she closed her office door, drew in a deep breath and keyed Unknown Number into her cell phone.

"Hey, you, it's me," he said on the first burr.

She heard a smile in his voice, but his answering so quickly caught her off-guard. "Oh. Uh, hi. I didn't expect…I got the flowers. They're beautiful….I didn't expect them. So thanks."

She scowled. She sounded like a silly fool.

"You're welcome. The card was with them or you wouldn't be calling."

"Yes. Yes, it was."

"What do you think?"

"Well…I don't know. I did think about it. All night, to be honest."

"And?"

"Well…I sort of thought…I mean, maybe we could get together and talk about it."

His deep chuckle came across the line. It sounded soft and intimate. "Fine with me. I like talk."

She nodded, as if he could see her, her self-confidence restored by his buoyant attitude. "So you said. I was thinking, if you still want to come down here for dinner, there's a new steak house out on the north end of town, by that new grocery store. It's called Rio Brazos Steakhouse. If anyone asks, we could, like you said, tell them you're shopping for a house."

"When?"

"I'm busy over the weekend, but I could do it tonight. Or even tomorrow night."

"Great. I can be down there this evening. How's six o'clock?"

OhmyGod. She hadn't expected him to be so agreeable. "Uh, fine. But I can't stay late," she added quickly, just so he would know she expected this to be a short meeting.

"Not a problem."

And just so he would know there would be no repeat of the episode in the parking lot behind *Casa Familia*, she cleared her throat and added, "Okay then. I'll, uh…I'll park out front."

Drake disconnected, jazzed and unable to remember the last time he had been this interested in pursuing a woman. Most of the time he didn't have to. They just seemed to appear. And depending on their looks and personalities, he hooked up and rode until the end of the line. Or not.

As he checked his watch, counting the hours until six o'clock, a soft rap sounded on his office door. "Come in."

Gabe Mathison's head poked through the doorway. "Hey boss, got time for lunch?"

Gabe's calling him boss was a joke attributable to Gabe's inexperience. The fact was that his real estate broker's license made him his own boss. He hadn't been at the game long enough to absorb that. "You bet. You got the info together on that Camden County property?"

"Ready to roll. Already got a contract written. At first I wanted to sell it to somebody, but now I'm thinking we ought to keep it in house. Do it ourselves. Strip mall. Lease to small businesses."

Drake liked his attitude. At this point in his young career, Gabe hadn't gotten so greedy that he wasn't a company man. A couple of years from now, he would be a hundred eighty degrees different. "Sounds good," Drake said. "I don't mind adding another strip to our inventory."

Over lunch at the Petroleum Club, they reviewed Lockhart Concepts' offer to purchase 5.17 acres on the corner of two state highways in Camden County and Drake made a mental note to give it a windshield appraisal as he passed it this evening on his way to dinner with Shannon.

As they left the club, Drake asked, "What did you learn about the surrounding property?"

"It's about thirty acres. It's owned by one woman. I'm betting some little ol' lady inherited it from her deceased husband. Probably can't wait to sell it. The holidays have got everybody's schedules screwed up, but I'll follow up on it after the first of the year."

"Great. Go for it. You'll have to do most of this deal yourself. I'm planning on taking some time off after the holidays. If you have any problems, take them up with Debra or one of the other guys in the office. But keep me in the loop."

Outside the building, they both pulled on coats and parted ways. As Drake walked back to his own office, his cell bleated and he checked the screen. Mom. She told him she had decided to go to the Double-Barrel for Christmas after all. She wanted to ride down with him.

He was puzzled, but he said, "Good, Mom. I'm going next Wednesday. That okay?"

"I'll be ready."

"What made you change your mind?"

"I want to spend Christmas with my family. And I believe Kathryn needs us all to be together. Going to Santa Fe wasn't a good idea in the first place."

"That's great, Mom. So you and Dad made up, huh?"

"We've been talking. I told him I might reconsider a reconciliation. It's a big step after so much time has passed. I've gotten used to living alone and I'm sure your father has acquired many friends."

Friends meant girlfriends, Drake translated. He made no comment.

"I'm hoping we'll have a chance to talk some more over the holiday," she added.

She sounded happy, almost giddy. "Mom, that's great. Every single one of us would be glad to see that happen. They miss you at the ranch."

"Your father's in a good mood. He even agreed to a winter vacation in the tropics, so I'm researching possibilities."

"No kidding? He's taking you on a cruise?"

"No. He refuses to get on a boat. As you've reminded me, he's afraid of water. We'll fly somewhere. Anyway, he's making me think about a lot of things. He's different lately."

"Maybe he's getting smarter in his old age."

"Your father will never be old" she said, laughing. "And he has always been smart. Your mother will never be old either."

Drake laughed, too, happy at the prospect of his parents getting back together. If they did, maybe the family could return to being like it used to be before his mom left the ranch and his dad went nuts. "That's the truth, Mom."

❧

Despite being busy, an anxiety thrummed within Shannon. How could she be so nervous about a face-to-face dinner with a man who had seen her naked, touched her and kissed her everywhere and with whom she had already had sex twice?

Her team was gone by five and at last she was alone. For the first time all day, she had the quiet time to think. The person she used to be flashed in her memory. Ten years ago, maybe even five years ago, she would have thought so much mental fuss over a roll in the hay with a hot guy silly. Back then, she had been more like her alias, Sharon Phillips at the Worthington Hotel two weeks back. But these days, she was no longer that person. She was the caretaker for an elderly woman and she owned a successful small business. She could no longer ignore the consequences of irresponsible behavior.

She freshened her makeup, checked her email messages one last time, then idly surfed the Internet, killing time until 5:45. The Google logo in the corner of her screen jumped out at her. Other than knowing Drake Lockhart was a rich minor celebrity, had a permanent frown line between his brows, a toned and sinewy body and astonishing stamina in bed, she knew little else about him.

What else is there to know? Christa would say, which made Shannon smile.

She typed Drake's name into the Google search box.

A dozen listings popped up on William Drake Lockhart, III, Fort Worth real estate investor and developer. She followed a link to a short blurb on Wikipedia about Lockhart Concepts, a privately held company with locations in both Fort Worth and Dallas. In fewer than ten years, under the leadership of its owner and CEO, William Drake Lockhart, III, it had acquired or constructed roughly forty properties—shopping centers, office buildings and apartment complexes, one in Midland, two in Austin, but most of them in the Dallas/Fort Worth Metroplex. The company's assets were valued at a staggering amount of money. She knew Drake was wealthy, but she hadn't known just how wealthy.

She read another paragraph about his being a stakeholder and the CFO of the legendary Double-Bar L Cattle Company, a ranch that consisted of approximately 315 sections of grazing land and thousands of cattle in North Central Texas. She did some quick arithmetic in her head. 315 sections equaled over 200,000 acres. That number wasn't surprising. She already knew the Double-Barrel Ranch was huge, but the role Drake played in its management was new information.

The family also owned thousands of acres of farmland in West Texas. With such large numbers bandied about, she couldn't keep from feeling silly at how concerned she was with one tiny five-acre corner.

She sped through the information. He was the oldest of four siblings, had graduated from SMU summa cum laud, then earned an MBA from the university's prestigious Cox Business School.

Summa cum laud. Shannon didn't know what that meant. She Googled the phrase and found it, too, on Wikipedia.

Oh, hell. Not only was he unimaginably rich, he was really smart, which she had feared. And he was an MBA.

A sense of inadequacy struck her and she questioned again why he had an interest in someone like her, whose high school diploma had come via GED. Her college education consisted of the classes necessary to qualify for the state real estate exams, most of which she had taken at night or online. Involuntarily, her fingers flattened against her lips, as if they wanted to hold back a groan.

She continued to click on links and found the *Texas Monthly* puff piece identifying him as one of the state's most eligible bachelors. It didn't mention that the title had been bought in a PR campaign. If a person had enough money, she supposed he could buy anything, even a phony title.

The article consisted of more pictures than words. She skimmed through it. With his unusual eyes, his chiseled jaw, his mysterious smile that almost wasn't a smile, he was very photogenic. Several of the pictures of him in various poses made her stop for a second look—shirtless and swinging an axe against a downed tree; roping a calf from the back of a galloping horse. Shirtless again, he lounged in a bathing suit on the deck of a big boat. The last picture showed him boarding a private jet, wearing a dress shirt and tie.

Does he own an airplane? Of course he does, she answered herself. *Maybe more than one.*

Every close-up, even the smiling ones, showed the deep frown line between his brows. At the time of the article's date, he had been thirty-two years old. A crease that deep at that age came from its being there constantly. Why? What made him constantly frown? Just something else she didn't know about him.

An old article from the *Fort Worth Star Telegram* announced his engagement to Tamara Lynn McMillan. The bride-to-be was blonde and beautiful. She looked like Brittany Spears. The date was fifteen years ago, which meant he had been engaged at a young age. Had he been married? She had never heard.

She read on. His fiancé was the daughter of another ranching family in Treadway County and a student at TCU in Fort Worth. They must have known each other their whole lives. That probability raised a new list of questions in Shannon's mind. Had they gotten married, then divorced? Did he have kids? Or if he and his fiancé hadn't married, why not?

She moved on to a link to *Fort Worth, Texas* magazine where someone had written about the construction of Lockhart Tower. She had lived in Fort Worth when he first bought the old Millennium Bank building. She vaguely remembered the publicity as he remodeled it into a showplace. Some report about him or the building had been on TV news every night.

Her interest piqued, she clicked on the link to the article and saw a full-page color portrait of him in jeans and boots, astride a roan horse. Lockhart Tower's off-white color, its long line of azure windows climbing in a straight line toward a brilliant blue sky filled the background. *Cowboy*, she thought and smiled. She had always been a sucker for cowboys. At least he wasn't a drugstore cowboy. At least he was connected to a real ranch. He could probably ride the horse he sat on.

The story began with some short paragraphs recounting the bank building's history. After the bank had gone broke, the building had been vacant and for sale for years. Because of the asbestos used in the original construction, it couldn't even be torn down. The estimates for doing nothing more than removing the asbestos to the EPA's satisfaction came to a huge amount of money. City officials had offered generous incentives to anyone who would present a plan to deal with it, but had no takers. Everyone was afraid of it. Many potential buyers had come and gone.

Then, a few years ago, a tornado had crashed through downtown Fort Worth. A flashback of that horrific evening whirled through Shannon's mind. Back then, her home had been a twenties-vintage rental house on Fort Worth's west side. She had spent the nightmare storm alone and terrified, crouched under a mattress in an ancient porcelain bathtub in the old house's only bathroom.

The deteriorating bank building had been irreparably damaged. Most of the windows had been blown out. Someone had slapped uncountable plywood patches over the gaping maws. Not only were they ugly, they were nowhere close to being waterproof and the building's condition had gone downhill even faster. The need for something to be done about the thirty stories of concrete, steel and asbestos right in the center of downtown became urgent.

Then, from out of nowhere, Drake Lockhart, young real estate broker, developer and speculator—an upstart unheard of by most of the Metroplex movers and shakers—had bought the bank building from an East Coast holding company for pennies on the dollar and presented a plan for its future and the city council had accepted it. Every professional journal in Texas had published commentary on what would finally become of the "old Millennium albatross" and its young new owner who apparently had more money than brains and experience.

"He was undaunted by the ridicule of the naysayers," the article said.

Undaunted. A word that suited what little Shannon knew of Drake.

After removing the asbestos and modernizing the building, he had turned the bottom two floors and a mezzanine into a mall of upscale boutique retail shops and trendy restaurants. The upper floors became luxury high-rise condominiums. He had spent a small fortune and he had plastered his name across all of it. In her mind's eye, Shannon could see the name LOCKHART TOWER standing out in the daytime and highlighted by architectural lighting at night.

Currently, no one jeered about Lockhart Tower. It was one of the highlights of the Fort Worth cityscape and a sought-after home address. Every square foot of commercial space was leased and had a waiting list. Every residential unit had sold for an astonishing price.

The article continued to trumpet Drake's accomplishment. In a good real estate market, he had done the difficult. In a market trending down, he had done the impossible. Fort Worth city leaders called him a hero. A true Texan with that old-fashioned Texas can-do spirit, a man who marched to his own drummer.

Shannon clicked a link to a short article in a real estate magazine. Value of the condos had nearly doubled since they first came on the market. The smallest unit in the building had resold a few months ago for more than half a million.

She sat back in her chair, reeling from the knowledge that he must have been younger than thirty when he bought the bank building. The realization of just how smart and daring Drake Lockhart was amazed her. But after more thought, that information wasn't so stunning. She'd had a firsthand experience with how persuasive he could be when he wanted something. She, as much as anyone, should know he was someone who seized opportunity.

Now she was even more puzzled by why a man like him would be attracted to her—ordinary, white bread Shannon Marie Piper. Other than being in the same business—sort of—what did they have in common?

She remembered the moment their eyes had connected at the TCCRA party, the arcane link between them, as if he were a magnetic force too powerful for her to resist. And how sexual arousal had been her first reaction to him. The fact that he was who he was had not been part of that.

And he had said he felt the same....*I knew it'd be good....The minute I saw you, I knew.*

Well...that wasn't exactly saying he felt the same, but she took it to be close enough.

Chapter Twenty-Two

SHANNON ARRIVED AT Rio Brazos Steakhouse promptly at six. Drake's silver sports car was already parked in a far corner of the parking lot. She still didn't know what kind of car it was.

She found a slot beside handicapped parking in front of the entrance. "No chance for hanky-panky in this spot," she mumbled as she scooted out of her Sorento. She dragged out her briefcase and carried it in for show, just in case some Camdenite she knew might be inside.

Sure enough, the young hostess who greeted her was an acquaintance. "There's this guy waiting for you. He said y'all would be talking business. I put him in the back in a corner where it's quiet."

"Thanks, Stacy."

Shannon followed her, happy to see no one she knew among the diners.

Drake stood as she neared the table. He had on typical cowboy garb—butt-hugging jeans and boots and a long-sleeve button down shirt. Today, it was a lovely gold and pink and green plaid. After seeing the magazine spread, she had concluded that this style was his usual dress. Did he choose his own clothing? She couldn't imagine him doing something so mundane as shopping for clothes.

Now that she could see him in a more ordinary environment, he seemed ordinary. Nothing like one would expect from a man who had done all that he had done and owned all that he owned. He held a chair for her. She sank onto it, set her briefcase on the floor, slipped out of her coat and let it fall across the back of the chair.

Stacy came to take their order for drinks, but they both declined. Stacy handed them the menus and hurried away.

"I went to high school with her oldest sister," Shannon told Drake about Stacy. "So you see why I keep my nose clean in Camden?"

"I know how it goes," he said, smiling in that almost-shy way he had. "I grew up in a small town, too, you know."

That was one of the few things they had in common as far as she could tell. It struck her that they would have been teenagers at about the same time, but she didn't mention it. Those years had been miserable for her.

Drake diverted his attention to the menu. "So if this is a steakhouse, the steak must be good, huh?"

Shannon quickly scanned the menu. "Maybe. I've never eaten here." She sat back and crossed her hands on her lap. "I'll have the tortilla soup."

Drake looked up at her. "In a steakhouse?"

She shrugged. "I've gotten used to eating light at night. My grandmother says she sleeps better if she doesn't eat a big evening meal. She does most of the cooking, so I eat whatever she fixes. I think she's right about that anyway.

Stacy returned and Drake ordered soup for both of them.

Shannon gave him a look. "You don't have to order soup just because I did."

"You're not the only one who thinks your grandmother's right."

They sat in silence for a few beats. She had never felt so awkward. She could think of absolutely nothing to say.

"This is quieter than happy hour at that Mexican joint," he said at last.

On an inner sigh, Shannon resigned herself to the fact that they might, after all, discuss that Saturday night after the TCCRA party. She ducked her chin and focused on straightening her napkin in her lap. "You've probably figured out that I took us there because I knew it'd be too noisy to talk. I was so surprised to see you. I knew you'd ask me questions I couldn't answer. And I didn't want to talk about that…that night."

"I did figure it out. Eventually."

She looked up. "There's no point, right? We both know what happened. We got a little drunk and went off the deep end."

"I wasn't drunk. And you weren't either."

He was right. She had tried to convince herself alcohol was a factor, but in truth, it wasn't. She looked away.

"So, uh, how is it?" he asked. "Did you do a test or something?"

Heat crawled up her neck. She couldn't believe she was having this conversation with a man she barely knew. "I don't need a test. My calendar's good enough."

"You sure?" he asked.

"I'm sure." She slid furtive looks around, to see if anyone could hear them, was relieved to see the nearest diner three tables away. She refocused on his face. "Can I ask you something?"

"Can I refuse to answer if I don't like the question?" He smiled then. "Of course you can ask me something."

"Tuesday night at *Casa Familia*. Has that happened to you before? Have you gotten caught doing the wrong thing at the wrong time?"

His expression remained inscrutable. Finally, he ducked his chin and rearranged his napkin. Obviously he didn't want to discuss this subject. "Once. Some years ago."

"How did you handle it?"

"It didn't have to be handled. It was a false alarm. I think I said before, I'm usually careful. I don't have an excuse for Tuesday night."

Stacy reappeared with their soup. Shannon waited until she placed their bowls and left. "When you said if anything happened, we'd take care of it, did you mean you'd expect me to have an abortion?"

"No," he answered sharply, giving her a frown. "Why would you think that?"

"I just assumed—"

"Don't assume. My God, my family's in the animal breeding business. If something needs to be aborted, Mother Nature takes care of it. She's a helluva lot better judge than I am." He tucked into his soup.

So much for the abortion question. But if he wouldn't want her to have an abortion if she got pregnant, what *would* he want? What would *she* want? With the sex so hot and evidently irresistible for both of them, the outcome of an accident was something to consider.

Setting the sticky topic aside, Shannon tasted her soup. "Soup's good."

He put down his spoon and looked at her. "Shannon. It's been a long time since I've met somebody I felt like telling I wanted her company more than anyone else's. I don't know what it means and I'm not trying to attach anything high-flying to it. I'd just like for us to spend some time and get to know each other."

He gave a little-boy smile and a soft laugh "Not that I'm turning down the awesome sex....I mean, I'm not crazy."

He was so damn charming she almost couldn't bear it. She released a sigh. "I have to ask, Drake, why me?"

"Why not you? You're interesting. Most of the women I meet are phony. I figure that out in ten minutes. You're different. You keep surprising me. And I believe we've got more going for us than you know. Maybe even more than I know."

She shook her head. "How could that be? We come from two different worlds."

The line between his brows deepened. "I don't pay much attention to stuff like that. People either like each other or they don't. And if they do, they make things work out. Everything else is superfluous."

"But you must know a lot of women who have more to offer someone like you than I do. A hundred of them must have been present at that party."

He gave a little grunt, obviously frustrated. He leaned forward, his eyes intent on hers. "Okay, this is weird, but I'm going to say it anyway. That night, when I saw you, every other woman disappeared. Something I can't explain came over me. All I knew was I had to have you."

Shannon had never had a conversation like this with any man she had ever known. What he had said in the *Casa Familia* parking lot about chemistry came back to her. She grimaced and looked away. "Well, you're right. That's weird."

"Look, I'm not a bullshitter. I'm no saint and I won't tell you I've never been involved in a one-time deal with a woman. But not in years. I'm trying to believe I've grown up."

She couldn't hold back a laugh. "What do you expect me to say?

"You can admit that you felt something yourself. Otherwise, you wouldn't have gone home with me and you wouldn't have gone to bed with me. So I think something beyond both of us was influencing us."

Shannon had never let herself believe in the unbelievable. Now she was more nervous. She managed a little laugh. "I was hungry. And you have to admit, you were persistent. You didn't exactly take no for an answer."

"But I would have if you'd meant it."

Oh, God. Had she been that transparent? She gave another nervous laugh. "Thanks for reminding me how weak I am."

"I don't know you that well yet, but I suspect being weak had nothing to do with it."

She hesitated, letting her aim to be tough go ahead and collapse. "Okay. You got me." She looked down and fingered the hem of the napkin in her lap. "I felt the attraction, too. I still do. But acting on every wacky impulse that comes up can get you into trouble."

Stacy halted the conversation by showing up and asking if they needed anything else. Shannon welcomed the interruption and a chance to change the subject. After Stacy walked away, Shannon said, "I saw your car in the parking lot. It's a beautiful car. I didn't hear you say what it is."

"Aston Martin."

Oh, my God. James Bond. She didn't know the cost of an Aston Martin, but she suspected six digits. "Ah. No wonder you parked so far away. If I owned a car like that, I might carry a plastic bubble to put around it when I parked it somewhere."

He grinned. "Wanna hear its story?"

"Sure."

"I was valedictorian my senior year in high school. In Drinkwell, there weren't that many kids in my class to compete with, but still…"

After what she had read about him earlier, this wasn't surprising information. She already believed he was the smartest man she had ever known personally. She would much rather hear personal information about him than eat soup. She put down her spoon, tilted her head and gave him rapt attention.

"…my parents were so proud," he went on. "I was afraid Dad's shirts weren't going to hold his puffed up chest. You know that small town gossip you're worried about? Everybody in Drinkwell said my dad bought me that honor. I hated people saying that about me. And about him. I got it because I studied my ass off."

He swallowed a spoonful of soup, then continued to talk. "My parents knew I had earned it. One day when I came home from school, a new Corvette was parked in the driveway in front of the house." His face broke into a beaming smile. "It was shiny as a diamond and fire engine red. I knew it was for me. I nearly tore the front door off getting into the house."

"Wow, how nice," Shannon said, returning to her own soup, and suddenly wondering how it would be to have a father who would reward you with even a small gift. As far as she could remember back, even before hers died, he had hardly known she existed.

"What I didn't know at the time was that before I got there, my dad and mom had a big fight over Dad buying it. I barely got through the front door before Mom said, 'Do not get used to that car. It's going back where it came from tomorrow.' I thought she'd lost her mind.

"Score one for Mom because Dad didn't even argue. Sure enough, the next morning, she drove the Corvette back to Fort Worth, I followed her in my old truck and she returned the car to the dealership. I had all I could do to keep from bawling."

"So you never got over it and now you own a sports car."

He lifted a finger. "Ah, but the one in the parking lot I bought myself, with my own money. That day, on our way home from the dealership, Mom told me something. It seemed unimportant at the time, but it's something I want to tell my own kids someday."

Remembering the engagement photo she had just looked at online, Shannon looked up. "How many kids do you have?"

"None. I've never been married."

A little happy dance erupted in Shannon's chest. "So what did your mom tell you?"

"She said, 'Son, you have to understand, our pride in you doesn't call for an extravagant material reward. It lives in our hearts and always will because we love you, whether you're the smartest boy in Drinkwell or not.'"

Shannon smiled, liking his mother. "Aww. Your mom sounds like a wise woman."

He dabbed at his mouth with his napkin. "I was pretty pissed off at her that day. I pouted all the way back to the ranch. She told me something else I've never forgotten. She said, 'I'm not saying you can't or shouldn't have a sports car. You can have any extravagance you want so long as you earn it and pay for it yourself.'"

He paused a few beats as if waiting for a reaction, but Shannon had no clever remark.

"You see, my mom wasn't like my dad," he continued. "She didn't grow up with the material advantages he did. Her parents—my grandparents—were hard-working blue collar types. My grandpa was a handyman around Drinkwell. He got called on to fix damn near everything. And my grandma cooked in the school cafeteria.

"Dad always wanted to help them financially. He could've made their lives easier, but they refused his help. They're proud, common-sense people. Coming from that environment, Mom saw life in a different way from Dad. Or at least she did back then."

"You mean she's changed?"

"She and Dad have been married thirty-five years. I don't think you could live in the Lockhart family that long without its influence rubbing off on you."

"Ah, I see," Shannon said, nodding. But she didn't see at all. Was something wrong with the Lockhart family?

"So that's the story of my sports car," he said. "It's a prize I gave myself. But it wasn't until a couple of years ago I thought I'd earned it."

Thanks to his mother, perhaps he hadn't grown up a spoiled rich kid after all. "When you opened Lockhart Tower, you believed you had earned it?"

"Not even then. I had some heavy obligations at that time. I didn't dare declare success until they were settled. Only after the last unit was sold, the deal closed and my debts paid did I buy that sports car. So now, it's your turn. Tell me a story about you."

Most of the Shannon Piper tales of the past were dark, with nowhere near the cheery flavor of his. Nor the happy outcome. She didn't want to share them. "Don't know one," she said.

"I don't believe you. I'm thirty-five. You must be about my age."

"Thirty-three," she said, smiling and wagging her finger at him. "I'm only thirty-three."

"Whatever," he said on a laugh. "My point is you've got a story. You own your own real estate brokerage. Not many thirty-three year-old women can claim that. Getting to where you are couldn't have been easy, especially in a small town. Real estate, whether it's commercial or residential, is a take-no-prisoners game with a high attrition rate. And the market's been volatile for several years. Sounds like you've got what I call stickability."

Indeed, she had stuck it out, one plodding step at a time—when she had put in eighteen-hour days, working at a job full-time and going to school at night; when she had spent two years listing and selling houses, slogging through mud, dripping through rain, shivering through blue northers, learning everything she could about the business. When she had winged it through sticky-wicket deals involving big city lawyers and every time she had been crushed by losing a good listing or a buying customer to a competitor. And when she didn't know where her next mortgage payment might come from and it looked as if she might lose it all.

"I *have* worked hard," she said.

"And a story goes with that."

"When you spend all your time working, you don't have a life. So, no stories."

"What about your family? Why do you live with your grandmother?"

"Not much to tell there either. Grammy Evelyn's eighty-four. She's spry, but she needs someone. She has only a small income from Social Security. I pay the bills and the taxes and take care of the house and she lets me have a place to live. She owns one of those rambling old houses that's been designated a Texas historical home. It was built before 1900. Sometimes the upkeep on it gets to be a challenge. But so far, I've managed."

She laughed, thinking back to when she first moved back to Camden, into Grammy Evelyn's home.

"What's funny?" he asked.

"It must have been, oh, a couple of weeks after I first moved in that Grammy Evelyn got around to telling me she hadn't been able to pay the taxes for several years and the house was in danger of being seized by the county."

"Oops," he said.

"It was an oops moment, for sure. I was broke. I had just started working as an assistant to a real estate broker who was a friend of my grandmother's. The friend would've known what to do, I thought, but I was afraid that if I told her, Grammy Evelyn would be embarrassed. I wasn't making a lot, so I went to the tax assessor's office and tried to work out a payment plan. But the county's lawyers had run out of patience with my grandmother. They had no interest in an installment plan and I had no way to get the money in a lump.

"If the county had taken the house, I could've gotten along living somewhere else and I could've taken Grammy Evelyn to live with me, but moving out of her home would've been a blow to her. She's lived there since she first married my grandpa."

"I know how it is with elderly people," Drake said. "My dad's mother is ninety. What did you do?"

"When I couldn't think of any other solution, I had to go to my sister and brother-in-law and beg them to catch up the taxes. Gavin Flynn, my brother-in-law, is a lawyer here in town. He had the money to just pay the taxes and be done with it, which he did. But he put a lien on Grammy Evelyn's house."

The frown between Drake's brows deepened. "Why?"

Because he's an ass, she wanted to say, but didn't. "He and my sister Colleen are afraid that when our grandmother passes on, she might leave the house to me. They think I'm trying to undermine my sister. The lien was his way of making sure she gets a part of it. I think they're in a lather over nothing. I've never seen my grandmother's will, but I doubt she would leave my sister out.

"Anyway, him doing that pissed me off. Grammy Evelyn didn't understand what was going on. She worried about it. She was afraid

Gavin might take possession of the house at any time and kick her out. I couldn't make her understand that he couldn't easily do that.

"And I couldn't make him see, or care, that he was causing her stress. So I spent almost every extra penny I had for the next two years paying him back and getting that lien lifted. And pretty often, I had to hound him to get him to go to the county clerk's office and acknowledge that he got the money. Finally, after a particularly ugly confrontation with him and my sister, he released the lien."

"Nice guy," Drake said.

A wicked pleasure slunk through Shannon. Gavin would be mortified if he knew she had told something so evil about him to a man of Drake's status. "Something good came of it, though. As Grammy Evelyn has told me about a million times, when a window closes, a door opens, or something like that. That experience and her nagging are what got me interested in going into the real estate business. And here I am. So there's a story for you."

"What did your brother-in-law think when you paid him back?"

"I'm not sure he wanted to be paid back. I think he would've rather had the lien. He's controlling."

"The rest of your family?"

"Um, my dad's been dead for years. My mom lives in California. And that's about it."

She omitted saying that her mother was a fifty-five-year-old moon child on her fifth live-in to whom she wasn't married.

"There's bound to be more," Drake said. "Everybody wants to talk about himself. Why don't you?"

She frowned and cocked her head. "Because. Some stories are just better left untold."

He lifted his chin, his golden-brown eyes alight with mischief. "A woman with a past?"

"Well…I haven't killed anyone. Haven't been in jail, if that's what you might be thinking….Oh, and I haven't done drugs either. Consumed my share of alcohol, but no drugs."

Drake's face broke into a huge, white-toothed smile. "Same here. I partied a lot when I was younger, but I hardly drink at all now." He picked up his water glass and saluted her. "Someday."

"Someday?"

"C'mon. Lift your glass. Someday you'll trust me enough to talk about yourself. I'm counting on it."

Reluctantly, she picked up her glass and touched it to his with a soft clink. "We'll see."

They progressed to conversation about the real estate market in Camden. He briefly mentioned a luxury apartment complex he had under construction in Southlake. Time flew. Before long, they noticed that the waitress had cleared away their dishes, each of them had made a trip to the restroom and it was eight-thirty.

"It's time for me to get home," she told him. "My grandmother has this ornery cat and if he doesn't come inside before her bedtime, she goes looking for him. I don't want her doing that with me not there."

"You said you're busy this weekend?"

She nodded. "The Camden Realtors' Christmas party is Saturday night."

"Is someone escorting you?"

"I'm taking my grandmother. I've already bought tickets."

"Are you wearing that green dress?"

She snorted a laugh. "Our little gathering will be nothing like that shindig up in Fort Worth."

"You know where Stone Mountain Lodge is?"

Stone Mountain Lodge had once been Stone Mountain Ranch, fifty miles west of town. A real estate development group had bought it and built a plush private hunting lodge.

"Everyone in Camden County knows about Stone Mountain Lodge," she said. "I've even been there. When it first opened, the owners invited the Camden Realtors to a free lunch and a tour. They thought we might help them sell memberships."

"I'm planning to bird hunt there with some friends Saturday and Sunday mornings. Is there any way you could be my guest Friday night?"

A rock dropped in Shannon's stomach. So they were down to it. She had been so engrossed in reading about him on the Internet, she hadn't rehearsed how she would say what she had decided. "You're a member?"

He shrugged.

Of course he was a member. Stone Mountain Lodge was a chi-chi destination. Most of the Fort Worth upper crust who were sportsmen probably held memberships. "I don't shoot," she said.

"There are other things to do."

"Like hop into bed?"

He grinned. "Listen to you. I was talking about the spa. I haven't used it myself, but people who have tell me it's great."

"Were you planning on me having a separate room or what?"

"Is that what you want?"

He had given her a perfect opening. She hesitated, crafting an answer. "Okay, here's the deal," she said. "I've been thinking about this. What I don't want is to get involved. I don't mind a, um"—she cleared her throat—"an arrangement. As long as it doesn't interfere with my work or my life."

He cocked his head, angling a narrow-lidded look at her. "An arrangement?"

"Yes. We could just get together for sex occasionally and not bring feelings into it."

He sat back in his chair and crossed his arms over his chest. "A body can be pretty cold without the person inside it, don't you think?"

She didn't want to discuss the fine points. Instead of replying with words, she, too, folded her arms under her breasts and gave him a take-it-or-leave-it stare.

She saw the dare in his eyes. She should have known better than to challenge him. He hadn't become what he was because he ever relinquished control of a negotiation. A slow grin tipped up one side of his mouth. "I can handle that....If *you* can."

She couldn't let him get the upper hand. "You think I can't?"

They stared at each other a few seconds. Then he sat forward and rested his forearms on the table, his eyes leveled on her face. "Okay, but I want some ground rules. One woman at a time is all I want in my bed. I'd expect the same loyalty from you."

She gave a huff. "I just said how busy I am. If I barely have time for you, how could I have time for someone else?"

"I accept that, although I haven't seen much that makes me think I should believe you. So getting back to the weekend. No-strings, burn-down-the-walls fucking in a quaint, totally private little place. How about it?"

Shannon flinched inside at the blunt words. But she had thrown out the idea and the truth was the truth. "From what I recall of the lodge, those cabins are more than quaint and private little places. Isolated luxury is a more accurate description. But then, luxury is the norm for you, isn't it?"

He shrugged. "I've got one of them reserved. The dining room serves excellent food. We can have dinner, then go back to the cabin."

A visual of the cabins flitted through her memory—rustic décor, soft relaxing colors, a fireplace, floors of Italian tile. During the Realtors' tour, she and another Realtor had looked at the king size bed that almost filled the sleeping area and the bathroom's tub large enough for two and joked about where the emphasis had been placed.

"I'm flying down there tomorrow," he continued, "but I can get a car. I'll come over here in the afternoon, pick you up and take you back with me. Since you can't be seen with anybody, maybe we can sneak in and out of Camden on the back roads and no one will spot us."

"Now you're being sarcastic."

"Hey, I'm just trying to be accommodating. While I'm hunting Saturday morning, you can take advantage of the spa. My treat. The works if you want. I'll get you back to Camden in time for the Christmas party Saturday night."

Unless something had changed, the spa treatments started at two hundred dollars for a single treatment. She could spend a thousand dollars easily. But if she took advantage of his offer, what did that make her? For that matter, what did this entire arrangement make her even if he didn't throw in the spa treatments? *Damn.* She should have given this more thought.

Still, she refused to back down. She drew a deep breath. "Getting away overnight is hard for me."

His eyes leveled on hers. "Turning chicken?"

She refused to blink. She stared back at him. "I have obligations. I told you, I don't like leaving my grandmother alone in the evening....And now, I really do have to go."

She stood and lifted her coat off the back of the chair. He stood, too, took it from her and held it while she slid her arms into it. She picked up her purse and briefcase and looked up at him. "I'll call you and let you know."

"I'll be waiting." He shrugged into his own coat and picked up the check.

She waited while he paid. Outside, he followed her to her SUV's door. As she started to pull on the latch, he covered her hand with his and stopped her. "I don't give a damn who's watching." He bent down and kissed her, then looked into her eyes. "I'll be waiting for your call. Don't disappoint me." He turned and strode across the parking lot to his car without once looking back.

She watched him, chewing on her bottom lip. *Dear God. What have I gotten myself into?*

Could this get any crazier?

As Drake drove toward Fort Worth, he tried to digest the after-dinner conversation he'd had with Shannon. She couldn't be serious about wanting just sex. No woman he had ever met would be content with that.

An emotion churning within him made him uncomfortable. He couldn't identify it. It felt like rejection. But it wasn't rejection because they would meet again. For just sex.

Why couldn't he be satisfied with that? An occasional hot, easy, no-strings-attached coupling with a drop-dead gorgeous female? Not too many years ago, that was all he had wanted. Why did the prospect of that arrangement with Shannon, a woman he hardly knew, leave him feeling empty and adrift instead of relieved?

...I haven't had sex in over two years....

Her statement in the Mexican restaurant parking lot. He couldn't get it off his mind. If it were true, it said something about her, but what? It flew in the face of what he knew of her from the time they had spent together.

He had never had a woman more willing or giving in bed. Was that something special that applied to him only? Ego made him want to believe it was.

Or had she been that way with every guy she had ever slept with? And how many were there? The question usually didn't come up with the women he saw. He had never expected women over thirty years old to be virginal. But then, he typically didn't run into one who stated outright that she wanted only sex from him.

His thoughts veered from speculating about her motives to trying to figure out his own. What drew him to her? His past included career women with advanced degrees and lists of accomplishments to brag about. And they did brag. And most of them were also agenda-driven, hard-to-please and determined to steer him or bend him to their wills. He classified those affairs as hookups where he gave only as good as he got. They had never lasted long.

He suspected Shannon was nothing like those women. Though she had told him numerous lies, she came across to him as being honest to the core. Then what he liked about her dawned on him. She had a raw instinct and an innate fearlessness, a self-confidence that came from a place so deeply ingrained, she didn't even know she had it. Gut-level traits he couldn't keep from admiring, especially in a woman. She reminded him of himself. And that could be what had him so antsy about her.

Be cool, man, he told himself. *Just be cool. Take one step at a time.*

He could play her game for now. If sex was all she wanted, he could handle that with pleasure. He already knew she liked fucking and she had liked fucking with him. She would call him for that, if for no other reason. She would figure out a way to meet him at Stone Mountain Lodge tomorrow. He had already made her howl at the moon. And he could do it for as long as necessary.

Necessary? Necessary for what? What did he expect from this?

Chapter Twenty-Three

OKAY, NOW WHAT? That was Shannon's first thought when she awoke early Friday. Sleeping all night with a guy and waking together was different from just having sex. And those cabins at Stone Mountain Lodge were really small with really close quarters.

She shut down those thoughts and veered to the logistics of spending Friday night away from home. These days, because of Grammy Evelyn and Arthur, Shannon was rarely away from home at night. Her grandmother didn't really need a babysitter, but Shannon wanted someone to look in on her in the evening in case she went outside to look for Arthur and fell.

Christa usually did her this favor if needed, but she was leaving work early on Friday to take her sons to a football game and wouldn't be home until late.

Shannon tried to keep her private life out of her office. She never asked the women who worked there to do a personal favor. One thing she had learned in six years was that unlike relatives, real estate agents came and went. And just as they brought gossipy tales with them, they took them when they left.

The next choice was her uptight older sister. Colleen would keep a secret, if for no other reason, because she feared Shannon's social life might affect her or her husband in some negative way. Not a nice thought about her own sister, but a fact nevertheless.

Colleen's husband usually went into his office early. By the time Shannon was ready to leave the house, he would be at work. She hurried through her morning ritual and breakfast with Grammy Evelyn, then headed for her sister's house fifteen miles out of town. As one of the few lawyers in Camden, Gavin, as well as Colleen, felt they had a certain cachet to uphold, so they lived in one of Camden's several gated lakeside communities.

Shannon rehearsed her speech all the way to her sister's sub-division.

Colleen and Gavin's home was so new the lawn was skimpy and the yard plants still had a freshly-planted look. Colleen invited her in and offered her a cup of coffee in her sparkling white kitchen with its accents of spring green. Most people with whom Shannon was acquainted served coffee in mugs, but not Colleen. Like Grammy Evelyn, she handed Shannon coffee in a china cup sitting on a matching saucer.

Colleen's appearance was as stiff as her personality. She was thin to the point of being bony, shorter than Shannon and eight years older. Her hair had once been red, thick and naturally curly like Shannon's, but these days, to cover gray, she dyed it a color that was almost burgundy. A short wedge cut made it look as if a triangular turban encompassed her head. Every time Shannon saw her, she wanted to recommend that she get a new do, but enough friction existed between them without Shannon expressing an unrequested opinion about her hair.

Today, Colleen's flat chest was covered by a white sweater dotted with red poinsettias. Breast size was one more area where Shannon and her sister had nothing in common.

Colleen and Gavin had no children and their tidy home adorned with expensive decorator touches reflected that. A small Christmas tree stood in one corner of a sunlit breakfast room adjoining the kitchen. Colleen put Christmas trees in several rooms. Shannon herself was lucky to get one Christmas tree standing and decorated in the parlor of Grammy's house.

Shannon could see by her sister's behavior that she wasn't fooled by this uncommon visit. Colleen knew she wanted something, so as they sat at the white granite breakfast bar, Shannon set her cup on its saucer and went straight to the point. "I need a favor. I'm going to be out of town overnight. I need someone to look in on Grammy this evening and again tomorrow morning. I worry about her going outside after dark to look for Arthur, especially when it's so cold at night."

Colleen set her own coffee cup on its saucer and rested her folded arms on the counter. "Where are you going?"

"Just...somewhere, Colleen. What difference does it make?"

"My God. It's a man, isn't it? You're going off to spend the night with some guy, like you used to do with that Justin Turnbow. I thought you had cleaned up your act. Who is it this time?"

Shannon bit back a sarcastic comeback. "A friend from Fort Worth. No one you'd know."

Colleen picked up her coffee cup, her face contorted into a pinch-mouthed expression. "Well, I hope he isn't married."

"Oh, Colleen, give me a break here."

"I thought you'd learned your lesson. Living there in Grammy Evelyn's house, showing off as a respectable businesswoman and risking everyone in town finding out you were sleeping with a married man. I still don't know how you look yourself in the mirror."

"It was two years ago, Colleen. Justin and his wife were separated. Can't you just leave it alone?"

"Don't you ever stop to think that what you do affects your family, too?" Colleen said indignantly. "What if Gavin decides to run for office? What would we tell everyone? Most of the people in this town are honest and God-fearing. They don't cheat—"

"Oh, grow up. Half the married couples in this town cheat. They don't have anything else to do. And what I do in my personal life won't endanger Gavin's political future."

"I still say, this is Camden, Texas. What honest citizen wants to do business with a—"

Clack! Shannon set her cup on its saucer. Anger boiled through her. She glared at her sister. "Don't say it, Colleen. Don't you dare say it. I don't need a lecture or to be called names. All I want you to do is check on Grammy. Surely you could do that for *our* grandmother regardless of what you think of me."

Colleen's reply was an exaggerated sniff.

Out of patience, Shannon stood up and picked up her coat from the stool where she had laid it. Her sister hadn't even offered to hang up her coat. She could think of no one else she wanted to ask to look after their grandmother, but she said, "Never mind. I'll find someone else—"

"I didn't say I wouldn't do it. If you get someone else, everyone in town will know what you're up to."

Shannon's jaw clamped tight as a vise, but relieved to get Colleen's cooperation, she held her tongue and slipped into her coat.

"So tell me, Sister," Colleen said. "If I babysit Grammy, would that mean I might get that pair of diamond and opal earrings I've always wanted."

Shannon stopped and gave her a look. "What diamond and opal earrings?"

"The ones Grammy said she wore when she and Grandpa got married."

"I don't have them, Colleen, if that's what you're saying."

"Hm. Well you've gotten everything else from her. I just assumed you'd gotten those, too."

This was the way most meetings with her sister went. Sooner or later, she grumbled and complained about Grammy's personal belongings. "I don't have them," Shannon said firmly. "I imagine they're in her jewelry box. If you asked her, she'd probably give them to you." She started for the door. "I have to go."

Colleen followed. "Don't worry about Grammy," she said sourly.

Shannon nodded, freeing her hair from her collar and hanging her bag on her shoulder. "I appreciate your looking in on her."

After their quarreling, saying good-bye was awkward. As she walked toward the front door, Colleen said her name and Shannon looked back.

"I hope it's worth it," her sister said.

"Worth what?"

"What you're doing. I just hope it's worth it."

With that, Shannon found herself standing on her sister's front porch with the door closed in her face.

All the way back to town, Shannon brooded over how poorly she and her only sister got along. Trying to have a cordial relationship with her was futile. The age gap between them was wide enough for them to never have been friends. When Shannon was a little girl, Colleen had been her babysitter while their harebrained mother did who knew what. The responsibility had kept Colleen from socializing with her friends. She had resented it then and maybe she still did after all these years. Asking her for help had been a mistake.

Shannon stopped by her office to catch up on some last minute Friday housekeeping chores before calling Drake. Only Chelsea was present. As she sat at her desk shuffling through the pages of a contract Terry had left on her desk, the bell on the front door dinged. Seconds later, a tap came on her office door and Chelsea stepped inside.

"There's a couple out there that wants to look at houses," Chelsea said, her mouth flatlined. She looked down at a piece of paper in her hand. "Martha and Art Springer."

"Today?" Shannon asked.

Chelsea nodded.

"Call Kelly or Terry to come in. I'm fixing to—"

Chelsea's head shook.

Oh, hell. "They aren't available? Don't tell me."

The receptionist's head shook again.

"Great." Resigned to the change in her plans, Shannon put out her hand for the note. "Tell them I'll be right with them. And do me a favor, will you? Call my sister and tell her I won't need her help. I'm not going out of town after all."

Chapter Twenty-Four

THE SPRINGERS WERE yakkety customers who peppered Shannon with a non-stop barrage of stories and conversation. As the appointment dragged into the evening hours, Shannon worried about Grammy Evelyn at home alone. She barely found an opportunity to call and check on her, much less place a call to Drake. After parting from the Springers at 10:30, she sent him a text message rather than risk waking him. He seemed to be such a hip guy, she couldn't imagine that he didn't text.

Saturday began early and was a repeat of Friday. Drake hadn't replied to her text. Worried that he might not have gotten it, she managed to find a few minutes to call him. He didn't answer, so she left a voice message.

Fortunately, the Springers found a home they liked and put in a bid on a $400,000 purchase, to which the seller finally agreed. The sale wouldn't close until January, but that was okay. Shannon needed commissions in January, too. And this one she didn't have to split with another agent.

She barely made it to the Camden Realtors' party. If she hadn't bought the tickets early and hadn't promised to take Grammy Evelyn, she wouldn't have gone at all.

She awoke Sunday morning exhausted and lay staring at the ceiling. Drake was probably mad as hell. She dragged herself out of bed and checked her phone for a reply from him. Nothing. *Yep, he's mad.*

Saturday morning. Drake checked his cell phone for messages and saw two from Shannon. She had sent him a short text message last night: *Sorry. Can't make it. Tied up.*

The voice mail said almost exactly the same thing, then the line went dead.

Tied up? What kind of game was she playing with him?

Anticipating hearing from her again, he carried his phone with him when he went out to shoot, something he never did. Half way through the hunt, his phone fell from his vest pocket and he stepped on it and crushed it. Frustrated, he agreed to join his hunting pals for lunch, followed by a golf game.

After pulling herself together, Shannon took Grammy Evelyn to church. Colleen and Gavin made cursory conversation before the service. Shannon could tell her sister was dying to ask why Chelsea had called and canceled the need for someone to look after Grammy Evelyn.

As the preacher droned on, Shannon fought not to doze. Thoughts and memories floated in and out of her half-hypnotized state. It was just as well she hadn't been able to go to Stone Mountain. Why take on a battle? And she was sure a battle was what it would have been. Him tormenting her with bone-melting sex and her trying to be blasé and not care about him.

She could already see the not caring part wasn't working. Because she couldn't erase him from her thoughts, couldn't keep from wondering where he was and what he was doing. Did he go to church on Sundays?

After church, she and Grammy exchanged another short conversation with Gavin and Colleen and some of Grammy's friends, but the north wind was chilly and no one wanted to stand around outside and chat.

At home, Grammy had left a pot roast cooking in the Crockpot. As Shannon helped her with lunch, her thoughts drifted to Drake again and the Lockhart family. Grammy had been born and raised in Camden, and the Lockhart family had lived in Drinkwell for generations.

"Grammy, do you know the Lockharts from Drinkwell?" she asked.

Her grandmother stopped what she was doing and turned. "Oh, lands, yes. Everyone knows them. Why do you ask, dear?"

Shannon's pulse quickened. She nearly dropped the silverware she was picking from a drawer. "Oh, no special reason. I just heard something about one of them a few days ago."

Her grandmother returned to lifting potatoes out of the Crockpot. "I'm not surprised. There's always been a lot of talk about that family. Most of it not good."

She topped off the bowl of steaming potatoes with steaming carrots and onions and carried the bowl to the table. "My Lloyd and Bill Lockhart Senior were the same age. When both of them were still alive, Bill Senior bought hay from us. We grew wonderful hay and he sometimes bought the whole crop."

"No kidding," Shannon said, intrigued that her family had a remote connection to the Lockharts. But then, many probably did. They were the most influential family in the whole area.

"Bill Senior was a hard man," Grammy Evelyn continued. "I learned something from doing business with him. Rich people always do and get what they want to, regardless of the damage they might leave behind them. They have no conscience about trampling daisies.

"What do you mean, Grammy?"

"When Lloyd and Bill Senior negotiated for the crop, it looked to me like it always went in Bill Senior's favor. But Lloyd thought he was fair. I don't know if he was or not, but I know a number of people from Treadway County who thought he was crooked as a dog's hind leg. Since he owned most of the land in that county, he also owned the officials."

Shannon looked up from setting the table, now eager to pick her grandmother's brain. "Do you know any of the younger family members?"

Grammy Evelyn was back in the kitchen, lifting the roast out of its gravy. She set it on a platter and picked up a knife.

Her grandmother's hands weren't as deft as they had once been and she dropped things. Shannon walked over and put her hand out for the knife. "Let me slice it, Grammy,"

"I never knew any of the other Lockharts," Grammy Evelyn said, handing over the knife. "Bill Senior had only the one son. He and his wife thought they couldn't have children, you see, so their boy came along when they were older than most starting a family. Some people thought Sarah Lockhart never got pregnant because Bill Senior didn't spend enough nights at home."

Shannon laughed. "Grammy, you wicked thing."

"Well, that's what people said, dear. And when they finally had their son, they called him Bill Junior. People still call him that to this day. Imagine that. Couldn't even give him his own name." She shook her head. "So much arrogance."

As Shannon carried the platter of sliced roast beef to the table and set it alongside the bowl of vegetables, her grandmother walked over to the dining room window and looked outside toward the square. Shannon could almost see her memory spinning backward.

"Bill Junior was a golden child all right," Grammy Evelyn said. "The sole heir to the whole Lockhart empire. The land, the cattle, the oil wells, the cotton farms. And everything else that went with it."

"Wow," Shannon said, imagining the barrier between her and Drake growing higher yet.

"Bill Senior was ruthless. There was always talk about how he cheated his brother and sisters out of their share of that ranch. He was not an only child, you see. He had a brother and two sisters. I don't think a one of them still lives in Treadway County."

She sighed and played with the edge of the crocheted curtain that covered the window. "There was a lot of bitterness. Even some lawsuits. But I lost track of them after Lloyd died and the farm left our family."

Grammy Evelyn rarely said anything about the Lloyd farm, which Shannon knew had consisted of hundreds of acres on the banks of what was now Camden Lake. She picked up the salad she had made and carried it to the table. "What happened with the hay? Did they just stop buying it?"

"There wasn't any to buy. After Lloyd passed away, your daddy and I leased out the farm. And that was just a terrible mistake. The tenants were from Louisiana. They didn't know much about farming in this area. They didn't want to grow hay. They tried several other crops, but it didn't work out. They were so inept they couldn't have grown weeds, much less good hay. They forfeited on the lease and we had to sue them. With Danny sick, it was a great hardship and very stressful."

"I've never heard you say you leased the farm," Shannon said, back in the kitchen and dumping ice cubes into glasses and pouring tea. "If my dad was still alive then, why didn't he take it over and farm like Grandpa did?"

"Your daddy never did want to farm, dear. He went to college to be an engineer. He was more interested in his job at the bomber plant in Fort Worth than he was the farm."

Shannon scarcely remembered her father, Dan Piper. But everyone who did still talked about how smart he was. And how selfish. He had contracted pancreatic cancer and passed away not long after Shannon's grandfather's death. She was fifteen when he died, but her mother had divorced him several years before that.

"When those tenants finally gave up," her grandmother continued, "Danny's doctors weren't giving him any hope. So with Lloyd already gone and Danny soon to leave me, I just sold the place. We needed the money. I had a big farm auction and got rid of all the equipment. Then I sold the land to those Dallas real estate people."

Shannon had to laugh inwardly. Grammy Evelyn always said "those real estate people" as if she had just bitten down on a bug. "Grammy, don't forget, you have a good friend who's a real estate person and I'm one, too."

The little elderly woman turned away from the window and planted a skinny hand on one hip, defiance showing in her eyes. "Well, I hope you aren't like them. They nagged Lloyd for years. We had several miles of frontage on the highway through town on one side, you know, and the lake on the other. They were pushy enough when he was alive, but after he went, they were like starving dogs after a big bone. I've always believed those men took advantage of me."

"Sit down and let's eat," Shannon said, eager for her grandmother to keep talking. She knew so little of her family's history.

"I was so weak then," Grammy Evelyn said, taking a seat at the table. "All I could think of was trying to get Danny well. I wasn't very smart either. Lloyd always took care of our business." A wistful expression crossed her face as she spread her napkin in her lap. "We had beautiful land. Such bountiful peach trees and pecan trees. Huge ancient live oaks. Those real estate rascals were just itching to get their hands on it so they could put buildings on it. And now look at what they've done to it."

Camden's only strip mall sat on part of what had been the Piper farm. So did several big box retail stores, as well as smaller businesses. At some point, Grammy Evelyn must have been paid a lot of money for such valuable real estate. But now, she had nothing but the roof over her head and wouldn't even have that if it weren't for Shannon. "If it made you unhappy, I'm sorry it worked out that way, Grammy."

"Your daddy's passing showed me how short life is, Shannon. He was only forty-one years old. You probably don't remember those days. Your mother wasn't speaking to us and she didn't allow you and Colleen to come around us. She thought we were backward old farmers. Hicks, she called us."

Shannon had heard those very words, among others, about Lloyd and Evelyn Piper from her mother. During her years growing up, she'd had almost no acquaintance with her father's family. After she became an adult, she had learned that much of what her mother had told her about them was untrue.

Now that Grammy Evelyn had started talking, she didn't appear to want to stop. "Danny's treatment cost us so much. The insurance we had didn't begin to cover it. I took him everywhere, trying to save him. After he passed, I tried to make some of the money back with investments. I might as well have taken it to Las Vegas. I lost so much. I didn't know how to invest. I didn't know where to go to get advice. In those days, there weren't any smart financial people in Camden and I didn't trust the banker. I gave up being an investor before I lost everything. I took what was left and tried to enjoy life."

As Shannon recalled, her grandmother had indeed enjoyed life and had little contact with her only two grandchildren. She traveled everywhere, bought expensive clothing and jewelry, went on luxury cruises. And that was what Shannon was aware of. She couldn't guess what Grammy Evelyn had done that no one knew about. There had been times when Shannon barely had enough money for food, but all she had heard from her grandmother was that she had gone to the Mediterranean or New Zealand or some other exotic place.

Still, Shannon held no resentment. After all, the money belonged to her grandmother to spend as she wanted to. She reached over and covered her grandmother's aged hand with her own. "I hope you did enjoy it, Grammy."

A little old lady heh-heh-heh erupted. "Oh, I did, dear. I surely did. Unfortunately, I've outlived the money. And now you're having to take care of me."

"I'm not complaining. This is as close to a real home as I've ever had."

Grammy Evelyn gave her a direct look. "I like hearing you say that, Shannon, but I know I didn't do right by you and Colleen when we were all younger. After Lloyd, then Danny, passed so close together, I was a lost person for a long time. I lived in a fog of grief. I didn't know what I was doing half the time. And now, taking me on is keeping you from enjoying your own life. You work so hard. You have no social life. You should have a boyfriend while you're still young."

"No time," Shannon said. "Maybe I'll get around to it later."

And after hearing about the Lockhart family, it would be much later. Shannon no longer felt so guilty about not making it to Stone Mountain Lodge.

Sunday afternoon, Drake stopped at the registration desk and arranged to be driven to the airstrip where the family's Gulfstream awaited him. He was taking packages of frozen quail home with him—his own that he had shot and those of some of his buddies'. Their motives for going to Stone Mountain Lodge were different from his. He went to shoot, challenge his hunting skills and wind up with meat he liked, but with all of them married, they had been on the loose on an all-male weekend. Had they been in a place populated by flocks of women instead of birds, at least a couple of them would have been on the make.

Drake wanted to believe that if he were a married man, he wouldn't behave that way. God knew, he had seen the aftermath of his parents' cheating and had heard about it in his grandparents' marriage. He wanted to believe marital infidelity and family dysfunction were not programmed into the Lockhart DNA. He wanted to care enough about the woman he married not to want to cheat on her.

The lodge's car soon picked him up. "Where can a guy get a phone on a Sunday?" he asked the driver.

"Walmart in Camden," the guy answered. "But that's fifty miles from here."

Shit.

Five minutes later, Drake was buckling himself into the plane's seat without a phone. He rested his head against the cool leather headrest and closed his eyes. The flight to Fort Worth would be short, but with no phone to disturb him, he hoped to catch forty winks.

His head felt like a basketball. He and his hunting pals had closed the bar last night, all five of them getting shitfaced. These days, he rarely drank enough to get drunk, but last night, he had sought a change of mood in a well of whiskey. Bad idea.

All of his pals had heard the rumor about his marrying Donna. His association with her and her elite family and what it would do for his future spawned plenty of jokes and hoo-rah around the table. Drake had absorbed their teasing without bothering to discuss it. What went on between him and any woman was his private business. And as for his future, nothing he did in his professional life had anything to do with Donna's uber-rich and influential father.

As the engines revved and the plane began to taxi, his swirling thoughts finally circled back to the source of his irritation. Shannon. That woman had gotten under his skin in a big way.

...I'll call you and let you know....

Well, she had called all right. More than twenty-four hours after he had expected her to.

A frown tightened his brow. Meeting her had been fucked up from the git-go and now she was fucking him up, too.

Fortunately, he didn't have time to dwell on it. The end of the year dictated tasks he had to accomplish on his various projects to avoid income tax disasters. He had to put Shannon—and all women—out of his mind for now.

He wouldn't call her. Wouldn't even think of her. What he had to think of now was getting as much as possible wrapped up by Christmas so his mind would be free and he would be able to enjoy the holiday at the ranch with his family. This year's Christmas was shaping up to be great. His parents might be on the verge of putting their marriage back together after seven tumultuous years. If he could contribute anything that would expedite their reconciliation, he wanted to do it.

He could do just fine without calling Shannon. He might give her a buzz after Christmas. Or by then, he might forget her altogether and be freed from the seemingly irresistible conundrum she presented in his life.

Back in Fort Worth, on his way home from the airport, he stopped at a Walmart store and bought a new phone. At home, he sat down to tinker with it and at the same time, watch a football game on TV, but Shannon refused to leave his head. At half time, he could stand it no longer. He walked into his bedroom, pulled her business card out of his wallet and called her on her cell.

She came on the line with a laugh. "Is this Unknown Number?"

"Yeah," he said, strangely elated to hear that she sounded happy to get his call.

She didn't say anything right away, then "Listen, I couldn't get away on Friday. Did you get my messages?"

He wanted to ask her what she had gotten so busy doing, but if she wasn't forthcoming with the information, he hated sounding like a fool by asking her or even discussing it. He curbed the sarcasm that tasted bitter as bile. "You missed a nice weekend."

"I know. I really am sorry."

"Look, I'm planning on going down to Drinkwell on Wednesday and I'll be down there for a week. I won't be able to stop off in Camden. I'd like for us to get together before then and—"

"For sex?"

He frowned, taken aback by the bluntness of the question and too aware that with her, nothing was a foregone conclusion. "Isn't that the agreement?"

A pause. "Um, yes. Yes, it is."

"Tuesday evening. We can have dinner. If you'd like to come up to Fort Worth, I can drive down and pick you up or I can send a car for you."

Silence again. Then, "You don't have to do that. If I decide to go up there, I can drive."

If, if, if. Here we go again.

So much evasion was starting to annoy him. He couldn't picture himself cooling his heels all day another day waiting to hear from her.

"Let's get something out in the open and be done with it. If you want to come up and spend some time with me tomorrow evening, I'll do whatever I can to make that convenient for you. But if you're not interested or you want to renege on our arrangement, the sky won't fall. Don't give me a song and dance. Just say no."

He hoped his tone that traveled across the phone lines sounded neutral rather than expressive of all of the aggravation he felt.

Silence. Then, "That's fair." More silence. He waited, rubbing the crease between his brows with his fingers. Was she going to say no? Then, "Actually, I wouldn't mind an evening out. But I won't have much time."

Drake closed his eyes and drew a breath through his nose. "Okay. If time's an issue, instead of going out, I could cook outside on my balcony. I don't think it's too cold."

"That sounds good."

"When should I expect you?"

"I'll have to call you and let you know." Then she added quickly. "But I can't spend the night."

"But you'll be able to stay later than eight o'clock, right?"

"I promise I'll try."

"Fine. I'll be waiting for your call."

Had he just said that?

They disconnected. He sat there staring at his new phone, no longer interested in playing with it or watching the football game. He had never bent over backward so far for a dinner, an evening or a night with any woman. But what had he made a date for? Food or sex? He wasn't sure.

Chapter Twenty-Five

THE NEXT DAY, noon came and went and Shannon hadn't called Drake back. Three days had passed since dinner at the Rio Brazos Steakhouse and she was waffling again. Why had she promoted such a stupid arrangement? A tryst here and there based on nothing but sex had sounded doable when she had talked about it with Christa, and even when she had suggested it to Drake at dinner at the steakhouse. But now, it sounded sleazy and unrealistic. She had never done anything like that. Her past liaisons might have been wobbly, but they had included at least a modicum of caring.

But with the caring path being rocky and uncertain, an uncaring approach was the only way she could continue with Drake.

Her apprehensions went beyond the threat to her well-being. Besides the emotional pain he could cause her, nowadays, punctuating every move she made were the memories of the years she had been desperate for money. Still clear as if they were yesterday were the times she had stood in the cosmetics department at Walmart and debated if she could afford a new lipstick. And the times she had relied on payday loans to buy gas for her worn-out car even when she knew a payday loan was a rip-off.

A part of her wanted a man like Drake all right, but her alter ego had piped up and thrown cold water in her face: *He's too far out of your reach.*

Her common-sense self had to agree. If she let herself fall for him, she risked becoming distracted to the point of neglecting her business and losing her and Grammy Evelyn's livelihood, then eventually, the affair falling apart and leaving her with nothing.

And it would fall apart, her alter ego said. *It always has.*

Those negative thoughts carried her through the end of Monday. Then, finally, on Tuesday morning after the Multiple Listing breakfast, her will power retreated for a few seconds, what she really wanted won her inner battle and that pesky alter ego remained silent.

She called Christa and asked her to check on Grammy Evelyn before bedtime. Then she called and left a message on Drake's voice mail that she would be at his condo by six o'clock. She also repeated that she couldn't spend the night. They hadn't made it clear on the phone if they would be meeting for dinner or for sex, but she suspected they wouldn't have enough time for both, which was just as well. She had no interest in another slam-bam episode like the one in *Casa Familia's* parking lot.

She left her office at two and went home. She told Grammy Evelyn she was meeting friends in Fort Worth for dinner and that Christa and her two sons would come by and see if she needed anything and to take Arthur outside. Then she withdrew to her bathroom to shower and dress.

Before she finished styling her hair, Grammy Evelyn came into the bathroom. She closed the toilet lid and took a seat, as she often did while Shannon dressed and primped. "You've got your mother's hair," she said. "She had such pretty red hair." She got to her feet and came to stand beside Shannon, looking into the medicine cabinet mirror. She touched her own hair, which was snow-white, short and permed. "I always wished I had naturally curly hair."

Shannon put the finishing touches on her curly do. "It's a big pain most of the time, Grammy."

Shannon switched off her flat iron and set it on the side of the sink. "Listen, Grammy, don't go outside after dark to look for Arthur unless Christa's here with you, okay? If he doesn't come back into the house at a reasonable hour, let Christa's boys go out and look for him."

"It's such a lot of trouble for Christa to come over and fool with me."

"She doesn't mind. She's a good friend and she likes you. And her boys like watching your TV." Last Christmas, Shannon had bought her grandmother a large flat-screen TV in front of which she spent much of her time watching while she crocheted. "She's going to just drop by. And if her boys don't find Arthur, just let him stay outside."

"But dear, he might get chilled. Then he'd be sick and I'd have a vet bill."

"It'd be nice if Arthur didn't have so many girlfriends." Then, fearing she might have sounded harsh when she hadn't meant to, Shannon smiled at her grandmother, looped an arm around her narrow shoulders and gave her a little hug. "But tell you what. If he stays outside and gets sick and has to go to the vet, I'll pay for it. Better to pay for a vet bill for him than have you hurt yourself."

Grammy Evelyn shook her head. "Catting around is such a waste of his time. He's been fixed, you know, all the way back when he was a kitten. I try to tell him he wouldn't know what to do with a pretty little female even if he caught her."

Shannon couldn't keep from laughing. "You just keep telling him that, Grammy."

The elderly little woman raised her palms. "Oh, I tell him, believe me. But he's just like all men. He doesn't listen." She started for the door again. "Well, I'd better let you finish. You should hurry. You don't want to keep your friends waiting."

More mysterious talk about men from Grammy Evelyn. Shannon paused a few seconds, watching her, wondering if she'd had a fling after Grandpa died and thinking how close they had become since they had been sharing the same house. She regretted that she hadn't known her that well growing up. But so much had been going on in the family in those years.

Soon she was on her way to Fort Worth. All morning, she had pondered taking Drake a Christmas gift. But what could someone one like her give to a man she hardly knew, who had everything money could buy?

She had settled on a fruit basket, a housewarming gift she usually gave her customers. Everyone, even the rich, liked to eat. So at the outskirts of town, she stopped off at Camden's small farmer's market and picked up a gift basket of premium Washington apples and California oranges festively wrapped. The stop-off made her leaving Camden half an hour later than she originally planned.

At Lockhart Tower, she drove into the underground parking and to the slot the attendant told her was reserved for Drake's guests. *Guests? Who came to see him?* As complicated as it was to get through the security between the building's lobby and his condo, she couldn't imagine that he had a parade of visitors. In fact, she wondered how *she* was going to reach his front door.

Before switching off the engine, she hesitated recalling the conversation with Grammy Evelyn: *...rich people always do what they want to, regardless of the damage they might leave behind them. They have no conscience about trampling daisies....*

Wisdom from your grandmother, her cranky alter ego said. *Don't forget it and do something foolish, like letting yourself believe this arrangement could turn into something more.*

"Right," Shannon said aloud. She and Drake Lockhart functioned on two different social planes and the likelihood of a merger in thought, philosophy and status was far-fetched to say the least. They meshed on only one level.

She took the elevator from the parking garage up to the main lobby. The doorman, guard, or whatever he was, met her. He knew her name, told her Mr. Lockhart was expecting her and would meet her at the elevator door on his floor upstairs.

And he did, wearing Wranglers and a lavender button-down with a narrow green stripe and a signature logo of some kind. He had exquisite taste in shirts and lavender made him look good enough to eat.

He gave her a peck on the cheek. She thrust the fruit basked into his hands. "For the man who has everything. Merry Christmas."

"Thank you," he said with a huge smile as he examined the basket. "Looks good." Then he tucked it under his arm, grasped her elbow with his opposite hand and hurried her along the hallway toward his door. "You're late."

"I couldn't get away as soon as I planned. And stopping for the fruit basket took extra time. Hope you like apples and oranges."

"Love fresh fruit," he said.

Inside his condo, Alan Jackson's voice from the entertainment center and the smell of something cooking in the kitchen met them. "Honky-tonk music?" she asked.

He set the fruit basket on his entry table, then helped her out of her coat and hung it in his coat closet. "Takes me back to my wilder days." He pulled her close, locked her into an embrace and stamped a kiss onto her mouth. "Hi," he said and smiled.

"Hi, yourself," she said, smiling back and sliding her arms around his neck. "Smells good in here. Whatcha cooking, cowboy?"

He nibbled at her lips. "Potatoes."

"Hmm. Baked?"

They continued little nibbling kisses. "When there's time…I like potatoes…baked… instead of…microwaved." He nuzzled beneath her ear, flicked with his tongue. "Damn, you smell good, too."

He pulled back, released her and picked up the fruit basket, then reached for her hand and led her to the kitchen. Okay, dinner instead of sex. In one way, she regretted that. The *Casa Familia* parking lot episode did need closure in her mind. But in another way, she was relieved because she now realized she would never be able to hold up her end of this goofy arrangement. It was a silly idea anyway and it was her fault.

A small, but long and narrow package with a little red glittery bow lay on the end of the dining table. He set the fruit basket on the eating bar between the dining room and kitchen, picked up the package and handed it to her. "I've got something for you, too."

She blinked. Though she had thought of giving him a present, that he would have one for her hadn't occurred to her. "Wow. I didn't expect—"

"Open it," he said, hovering at her side as if he couldn't wait for her approval.

She didn't have to be a genius to figure out it was a pen. She unwrapped it, opened the box and saw an exquisite silvery blue Mont Blanc, the distinctive white flower on the top of the cap unmistakable. Her breath caught. She had never expected to own a Mont Blanc pen. Having worked in retail for years, she knew the price of it. She would never spend so much for something to write with. In her plebeian thinking, a BIC worked just fine.

Finally, she found her tongue. "It's beautiful." She looked up into his amber eyes and saw happiness. *And your eyes are beautiful, too.* "But it's too much," she said.

"A successful professional woman should have an excellent pen," he said.

She had received few presents in her life, Christmas or otherwise, that she believed were purchased with thought of who she was or what she did. His gift filled her heart with so much emotion, she had trouble speaking. "Thank you for saying that. And thank you for the pen. I'll guard it with my life."

He chuckled. "You don't have to go that far. It's just a pen."

Everything truly is relative, she thought. In his world, the price of a Mont Blanc pen was chickenfeed.

"Let's eat," he said, picked up her hand again and led her on into the kitchen.

Two thick, deep red filet mignons rested on a plate on the cooking island. Just like that, a visual came to her of herself spread before him like a dinner to feast on. Lust, raw and pure, zoomed to her nether regions and her knees trembled.

She must have had an odd expression on her face because he said, "What's wrong?"

"Um, nothing." She picked up a bottle of red wine standing beside the steaks and stared fuzzy-minded at the label. "I don't think I've ever seen this one in a grocery store," she said tightly.

"You wouldn't." He took the bottle from her and removed the cork. He poured two stemmed glasses half full and pushed one toward her.

She picked it up and sipped. "It's really good."

As she returned the glass to the counter, her eyes strayed to his fly. It was bulging. Yet another image came to her of him standing in this very spot, fly open and erection jutting only inches away from her sex. And her naked and whimpering and pleading and reaching for him. She was anything but cold, yet a shiver slithered up her spine. She tried not to look at him, but she couldn't stop herself.

"What?" he asked.

Tension—*sexual* tension—thrummed between them. She turned away. "Nothing."

He leaned down, lifted her chin with his fingertips and tenderly kissed her lips. "Don't do that to me," he said softly. Tell me what you're thinking."

"I wouldn't dare."

His eyes captured hers, his delectable lips inches away. "Coward."

"Totally."

"Don't you know I'm remembering the same thing?"

Sex on the cooking island? Did he really remember?...Or had he read her mind?

Drake knew what she was thinking. Ever since the night of the TCCRA party, he hadn't been able to go into his kitchen without experiencing a visual of her stark naked under the light that hung above the cooking island. He reached for the button on her jeans. And just like that they were kissing and undressing each other.

In a matter of minutes, they were half naked on the living room sofa and she was astraddle his lap. His shirt was undone, her chest was bare, his mouth was latched onto one of her firm rosy nipples and his marble-hard cock was buried in her wet, hot pussy all the way to her heart. They huffed and pumped to breathless orgasms.

Afterward, they sprawled on the sofa in a full frontal body hug, both spent. "Not quite as edgy as that Mexican joint parking lot, but close," he rasped out.

"The temperature needs to be colder," she said.

"I'm glad I had a rubber in my wallet."

"You didn't have one in the parking lot?"

"Nuh-unh. I don't carry them. But I put one in my wallet after that parking lot.

She giggled. "I wonder if I should believe you."

"You can always believe me. I'd never lie to you."

She gave him a look, wishing she could say the same thing. "Okay. I appreciate that."

"Are you hungry? We still have time to eat and those steaks are calling my name."

"Sure am. But I didn't think we'd have time for reindeer games and dinner both. There's something to be said for efficiency, huh?"

He loved her sense of humor. He laughed and stamped a kiss on her lips.

She sat up and bent forward, sorting her clothing. She was still wearing one leg of her jeans and panties. He propped himself on his elbow watching her, relishing how the firelight cast shadows on her flawless skin and her lush breasts. He loved her large nipples and their unusual color. Before she put on her bra, he leaned and kissed one, then her tattoo. "My yellow rose of Texas."

"I hate the thing," she said as she hid her beautiful breasts in the beige lacy cups of her bra.

The rose still peeked out from behind the lace. He traced it with his fingertip. "Don't hate it. I think it's sexy. And I don't want you to share it with anybody but me."

She gave him her back. "Do me." He sat up and worked at hooking her bra. "Believe me, I do my best not to share it. Ever," she said. "I've always hated it."

"Why did you get it?"

"Too many beers, too few brains. It seemed like a good idea at the time." She reached for her sweater on the floor and pulled it over her head.

"I was afraid you weren't going to show up tonight," he told her, helping her tug her hair from her sweater neck.

She pushed her foot through the panties and jeans, stood and pulled them up. "Why? I said I would."

"You were so hesitant on the phone. And when you were late, that convinced me."

"Would it have mattered so much if I hadn't made it?"

"Yes."

"It'll always be that way, you know. I have to consider my business and my grandmother before I think about what I might want to do. Since it's just sex, I guess it's no big deal if it has to wait at times."

"Right," he said curtly, wishing they could skip dinner and move from the sofa to his bed. But he stood up, dealt with the rubber and tied it off, then pulled his jeans and shorts over his butt and started for the bathroom. "Those potatoes must be charred by now."

"I'll hurry," she said and quick-stepped toward the guest bathroom in the opposite direction.

He hadn't expected sex tonight, had resigned himself to the fact that they wouldn't have time. She never stopped surprising him. Washed up, he returned to the kitchen and was removing the potatoes from the oven when she came in. "I don't know if they're edible," he told her.

Wearing a thick oven mitt, he took the potatoes to the cooking island, laid them on a piece of foil wrap and enclosed them into a foil package. Then he looped an arm around her shoulder and her arms came around his middle. "Why did you go to the other bathroom?"

"I don't know. Privacy?"

"You don't think what we just did was private?"

"I guess I'm not ready to share a bathroom."

"We'll work on that." He began to season the steaks with a one-handed flourish.

"I didn't know you could cook."

"Just easy stuff. I have to. I can't eat every meal in a restaurant. I don't even enjoy going out that much. I'm putting you in charge of the salad. Everything's in the fridge."

"Peeling and chopping. Woman's work, huh?" She left his embrace and walked over to the refrigerator. It was full of food. "Wow. I don't believe for a minute you went to a grocery store and bought all of this."

"Think I'm too dumb?"

"I think you're too busy."

"My housekeeper takes care of the groceries. She shops on Mondays."

"Oh, well, that explains it."

As she bent over the refrigerator shelves, he walked behind her and slid his arms around her waist, fit his groin against her bottom. "Most of it will probably get thrown away since I'm leaving town tomorrow.

"Too bad," she said, reaching into the refrigerator, her bottom tight against his groin. He was getting hard again.

"How hungry are you?" he asked. "I could be persuaded to go without dinner."

She giggled. "Come on, now. I hate to see good food wasted. You know what? Since you're going to be gone a week, you should take all of this with you."

She dragged out lettuce and tomatoes, a cucumber and a green pepper and salad dressing, then straightened, her arms full of victuals. She turned in his arms and thrust the bottle of salad dressing between them. "Grab this before I drop it."

He did, his fingers brushing her breast. They carried everything to the cooking island. He picked up the steaks and his glass of wine. "Back in a jiffy," he said and started for his balcony.

As Shannon tore and chopped vegetables, she thought about privacy. And intimacy. And doing it on the Drake Lockhart's cushy leather couch, then casually sharing the preparation of a home-cooked meal. Having an understanding and making an agreement to be his mistress, more or less.

The whole thing was almost as much a surreal experience as the evening after the TCCRA ball. She grabbed her own wine glass and swallowed a huge gulp. "Lord," she mumbled to the air, still unable to believe she was doing this.

He returned to the kitchen and pulled placemats and silverware out of drawers. "If you want bread, I picked up a loaf of fresh sourdough from the deli below my office."

"Not necessary. I try not to eat too much bread."

He went outside again and soon returned with the steaks that looked to be grilled to perfection and they sat down to eat.

"How was the weekend?" she asked him, then instantly regretted bringing it up.

He had already cut into his steak. "It was good. A lot of birds this year. All of us limited out. Do you like quail?" He popped the bite of steak into his mouth and chewed.

Now he was casual. The intensity was gone.

"I never get a chance to eat it." She tasted her own steak. "Lord, that's good steak," she said.

"Hm. I got it at a butcher shop out on the West Side. The butcher's a friend of mine. If I call him, he picks out choice cuts for me."

"Cooked to perfection," she said, giving him a smile.

"How was your weekend?" he asked. "The Realtors' party in Camden?"

His tone had an edge. "Good. I was worn out, but my grandmother loved it."

"Worn out?"

"I guess I didn't tell you the details. I had drop-ins on Friday. I was the only one in the office, so I showed them property all of Friday and into Friday night. And all day Saturday."

He sat looking at her, then finally said. "I see."

"I sent you a message that I was tied up. What did you think I was doing?"

He cleared his throat and sipped his wine. "What I thought doesn't matter. Hope you wrote a deal."

"I did. A good one. Drake, it does matter. You thought I lied to you. I didn't get home until nearly eleven o'clock Friday night. And I worked all day Saturday. I barely had time to get dressed for the party. Grammy Evelyn and I met my sales team and their husbands, who were arm-twisted into dancing with me and even with her so that we didn't feel left out. I went home alone to my lonely bed."

"Okay, fine." He smiled. "Thanks for clearing the air."

He stood and picked up his plate, started for the kitchen. She had finished eating, so she stood, too, picked up her own plate and followed him. "I said I'd be loyal in this pact. And I will. I wouldn't have made that promise if I hadn't meant it. If I find that I can't keep doing it, I'll say so."

His taut jaw relaxed. "Shannon, I—"

She stood on her tiptoes and kissed his lips. "Don't say anything. We don't have to talk it to death. We understand each other. Let's just get these dishes cleared away. It's time for me to go home."

"I hate that," he grumbled. He drew her into his arms and kissed her and she kissed him back, facing how much she enjoyed his kisses and his company.

They dealt with the rest of the dishes together, quickly and in silence. When everything was either put into the dishwasher or stacked in the sink, she said, "I really do have to go." She reached for his hand. "Walk me to the door? Tell me good-night?"

They walked together to the front door, he pulled her coat out of the entry closet, helped her into it, turned her and kissed her again. "Merry Christmas," he said softly, clutching her coat collar under her chin.

"You, too." She smiled up into his eyes. Casual. Nothing heavy when they were saying good-bye. "You're going to your family's ranch tomorrow?"

"I'm taking my mom down. It's always kind of a family reunion. You?"

"Grammy Evelyn and I'll be going to my sister's. She always cooks Christmas dinner."

"I'll be back next Wednesday," he said.

Instantly Shannon's thoughts shot to her offer on the five-acre corner. Wednesday was after Christmas. The owner should be back in town and she would learn about her offer to buy the property. Her entire life could change just that quickly.

"I'll call you," he said. "We can talk about New Year's."

She hadn't given a thought to a New Year's celebration. "What about it?"

"Spend it with me?"

Her pulse rate bumped up. "Where?"

"Here. I hate going out on New Year's Eve. Everybody's drunk and insane. It's on Saturday. Stay the weekend with me. I'll come get you and take you home on Sunday. I promise you we'll sleep in a real bed and take all the time we want to. I'll try to figure out how to fetch you without being seen. We can have dinner delivered and watch a movie....And whatever else comes up."

That could mean another lecture from Colleen, but she laughed. "I'd love to spend New Year's with you. Especially the whatever comes up part."

He laughed. "I'll call you when I get back after Christmas and we'll make a plan."

She pulled away and looked into his face. "I have to go."

"I know," he said. "I hate it, but I know."

They kissed good-bye again before opening the front door, a long deep kiss that left them both full of longing. He rode the elevator downstairs with her and walked her to her Sorento.

"Buckle up," he said as she positioned herself behind the wheel. She obeyed and buzzed down the window. "Be careful driving," he said. "Now that I've found you, I don't want anything to happen to you."

"Thanks for dinner," she said. "Best steak I ever had. Wine was good, too." He gave her a lopsided grin. "Everything else was good, too," she added, grinning back at him.

"Be careful," he said again and she drove away.

His words echoed in her mind and heart all the way back to Camden:

Now that I've found you, I don't want anything to happen to you....Now that I've found you, I don't want anything to happen to you....Now that I've found you, I don't want anything to happen to you.

She was suddenly brimming with Christmas spirit. Tomorrow she would go shopping for sure and buy gifts for everyone.

And she could hardly wait for New Year's Eve.

Chapter Twenty-Six

THE NEXT MORNING, Drake awoke in a great mood. Last night with Shannon had been more than he had expected. Despite the holiday and the trip to the ranch looming before him, he couldn't get her off his mind He thought about her through his shower and breakfast. Before leaving his condo, he sent her a text: *Merry Christmas again.*

A few minutes later, a text came back: *Ho, ho, ho to you, too.*

As forecast, the day was bright and sunny, with a temperature in the sixties. The trip to Drinkwell for the holiday was an opportunity to drive his Virage. All the way to his mother's home, he continued to think of Shannon. How could he not? In the passenger seat rode two plastic bags of food from his refrigerator. If Shannon hadn't said he should take it with him, he wouldn't have thought of it. She was right. It was a shame to waste food.

At his mother's house, as he loaded her bags and gifts into his car, she saw the bags of groceries. "Good heavens. What's this?"

"Food out of my refrigerator," he said. "I don't want it to go to waste."

His mom laughed. "I'm so proud of you, Son. I'm glad to see that what I used to tell you kids when you were little made an impression."

Drake grinned inwardly. Sometimes his mother's humble beginnings sneaked through and presented a dichotomy to the way she now lived. "I well remember it, Mom. 'Eat all of your food and consider yourselves lucky. Somewhere in the world, a hungry child would like to have this much to eat.'"

"That's right," she said. "And we should never forget it, especially in this season of giving."

Her bags and gifts filled the sports car to its roof and he barely found space in the back for his bags of groceries. The family custom was to give generously to the Treadway County food bank and to various charities instead of exchanging gifts with each other, but Mom always gave small personal gifts to each of them, along with homemade cakes and candies. Fortunately, he kept plenty of clothing and personal items down at the ranch because he had no room to haul another single object.

"I swear, Son, it would be easier to take my Escalade."

"We're fine, Mom. I don't get to drive this car much."

She was jolly and chatted cordially as they motored out of Fort Worth, headed southwest.

When they reached the outskirts of Camden, Drake did his best to not so much as look at Shannon's billboard rising beside the highway.

But his mother saw it. "Piper. Pretty girl. That name sounds familiar. Do you know her?"

"I rarely run into residential Realtors," Drake answered, glad to be speaking the truth.

"You're in the same business. I just thought—"

"Commercial brokers and residential brokers don't do the same thing," he said, hoping to end the conversation.

"I remember some Pipers in Camden," Mom continued. "I seem to recall Bill Senior buying hay from them."

Drake dared not follow this thread. Lest he reveal what he considered his personal business to his mother, he didn't respond.

He slowed as he drove on into the heart of town and the heavier traffic. He stopped at a red light in front of Camden's only strip center and almost directly in front of *Casa Familia*, where he had gone to supper with Shannon.

"This shopping center," his mom said, pointing toward the strip mall. "I believe it used to be Piper land. The Walmart store, too. I remember when this was all a hay field on both sides of the highway. Pipers irrigated out of the lake, which was what made their hay superior to most."

Had he just learned something about Shannon's family's history from his mother? "Common story with these old farms, Mom. One by one, they're being sold off and turned into shopping centers and subdivisions."

"I know. And it worries me. If we cover up all of our good farmland with buildings and asphalt, where will we grow our food? And cattle? My God, you know how much land it takes to feed a cow."

With his family's livelihood being agriculture, Drake had had similar thoughts about real estate development. Still, the cheapest and most easily developed land he could find, which invariably turned out to be farmland or pastureland, was what he sought to buy for his projects. A site that was flat and easy to work with was what all land developers wanted.

That inconsistency in attitude made him a hypocrite, but he had learned to live with it. "It's all about money, Mom."

"Everything's about money. If you've got it, you're trying to keep it and if you don't have it, you're trying to get it. I might not have a business head like your father, but I lived with him long enough to figure that out."

As they got closer to the Double-Barrel, his mother began to talk about his dad and how wonderful their marriage had once been. She hoped to reclaim that happiness. And she didn't miss the opportunity to remind Drake that he was now thirty-five and missing a lot in life by being a workaholic and a bachelor.

When they came to a stop in front of the ranch house, Dad was on the front porch. He saw Mom in the car, strode straight to the passenger door and opened it. "Betty." he said, offering her a hand out of the low-slung car.

She beamed a thousand-watt smile at him. "How are you, Bill Junior?"

Dad smiled back at her. "Better, now that you're here." He offered a crooked elbow, she tucked her hand into it and they started for the house, leaving Drake to unload the car.

Pic came out of the house and helped him. "What came over Mom?" he asked.

"Your guess is good as mine," Drake said. "But something's going on with those two."

Pic laughed. "Well, Merry Christmas."

Drake's parents spent the next three days moon-eyeing and hand-holding. Dad was at Mom's elbow constantly. Drake caught them exchanging air kisses once. She occupied one of the guest bedrooms, but Drake wouldn't be surprised to learn she was sneaking into Dad's bedroom at night. There had been a time when his parents had had a sexy relationship. As teenagers, he and Pic had made jokes about it between themselves.

With the days sunny, balmy and pleasant, Drake, his dad and his brothers hunted in the early mornings. In the afternoons, he rode the pastures with Pic, inspecting the cattle and the fences. He had a productive meeting with Kate that was less emotional than the last time he had seen her. He even had coffee with Blake Rafferty and caught up first hand on the arson investigation.

Christmas morning came and Drake awoke to delicious aromas, a replay of his childhood and one of the reasons he loved coming to the ranch for the holidays. He rose early and met the family in the kitchen. He hadn't sensed this much good will among the family members since before Mom had left seven years ago. He felt upbeat.

With the holiday meal to be served in the early afternoon after the gift exchange, Johnnie Sue and Mom made him, Pic and Dad a light breakfast. Afterwards, Pic went to town to pick up Mandy and their Grandmother Lockhart at the retirement center where she lived. Troy soon showed up, bringing a huge basket of meats and cheeses.

Today was the first time Drake had seen his little brother except on the back of a horse since Thanksgiving. Pic had already said that Troy and his horse came in second in the futurity finals.

Drake and he man-hugged. "Congratulations. I saw your performance early in the competition. Impressive. How long did you work with that horse?"

"Not that long," Troy answered. "Few months maybe. Somebody else had her before the owner brought her to me. She's a helluva horse. Smart. She's got cow, for sure. Did Mom make eggnog?

"In the living room." Drake led the way into the room that was rarely used.

An elaborate Christmas tree larger than the one in the den took up the corner to one side of the rustic fireplace, flooding the room with holiday ambiance. A punch bowl filled with bourbon-spiked eggnog sat in the center of a long table in one end of the room. Troy spotted it, walked over and dipped a cup for himself and one for Drake. He picked up the bottle of bourbon that sat on the table. "Let's have a Merry Christmas toddy, Brother."

Drake took the cup. Troy poured a dollop of bourbon in both his and Drake's cup, they lifted the cups to each other and Drake sipped. "Pic said you were only a couple of points behind the winner."

"Yep. Shit happens, doesn't it?"

"Too bad. Still, even with coming in second, her foals will bring a healthy sum."

"Oh, yeah. She's as good as the horse that won. Next time, she might be the winner. It was that close. Owner's a nice guy, too. He's a car dealer in Kansas City."

"I hated to miss the finals," Drake said, "but I had to get to Lubbock."

"How'd it look out there?"

"Not bad. They're drilling again."

Troy's mouth twisted into a smirk. "I wasn't talking about oil wells, smartass. I was talking about the windmills."

Drake chuckled. "Well the wind's still blowing if that's your question. I'm going back the end of January to wind things up. Listen, have you had a chance to spend any time with Kate?"

He nodded. "She's doing okay, considering. She's back to working with the horses, which I think is the best thing for her."

Drake nodded, too. "She's tougher than I thought she was."

"She's going through the motions of enjoying the holiday," Troy said, "but her heart will be a long time healing. Pic and I finally got all the rubble and debris either hauled away or buried, but I still feel like ants are crawling on me every time I go around where that barn was. We just need to find the fucker who lit it up. I'd like to get a piece of the sonofabitch."

Drake didn't doubt Troy's ability to settle scores. He was slightly smaller than either he or Pic, but he was a mass of solid muscle.

Besides spending his days horseback, he jogged and worked out. Years back, when he was still a college student, he had decided that living in the ranch house with Pic and Dad put too many restraints on his social activities. He had moved into one of the vacant ranch hand's houses a few miles from the main house. He had set up a room as a gym even before he bought any furniture and he often used the workout room just off the main house's garage.

"Blake Rafferty's on top of it," Drake said. "Let the law handle it. No need for any of us to get personally involved. Like you, I just want those cops to hurry up and find the bastard.

A commotion and pleasant conversation came from back in the entry and he and Troy returned. The woman Johnnie Sue had hired to help with the meal had arrived, followed by Will Harrington and Kate. Their sister no longer wore bandages, but other evidence of her ordeal was still present.

At almost the same time, Pic showed up with their grandmother and Mandy. Brunette with soft brown eyes, Mandy was even prettier than she had been in high school. She was his brother's refuge when life at the Double-Barrel became more than he could stand. In a way, Drake envied the intimacy obvious between her and Pic—the tender touches, the smiling glances, how they behaved like two peas in a pod.

And he couldn't keep from thinking of Shannon.

Dumb thinking, hoss. Pic and Mandy had known each other since they were kids. They had history together, though not always smooth. Drake had seen Shannon three times. Yet, he felt as if he had known her forever and wondered if she would enjoy this family gathering.

The importance of family came to him. Meeting a woman to whom he felt connected and seeing his mom and dad working on reconciliation had made him sentimental in a way he had not expected. Perhaps he was merely affected by the season of peace and joy, but for the first time in his life, he felt an urge to have a family of his own.

The women, except for Kate, eventually relocated to the kitchen. Kate was beautiful, talented and smart in many ways, but she didn't have a domestic bone in her body. She gathered everyone who wasn't occupied with meal preparation around the Christmas tree in the living room for Karaoke Christmas carols.

And caroling around the Christmas tree was where they were when the doorbell chimed. Troy left the group and answered the door. The next thing Drake knew, Mona Luck was standing in the living room doorway, wrapped in a fuzzy red coat, a bottle of Jack Daniel's in one hand. "Bill, baby! I brought you a Christmas present!"

Drake's stomach did a somersault. He started for Mona, at the same time mouthing to Troy to get to the kitchen and stop their mother from coming into the living room. Mona was at Dad's side before Drake could reach her. Obviously drunk, she fit her body against Dad's, slid her arms around his midsection, stood on her tiptoes and planted a big one on his lips, leaving a huge red smear. "Just want you to know I ain't mad at you, baby. You can sleep it off in my bed any ol' time you want to. We had fun, huh?"

Dad looked sheepish and confused. "Merry Christmas to you, too, uh, Mona." He patted her back, then peeled her off his side and set her at arm's length. "Uh, honey, you need to go home now."

"But I ain't got nobody at home, Bill," she whined. "It's Christmas and I'm all by myself. Wanna come home with me? I'll give you a real special Christmas present."

Crash! All eyes swung to the doorway. Mom stood there, bug-eyed, shards of a broken dish and a puddle of liquid spreading around her feet on the tile floor.

"Hey, Miz Lockhart," Mona said, thrusting the bottle of Jack Daniel's in Mom's direction. "Merry Christmas."

Mom's round-eyed gaze swung to Dad. "You bastard! You good-for-nothing, lying, cheating, fucking bastard!"

She charged up the hallway toward the bedrooms, tearing off a white frilly apron as she went.

Dad shot off after her, pointing a finger at her back. "Don't you dare say a damn word to me! You never said you were gonna show up. You kept dragging it out. I never know what the hell you're doing. You expect me to read your goddamn mind? How the hell did I know Mona was gonna come out here?"

Pic, who was nearer to Mona than anyone else in the room, spoke up, taking Mona's arm. "Miz Luck, you've had an awful lot to drink. Let me take you back to town."

She yanked her arm away, teetering on her spike heels, her mouth horseshoed into a scowl. "I'm not ready to go back to town."

Troy quickstepped to her side and caught her around the waist to keep her from falling sideways.

"Bill Junior invited me for Christmas dinner," she said to him.

Mandy stood calmly, her hand wrapped around a cup of eggnog. A Lockhart family fight was nothing new to her.

Loud voices and thumps erupted from the bedroom area. Mere minutes later, Mom marched back into the living room, pulling her wheeled suitcase, articles of clothing partially hanging out of the zipper opening. She stopped in front of Drake. "Son, take me home. Take me home this instant. I want to leave this"—she raised a clenched fist and shook it—"this den of iniquity."

Before anyone could reply, Dad stamped back into the living room, pressing a handkerchief against his forehead. Everyone in the room stared at him.

"Wait a minute! Just a goddamn minute, Betty!"

Mom spun around to face him, roasting him with a bug-eyed glower. "Don't you cuss at me, Bill Junior! And don't you tell me to wait a minute! You know what you can do with all your talk about making up and putting our marriage back together? You can stick it up your ass! I have lived with this…with this…with you…"

Oh, God. Mom was sputtering. Bad sign. Drake had to get her out of here. He lifted her suitcase onto the sofa seat, unzipped it and began gathering and piling her loose-hanging clothing into it.

On a growl, she turned back to Drake. "Take me home! Now!"

"You are home," Dad roared, lowering his handkerchief. An egg-sized red lump showed at his hairline and the red lipstick smear still marked his mouth "Drake, you stay where you are! You're not taking her anywhere!"

"Go to hell, Bill Junior," Mom shouted. "My home is in Fort Worth!" She turned back to Drake. "Son, take me home."

Drake now had Mom's overstuffed suitcase re-packed and was struggling to close the zipper. "Okay, Mom, okay. Just give me a minute."

"Betty's going home?" Drake's ninety-year-old grandmother asked from the other end of the sofa, her rheumy eyes huge behind her thick glasses lenses.

Mandy rushed to sit beside her, picking up her hand and patting it.

Kate came over to him, tears in her eyes. "You're going back to Fort Worth, Drake?"

"Kate, honey, I've—"

"TAKE! ME! HOME!" Mom's voice came out a shriek from a red mask of rage. "Son, if you do not take me home this very minute, I'll cut my wrists!" She turned in a circle, her hands raised in the air, her fingers rigid and splayed wide. "Just give me a knife! A pair of scissors! A nail file!"

"All right, goddammit," Dad bellowed. "Take her ass back to Fort Worth if that's what she wants!"

Kate began to sob, dropped to the sofa beside Mandy and buried her face in her hands. Mandy looped an arm around her shoulder. "Now, now, Kate. Don't be upset."

Pic threw up his hands. "This is the shits. The drizzling shits." He stepped in front of their mother, in her face, staring down at her. "Where do you get off, coming down here and acting like you're so goddamn good when we all know you've got a boyfriend up in Fort Worth?"

"Betty's got a boyfriend in Fort Worth?" their grandmother parroted.

"No, Mrs. Lockhart," Mandy told her. "He said Betty has a lot of friends in Fort Worth."

Pic raved on at Mom. "You think I don't know you're sneaking into Dad's bed at night, making him think you care about him? My room's just up the hall. You think I'm deaf? You think I don't hear all that shit going on in his bed? Y'all are worse than wild horses."

Mom moved against him, punching his chest with her finger, forcing him to step backward. "I am your mother. I bore the pain that gave you life. Don't you dare disrespect me. You've never supported me. You've always taken your father's side."

Pic had backed up under Mom's attack, but Drake could see his normally easy-going brother was ready to explode. "C'mon, Mom," Drake said. "Don't drag Pic into your fight with Dad."

"Stay outta this," Dad yelled at Pic. "You don't know what the hell you're talking about."

Pic turned on Dad, eye-to-eye and stabbing the air with his finger. "You and Mom have royally fucked up Christmas for everybody. Neither one of you ever considers a goddamn soul but yourself. You know what I think of the whole friggin' circus? I'll show you what I think."

Before anyone could move, Pic strode to the Christmas tree, shoved his hands among the branches and grasped the trunk. He picked it up in a mighty lift and stomped to the front door. Electric cords, lights, tinsel and assorted ornaments trailed behind him.

Drake grabbed at his brother's arm. "Pic, stop…"

Pic swept the door open and with one great heave shot the tree into the yard as if it were a javelin. It landed on its top, then fell over with a whoosh and a chorus of tinkles. Like a vanquished warrior, the angel tree topper rolled off to the side in the beige grass. A breeze picked up tinsel and icicles and carried them toward the barn.

Pic yanked the door back against the wall, slammed it with a *Crash!* He turned to the speechless room. "There, goddammit! Christmas is over!"

All the way from the Double-Barrel to Camden, Drake said not a word. Mom sobbed and cussed. By the time they approached Camden, Drake's stomach was tighter than a bloated horse's cinch. He didn't even look up at Shannon's picture on the billboard.

Finally, on the last leg of the trip, from Camden to Fort Worth, Mom began to get control of herself. "Let this be a lesson, Son. This is what happens when someone in your life becomes an obsession. I lived in your father's shadow from the day we married and spent most of my time trying to live up to his style and standards. I was obsessed with him for nearly thirty years and it was a very unhappy situation. I think they call it co-dependency."

Drake's memory spiraled backward. He had taken psychology in college. He must have studied co-dependency, but at the moment, nothing solid registered.

"Now that I'm away from the ranch," she said, "I'm finally getting over those years and learning to live on my own, without him dictating my life." She blew her nose and coughed and cleared her throat.

"Unfortunately," she muttered sourly, "the jackass still has the power to talk me into just damn near anything, even things that are out of character for me."

Shannon Piper popped into Drake's thoughts and the realization that she had driven him to behave in an uncharacteristic way. Each encounter with her had been more bizarre than the last. Her failing to show up at Stone Mountain Lodge had driven him to get stinking drunk in the bar, something he hadn't done in years.

Prior to that, he had walked to the jewelry store near his office and spent five hundred dollars on a pen for her when he hardly knew her. She might have already hocked it.

When she was half an hour late arriving at his condo Tuesday night, hc had felt like a jealous fool and barely stopped short of interrogating her And when she had scolded him about not wasting food, he had piled most of the contents of his refrigerator into a damn sack and hauled to the Double-Barrel.

Was Shannon Piper becoming his obsession? His hands tightened on the steering wheel and he made a vow. No woman would ever have control over him or maneuver him the way he had seen his parents manipulate each other.

"I should've gone to Santa Fe with Barron," his mom said, her nose stuffy from crying. "I just hope it isn't too late for us to go on that cruise in January."

Drake's jaw clenched. The knot in his gut might not un-kink until spring. "Jesus Christ, Mom. You're thinking about a cruise with your boyfriend after you and Dad trashed Christmas and upset the whole family?"

"I should've never believed your father. I should've remembered what a lying, cheating philanderer he is. And he'll never be anything else."

Drake couldn't keep from remembering a few things himself, like the morning he and Pic had hauled Dad out of Mona Luck's house and the shape he was in, and snippets of Pic's words: *...waltzes him around...telling him she'll come back, then not doing it...tells him she loves him...keeps living up there in Fort Worth...hanging out with her friends...*

"Mom, give it a rest," Drake said. "I don't want to hear it."

At last, he pulled into her driveway and parked.

"Come inside," she said. "I'll make something to eat."

He killed the engine and turned to her. "I never thought I'd hear myself say this, Mom, but why don't you and Dad just get a divorce and be done with it? What you're doing is unfair to everybody. And it keeps the family torn up all the time."

Her head slowly shook. "I'll never divorce your father, Drake. And he'll never divorce me. Neither he nor I can afford it. For that matter, you children can't afford for us to divorce, either. You know better than anyone how complicated the Lockhart family finances are. What Bill Junior and I have to do is learn to live without contacting each other. He needs to stay out of my life and I certainly need to stay out of his."

"But he's not in your life. Not much anyway."

She didn't reply, just turned her head to the right and looked out the window.

Drake had always suspected his parents saw more of each other than he and his siblings knew. He leaned forward, seeking eye contact. "Is he? Is he in your life? Is something going on that I don't know about?"

After a pause, she looked back at him, her gaze direct and daring. "All right, I'll tell you the truth about myself and him. Your father has a powerful libido. I excused his cheating for years by telling myself that one woman simply wasn't enough for such a highly-sexed man. He always was a—a wonderful…I'll put it this way. I enjoyed the physical part of our marriage immensely. But I've…I was naïve."

Drake's cheeks flushed. This was more information than he wanted to know about his parents. "Mom, c'mon, I don't—"

"Be quiet, Son. I'm trying to tell you something you need to know if you haven't already figured it out. Only in recent years did I face that it isn't sex that drives Bill Junior to cheat on his wife. What motivates him, Drake, is arrogance and selfishness. The belief that because of who he is, he can have whatever he wants, whenever he wants it no matter who he hurts. And he assumes he can clean up the mess later with charm or money or connections of some kind. That attitude was instilled in him by his own father. Bill Senior was an overbearing ass who rolled over people like a thrashing machine plows through wheat."

Drake memories of his grandfather included a lot of liquor, loud talk and him constantly telling Grandma to shut up. "Mom, I don't feel like—

"And I'm going to tell you about Christmas. It isn't pretty. I had every intention of going to Santa Fe with Barron. I decided to go to the Double-Barrel instead because your father came up here last week and stayed with me three days. He seduced me into going to the ranch for Christmas."

Her head turned and she stared out the windshield "He made me believe we could have things back like they used to be," she said bitterly. "I succumbed. He knows how sentimental I am. Where he's concerned, I'm just weak. And those are the cold hard facts. As I said, he can talk me into almost anything."

An understanding came to Drake, surprising him. Or maybe it wasn't so unexpected. Maybe it had been present all along and he had ignored it. He sighed. "Damn, Mom. I don't know where all of this leads."

She looked at him again, a plea in her eyes. "Please, Drake. Come inside and let me make us supper."

He was starved, he had to admit. Breakfast at the ranch now seemed like last week. He hadn't had any food since except eggnog and bourbon.

"I'm just going to go home and kick back, Mom. Let's take your stuff inside."

On a huge sigh, he pulled on the door latch.

Chapter Twenty-Seven

DAYLIGHT. DRAKE FUMBLED around his kitchen brewing coffee. He threw in an extra scoop, needing the caffeine jolt. He had left his mother's house yesterday, come home and gone straight to the refrigerator, only to remember that he had taken most of the food that had been in it to the ranch. He had found some cheese and made a sandwich with stale bread and mayonnaise. After that, mind-numbed, he had watched TV until late, followed by fitful sleep.

He thought he had consigned the memories of his parents' past battles to a locked emotional closet, but last night, all night, they had escaped and come full frontal. He had been through many a storm between them, but until yesterday afternoon, he had never heard anything like what his mother had said in her driveway. That brief conversation hadn't even scratched the surface of her and Dad's problems. Some psychologist could spend the rest of his career trying to straighten them out.

How might his own attitude toward women and marriage—and that of his siblings—be different if his parents had been different? With them as an example, having positive thoughts about settling down with one woman was hard.

He rummaged through the refrigerator again looking for food. Today being Monday, usually his housekeeper would come and do the grocery shopping, among other tasks, but with today also being the day after Christmas Day, he had given her the day off.

He had no desire to get dressed and trip off to some restaurant for breakfast this morning. Nor was he in the mood for stumbling through culinary endeavors. If he had the right woman in his life, she would know how to deal with this situation. She would simply cook something edible.

In the freezer, he found a box with a picture of sausage and scrambled eggs on it. While it turned in the microwave, a visual of his mother from years back came to him. When he, Pic, Kate and Troy were kids, she had been on their asses constantly: .... *Just because you're a Lockhart doesn't mean you can do this or do that...Being a Lockhart doesn't make you immune from common courtesy....Just because your father said you can do it doesn't make it right.... Blah, blah, blah...*

She'd had a different mindset from dad who was of the if-it-feels-good-do-it crowd.

According to Silas Morgan, Mom's parents hadn't wanted her to marry Bill Lockhart Junior even though she was pregnant. Drake didn't know why the Picketts had felt that way and might never know, but he suspected that they, like most of the citizens of Treadway County, believed everything Bill Lockhart Senior did was crooked, so they believed the same about his son. And they were intimidated by the Lockhart wealth and influence.

Even now, after all these years, his mother's family had little to do with her. Drake had admired and respected from afar his only uncle, Mom's brother, who had been a helicopter pilot in the military.

He couldn't remember his mom ever having many friends. He had sometimes thought of her as floating in a moat, with the castle on one side and a barren field on the other. Back when he and his siblings were kids, though she appeared to be wrapped up in Dad and the family, a part of her must have been lonely. He related. He didn't have a long roster of friends himself. His company and the family's business consumed most of his waking hours.

Bottom line, Mom had worshipped Dad, but never felt quite good enough to be his wife, even after giving birth to his three children. Drake believed that until Barron Wilkes, she had never slept with another man.

The coffeemaker pinged and he poured a mug, his thoughts switching to his dad. Drake adored him. The man had always had an aura. Always had more energy, more charisma than anyone else Drake knew. He filled a room. Until recent years, Drake himself had been intimidated by the sheer size of his dad's personality. As far as he was concerned, though his dad had failed as a husband, he couldn't have been a better father. With a steady, but gentle hand, he had raised his children to be good citizens.

Pic, Kate and Troy felt the same. They had never given much thought to the disconnect between their love for him and the way he had abused their mother's affection and disrespected her as his wife. It had taken some time for Drake to see it, but he had eventually recognized that her leaving him was the only thing she could do.

The microwave chimed, halting his musing. He carried his breakfast and a fork to the table. He sat in the same chair where he had sat when he and Shannon had had dinner on Tuesday night and an image of her sitting to his right came to him. What had her Christmas been like? Not like his, for sure, though it might have been unpleasant if she shared it with her sister and brother-in-law, whom she seemed not to like very much. Fucked-up family was something they had in common. They should have spent Christmas together, just the two of them.

Not enjoying either breakfast or his thoughts, Drake picked up his mug and left the table. He ambled over to the window wall and looked out. The streets were deserted, but the sun was shining and the daytime temperature still hovered in the sixties. With good weather and the holiday continuing through today, downtown activity would pick up later. Off-work people would drift in to go to the movies or eat in the restaurants. The merchants would have a good day.

As Drake sipped at his coffee, he couldn't keep his thoughts from swerving back to his parents. He believed Dad when he said he was miserable without Mom and wanted her to return to the ranch. But if he ever persuaded her to do it, would he consider the war won and go back to carousing, staying away from home days at a time and having strange women show up unexpectedly on his doorstep? Mona Luck wasn't the first.

Feeling a profound surge of sympathy and warmth toward his mother, Drake returned to the bedroom, picked up his phone and called her. "Hey, Mom, whatcha doing?"

"Just getting up and around. How are you this morning?"

"I'm good, Mom"

"I'm so glad the holiday is over. Next year will be different. I will not be at the Double-Barrel. And nothing your father does will persuade me otherwise. Have you spoken to your brothers? Or Kate?"

Drake heard anxiety in her voice. After Pic had hurled the Christmas tree into the yard, the whole family except for Grandma and Dad had roared away from the ranch like a parade on steroids. Knowing his siblings, they might not call Mom for weeks. "Not yet. I'll call them today though. Don't worry. I'll smooth things over. Listen, Mom, we didn't get around to eating yesterday. Why don't I pick you up and we'll go somewhere for Christmas dinner?"

For Shannon, Christmas had come and gone uneventfully, with the traditional turkey and trimmings at Colleen and Gavin's house and cousins from Austin seen only on holidays. Colleen showed no hint of the cattiness that had underscored most of their one-on-one conversations for years. Colleen wanted their grandmother and cousins to see her as a gracious hostess.

From her collection of jewelry, Grammy Evelyn had given Colleen an aquamarine pendant for Christmas. Colleen had gushed over it. Shannon had felt no envy. Colleen's craving for things, and not just from their grandmother, had a malevolence to it Shannon had never understood.

With most businesses in town closed, Shannon didn't open Piper Real Estate either. Yesterday, when leaving Colleen and Gavin's house, Grammy Evelyn had invited their Austin cousins to visit and have lunch before they returned home. Today, Shannon planned on spending the morning helping Grammy bake fancy chicken potpies in little individual dishes.

And underlying all of that activity was her anticipation of tomorrow. After today, Christmas was over. The seller of her five-acre corner would be back from his vacation. By tomorrow night, she would know if the was the new owner of the five-acre parcel that would change her life.

The cousins' visit turned out to be an exercise in patience. They were from Grammy Evelyn's side of the family and Shannon scarcely knew them. They were closer to Grammy Evelyn's age than hers and she had little in common with them. She thought they would never leave. The whole time they sat at the table talking, she had to force herself not to leave her chair and pace.

Tuesday morning, she was in her office early and waiting for a phone call from the Dallas Realtor. By lunch, she still hadn't heard from him. By mid-afternoon, she could stand it no longer. She called.

"Sorry, honey," he told her, "but another offer came in late last Friday."

Mental snarl. She hated being called "honey" in a business conversation. She was as much a professional as he was. "And you didn't call me and let me know you received it?"

"Come on. I'm not obligated to call you. It was hectic last week.

"Can you tell me what the offer is?"

"You know I can't do that."

"Can you tell me who's trying to buy it, besides me, that is?"

"Hey, I thought you were a professional. You ought to know I can't do that either."

Shannon had known the answer to both questions before she asked them, but she had hoped the agent might be as unethical as some of the other high-roller types she had met. She made a loud sigh, venting her frustration into the receiver. "This is really important to me."

"Honey, all real estate deals are important to somebody. But okay, I'll tell you this. You've been outbid. That's it. That's all I'm sharing."

"Okay, thanks," she told him. "I'm going to put in another bid."

"It had better be today," he said in a warning tone.

"I'll get back to you. Just wait for my new bid."

She hung up, leaving him to fret. He would wait. He might not be obligated to pass information on to her, but he was obligated to get the best deal he could for his seller.

This was a revolting development. Whoever it was who wanted to buy that piece of property, he or she couldn't possibly want it or need it as much as she did. She called her loan officer. He agreed to back her up to a point. She wrote a new offer, upping her bid, and faxed it to the Dallas Realtor. To her dismay, she was now engaged in a bidding war.

She could still find something to be upbeat about. She'd had a good, quiet Christmas with no drama and she had New Year's weekend with Drake to look forward to. All she had to do now was endure asking her sister to look in on Grammy Evelyn.

On Wednesday, Shannon began to expect Drake's call. Hadn't he said he would return to Fort Worth on Wednesday? The call from Unknown Number came late in the day.

"Run into any problems getting away for the weekend?" he asked.

"All taken care of," she answered.

"I was thinking of ordering something good for dinner and watching a movie or two."

"Hm, dinner and a movie, huh?"

He chuckled. "I'll choose the food. You can choose the movies."

"Great," she said brightly.

He told her he would drive to Camden and pick her up on Friday afternoon. Or he would send a car or even an airplane. In the end, she laughingly told him none of that was necessary. She hung up with joy dancing all through her. Not because she cared so much about celebrating New Year's Eve, but because he hadn't forgotten. And he hadn't found someone else he would rather spend the holiday with. She was forced to acknowledge just how much she had wanted to hear from him and see him again and it had nothing to do with just sex.

You're such a sissy fool, her cranky alter ego hissed.

She picked up the phone and called her sister.

She left for Fort Worth mid-afternoon on Friday. Only Christa knew her destination. In her bag, she had several movies. Two westerns she thought he might like and two chick flicks for her, although she doubted they would spend much time in front of the TV set. After all, ten days had passed since they had seen each other. Sexual tension teemed even in her SUV. She couldn't wait to get her hands on him.

On the outskirts of town, she passed her corner and a note of anxiety tweaked her. She would know in a matter of days, maybe even hours.

When she reached Lockhart Tower's marble lobby, she found him waiting for her. In the elevator, they made out all the way up to the twenty-eighth floor, with him clutching her bottom and her pressing her pelvis against his erection. "Ten days is too long," he mumbled between tongue-dueling kisses.

"Mmm," she agreed.

Minutes after closing his condo door, they were in his bed for a blistering episode. Afterward, she lay in his arms, her cheek pressed against his firm, warm shoulder and her smooth legs entwined with his hairy ones. "I had a feeling this was going to happen, so I shaved my legs extra close."

He ran his arch up and down her calf. "Feels good." He smoothed a hand over her bottom and pulled her closer. "All of you feels good." His hand came out from beneath the covers and he rubbed his nose hard and quick.

"Is my hair tickling your nose?"

He wrapped one of her russet curls around his finger. "I like your hair. It suits you. It can tickle my nose all it wants."

"Thank you. And my hair thanks you." She placed a kiss on his shoulder. "After you said we were staying in, I let it dry naturally and gave it its freedom. No hair products, no flat iron. What you've got tonight, cowboy, is the real me."

"Works for me," he said. "I like things that are natural. People, too."

"People can't get any more natural than me. When I was a little girl, my hair was so curly, my dad called me Orphan Annie."

"I'll bet you were a cute little kid."

She snuggled closer, rested a hand on his chest and heaved a huge sigh of contentment.

"What was that about?" he asked, rubbing the back of her hand with his fingertips.

"Nothing. I just feel good. The holidays are over. Everything will settle down and I can get my team back to thinking about work."

"Since it's a new year, I want to say something," he said.

Uh-oh. A tiny tremble zipped across her mid-section. A serious statement after boiling sex couldn't be a good thing. "Do I need a stiff drink to hear it?"

He replied with a little laugh.

Her quip about a stiff drink had been a joke. She never tried to drown her setbacks in alcohol, but now she wondered if she might need it. She paused for a few beats, steeling herself for what might come next. "Then go ahead and say it."

"How do you think this plan for just sex is working out?"

"It hasn't had much of a chance."

"Is it still what you want?"

She raised her head and angled a narrow-lidded look at him. "Why are you asking me this?"

"We don't want feelings to get in the way, right?"

She back-pedaled, her own words flying in her face. Of course, she wanted him to feel something. And if she said she felt nothing, she would be lying. "We don't have to take it to extremes. We can feel *something.*"

"That's my contention. A few emotions make the sex better, don't you think?"

"You're confusing me. You picked me up and brought me home with you when you had no idea who I was. And it was for sex. No emotions. I thought you did that all the time. What are you trying to tell me?"

He propped himself on his elbow and faced her.

"That I don't like wasting time on superfluous bullshit. Thinking about how I want this weekend to turn out has been giving me hell since before Christmas. So here's where I am. I don't like this just sex idea. I think it's a façade anyway."

She frowned. "A façade?"

"I don't think it's how you really feel. I want us to give this a chance. To see if it's real. And to be up front and honest with each other. But if we can't do that, or if I'm wrong about us, we just admit it now and stop. I won't call you anymore."

She wasn't prepared for such a frank conversation. "Why can't we stick to what we talked about in the restaurant? Last Tuesday was good. We enjoyed each other and didn't get all caught up in feelings."

His head shook. "When I was twenty-five, I would've gone for an hour or two of fucking and going on my merry way until the next time. But I'm not that kid anymore. I can't imagine that you really mean that's what you want from me. Or from any man."

"No! I don't. Honestly, I don't. I don't know what I want."

He cupped her jaw in his palm, leaned and tenderly fastened his lips to hers. When he pulled back, his eyes locked on hers, the crease between his brows deepening. "I'm a man who lives by his instincts, Shannon. In all parts of my life. At the hotel that night, it wasn't just a pickup. There was something else there or it wouldn't have gone as far as it did. I promise you I'm not a fool whose dick dictates his behavior. I might've been once, but not anymore."

She heaved a sigh and turned to her back, stared at the ceiling. She hadn't been thinking of the night at the Worthington Hotel until he mentioned it, but now Donna Schoonover waltzed into her mind and how she had appeared to be his girlfriend, his fiancé or something one minute and the next minute she wasn't. Shannon had always suspected that whatever happened between Drake and her after they left the party had been instigated by Drake. If someone with as many positives as Donna Schoonover hadn't been able to hang onto him, how could Shannon Piper?

"Do we have to talk about it on New Year's Eve?" she asked meekly.

"I'm not letting you off the hook. You have to tell me the truth."

She turned onto her stomach and hugged her pillow, still looking into his face. "It seems like it's too soon to be talking about feelings. A month ago we didn't even know each other. We still don't."

He stroked her hair back from her face. "I know what I need to."

"How could you?"

"I told you. I'm good at sizing up people. My gut's never wrong."

"I'm at a disadvantage with you. You've lived a life different from mine. You've grown up rich and—"

"Most women like that I've got an extra nickel or two."

"I'm not opposed to it. I'm just repeating what I said. We don't have much in common. You're a celebrity of sorts. I'm an ordinary woman—"

"You're not an ordinary woman. And I'm not a celebrity."

"There's that other thing I already told you. I can't let getting involved with you, or anyone, do damage to my business. I just can't. I've worked too hard for it and it means too much to me. I know myself. I'm sort of an all-or-nothing kind of person. Here's what happens, you see. I fall head-over-heels for you, let my feelings get all involved, can't think about anything else, have no interest in doing anything else except being with you and—"

"Sounds good to me," he said, grinning.

"Let me finish. And the next thing I know, I've neglected business and I'm not making enough money to pay my mortgage on my office or pay my help and so on. My real estate company is it for me. I've put my whole heart and soul into it. For the first time in my whole life, I feel like I've finally gotten a break and I don't want to blow it."

"What if I say I'll give you plenty of room to do your own thing? And if you get into trouble, I'll even help you."

"I don't want your help. I don't want to be obligated. And I don't want to get hurt."

"I'm not planning on hurting you."

"Most people don't plan to hurt each other. It just happens."

"Do you have an argument for everything?"

"I'm not an argumentative person, honest. But I know that people make choices on the spur of the moment."

Like Shannon Piper has done too often in the past, she thought but didn't say.

"Then later, minds change. Circumstances change. People start to learn that maybe they made a mistake. Or they meet someone else and start thinking the grass looks greener."

Like Drake Lockhart did the night of the TCCRA party.

"Or one or the other gets bored or puts their own interests first."

Like Drake Lockhart has probably done a hundred times."

She gave him a direct look. "I can't keep from thinking about the woman who was with you at that Realtors' party."

He flopped to his back, locked his fingers behind his head. *Oops*. She had touched a nerve.

"This conversation seems to be going in a circle," he said. "Let's move on. So how's business?"

She was more comfortable discussing something of which she had more knowledge. "Rotten. It's always been slow over the holidays. I'm hoping for a good January, but the way the market is right now, January might be lousy, too. My team does have a couple of closings though and I'll be closing on that sale I made before Christmas. How's your business?"

"I'm expecting a couple of things in Lubbock to come to a head, one way or the other. I planned on getting a deal together out there in December, but I had to get involved with something at the ranch. I'm going west around the first of February.

"Oh," she said.

"When was the last time you were in Lubbock?"

"Hah. I've never been to Lubbock. I've never been west of Weatherford."

"Go with me?"

"To Lubbock?"

"You said you're expecting business to be slow. Maybe you can break away for two or three days. Ever seen a wind farm?"

Now this interested her. "Only in pictures."

"Go with me and I'll give you a first-hand look at ours."

Immediately, she started plotting how she could travel out of town for a few days in February. "I'll think about it."

He turned back to his side, braced on his elbow. He trailed a finger down her neck to her collarbone and kissed the pulse that beat there. "Not that it's a big deal, Shannon," he said softly, "but I've never taken anyone on a business trip with me. If you'd go, it would be a new experience for both of us. A test, maybe."

A test of what? If that were true, his inviting her had to be meaningful. "I'd have to find someone—"

"To look after your grandma," he finished. "People get paid to do things like that. I'll ask my assistant to find someone."

Shannon couldn't imagine what a babysitter for an adult would cost. "No. I'm responsible for her."

"Okay, I understand."

She shrugged, still unable to give him a yes or no answer.

He reached for his watch on the bedside table and glanced at it. "It's getting late. The restaurants will be packed tonight. We should order supper."

Chapter Twenty-Eight

SHANNON HAD DROPPED her bag on the floor near the bed. She picked it up as she started for the bedroom door. "Where you going?" he asked.

When she had come here after the TCCRA party and last Tuesday night, she had used only the guest bathroom. She stopped and looked at him. He was lying on his back, uncovered to the waist. His hands were locked behind his neck, his biceps bunched. His armpits showed tufts of dark brown hair, which also sprinkled his chest. He looked sexy and predatory and delicious. Just minutes ago, she had teased his brown nipples with her tongue and teeth and had loved his response.

"To the other bathroom," she answered.

"Why?"

"I just want to." She padded out of the room before he could talk her out of it.

"What's the big deal?" he yelled behind her. "I've seen you naked."

"You've done way more than that," she hollered back, grinning as she trekked through the dining room, the living room and up the hallway.

On a hunch, she had brought sweats and warm socks. Washed and dressed, she met him in the kitchen. He had put on flannel PJ bottoms and a long-sleeved T-shirt. She was still awestruck that she and the charismatic and almost-famous Drake Lockhart were spending New Year's Eve together, dressed in flannel and sweats. No one would believe it. She could hardly believe it herself.

He dragged a bottle of champagne out of the refrigerator and expertly opened it. Two champagne flutes sat on the cooking island, the light glinting off the rims. Oh, yes, they were real crystal. He poured them full, then picked his up, lifted it to her and sipped. "To an exciting year ahead. It's already beginning to show promise."

Returning his gaze, she picked up her glass and touched it to his. "To an exciting year."

They sipped, he looped his arm around her shoulders and side by side, they carried their glasses over to the wall of windows and stood in silence as they looked out over the city lights. She would love to know what he was thinking, although at this moment she couldn't begin to sort her own jumbled thoughts.

The food was soon delivered. Together, they removed the servings from a thermal carrier and placed them on the table. He opened a thick warm box and steam and delicious smells arose from two of the largest lobster tails she had ever seen.

He had already set the table with placemats and silverware. He had even placed a candleholder with tapers in the table's center. He lit them, then steered her to the chair to the right of the end seat. As he took the head-of-the-table seat, she tried not to read symbolism into the arrangement.

They served each other a fresh vegetable salad and a potato dish that looked and smelled heavenly. Though they had eaten together only once before, they behaved as if they knew each other's mundane habits.

She doused a bite of lobster in melted butter and closed her eyes as her taste buds sang. "Wow. When you said something special, you meant it."

"Good, huh?" He cut into his own lobster tail. "There's lobster, then there's *Maine* lobster."

"I've seen it on menus. Most of the time, you have to ask the price. You know what they say. If you have to ask the price, you can't afford it."

"Hm. I didn't know they said that," he said.

"See? That very statement is a good example of what I've been trying to tell you. You never have to ask the price of anything. Whatever its cost, you can afford it. I can't imagine what it's be like to be you and you can't imagine how it is to be me. That's a huge obstacle between us."

He chuckled. "Okay, from now on, we'll eat cheap. Will that improve the odds we can make this work?"

Covering her mouth with her napkin, she laughed. God, she loved being with him. He never gave up. "Don't laugh at me. I'm just trying to point out—"

"I know what you're doing," he said firmly, holding her gaze. "And I'm saying superficial differences don't reflect or affect who we are inside."

But he was wrong, Shannon knew. No matter what he said, differences such as growing up with wealth and power went far deeper than superficial.

After the scrumptious meal, they danced in the firelight in his living room. He held her close. They swayed to the music, but their feet moved no more than inches. They spoke in soft voices and touched lips often. They never got around to the movies. Instead, they drank champagne and watched the ball drop in Times Square on TV. At midnight, they kissed, crossed wrists and toasted.

"To the new year," he said, smiling down at her. "And our new understanding."

"To the new year," she replied, still uncertain what their understanding was.

They returned to bed and after ushering in the new year with bone-melting sex, they drifted to sleep in a tangle of arms and legs. Then later in the night, they found each other again. When they awoke mid-morning, their desire was even more fervent. After a deeply emotional joining, they held each other for a long while. He stroked her hair and tenderly kissed her. She hummed and cooed words she had never said to any man she had known.

You're letting things spin out of control, dearie, her alter ego warned.

Later, before she had a chance to leave the bed for the guest bathroom, he rose and tugged her out of bed. "We're going to test bathroom sharing," he said.

He led her to the bathroom off his bedroom. The room was huge, with mirrors all around. The floor was tan marble and tile. Everything was unbelievably clean and exquisitely fragrant, with a scent like the guest bathroom.

Having been in countless homes of all prices, Shannon had come to believe bathrooms revealed a lot about the people who owned them and what she read in his was that he was not the vainglorious egotist that Jordon Palmer had said. A single hand towel hung from a bar on the wall beside one sink. No monogram. A mechanical teeth cleaner of some kind sat on a little holder. A brown design circled the inside rim of the oval sink's white porcelain. Looking closer, she deciphered two parallel horizontal bars and a capital L. Double-Bar L. Cattle brand. In Texas, anyone who owned two cows had a brand. A few feet away, a second identical sink looked unused.

She ran her fingers over honey-colored woodwork polished to a sheen. She had already concluded he had a very good housekeeper. "Wow. To someone whose bathroom used to be an outdoor porch, this is something."

"C'mon. Don't be critical of your grandma's house. It was built before houses had indoor bathrooms."

"We have a plaque beside the front door that says so. And I wasn't being critical. I like her house. Sometimes it makes me feel like Scarlett O'Hara."

She spotted a louvered door in one end of the room. "What's that, a closet?"

"Take a look," he said, opening the door and urging her to peek inside.

Giving no thought to her nakedness, she stepped in front of him, her body touching his warm skin. His hand rested on her shoulder as she perused a dressing room with drawers and shelves as well as multiple cubicles holding many neatly hung shirts and pants, a boot cupboard and many pairs of cowboy boots. "All this storage." she said.

He cupped her neck, turned her and kissed her. When their lips parted, he said, "Let's shower. You must be hungry."

He led her across the room to the shower. Besides the dressing room that was as large as a bedroom in many houses she had seen, the other blatant extravagance was his shower. The glass and marble enclosure was only slightly smaller than her whole bathroom. A rain shower fixture hung overhead and massage fixtures protruded from the wall. Also outlets for steam. A bench spanned one wall. She saw what she thought was a radio. "Holy cow," she said in awe. "Is this where you bathe your harem?"

"Harem?" He frowned and steered her inside, at the same time punching buttons.

Water at a perfect temperature began to pour over them and steam began to fill the space around them. "I designed it myself," he said, grinning, obviously proud. "Well, I didn't actually design it. I had the idea and a real designer put it together. Cool, huh?"

A veil of steam began to enshroud them. "This is a first for me," she sputtered, slashing water from her eyes with her fingers. "I can't say that I've ever been steam-cleaned."

He poured eucalyptus-scented bath gel into his palm, then handed the bottle to her. "You sell high-dollar homes. I know you've seen steam showers."

"Well, yes. But I've never seen them work. And I've never been in one. Just because I list the house doesn't mean they let me use the shower." She laughed.

"This the latest in luxury bathrooms. All Lockhart Tower homes have the latest amenities."

"Now you sound like a salesman."

"Darlin', I *am* a salesman. First and foremost. Smart as you are, I thought you would've figured that out. Marketing is what I'm best at."

She smiled up at him and crossed her wrists behind his neck. "Oh, yeah? After last night, I might argue that point. But if you have a bridge you want to tell me about, I'll consider it."

They began to wash each other. She loved the feel of her soap-slicked hands sliding over his firm shoulders, his sinewy back. His erection pressed against her and she marveled that he was getting hard again. "Sex god," she murmured.

"It's you. You drive me to exceed my limits."

Sliding her front against him, she rose on her tiptoes and kissed him deeply. After they parted, she lathered soap between her hands, then began to soap his front. "I love touching you," she said softly.

"And I love having you touch me."

"Your body's so perfect." She smoothed her hands over his solid chest, his washboard abs, his hairy flat belly. She gently soaped his genitals.

On a hum, he pulled her close and soaped between her legs. "Sore?"

He was athletic and strong and no matter how gentle he was, a whole night of unbridled sex with him had been physically demanding. "A little. Are you?"

His hands moved up and began to soap her breasts, paying extra attention to her nipples. To her astonishment, the nerves inside her sex quickened.

"A little," he answered. "I haven't been good for three times in a night in a while."

They kissed again. Their lips parted on a hum. "Hmm. And all three were notable."

"I thought so. I'm damn proud of myself."

"Is that too much? Did we overdo it?"

"With you, I could never overdo it."

"Hmm," she said again. "You're dangerous. You're too good with flattering words."

She looped her arms around his neck again and pressed her slick breasts against the hard wall of his chest. "How come you're in such good shape? You must not sit at a desk all day. You must work out."

He caressed her bottom, began nibbling at her lips. "Sometimes. Lockhart Tower has a gym. And a pool. I don't swim, but I use the gym." He covered her mouth with his for another luscious kiss. "You didn't say what you thought of the shower."

"Fantabulous."

"It is. Especially with you in it."

She tilted back her head and began to shampoo her hair. His tongue traveled along the underside of her arms, ended up at her nipples. He closed his mouth over one nipple and that tingle inside her sex became a zing. "Hmm."

"I love your nipples," he said, gently sucking one.

That familiar clenching began inside her sex. She made a soft moan." He slowly sank to his knees, his lips moving down her wet belly. "Your body's so beautiful."

When his mouth reached her pubic hair, her pulse rate picked up and she could no longer concentrate on her hair. "Drake," she mumbled.

"Hmm?" He parted her labia with his thumbs and the tip of his tongue found her clitoris. Sensation shot through her. Her sex instinctively pushed toward him, making her helpless and needy anew. A little keening sound blurted from her throat. His agile tongue flicked and laved until she shattered in orgasm and went weak-kneed. He caught her in his arms, rose to his feet and smothered her mouth with a devastating kiss. Their lips parted and he said, "So what do you think? Sharing a bathroom is fun, huh?"

"You're such a devil," she replied.

They left the shower, with her feeling sated, shampooed, scrubbed and cleaner than she had ever felt in her life.

On their way to the kitchen, she stopped and looked outside. The sidewalks and streets were empty. The gray sky looked tumultuous. A norther had been forecast and apparently it had arrived overnight. No wind could be heard from inside the condo, but it could be seen in a fully unfurled flag in the distance and in the Christmas decorations that brutally lashed the light poles down on the sidewalks. She imagined its icy bluster whistling and howling up and down the brick streets that ran between the multistory buildings.

"Looks like we're going to be housebound today," she said. "We'll have to watch the movies I brought. Or football." She looked at him and grinned. "Or I can get even with you for what you did to me in the shower.

"Hold that thought for later. I've got a plan."

"What is it?"

"I'll show you after we eat."

Shannon straightened the kitchen from the night before as he pulled eggs and bacon from the refrigerator. "I had to go shopping so we'd have something to eat," he said.

Shannon couldn't imagine him in a grocery store, but then, he could probably handle anything, even a trip to a supermarket. "No way," she said.

"I took your advice and took all of the food down to the Double-Barrel. Since I gave my housekeeper the day after Christmas off, I had nothing in the fridge."

While they cooked, the Rose Parade showed on the small kitchen TV that hid behind a door in one of the cabinets. Calls began to come, all from his family members, wishing him a happy new year. She hadn't heard him say how large his family was. She hadn't given it much thought before, but it dawned on her that she had never received a happy new year call from her sister. They probably wouldn't even spend Christmas together if it weren't for Grammy Evelyn.

"How was Christmas with your family?" she asked him as she manned skillets of sizzling bacon and scrambled eggs.

He waited for toast to pop up. "Interesting."

She glanced at him across her shoulder. He was focused on buttering the toast. "Interesting?"

"I started to say entertaining, but that would be the wrong word for sure. How was yours?"

He laid the butter knife beside a stack of several slices of toast and reached inside the cupboard. Apparently he didn't want to discuss Christmas with his family.

She scraped the scrambled eggs into a bowl. “Well I couldn’t say it was interesting. Dinner at my sister and brother-in-law’s house. Some cousins came from out of town.”

“The Houston side of the family, huh?”

Oh, hell. She looked up from lifting the bacon from the hot skillet, feeling her cheeks heat up. He was grinning. He winked.

She laughed then, feeling guilty as she turned off the burner under the skillet. “Okay, I fibbed a little that night. I don’t have any relatives in Houston.”

He came to her and placed his hands on her waist. “Someday you’re going to have to tell me why you did that.”

“You don’t have to wait until someday. I’ll tell you now. I was confused and conflicted. I wanted to be with you, but I couldn’t stand for you to think I was bad.”

He was still grinning. “But you *are* bad. In a good way.” He pulled her close and nipped her bottom lip with his teeth. “You’re the baddest woman I know. You turn me into a wild man. Make me feel like I’m eighteen again.”

They kissed again, a long languid joining, all minty-tooth-pasty and sweet, with her arms around his wide shoulders. She could feel his erection through his sweats. She playfully wriggled against him. He caught her hand, placed it over him and she felt his firm shape through the soft knit.

“We should go back to bed,” he said huskily. “Let me set a record.”

“If we spend so much time in bed, don’t you think we’ll get tired of each other?”

“Not a chance.”

They kissed again until she pulled away and smiled up at him. “We should eat, cowboy. Breakfast is getting cold. And I didn’t slave over this hot stove to end up with cold breakfast.”

After breakfast, they tidied the kitchen, then they bundled up. He produced a skullcap and pulled it onto her head and wrapped a knitted muffler around her neck. His attention and concern for her comfort touched her. They left the condo and strolled the city streets, something Shannon had never done in spite of living in Fort Worth for years.

Most of the retail stores were closed, but all of the eateries and bars were open and festive, with big-screen TVs showing the day’s events. Drake knew the business people and they knew him. Everyone greeted him enthusiastically. At noon, they had beer and deli sandwiches and talked football with a group who had come to spend New Year’s Day downtown. Before leaving, he told her he owned the building and his offices were on the upper floors.

As the day waned, they returned to his condo. Cuddling under a blanket on the oversize sofa in the living room, they attempted to watch the Rose Bowl game, but soon became so absorbed with pleasing each other, they missed most of it. Indeed, she did get even with him for what he had done to her earlier in the shower.

They slept in each other's arms again Saturday night, and on Sunday morning, she prepared to say good-bye. As she shrugged into her coat just inside the front door, he said, "I'm taking some time off in January. Kicking back a little. Can you get free this week?"

Since her marriage, she had never spent that much time all at once with a man. "For a whole week?"

"I know you can't get away at night. Maybe we could do some day dates."

"Maybe," she said. "You can call and let me know, I guess, and I'll see if I can do it."

"Good enough."

They embraced before opening the front door, preparing to kiss good-bye. "Don't kiss me hard," she said softly. "If you do, I'll want to stay."

He pulled her tightly against him and kissed her fiercely. When they broke to breathe, she choked out, "I was just kidding."

"I wasn't." He kissed her again.

"If we don't stop, we'll be back in bed."

"I know."

They kept kissing.

Finally, she stepped back, putting two feet of distance between them. "Drake. I have to go."

He walked her up the hallway, rode with her on the elevator and walked her to the parking garage. "Be careful driving," he said.

She slid behind the wheel, closed her door and buzzed down the window. "Thanks for the weekend" she said, as she fitted her bluetooth against her ear.

He bent to the car window's level and pointed to it. "Don't let that thing distract you. I don't want you to have a wreck."

Again, the concern for her well-being touched a deep place within her. It had been years, if ever, that someone "cared" about her. She was still grinning like an idiot. "I won't, Dad."

He gave her his little-boy grin. "Okay, okay. I told you I'm possessive." He straightened, still looking down at her, then bent again and kissed her again. "Good weekend."

Oh, it was more than good. It had been glorious. And it had completely destroyed her idea of classifying their meetings as just sex. "The best," she said softly.

She buzzed up the window and backed out of the parking slot. He was still watching when she pulled out onto the street into the traffic.

Forty minutes later, as she entered the Camden city limits, her phone warbled and she keyed into the call.

"I've been studying my schedule and the weather," he said. "Wednesday's a good day. How does lunch on the Gulf sound?

"The Gulf of Mexico?"

"Do you know another Gulf?"

"Uhhh, no. No, I don't. It sounds great, but you said day date."

"Airplane, darlin'. Airplane.

A little squiggle slithered through her stomach. *Oh, my God.* They were going to the Gulf on his airplane. For lunch!

Chapter Twenty-Nine

IN THE AFTERNOON the next day after New Year's Day, as Betty Lockhart neatly folded her new shorts and tops into her suitcase, she was thinking about her family. Except for Drake, she hadn't heard from a one of them since the Christmas Day fiasco at the Double-Barrel. They hadn't even called to wish her a happy new year. As usual, they probably were mad at her instead of the person they should be mad at, Bill Junior.

She'd had a horrible New Year's Eve, which had included a rubber-chicken dinner with Barron at his country club. Who were they trying to kid, calling that atrocious food fine dining? Dancing to a geriatric band with an accordion had followed the heartburn-generating meal. She had asked Barron to bring her home before the midnight hour. They had hailed the new year over a cup of coffee in her living room. She only hoped the evening wasn't a harbinger of the coming year.

Ever since she had moved away from the Double-Barrel, a new year had put her in a melancholy mood and so far, this year was proving no different. Thirty-five years ago when she had married Bill Junior, she hadn't been able to imagine her future, but she must have believed that by this point in her life, her family would all gather on holidays and everyone would be filled with love and happiness. So much for teenage dreams. Reality had set in early in her marriage.

She hadn't even seen her own parents at Christmas. They had never come to the Double-Barrel for holidays and the past Christmas had been no different. Nowadays, they spent the winter traveling in their RV they bought after they both had retired and sold their home in Drinkwell.

Bill Junior had probably spent New Year's with that Luck woman and most likely had not been bored. He was never bored. Or boring. He made things happen. Damn the bastard anyway. She wanted to hate him, but she couldn't hate the father of her three smart, wonderful children. Not only could she not hate him, she had a hard time staying mad at him, even when she needed that anger to keep her heart from being ripped from her chest.

She returned her attention to her packing, trying to shut him and her kids out of her mind. She had a lot to do. She and Barron were scheduled to fly to Florida on Saturday, where they would board a cruise liner for the Caribbean, then Cancun and points south. She could hardly wait. A luxury ocean cruise was one of her greatest fantasies.

Of course she could have already gone on a cruise if she had wanted to. She certainly had the money available to her. All she had to do was call the Double Barrel's accountant and someone would arrange the whole thing for her. But what fun would doing alone be? Dozens of times she had wished Bill Junior would consent to share the experience with her.

Or perhaps Kathryn. But her daughter was so wrapped up in horses and cowboys, she would be bored to tears on a boat in the middle of the ocean. Betty had never nagged her daughter about it because she was empathetic. She knew more about boredom than most people. She spent a great deal of her time in that state.

The warble of the phone took her from her task and her woolgathering. Checking Caller ID, she saw a number she didn't recognize, but picked up anyway. She was expecting several phone calls.

"Hi, Betty. How are you?"

Betty recognized the voice at once. Donna Schoonover. She didn't know Donna well, had only seen her a few times here and there when she had been with Drake and had talked to her on the phone a few times. As far as Betty knew, Drake was the only mutual interest she and Donna shared. "Why, I'm just fine, Donna. How are you?"

"Wonderful. How were your holidays?"

"Wonderful," Betty lied. "How were yours?"

"Fantastic. Mama and Daddy and I had a fabulous Christmas. Just the three of us. Mama gave the help the weekend off and we flew up to Aspen. It was marvelous. Aspen is so amazing. It's gorgeous this time of year."

Betty closed her eyes and rubbed her forehead with two fingers. Sometimes this young woman's hyperbole made Betty's ears want to ache. She had never heard anyone Donna's age use words like she used. All of that European education she'd had, no doubt. "Oh, I'm so glad you had a good time."

"Listen, I'm hearing some juicy talk about your son. I confess I called to pick your brain. I hope you don't mind." A titter came across the line.

Betty's interest piqued. "About Drake? What kind of talk?"

"His new girlfriend. No one knows who she is or where she came from. People are wondering if she landed from Mars." Donna laughed.

Drake hadn't mentioned a word about a new female in his life. "Well, my goodness. I don't know who she is. Who told you?"

"Oh, a little bird." Donna tittered as if she had just said something cute and funny instead of throwing out an age-old cliché. "Actually, a son of one of Daddy's friends went hunting with Drake at Stone Mountain Lodge before Christmas. He said Drake was super-bummed out because some woman he was really interested in stood him up. And he got terribly drunk."

Betty's hand tightened on the receiver. She could count on her fingers the number of times in recent years she had seen her serious-minded son drunk. In that regard, none of her children were like their father, thank God. "Drake got drunk?"

"And that's not all. Mitzi saw him downtown yesterday with a redhead—I presume it was the same woman—and they were practically molded together, if you know what I mean. Mitzi said her hair looked absolutely awful, like it had been combed with an eggbeater." Donna laughed raucously. "Mitzi is so funny."

No wonder he had cut the conversation short yesterday when she had called him to wish him a happy new year. His girlfriend must have been with him. "Well, my goodness," she repeated, mystified.

"You really don't know about her?"

"Well, no. But then I've been busy. I'm getting ready to go on a cruise with Barron."

"Oh, that's just marvelous," Donna exclaimed. "You'll have the most amazing time you've ever had. I just know it. It's too bad you don't know anything about Drake's new friend. I was relying on you."

Her tone of voice changed to a whine. "You know, I miss him so much. He's such a sweet guy and he treated me just wonderful. I know he didn't like me drinking so much gin. I've been talking to Mama's therapist and I've cut waaay back. I've quit smoking, too."

"That's good," Betty said absently, distressed that Drake hadn't confided in her. There had been a time when he had talked to her privately about his friends and activities.

"I know I could put things back together with him," Donna was saying, "if he'd just give me a chance. But he doesn't even return my phone calls.

"Oh, my. It isn't like Drake to be rude."

"If you have any tips how to get his attention, I'd love to hear them. Or if you could say something…"

Betty couldn't believe her ears. Donna Stafford-Schoonover had to beg few people for attention. As for tips? Half the time Betty didn't know how to get along with Drake herself. "What kind of tips?"

"The name of his new friend, hmm?"

"How can knowing her name help you revive your relationship with my son?"

"If I knew her name, I could find out who she really is. What my competition is, you know? I have all kinds of resources. For all we know, she could be a terrible gold digger. And I know you don't want that for poor Drake."

"No, I don't. I suppose I could ask."

"Would you? That would be fabulous. Well, you have my number. Just let me know what you find out. You can call me any time."

"Of course," Betty said.

"We should do lunch. When you get back from your cruise. You can tell me all about what an amazing time you had."

"Yes, let's do," Betty said.

They disconnected and Betty stood there a few seconds, wondering what Drake was up to. She thought a few more seconds about how to open a dialogue with him. Yesterday, she had tried to tell him about her upcoming cruise, but he had practically hung up on her. Well, she could tell him today. Just because the rest of the world considered today a holiday didn't mean he did. She speed-dialed his cell.

He came on the line with a cheery "Hey, Mom."

Maybe he was glad to hear from her. "Listen, Son, in case any of you are interested in my whereabouts the next couple of weeks, I want to let you know—"

"C'mon, Mom. Don't play the pity card on me. You know we're all interested in where you are and what you're doing."

"I want to let you know Barron and I will be leaving on our cruise the end of the week."

Silence. "Well that's something you've been wanting to do," he said at last. "What day are you leaving?"

"On the eighth. I also want to ask you something. One of my friends told me she saw you downtown yesterday with a woman. She said the two of you were cuddled up like lovebirds. Do you have a new woman in your life?"

More silence.

"Drake?"

"So that's what this call is really about?"

Damn. How could he read her mind over the phone? "Of course not. I just wanted—"

"I don't know who saw me, Mom, but what I'm doing or who's with me is nobody's business."

"But surely you can tell your mother what's going on."

"How's this? If there's something to tell, you'll be the first to know."

"Well, my stars, Drake. You're being so secretive. You won't even tell me her name?"

"I don't know if she'd appreciate that. She might like her privacy."

Tears rushed to Betty's eyes, but she sniffed them back. "Oh. I see. Well, whatever. I guess that's a good thing." She sniffed again. "Listen, since I'm leaving town, can we have lunch this week?"

"Let me check."

She waited, knew he was scrolling through his BlackBerry. Drake's whole life was programmed into that damn machine. These days, he hardly did anything spontaneously, even lunch with his mother. Why did so many women put up with it?

He soon came back on the line. "How about tomorrow?"

"Good. Where shall we eat?"

"Rusty's Grill okay?"

Betty frowned. She hated trying to have a conversation in noisy bistros. Drake knew that. Had he chosen that café for just that reason? "I'd rather go somewhere a little quieter."

"Okay, there's Reata. One o'clock?"

"Good. I'll see you there at one."

They disconnected, with Betty more curious than ever. Why in the world would he hide the identity of a new woman in his life? He had never done that before. Well, she might have struck out with this phone call, but she could ask him more questions at lunch.

Chapter Thirty

THE NEXT MORNING, Betty dressed in casual navy slacks and a light blue sweater and drove downtown to Reata, arriving before one o'clock. She had already been served coffee when her punctual son strode purposefully toward her table, speaking to several diners along the way. Everywhere he went, he knew people and they knew him.

He walked up beside her, leaned down and kissed her cheek, then took a seat opposite her. She could tell before he said a word that he was in a good mood. A waiter appeared immediately with both water and coffee carafes.

"You certainly look chipper," she said to her son.

"I am," he replied, waiting for the waiter to fill his glass and his cup. "Starting the new year off right. Got projects going, deals cooking."

"And a new girlfriend?"

"Mom, this lunch isn't going to be about that, is it?"

Betty retreated. "No, no. I just wanted to see you before I leave. In case our boat sinks, you know?" She gave a silly laugh.

"C'mon, Mom—"

"It's been known to happen."

Just then, a waitress came and took their orders. Drake ordered the house hamburger for which Reata was famous. Betty ordered soup. After the waitress hurried away, he asked, "How long did you say you'll be gone?"

"Ten days. We'll make a stop in Costa Rica. Barron owns property there. He's even thought of moving there."

"Hm," Drake said, sipping his coffee. "Ran out of people to screw over up here, huh?"

"Now, Drake—"

"I'm kidding, Mom. I'm kidding. Who you spend your time with is none of my business." He set down his cup and gave her a direct look. "Just as who I spend my time with is none of yours."

Betty exhaled a sigh. "There you go being tacky again. Why won't you tell me about your new girlfriend? Surely you can tell me her name. Am I going to get to meet her?"

"I don't know. If it comes around to that, I'll leave that kind of stuff up to her."

Her mother's instinct went on alert. "My Lord, Drake. You sound serious."

"I might be. I just don't know yet."

Surprised, she sat back in her chair. He hadn't said he might be serious about someone since his engagement to Tammy. "Is she from Fort Worth?"

Sipping his coffee, he shook his head. "Camden."

For a reason Betty couldn't explain, even to herself, the image of the red-haired woman on the billboard outside of Camden charged into her memory and collided head-on with the description Donna had given her on the phone. Drake had dated heiresses, actresses, doctors and lawyers and God knew what other women who had reached stratospheres of success. He had never dated a... *a real estate salesman.*

Why, this woman was in the same category as a used car salesman. Betty wanted more for Drake than a money-grabbing bimbo like Pic had married. *Oh, dear Lord.* This was a serious situation.

"Camden," she said, dumbfounded.

"Yep. She's been right under my nose all this time. And I'm not saying any more about it."

Betty had enough sense not to push further. She wanted this meeting to be cordial, without her nagging and irritating him.

She reached home mid-afternoon, went straight to the bedroom she used for a study and dug out the regional phone book she kept in case she wanted someone's number in Drinkwell or the dozen other small towns around it. Prowling through the yellow pages, she found an ad and the name she was looking for: Piper Real Estate Company, Shannon Piper, broker and owner. She couldn't explain why, but she believed she now knew her son's new girlfriend's name.

She picked up the phone and scrolled through its log for Donna Schoonover's number. But before she found it, she stopped. Donna was no friend to her. In fact, Betty had seen no evidence that Donna was a friend to anyone. She only gave Betty Lockhart the time of day because she wanted to know about Drake.

Besides that, she wasn't sure Shannon Piper was the right person. What if she gave that name to Donna, then she turned out to someone who had never heard of Drake Lockhart? Although Betty couldn't imagine who had never heard of her son. He was almost famous. Nevertheless, how embarrassing might a mistaken identity be?

And she had to consider that Drake would be murderously angry if he knew his mother had reported on him to one of his former women.

She wouldn't call Donna right this minute, she decided. She needed to think about it more, needed to ponder if she wanted to risk her son's ire. Still, she did want to know if who he was seeing really was that real estate person from Camden.

Aside from debating all of that in her head, she was intrigued by the idea that Donna had ways of learning about skeletons in someone's closet. Betty wished for the same connections. Enough money could buy anything. She had seen that happen often enough. Good Lord, Bill Junior's father had bought every politician and public servant in Treadway County and a few in the Texas legislature. At one point in their past lives, Betty had believed he owned the governor.

Well, it would wait, she finally decided. Donna wasn't expecting to hear from her until after she returned from the cruise.

Wednesday morning came. Shannon had relented and allowed Drake to send a car for her. When a black Lincoln Town Car stopped in front of Grammy Evelyn's house, before the black-suited driver reached the front door, Shannon dashed outside and met him on the sidewalk. She climbed into the spacious backseat and a buttery leather interior with trim that looked like polished wood. She felt like a queen. At the same time, she had never felt so out of place. She would have to somehow explain the limo to her grandmother.

She found Drake waiting for her. He drove them in his pickup to a private Fort Worth airport. There, they boarded a private jet, the same one she had seen in the photograph of him in the *Texas Monthly* spread. It was outfitted with padded leather captain's chairs the color of a latte, two sofas that made into beds, a wet bar and a bedroom.

"Wow," Shannon said. "This looks better than living rooms I've seen."

"And you've seen a lot of them, right?" He guided her to a seat and helped her fasten her seat belt, then sank to a seat beside her.

The engines came to life and they began to taxi. That tilt in her stomach that flying always gave her struck her with force. Drake picked up her hand and interlocked their fingers. "Nervous?"

"I've never flown on a plane like this."

"Only way to travel. Too much hassle and wasted time with the airlines and airports."

They stopped for a few seconds on the taxiway, then roared up the runway and thundered off to Galveston, where they dined on premium raw oysters in a tiny bistro on the ocean and lingered long after the meal.

"This is wonderful," Shannon told him. "I've lived in Texas my whole life and never been to Galveston. Really, I've hardly been anywhere in Texas. Although I did go to Austin to take the real estate exams."

"Never been to San Antonio?" Drake asked.

"Nope.

"Then you've never seen the Alamo. My God, every Texan should see the Alamo."

Soon, they flew back to Fort Worth, giving her the time to get home early enough to watch TV with Grammy Evelyn. They hadn't had sex. Hadn't even talked about it.

As they walked to the parking garage, he invited her for a three-day jaunt to South Texas.

"That's more than a day date," she said.

"I know. I'll hire a babysitter for your grandmother."

"I don't want you to do that. I'll figure it out."

She had to worry about more than caring for her grandmother; she had to *explain* to her. The elfin woman was old, not dumb. She would know she and Drake would be sleeping together. In all of the time Shannon had lived in her grandmother's house, she had never let her become aware that she had done anything like that. Not even when she had been seeing Justin Turnbow. Out of respect, she had kept her liaisons with men clandestine and short.

She believed Grammy Evelyn loved her so much she would support her no matter what, but she was a little old lady and Shannon didn't want her to be the target of gossip and snide remarks. Her own granddaughter, Colleen, might be the worst offender.

She rode home with dread, hoping that after she confessed her intentions, Grammy Evelyn wouldn't feel compelled to lecture her on the birds and the bees.

When she arrived, her grandmother had cooked a dish she called "slumgullion," which meant she had cleaned out the refrigerator and thrown all the leftovers into one pot. While they sat at the round table and ate, Shannon said, "Grammy, what would you think if I went on a trip with a guy?"

Grammy Evelyn smiled, a twinkle in her eye. "I think you should have a social life. Time doesn't run backward, you know. Who are you going with?"

"Drake Lockhart," she said, without looking up from her plate. "He's asked me to go to South Texas with him for a few days."

She waited for her grandmother to gasp, but she only said, "Lockhart's an unusual name. He wouldn't be from the Treadway County Lockharts, would he?"

"Uh-huh," Shannon said, turning her eyes to the plump roll she was buttering.

"Is that who sent that fancy car to pick you up?"

Shannon still didn't look up. "Uh-huh."

"Oh, my dear," her grandmother said. Shannon did look up then, and saw Grammy Evelyn's eyes huge and round behind her glasses lenses. "The Lockharts are very influential people. Wherever did you meet one of them?"

Grammy Evelyn had said "one of them" as if she were speaking of an alien species. "In Fort Worth at the Realtors' ball."

"Is it one of Bill Junior's children you're seeing?"

"Uh, I believe so."

"Which one?"

"His name's Drake."

"The oldest one. Oh, my dear," Grammy Evelyn said again, covering her thin lips with her tiny fingers.

"You don't have to worry, Grammy. I'm going to ask either Christa or Colleen to come by and visit you and make sure you have everything you need."

"Oh, I wasn't worried about myself, dear. It's you I'm thinking of. You must be careful. Those Lockharts, they're takers. I'm sure they're all brought up to be that way. They think the world belongs to them."

"In Texas, I guess a good part of it does."

Subconsciously, Shannon had already filed Drake in the "taker" category, though she didn't know him that well. But how could he not be a taker when the world was his oyster?

"I'll be careful, Grammy. Listen, if you have to go to the grocery store or the drug store or anywhere else, just let Christa know. I've already told her you get your hair done on Saturday. She'll pick you up and drive you to the beauty shop. And I'm sure Colleen and Gavin will be happy to take you to church."

"Christa's such a nice girl. We had the best time when you went up to Fort Worth on New Year's. We baked those cookies. She and Arthur got along very well. She brought him a cute little feather on a string. She knows a lot about cats."

Shannon laughed. "Christa knows a lot about everything, Grammy."

"Have you told Colleen where you're going? And with who?"

Shannon's shoulders sagged. "No, Grammy, I haven't. She'd...she'd judge me. And you know Gavin. He might try to make hay out of me knowing Drake Lockhart. I know we can't keep it a secret that I'm going somewhere, but we don't have to tell who I'm going with."

Grammy Evelyn reached across the table and patted her arm. "That part will be another one of our little secrets. Mine and yours and Christa's."

Shannon felt a mild relief. She didn't want cold water thrown on her good mood. She left her chair, walked over and pressed her cheek against her grandmother's. "Thanks, Grammy. You're the best grandma I ever had."

Grammy Evelyn gave a little-old-lady chuckle. "I believe I'm the only grandma you've ever had."

Indeed. Shannon's mother's mother had been out of the picture since Shannon was a child and she didn't even know why. "I believe you're right, Grammy." They both laughed.

"You just be careful," Grammy Evelyn said again. "Don't let him mistreat you just because he's a Lockhart."

The Town Car picked her up again on Thursday afternoon and delivered her to Lockhart Tower. She and Drake piled into his Aston Martin and roared off to San Antonio, where they slept in an historic old hotel near the Alamo.

The next morning, along with hundreds of other tourists, they inched through the most famous historical monument in Texas. Drake had visited it several times. At every exhibit, he stopped and expounded on the display and the related event. Until then, she hadn't known he liked history and knew a lot about it.

He seemed more relaxed than she had known him to be up to now. She loved every minute of seeing him as she suspected few people did. But as he told her historical facts and stories, that feeling of inadequacy flickered anew within her, reminding her that he was so much better educated than she was and had always lived in a different world.

After the Alamo tour, they browsed in the gift shop where she bought a collector's spoon for Grammy Evelyn's collection. Then they moved on to the Mexican market where she bought trinkets and jewelry for her friends. Drake showed no interest in picking up souvenirs and she wondered about his friends. If he had any, she had seen no sign of them and heard little about them.

They ambled along the Riverwalk, ate delicious Mexican food. When a strolling Mariachi band stopped and played a romantic Mexican ballad at their table, Drake reached across and covered her hand with his.

He had premium tickets to a music concert in Austin conducted by Texas country musicians. Tomorrow they would drive to Austin.

Late Friday afternoon, Betty Lockhart was scurrying around like a mad woman. She and Barron were leaving at noon tomorrow. She still had a million things to do. She was in Macy's at the cosmetic counter when her cell phone played a George Strait tune. She dug it out of her purse and keyed in to the call.

"Hi, Betty, remember me?" a female voice said.

Betty had heard that voice. Her brow tightened as she scrolled through her memory, but came up blank. "Um, no I don't think I do."

"It's Tammy."

"Tammy?"

"Tammy McMillan." The voice laughed. "Or I should say it's Tammy Harper now."

Betty could have been blown over by a feather. To unexpectedly hear from Donna Schoonover was one thing, but to hear from Drake's former fiancé of fifteen years ago was a monumental shock. "Oh, my God. Tammy. How are you?"

"Fine. I'm living in Fort Worth now and I heard you're living here, too."

"Well, my goodness. How did you find me?"

"I joined the Riverside golf club and I saw your name on the roster. I talked to someone who knows you and she gave me your cell number. It's really a small world."

"It certainly is. I can't believe you're here now. The last I heard, you had moved to Arizona." Betty deliberately omitted a comment about Tammy's husband.

"That's one of those long stories. I thought we might get together for lunch. Or dinner or something. We might even go for a golf game someday when the weather's pretty."

"I'd love that, darling."

Old times bombarded Betty. With the McMillans owning the ranch adjoining the Double-Barrel, Betty had known them most of her life. Once, the McMillans and the Lockharts had been good friends. For six years, they had anticipated they would join families until Tammy broke her engagement to Drake and married a pro golfer from Arizona. Betty had never known the whole truth of the breakup. To this day, Drake refused to discuss it.

"Where are you folks these days?" Betty asked.

"Still in Sedona. Still playing golf." Tammy laughed again.

Tammy's father had always been as much a Texas redneck as Bill Junior. Betty couldn't imagine him playing golf any more than she could Bill Junior. She distinctly remembered that the McMillans had moved to Arizona to be near their only daughter and her children. "My, my. And you're here now."

Tammy laughed again. "I know, right? Ironic, isn't it?"

"Ma'am, did you want to purchase this mascara?" the cosmetic clerk who had been helping Betty asked.

"Oh, excuse me, darling," she said to the clerk. "An unexpected call from an old friend." She handed over her credit card and returned to her conversation with Tammy. "I'm in Macy's, so I can't really talk. I'm leaving town tomorrow, but I'd love to visit with you for hours. Are you busy this evening?"

"Not really."

"Come to my house then. I'll cook dinner. I haven't cooked in weeks. But I warn you, it'll be something simple."

"Sounds good to me. Give me your address."

Soon Betty was speeding toward home, her thoughts churning. Tammy McMillan. *My God. What are the odds?*

After Tammy and Drake's breakup, the friendship between the McMillans and the Lockharts became too awkward to continue. Then, not long after Tammy moved to Arizona, the McMillans leased out their ranch and followed her.

Still, someday Tammy would inherit the MCM Ranch, lock, stock and barrel, and its dozens of producing gas wells. The MCM wasn't as big a spread as the Double-Barrel, but it was big enough and rich enough to make Tammy a wealthy woman.

When Drake and Tammy were engaged, Betty had thought them a perfect match—both beautiful people long-acquainted, both from old Texas families, both with small-town upbringing and deep roots in the cattle ranching business. Betty had expected them to spawn beautiful babies who would fill her hours and life with joy.

As she pulled into her garage and parked, she was so glad she hadn't called Donna Schoonover back. If she was going to broker a make-up date between Drake and any woman, that woman should be Tammy Mc-Millan.

Chapter Thirty-One

FOR SHANNON, THE latest chapter in the fairy tale ended on Sunday. The black Town Car appeared at Lockhart Tower to pick her up and take her back to Camden. She climbed into the backseat, closed her eyes and tried to nap.

But she couldn't sleep. Keeping her in a state of semi-consciousness was the fact that precisely what she feared would happen had happened. For four days, she had left the real estate office totally in Terry's care, hadn't even discussed it, had scarcely thought about it. She had even shoved the deal on her five-acre corner to the back of her mind. Just sex had flown out the window and all she could do was dwell on Drake's every word and action.

Her cranky alter ego beat a drum in the back of her mind that said this could not end well for Shannon Piper. Somehow, she had to get control of her emotions.

The first thing she would do to get herself back on track toward good sense would be to decline his sending a car for her. He was trying to do something good for her, but she felt like a "kept woman." She didn't like having it pull up in front of Grammy Evelyn's house. Everyone on the Camden square could see it and see her get into it and out of it. No doubt they were already talking.

After the Town Car disappeared from his sight, Drake lingered a few minutes in the parking garage, dreading going upstairs to his empty condo. Gloom weighted his shoulders like a heavy cape. He hadn't wanted Shannon to leave. And that was crazy. He had to get back to work and so did she. He had a planned trip to Honolulu coming up next weekend to watch a couple of his favorite golfers play in the Sony Open. Consequently, he had two weeks' worth of work to do in a few days.

Upstairs, unmotivated to work, he dragged a bottle of Perrier out of the fridge and sauntered over to the window wall. The weather was nice today, but another cold front was expected tomorrow.

The weather had been great while he and Shannon were in San Antonio and Austin, too. He couldn't believe she was over thirty years old and had never seen the Alamo. Or strolled the Riverwalk. He had done those things many times as a younger man. After Tammy had dumped him, he had spent many a weekend partying in the bars on the Riverwalk.

These days he hardly ever frequented tourist attractions, but he was happy he had chosen to entertain Shannon in that way. A sense of pure joy had filled him at her fascination with the Alamo and its rich history. She had loved the Mariachi band that played in one of the Mexican cafes on the Riverwalk. And she had loved the Robert Earle Keen concert, who was, by anybody's standards, a Texas music legend.

Now Drake knew what it was about Shannon that appealed to him. The way he saw her was exactly who she was. No phoniness, no airs, no ulterior motives. She was just Shannon. Beautiful, smart, fun, a quick wit laced with a touch of cynicism and a fascination for everything around her. He liked her more every time he saw her, liked being with her, liked making her happy. Making love with her took him to a depth of passion he had rarely known and drenched him with unadulterated bliss.

Whoa! When had just sex turned into making love?

When Shannon arrived at home, her grandmother was absorbed in one of her TV shows, her fingers busy crocheting a baby afghan. Shannon was glad because she was exhausted. After a brief chat, she went to her room and fell into bed.

Monday morning, she awoke with cramps. She didn't dare complain, lest the gods of retribution decided she deserved a comeuppance, such as a leaky condom or a miscalculation.

Though still worn out, she pushed herself out of bed. She was eager to get to her office and learn what had gone on in her short absence. Maybe one of her team had written a deal that needed her review and signature.

Maybe the owner of the five-acre parcel had made a decision.

She dressed and made her entrance into the kitchen. Her grandmother had oatmeal and hot tea waiting for her. An Asian friend of Grammy Evelyn's brought her oolong tea from an Asian market in the Metroplex and Shannon loved it.

Before leaving town on Thursday, she had again called on Christa and her two sons to look in on Grammy Evelyn every day, but she suspected that yesterday, Grammy had hitched a ride to church with

Colleen and Gavin. "How was church?" she asked as she scooped hot oatmeal into a bowl.

"Oh, I thought we'd never get away after the service. Gavin had to shake hands and visit with everyone he saw. He's decided to go ahead and announce for the legislature from this district. He's going to be a Democrat."

"Wow. How'd he come to that decision?" Shannon carried her oatmeal and tea to the table.

Her grandmother followed her and sat down opposite her. "He says Democrats outnumber Republicans two to one in this county. So the odds are better that he can win if he's a Democrat."

Shannon sipped the soothing tea. Nothing was better for her cramps than hot tea. She had no comment on her brother-in-law's political career.

"Colleen said a popular judge from Waco is running against him in the primary," her grandmother said. "I doubt Gavin will have much of a chance at winning. My Lord, he doesn't stand for anything."

Ain't that the truth, Shannon thought. She doubted he could win a race for dogcatcher, but she wouldn't trouble her grandmother with a catty remark. "Grammy, you didn't mention who I was with, did you?"

The little old lady's eyes twinkled behind her thick glasses lens. "Lands, no, dear. That's our little secret, remember? I just hope you had a wonderful time."

"We went to the Alamo."

"The Alamo?" The disappointment in Grammy Evelyn's tone couldn't be mistaken. "Oh, my. I thought you'd do something exciting."

Shannon covered her mouth with her napkin and laughed. "It was plenty exciting, Grammy. When I've got more time, I'll tell you about it."

Shannon found her office calm. Several showings had taken place in her absence, but no new business had developed. Disappointing. Chelsea reported no call had come from the Dallas broker either. Disappointing and annoying. So annoying, in fact, that Shannon called him, but got only his voice mail.

She went to lunch with her team. All three of them quizzed her about her new boyfriend. She gave them tidbits of information, but not a name. She swore them to secrecy and promised them she would reveal all in the near future.

All day, she expected to hear from Drake, but no call came. Anxiety began to build. She vacillated about calling him. With great effort, she did not. Wasn't a woman supposed to wait for the man to take the lead? *He's a busy guy, doing big deals*, she told herself. She would just have to learn to live with that. After all, they were only sex partners at his or her convenience.

But he could still call, if for no other reason, just to say hello, that pesky alter ego insisted.

Shannon began to slide back into a familiar pattern of doubt and insecurity where she had often found herself in dealing with men.

When he hadn't called by bedtime, she switched off her cell and went to bed. This was good that he hadn't called. If they were going to continue with this arrangement, they had to return to just sex. Or maybe they weren't going to continue at all.

She awoke on Wednesday, lecturing herself about being a slave to the phone and a spoiled millionaire's call. *To hell with him. If he can't call, then just to hell with him.*

Though the weather had turned back to being cold and windy, she put on her jacket and running shoes and did two miles before going to work. The exercise ended with her legs trembling and her lungs bellowing. If she didn't return to her regimen of running or walking at least three days a week, she would get completely out of shape. She hadn't run for the whole month of December, which proved her point about Drake Lockhart. Just knowing him was a distraction that took too much of her time and attention.

Midmorning, a call from *Unknown Number* came on her cell phone. An adrenaline zing went straight to her midsection. When she keyed into the call, the devil didn't even say his name, as if he expected her to know who was calling. "Can you take a quick trip next weekend?" he asked.

"Maybe," she answered guardedly. "I'd have to check my schedule," she quickly added, not wanting to appear too eager.

"Can you check it now? My assistant is making arrangements today for the Sony Open finals. And I'd like you to go with me."

Shannon had no schedule to check. "I guess I'm dense. I don't know what that is."

"Golf. It's a golf tournament. You like golf, don't you?"

Ah. Golf. Golf was big in Texas. Tournaments were played all over the state. The mid-January weather seemed chilly for it, but south of the Metroplex, temperatures were warmer. Perhaps she could manage another day trip to South Texas. She stalled a few seconds for effect, then said, "I could manage it, but I should tell you I don't know much about golf."

"You'll enjoy it. I'll see to it. We'll fly over there tomorrow and come back on Monday."

Quick calculation. *Five days?* Her brain homed in on *over there.* "Um, where is it?"

"Honolulu."

Her mind went blank for a full fifteen seconds. *Hawaii? Oh, My. God. Hawaii.* She had never been to Hawaii, hadn't expected to ever go. She had never been out of Texas except for a few trips to casinos in Oklahoma. Five days in Hawaii.

"Shannon?"

His voice brought her back to the moment. "I'll have to work on it," she said in a rush, "but yeah, I could go."

Dummy, that pesky alter ego snapped. *Can't you tell him no for a change?*

Not saying no to a trip to Hawaii, she told her nemesis.

"This is a good time to go," he said casually, as if he hadn't just left her speechless. "The weather's iffy here, but it's good over there. I can send a car for you this evening and we'll leave early tomorrow morning."

"Oh, that's okay. I'd rather drive my own car."

Some tough girl you are. That nagging alter ego refused to give up.

"Whatever you want to do," he said. "You know what to bring, don't you?"

"Is there something special I should know about?"

"This trip is strictly for relaxation. I'm not expecting anything we'd have to dress for."

"Right. Got it."

"I'll see you this evening. Try to be here by five-thirty or six. I'll have supper ordered."

"Sure. Fine. Got it."

He disconnected, leaving her mind in a blank space. No sweet talk, no small talk, not even a hello. Just instructions. Was this how "making this work" was going to be?

See? her alter ego said. *You've become his mistress, fated to wait at his beck and call. Even at the last minute.*

But before she could argue with herself about that, she thought about the five acres. *Oh, hell.* She had to get that deal wrapped up before the weekend so it wouldn't be on her mind while she was with Drake.

While she was with *the* Drake Lockhart!...In Hawaii!

She picked up the receiver and called Emmet Hunt, got his voice mail. All she could do was leave a message.

Now she faced a new dilemma. Six days and five nights away from home. Asking Christa to look after Grammy Evelyn was expecting too much of even as good a friend as Christa was. Shannon would have to call Colleen and tell her she was going to Hawaii.

"Who are you going with?" her sister asked.

"A friend," Shannon answered.

"The same man you went off with before?"

Shannon closed her eyes and repressed a sigh. "Does it matter?"

"It certainly does. We might need to get in touch with you for some reason. And we all need to get our stories straight."

Shannon could not let her sister's spitefulness derail her. All that was important was that Colleen keep tabs on their grandmother. After

Colleen agreed to help, Shannon spent the rest of the day preparing for the trip. She hurriedly brought her business up to speed so it could be handled easily by Chelsea or her sales team in her absence.

While getting her hair trimmed in Great Clips, she checked her messages. Nothing from the Dallas broker about the five acres.

She and Christa hit Walmart, which was a mistake because Christa talked her into spending money she couldn't afford. She bought new flip-flops and a sexy lace bathing suit cover-up, as well as a cute hobo-style beach bag adorned with fish and ocean waves.

Shopping took her mind off waiting for a call back about her latest offer on the five acres.

Late in the afternoon, she gave up on hearing from Emmet Hunt. She sent a text message to Drake letting him know she was on her way.

He met her in the Lockhart Tower lobby. Just like the last time, they made out all the way up to the twenty-eighth floor, filling the elevator cab with steamy desire. By the time they reached *28C*, they were fondling intimate places and tearing off clothing and they went to bed. Later, they unpacked the meal that had been delivered before her arrival. As her plate turned in the microwave, she wondered how many people re-heated filet mignon in the microwave.

The next morning, they boarded the Lockhart plane again and the jet zoomed into the western sky. Drake reached across the narrow aisle and held her hand. Once they smoothed out, her stomach began to settle. "Do you often just pack up and fly off somewhere on the spur of the moment like this?" she asked him.

"I rarely do anything on the spur of the moment," he answered. "I've got a lot of deadlines. Being that impulsive could cost me a helluva lot of money."

One side of her mouth quirked up. "I have to say, cowboy, that since I've known you, most of what I've seen you do is impulsive."

He laughed. "You cause me to behave in an atypical way."

"Wow, don't I feel special," she said, deadpan.

"Truthfully, I'm not usually an impulsive person. We haven't spent enough time together for you to get to know the real me."

"I want to know the real you," she said sincerely. "I wish I could know everything about you."

He gave her a mischievous grin. "You might not like the real me. A lot of people don't. They say I'm a bastard, a hard-ass. Among other things."

"I can see that in you," she teased. "Try me. Tell me something about the real you."

"I'll trade you fact for fact. You tell me something about you and I'll tell you something about me."

"You go first."

"Okay, see what you think of this. The real me is a dull turd. Stodgy and conservative. I see life in black and white, not much gray. I'm stubborn and set in my ways. My work and my BlackBerry, and sometimes my family obligations, rule my life. If I'm working a deal that calls for twenty-four seven, that's what I give it. If something related to the ranch goes to hell and needs my attention, that's where I put my focus. If I have to miss a party, it doesn't break my heart. When I work, I work hard."

"I don't see any of that as bad. Do you, really? But you can't work all the time."

"I relax. That's why we're going to Hawaii. So I can get away from everything. And I do mean everything. I don't even have my BlackBerry with me. And by the way, this trip isn't an impulse. It was planned. I blocked out the time several months ago."

"Ah. Then if the trip itself isn't an impulse, *I* must be an impulse. The woman I saw you with at the TCCRA party was who was *planned* to go with you."

He shook his head. "Nope. Until I met you, I had planned to make this trip alone and hang out with friends." He paused. "And for the record, I haven't seen her since that night."

Could that be true? Shannon's heartbeat stumbled. She smiled. "No kidding?"

Smiling back at her, he picked up her hand. "This trip is something I expect to enjoy. I wanted to share it with somebody I ca—I like. Somebody who doesn't put any pressure on me."

"In other words, I'm a pushover and I follow you around like a puppy."

"I don't mean to imply that. You've got priorities straight and you understand a little about my business."

She did understand that being a Realtor, if one were dedicated to it, was sort of like being an obstetrician. Your agenda was often not your own. And from her own experience in the business, she knew about sudden changes in plans and the pressure of waiting out a deal. "You can't kid me, cowboy," she said, laughing. "You like the hot sex. You're not exactly stodgy and conservative in bed, you know."

"Neither are you. We're a good match that way. It's all a part of the whole."

With that, he leaned his seat back and said, "Let's take a nap. We didn't get much sleep last night."

True. In fact, she was a little sore from making love all night. She drew a deep breath, leaned her own seat back and closed her eyes, proud of herself for diverting the conversation and not revealing even one piece of information about herself. She, too, soon dropped off.

When they awoke, a steward appeared and served them a cocktail. Her frugal mind tried to tally the cost of a trip to Hawaii in a private plane that included a pilot, a co-pilot and a steward.

A meal of poached wild-caught salmon and roasted asparagus followed the cocktail. "I hope you like salmon," Drake said. "I forgot to ask you when I called you."

"It's delicious," she said. And she meant it.

Soon after that, she was deplaning in a tropical paradise, hanging on to the arm of *Texas Monthly's* most eligible bachelor. *Look at me, World! Shannon Piper's in fairyland again!*

Drake had rented a fully-furnished condo on a private inlet. To say it was luxurious was an understatement. The night was the same as the night before had been in his condo back in Texas—hours of passionate, emotional sex.

They spent the next day in a tropical paradise walking and watching the world's best golfers compete for a fat prize at a magnificent golf course so manicured it looked artificial.

Drake dutifully explained the game to her as they followed the players. He offered to teach her to play or arrange a round of lessons from a pro. She declined the lessons, but told him someday she would let him teach her.

That evening, they dined in a restaurant with a superb location on a beach. He introduced her to at least a dozen of the golfers with whom he was personally acquainted. He had even played with some of them in various pro-am tournaments around the country. He made a golf date with one of them at some country club for the next time he was in Dallas.

As they returned to their hideaway, her alter ego piped up. *Girl, you are definitely not in Kansas anymore.*

Chapter Thirty-Two

SATURDAY WAS A repeat of Friday. A long day of walking, drinks and dinner with Drake's friends in a beach restaurant. Smart and interesting conversation about everything from sports to investments to politics. One golfer made a date with Drake to discuss investing in some building Drake was refurbishing in Dallas. Shannon was content to sit and listen and learn, but Drake constantly drew her into the conversation and asked for her opinions. He held her hand in her lap under the tablecloth for the entire evening.

Back in the condo, after they had taken each other to soaring ecstasy in the king-size bed, they lolled in the jet tub overlooking the ocean, her neck propped against a bath pillow on the tub's edge, her nostrils filled with lavender fragrance she had dumped into the roiling water.

He lay between her legs. His back rested against her torso, his head against her breasts, his body holding her legs apart and her sex open. The warm moving water gently pummeled, soothed and stimulated at the same time. After two days and nights of copious delicious sex, her clitoris had become a ravenous little fanatic, poised and wanting and waiting for more. Did Drake know he had done this to her?

Hmm.I could come like this. Her breathing grew shallow.

"So what do you think?" he asked. "Are we getting closer to your not being afraid of me?"

"What?" Frowning, she brought her mind back from its reverie, sat up and slid her hands down his chest. "What do you mean? I'm not afraid of you."

"Maybe I should've said trust instead of fear."

"Good grief, I've done things with you I've never done with anyone." She brought her feet up and hooked her legs around his waist, caressed his chest, bent her head and placed her lips near his ear. "Like last night," she whispered. "With that ice. Do you think I'd do that with someone I didn't trust?"

Chuckling, he laid his hands on top of hers. "Seriously, trust is the issue hanging between us. I get that. I've had some problems in that area myself, so I'm trying to convince you that you can trust me."

"You have trust issues?"

He hesitated long enough for her to think he wouldn't answer. Then she sensed he might be having difficulty with what to say. She brushed his neck with her lips. "You can tell me," she said softly. "We're thousands of miles from home. I've got big ears, broad shoulders and tight lips. Anyone who knows me will say so."

Finally, he said, "I was engaged once. A long time ago.…Not that it makes any difference anymore, but she dumped me. For a pro golfer. And I haven't put much trust in women since. I don't even have a lot of faith in my mom, even though everyone says I'm her pet."

Mama's boy. Jordan Palmer's words at the party flashed in Shannon's memory. "Why don't you trust your mother?"

"I see how she works my dad and creates chaos in the family. And I wonder if she stops with Dad. Perhaps she manipulates all of us and we refuse to see it because she's Mom."

Shannon would love to know specifics. She grasped a thick sponge and squeezed a trail of water down his front "Are you saying you trust me more than your mother?"

"I don't know. Maybe."

"Why would you?"

"Gut instinct. It's never failed me. In the real estate business, you live and die on instinct and trust. You're a good example. You rose to be a top producer in a highly competitive business. That's not easy. It shows that a lot of people have put their faith in you to act in their best interests. So if that many trust you that much, my gut says I should be able to, too. And you've got values I like."

Those words sent her heart soaring, not to mention her pride. "Like what?"

"You care about people. Your grandmother, for instance. You worry about her when you're not there with her. That's a selfless thing. I can tell from the way you talk about your employees that you care about them."

"Hah. I haven't cared about them much this month. I've left them with all the work while I'm playing around with you."

"I'll bet they don't mind."

"They never complain. They're more than just employees. We support each other. With such a small shop, we have to."

"See? You've put together that small business with good loyal people and made it go, apparently all alone. I'm impressed. I've got an MBA, but with the tough housing market we've got these days, I don't know if I could make a residential sales office profitable."

She squeezed more warm water over his chest. "It's a total accident."

"That kind of success is never an accident. It comes from hard work and discipline."

He was right about that much. She had never worked so hard in her life as she had trying to make her business successful. And she had never given up so much. Her head swelled even more, hearing that he recognized who she really was. "So working hard and being disciplined are what make you trust me?"

"That's not all." He sat up and turned to face her. His hair was wet and spiked in all directions. She reveled in the intimacy of seeing him like this. Smiling, he drew her toward him. "And I like how you are in bed. You don't back off, but you don't try to manipulate me."

Manipulation. That word stuck in Shannon's brain. Even in trying to sell property, she never tried to maneuver someone, believed the result was more positive if she let people come to their own decisions. She supposed being manipulated was something with which a man with so much money and influence had to concern himself, especially if he started out feeling his mother was manipulative. No doubt some of the other women he had slept with had wanted something more from him than sex.

But this was no time to be thinking about other women he had slept with. Tonight, he was with Shannon Piper and they were naked in a jet tub of fragrant warm water. In Hawaii. And who knew when or if she would ever be in this place again?

She floated onto his lap and twined her legs around his hips, wrapped her arms around his shoulders, pressed her body against his. She looked down into his beautiful caramel-colored eyes. "I can't imagine that any woman dumped you. Was she out of her mind or something?"

"Not at all." He repositioned her, then lifted one of her breasts with his palm and swirled his tongue around her nipple. The rosy bud became erect. A spray of tingles traveled all the way to her sex and she closed her eyes. He rolled it between his thumb and finger, played with it until it was unbelievably extended and almost purple. "Beautiful," he murmured, drew her nipple into his mouth and sucked her hard.

"Oohh....Drake—"

"That make you come?" he mumbled against her breast.

"Hmmm..."

His mouth moved across her chest to the other breast. "Have I told you I'm a breast man?"

"Several times....I'm glad....I love what you're doing."

As much as she loved his attention and relished his intimate words, what she really wanted, now that he was in a talking mood, was to hear about the woman he had planned on marrying. "Was your fiancé from Fort Worth?"

"Drinkwell...Her folks own a ranch...Next to the Double Barrel...Common fence line...We grew up together."

Just as she feared. *Damn.* A long-time relationship and a family connection. Bad news. But now he was stabbing at her firm nipple with the tip of his tongue and she was having a hard time keeping her mind on the question. She gave a soft moan.

"Good?"

"You know it is," she said huskily.

Even as she fought to keep her focus on her mission, she let her head tilt back and arched her back, lifting her breasts to him. "The prince and princess, huh? And then what happened?"

"Usual stuff…Dating, planning…I graduated…went to SMU…She graduated the next year…went to TCU…."

Rich college. Rich fiancé. For someone like him, that might be the usual stuff, but not for Shannon and most of the people she knew.

His fingers slipped between her thighs and searched. "Let me see. I'm looking for—"

She pushed off his lap and scooted away from him before he found what would end this conversation. "Wait a minute. I want to hear this story and I can't listen when you're doing that."

She captured his hands and held them so they couldn't roam and they sat there face-to-face with space between them, her thighs draped across his. "Now. She went to TCU and what?"

He grinned at her. "Think you've got me captured, huh?"

"And I'm not letting you go until you tell me what happened at TCU."

His shoulders lifted in a shrug. "She took golf lessons. Got into it in a big way. You know, playing in tournaments, going to watch tournaments, hanging out around golf courses, et cetera."

"And that's where she met a pro golfer."

He freed his hands from hers, clasped her waist and pulled her onto his lap again. "I like you better here."

She braced her elbows on his shoulders and combed her fingers through his wet hair, combing his spikes into waves. "Was it someone you knew?"

"I'd met him."

"And she just ended it, just like that?"

"More or less. It was a big deal for both our families. The wedding was already put together. People had already brought a roomful of presents."

"Oh, my God. You were engaged a long time?"

"Two years. But we'd been a couple for six years. My mom and dad, hers, the whole county, really, had been expecting us to get married for as long as I could remember. I couldn't imagine ever being with another woman. She was the first girl I'd had grown-up relationship with. Or at least I thought it was grown-up at the time."

You mean sex. Had he been a virgin until his fiancé? Had they learned about sex together? "What did you do after she called it off?"

"What I had to. I graduated from college. Then I went on to business school like I'd planned."

Shannon was dying to know all the details that led up to that unhappy ending, but she doubted she ever would. "You always do what you have to, don't you?"

"Always," he answered.

Struck by the irony of his story, Shannon scooted back again and looked into his eyes. "I guess you've got a right to hate golf, but you don't. I mean, we've come all this distance to see a golf tournament."

"I learned to play, too. Turned out I enjoy the game. It has nothing to do with her. Golf is a head game. And I like that. I'm pretty good at it."

She couldn't keep from grinning. "I'll bet. Something tells me your whole life is just one big head contest."

"I'm a competitive guy. Can't help it."

"So now you like golf, but you don't trust women. Is your ex still married to this golfer?"

"Must be. I haven't heard otherwise."

"Are your families still friends?"

"Not anymore. Her parents quit ranching and leased out their place. Moved to Arizona."

"Why? Texas wasn't hot enough for them?"

"The guy she married lived in Arizona. She's an only child. Her folks wanted to be near her, so they moved there, too. Pic says she hasn't been back to Drinkwell since they left."

"You're still keep up with her?"

"No. It's just local gossip you hear."

But Shannon wondered. Six years was a sizeable piece of life—longer than she had ever been with anyone, including the guy she had married. Six *months* of memories might fall into a black hole and disappear, but not six *years*.

An unexpected emotion surged within her. Possessiveness. Dark and overwhelming. She wished she hadn't questioned him about his ex-fiancé. Now he might be thinking of her and Shannon wanted all of his thoughts and desires focused on Shannon Piper. She clutched the sides of his head between her palms and kissed him fiercely, drew his tongue into her mouth and sucked it. "Make love to me," she whispered. "You promised to kiss me all over."

Perhaps she was manipulative after all.

The next day, the final round began. The golf course was a painting of brilliant green grass, turquoise ocean and azure blue sky. In a perfect balmy temperature, Shannon strolled in paradise with her prince. Life had never been better, but they would fly home tomorrow and the fairy tale would end.

They followed the leaders quietly. Drake often reached for her hand or watched from behind her with his hands on her shoulders and her leaning back against him. Sometimes one of the golfers would stop, shake hands and exchange a greeting with Drake.

That evening, they had more conversation over exotic drinks with Drake's sophisticated friends and acquaintances. Then they returned to the condo. The day, the entire trip had Shannon in a state of euphoria. Her chest almost wouldn't hold all of the emotions swirling inside it. She couldn't keep from thinking that this was probably as close to a honeymoon as she would ever know.

They had already undressed when Drake said, "We're going home tomorrow and we haven't walked on the beach. Want to before we go to bed?"

"Absolutely. How could I leave Hawaii without walking on a beach? Will anyone see us?"

"I don't think so. This is a private place."

"Good." She picked up her thin lacy bathing suit cover-up and pulled it on. "I've always imagined walking on a beach naked."

He grinned. "With that thing, you're pretty close."

In creamy moonlight, they strolled holding hands, the soft sand oozing between her toes. Covered only by her bathing suit cover-up, she felt wicked and free in a way she couldn't recall ever feeling before. A naked native on a tropical island.

A gentle breeze touched her face and ruffled her hair and made her nipples peak. The lushness of their surroundings swallowed her up, as if she had entered another woman's body or some other alternate reality. For a long while, they walked in silence.

This seemed like the perfect moment to tell him thank you, but that cranky alter ego spoke up. *What are you thanking him for? He's getting what he wants from you. Isn't unlimited sex enough?*

She shunned that cynical voice because she believed he wanted more than that from her. He had told her so.

"Having a good time?" he asked at last.

"Me having a good time? You forget what a hick I am. This trip has been a once-in-a-lifetime experience for me. Not just being in Hawaii, but being with *you* in Hawaii."

"You've made it special for me, too."

Another statement that sent a thrill all the way to her toes. *Why?* she wanted to ask, but she didn't want to sound like a needy fool. "Remember what we talked about New Year's Eve, about trying to make this work and being open and honest?"

"Hm."

"Since you shared something honest with me about your engagement, I think I should tell you I've sort of dropped the ball about myself. I think I owe it to you to let you know something about me."

"I'm all ears. I've been trying to find out about you since the first night we were together."

She didn't say anything right away, trying to sort through just how much she wanted to reveal about the person she had been. "I'm far from being a perfect person."

"Then you're just like me and everyone else I know. You said you used to be a free spirit. I'm guessing you still are."

"Maybe a little." On a phony laugh, she bumped his arm with her shoulder. "Like going to that Realtors' Christmas party where I was way out of my league and going home with a man I didn't know. That was the old Shannon Piper, for sure."

He chuckled. "Hmm. And I thought it was Sharon Phillips. How would I have met you if you hadn't done it? I don't leave much to chance, but I do believe there's a reason for everything that happens."

"As in fate?"

He shrugged, then dropped her hand and looped an arm around her shoulder, pulled her close to his side.

"Anyway," she said, "I hate having things hanging, so I'm just going to tell you. Mostly because I don't ever want to face the day that someone else tells you."

"I'm listening."

She drew a deep breath. "I was married once. And I was pregnant."

She glanced up at his profile, seeking a reaction, but she could see only his profile in the moonlight. He didn't reply, as if waiting for the rest of the story. She blundered on. "I got pregnant when I was seventeen. I got married and never finished high school."

"You have a child?" Shock was not what she detected in his question. Curiosity was closer to what she heard.

"No. I had a miscarriage a few weeks after we got married. The whole thing was…stupid. Just stupid."

They reached the condo's wooden deck and stepped up onto it. She sank to a lounge chair, glad for the shadows while she dragged out her dirty laundry. He sat down in the chair beside her and picked up her hand.

"The miscarriage could have put an end to everything, but after all of the commotion my getting pregnant caused in the first place and the hurry-up wedding we had, we decided to stay married. We didn't have a plan for the future, but I did make sure I got to a doctor and got birth control pills. I sure didn't want to find myself pregnant again."

"You don't like kids?"

"It wasn't that. I'd never even thought about having kids. I wasn't very bright back then, but I was smart enough to figure out that neither one of us had any business being a parent. We were kids ourselves."

"Good instincts, huh? We have that in common, don't you think?"

She glanced across her shoulder at him, still couldn't clearly see his face in the shade of the deck. "Really? You think so?"

He lifted her hand to his lips and kissed the back of it. "We have more in common than you think. Finish your story."

"It has a predictable ending. We stayed married a couple of years, then we gave up and got a divorce. It became final on my twenty-first birthday. There. End of story."

And she intended for it to be the end. No way did she want to talk about her struggling single days in Fort Worth and her various affairs. The marriage and divorce were what, in the far reaches of her mind, she had worried about his discovering. Public records existed of those events. They sat in more silence for a few beats.

"You left out the part between your twenty-first birthday and now," he said.

"I'd have to be a little drunk and in a really bad mood to talk about that. I call those years the lost years."

He interlaced their fingers. "Okay, skip that. So tell me about your husband. You didn't love him?"

I've never loved anyone but you, she wanted to say, but feared where vocalizing that might take them.

"That's as good an explanation as any," she said instead. "He was two years older than me. Rode a motorcycle. Wore leather clothes and earrings. That was back when most guys didn't wear earrings. I thought he was too cool. We dated almost from the time he enrolled in school.

"When I got pregnant, he was already out of school, but he didn't have a job. There weren't any jobs in Camden, so we moved up to Fort Worth to set up our happy home. We bounced from one minimum wage job to another. It took both of us to make enough to pay rent and eat. If I'd actually had a baby, I don't know what we would've done. After a few months, we started fighting. And then we started fighting a lot."

"What about?"

"Everything. Kevin felt trapped being married. So did I."

"That's his name? Kevin?"

"Kevin Barton. He was unstable, but I didn't realize it until we started sharing the same apartment. I sure couldn't see it when I was a high school kid. Back then, I thought the off-the-wall stuff he did was daring and cute. Later, I learned he's bi-polar."

"Was he abusive?"

"He didn't beat me up or anything like that, but he had a mean streak and a bad temper and he drank a lot. Plus, he was a lot bigger than me. And really unpredictable. He scared me more than once. If we'd stayed married, he might've gotten around to physical abuse.

"Even if he hadn't been bi-polar, he'd never learned how to behave or how to deal with something that didn't go his way. He was sort of one of society's throwaways. His mother did drugs. She never had looked after him very well. He'd lived in and out of foster homes. He didn't talk about it much, but I always wondered if he'd been abused himself.

"Anyway, it didn't take long for me to figure out I wasn't in love with either him or with marriage. And his problems were just too big for us to deal with."

"You didn't have any help? Parents?"

She shrugged. "He just had his mother and she couldn't help herself, much less anyone else. I was alone, too, for all practical purposes. My dad and mom got a divorce when I was around ten. Then my dad passed on when I was fifteen.

"My mother and I just never got along. She's a lunatic. A hippie a generation too late. Too self-centered to ever rely on. Soon after Kevin and I got married, she moved to California with some guy my sister and I didn't even know. She's still there. But I have to say, as nutty as she is, she's head and shoulders above Kevin's mom.

"So you see, Drake—and I guess this is what I'm really trying to get around to—I'm in that white trash category. Or at least I was until, thanks to my grandmother, I moved back to Camden and started over. That's the deep-down reason my grandmother means so much to me. She didn't do much for me or Colleen when we were kids, but after I got grown, she saved me."

He lifted their interlocked fingers and kissed the back of her hand again. "I don't recall that I've ever used that term 'white trash.'"

Maybe not. But after hearing her tacky story, he probably wondered what kind of mess he had gotten himself into. He was making such an effort to get down on her level, she couldn't keep from laughing. "It's okay, Drake. I've used it myself."

"I'm serious. I don't pigeon-hole people that way. I believe we're all what we want to be. We're all what we work to be."

"I'm not so sure about that. I've noticed that just a lot of people don't work to be anything."

"That's my point. Stop and think about it. Out of ashes, so-to-speak, you chose to educate yourself and become a successful businesswoman. You could've continued living a life of low expectations and making bad choices, but you didn't. An inner compass steered you to do what you instinctively knew was the best thing. The first time we talked, I saw that in you. I have the same instinct. We're lucky that way."

"I've had those thoughts at times. But there's a big difference between you and me. You haven't had to struggle for money. That makes a difference in someone."

"True. But there are degrees of struggle. Believe me, I've fought my battles. When I decided I didn't want to be a rancher, it was damn traumatic around the Double-Barrel for a long time. Years, in fact."

She turned her head and smiled at him. "But you're such a great-looking cowboy."

"A part of me will always be a cowboy. It's how I grew up. It's a life I love."

"That night in the Worthington, when I first saw you, you know who you reminded me of?"

"Who?" he asked, heightened interest sounding in his tone.

"It took me a while to put my finger on it, but I finally did. Hugh Jackman. Like he was in that movie, *Australia*."

He chuckled. "I remind you of Drover?"

"You saw the movie? You look like him. People must have told you."

"I've heard it."

"Your hair's like his. You even have that crease between your brows like he does."

He raised his hand and rubbed between his brows with his fingers.

"You must have frowned a lot when you were a little boy to get that."

"I was a pretty serious kid."

And he was a pretty serious man, she had already concluded even before he told her he was stodgy and conservative.

"Why didn't you want to be a rancher?"

"Don't get me wrong. I love the ranch, but I was never sure I could give it my undivided attention. I always had outside interests. The business world always drew me. Back then, when I was more tuned in to football, Roger Staubach was my hero."

"I don't know who that is."

"Pro football player. He was a quarterback at Navy. After his hitch in the service, he became the quarterback for the Dallas Cowboys. Then after his football career, he put together a successful real estate company in Dallas. I thought to myself, I could do that."

"And you did, huh?"

"I haven't caught up with Roger yet, but I'm, trying. But maybe as much as anything, I was tired of the brawling between my mom and dad. Being the oldest, I was always the peacemaker. I wanted to get away from it. If I'd stayed there, there would've been no escaping it. For Pic to want to stay with the ranch was a huge weight off my shoulders.

"Your folks fought a lot?"

"They still do, even though they don't live together. But I don't want to get into that. I don't want to fuck up the good time we're having by discussing something I can't fix."

"Their fights don't bother your brother?"

"Not as much as they bothered me. Pic's more like my dad. He accepts things for what they really are. Doesn't' try to rearrange them."

"And you do?"

"I used to, but not so much anymore. These days, my business consumes so much of my time and energy, I don't have the time or the inclination to get involved in anything other than the ranch's finances."

"How old is your brother?"

"The same age as you. Thirty-three. Two grades behind me in school. When he first graduated, he talked about joining the army. He thought that if Dad anointed me to run the ranch, there was no place for him. I was terrified. Even though I was in college in Dallas, Dad was still trying to convince me I wanted to be a rancher, still trying to persuade me to quit SMU and enroll in Tarleton."

"If your brother had enlisted, you'd have stayed in Drinkwell?"

"Oh, yeah. Too much was at stake to have both Lockhart sons jump ship. The Double-Barrel is a family corporation. Some Lockhart will always have to look after it. If Pic had left, I wouldn't have had much choice without throwing the whole family into turmoil. Lockharts stick together through thick and thin. We might cuss and brawl, but we function as a unit."

"I can't imagine that much family loyalty," she said.

"Let's go to bed," he said, abruptly changing the subject. "I've been sitting here picturing what's under that thin thing you've got on."

She gave him a grin and stood up. "Well you don't have to picture anymore, cowboy."

She slipped the cover-up off her shoulders and dropped it onto the lounge chair, leaving herself naked. Then she stepped off the deck into the moonlight that bathed the yard in silver. Turning in a circle in front of him, she lifted her arms above her head and swayed her hips like a hula dancer as she moved around the yard. "Do I look like you pictured?" she asked.

"Better," he said hoarsely.

She turned and faced him. He had been wearing cargo shorts and a loose island shirt, but now he, too, was naked. Even in the moonglow, she could see his erection standing against his belly and she couldn't take her eyes off him. Lust, as raw and primitive as she had ever felt it, sent little prickles of heat through her veins.

He stepped off the deck and came to where she stood. "My imagination's never as good as the real thing." He scooped her into his arms and carried her up the steps and into the condo.

They met in a tangled embrace in the center of the king size bed, their bodies cast in an eerie glow by a crescent of moonlight. They rubbed against each other sensually, kissing lusciously, stroking and caressing until their breathing became shallow and the air around them was awash with passion. Driven by mind-numbing craving, she urged him to his back and sat up.

"What is it?" he asked.

"Shhh," she whispered, leaning over him and blowing softly on his nipple. "Just be still." She trailed little suckling kisses over his hairy chest. "I'm an island goddess come to earth to give you pleasure." She licked the brown button around his nipple, then gently nipped the nub with her teeth, all the while lightly stroking his rigid penis with her fingertips.

She felt more than heard a catch from inside his chest. His hands combed into her hair. "God, Shannon—"

"Shhh," she said softly. "Don't talk. You're my captive. I'm in charge."

She turned. As she trailed her mouth down to his navel, she stroked inside his muscular thigh with her fingernails. A quiver ran along his thigh. She moved her mouth down to his solid belly, licking and kissing. She closed her hand around his hard penis. "You feel like velvet," she murmured. "And steel."

He gave a soft groan and opened his thighs, giving her access to his manhood. She cupped his hairy scrotum in her palm and gently fondled as she moved her mouth on down. His erection jerked with incredible strength against her cheek. When she reached her destination, she carefully drew one of his testicles into her mouth and wallowed it across her tongue, gently sucked it, enjoying every primitive sound that came from him. She even relished the pinch to her scalp as he gripped a fist full of her hair. Then she moved to his other testicle.

Finally, when she had him groaning and shuddering, she covered the head of him with her mouth. His hips jerked, he gave a deep grunt and clutched her shoulder. "Aw, goddamn…"

His grip was like iron, but she took her time, licking him, swirling her tongue around the crown of him, stroking his slit with the tip of her tongue, gently sucking the soft bulb. He whimpered and whined—but gruffly—and his hips lifted to her again and again, begging her for more. When she thought he'd had enough teasing, she slid her mouth all the way to the root of him and began to suck in earnest.

On a rumble from deep in his throat, he caught the back of her knee and urged it across his shoulders until she was kneeling astride him, her sex above his face. She felt herself open, felt his breath hot against her sensitive flesh, felt his fingers exploring…stroking…penetrating. A hum of pleasure traveled from deep in her throat.

Then, his whisker stubble rasped her delicate layers. His tongue licked into her and laved the length of her sex. Her deep muscles clenched. A shiver shot through her and she entered another realm, became a stranger to herself, uninhibited and on fire with need. His mouth suckled, his tongue penetrated, licked in and out. Her own breath echoed in her ears. A gravelly moan rose up in her own throat, muffled by his penis in her mouth. With no prompt, she began to suck to the cadence of his tongue and his pumping hips.

He grunted and puffed. She sucked him harder and faster. With each rise of his hips, his penis drove into her throat and his tongue penetrated again and again in a steady rhythm. Like an expanding balloon ready to burst, desperation grew in her belly.

When she thought she would surely go insane if he didn't allow her release, he drew the tiny core of her sex all the way into his mouth and sucked like a babe. She rocketed from the earth in mindless ecstasy.

Then, sucking him harder and faster. Tandem spasms of pleasure assaulting her. Starbursts exploding behind her eyes again and again. She wanted to beg, wanted him to stop, wanted him to never stop. Tears rushed in and an unidentifiable sound crawled all the way up from her belly.

His body stiffened and he grunted. His erection contracted with amazing strength and his salty semen shot down her throat, thick and salty. She swallowed but didn't leave him until he was empty and weak and gasping for breath.

She was almost helpless with weakness herself, but she lifted herself off him. Shaking and sniffling, she clumsily turned and found his mouth with hers. They kissed savagely with bumping teeth and punishing tongues and mouths that tasted of each other's flesh. His massive arms enveloped her in a tight embrace and they kissed and kissed. And all the while she sniffled.

This wasn't the first time sex with him had brought her to tears. The same thing had happened in his condo the very first time she had been with him. She didn't know where so much emotion came from. No man had ever driven her to tears. It could be only because their souls had joined.

He stroked her hair, her face, while she cried into his warm shoulder. "On, my God," he whispered. "You're so…You're so…Oh, my God, Shannon…"

She sniffled.

"I didn't hurt you, did I?" he asked.

"N—No."

"Shh-shh…don't cry, darlin'…It'll be okay….My God, you're just…Let's rest a minute. It'll be okay."

She could tell from his voice and the way his sweat-slicked body trembled, he was in no better shape than she was. But she didn't have to rest. She was already okay. She had absolutely nothing on her mind but the fact that she was secure in her dream man's arms and he just given her a sexual experience like none she had ever known.

They slept the night in an embrace, then made love again in the wee hours while they were still half asleep. They both were gentle and tender, with emotion more important than heat. Afterward, they stood melded together in the shower, kissing and caressing and her heart beating against his. Only after their skin had turned wrinkled and they were pressed for time to get checked out and in the air did they separate.

They made no conversation about the fact that they would be parting today, but a quietness had grown between them and their actions spoke louder than any words they could have said.

On the flight of several hours, he held her hand, but he was pensive and quiet. So was she. She had so much to think about. Something

Christa had said badgered her: *Sex with emotion is different from sex for fun*.

She must be in love with him, which made no sense. She had known him only six weeks, though she felt as if they had been one forever. And he surely didn't love her.

Still, whatever was going on between them was no longer about just sex. But if not that, then what *was* it about?

She knew only one thing for sure. A rollercoaster had taken control of her life. Should she try to stop it now or wait and risk it throwing her off its highest point?

Chapter Thirty-Three

BETTY LOCKHART RETURNED to her home on Monday. After nine days, she was glad to escape Barron's company. He was a lovely man, but he was an *old* man, who acted even older than he was. No amount of Viagra could turn him into a seething stud. He was nothing like Bill Junior who *was* a seething stud who could still ride a horse, flank a calf, climb a windmill, or do whatever he wanted to physically.

Wanting to re-anchor herself with the family, her first call was to Drake's office. Debra, his wonderful assistant, told her he was in Hawaii.

Drake hadn't mentioned a trip to Hawaii. "Hawaii? Did he go on business?"

"He finally took some time off," Debra told her. "He and a friend flew over there last Thursday to a golf tournament, but he's due back today.

Instinct pricked at Betty. "What friend? Who went with him?"

The assistant didn't answer right away. *Oops.* Betty realized she had overstepped. "Oh, never mind. I'll call him at home later. Thanks." She hung up and stood by the phone a few seconds, her thoughts in disarray.

Oh, dear Lord. Could Drake have taken that Piper woman to Hawaii with him? Betty made a mental inventory of Drake's girlfriends she had met. She knew how he felt about most of them, had even discussed some of them with him. She couldn't imagine him taking any one of them on a trip of several days. Good Lord, this was getting clear out of hand.

She hurried to her study where the regional phone book still lay on her desk. On a hunch, she thumbed through the yellow pages and found the Camden number of Piper Real Estate. Her pulse pounding, she hesitated, waiting for calm. After a few seconds, she pressed the number into the phone.

A young voice answered cheerily. "Good afternoon. Piper Real Estate."

"I'd like to speak to Mrs. Piper, please."

"I'm sorry. She's out for a few days. Can someone else help you?"

Betty's grip on the receiver tightened. "When will she return?"

"She'll be back in the office tomorrow. Could I—"

"Thank you," Betty said and quickly hung up before she said too much.

Her thoughts veered to Pic. He might know what Drake was doing. She called the Double-Barrel on its landline. To both her dismay and her delight, Bill Junior answered the phone. She closed her eyes and pictured him standing in the den, the phone pressed to his ear, his fist jammed against one slim hip, his starched jeans hugging his butt and muscular thighs, his masculinity making that sexy little bump at the bottom of his zipper.

Girding herself for a sarcastic exchange, she said, "This is your estranged wife. I have a question."

"You're estranged only because you want to be," Bill Junior said in his sexy deep voice. "I heard you went off on a boat with that old man."

How did he know that? She couldn't believe Drake had told him, but he might have told Pic, then Pic relayed the information to Bill Junior. Her children always conspired against her. Betty frowned. "I said I have a question."

"I've got one, too," Bill Junior said. "Did you sleep naked with that old geezer? I imagine you fucked him."

Betty made a mental gasp. "Shut your mouth, Bill. We are not having that conversation. I want to know who Drake took to Hawaii with him."

"How the hell would I know?" He laughed wickedly. "You know our Drake. That boy's got broads coming out of the woodwork. You'll have to ask Pic."

Betty rolled her eyes. Bill Junior was in rare form today. No doubt he was drinking. "Then let me speak to Pic."

"He's not here. Went to town. That's where I'm going pretty soon."

"Have you heard any talk about Drake dating a woman from Camden?"

"Nope. But I don't pay attention. I'm a whole lot more interested in who *you're* dating."

"My God, Bill. I'm over fifty years old. I do not date."

He gave a *heh-heh-heh*, the varmint. "I'm coming up to Fort Worth to the bull sale on Thursday. I'm planning on dropping by, so clear any stragglers out of your bedroom."

"I don't know what you're talking about. There are no stragglers in my home."

"That's *our* home, darlin'. If you care to ask the accountant, I believe he'll tell you the Double-Barrel owns it."

"Oh, really? Well I'm planning on playing golf on Thursday. You try to come into my house without my permission and you can deal with the Fort Worth Police Department."

"Cancel the goddamn golf. It's too fuckin' cold and it's a silly game anyway. I'll be there early. And get out that hot slick shit you got off the Internet. I'll be loaded for bear. I haven't had any since before Christmas."

Betty closed her eyes and let out a breath, recalling his pre-Christmas visit when she had introduced him to a pleasure enhancing product she had bought online. After the pathetic experiences she'd had with Barron Wilkes' shortcomings in their state room, the lure of Bill Junior "dropping by" was far stronger than her will power, but she told him, "Don't tell me what to do. I might or might not cancel my golf date."

Knowing she had just consented, Betty clenched her jaw and drew a measured breath through her nose. She had no pride. She was a fool, a sex-starved fool. Wasn't menopause supposed to kill your desire for sex? What the hell had gone wrong with her?

"And change the damn sheets," he ordered. "I don't want to lay down where that old man's been. I might catch something."

"You are such an ass, Bill Junior. I will not change the sheets. You come to my house, you take your chances." She slammed down the receiver with a loud *clack!*

She drew a deep breath, reining in her anger. Well, that conversation hadn't gleaned much—except a date for sex with her husband on Thursday. She checked her calendar, making sure she—they—would be undisturbed that whole day.

Next she speed-dialed Pic's cell phone, but got only his voice mail.

Even without more clues, she was convinced she knew who had accompanied Drake to Hawaii. Now she was even more frustrated. Once she had been acquainted with people in Camden she could call and ask questions. But no more.

She moved into her small study and her laptop and did a search online, but learned little more about Shannon Piper than she already knew—top producer, professional organizations, a few awards. Betty wasn't looking for any of that. She wanted dirt.

She had dismissed Donna's phone call of a couple of weeks ago, but in the back of her mind, she hadn't forgotten the heiress's boasting about her resources. But to take advantage of them, Betty would have to pass Shannon Piper's name to her. Betty's yen to know everything about Drake's girlfriend overrode her reluctance to give Donna the name. Before she had left on the cruise, she and Donna had talked about lunch. Betty scrolled through her contacts on her cell phone and pressed in Donna's number.

Shannon arrived back home on Monday afternoon. Grammy Evelyn was eager to hear about her trip. Shannon didn't get to bed until after ten.

She settled into bed, instantly missing Drake's warm body against hers and his arms around her. They had slept spoon-like only four nights, but it seemed much longer. It seemed as if she belonged in his embrace.

Her thoughts and emotions roiled. Something had happened between her and Drake. They had made love with a passion Shannon had known only with him. She had never had sex with so much deep emotion attached. She had never had a relationship with anyone where the very air around them teemed with awareness and anticipation of the next time and she wondered if other people could see it. They had made love morning and night and during the night for four days and nights and every time without a condom. That wasn't worrisome, as she felt safe, but she couldn't stop thinking of all that had been said between them. Dozens of tender words, even words of endearment. Except for the L word. But the emotion had been there, hovering in the ether. Several times she had almost said it.

She was in terrible trouble.

She flashed back to her departure from his condo. As she had bundled up for the trip home, he had handed her a silver American Express credit card:

"If you just have to drive up here, use this to defray the cost," he said.

Surprised, she looked at him. "To buy gas?"

"Anything you need."

She handed it back to him. "You keep it. If I need it, I'll let you know."

He thrust the card into her hand again. "But Shannon—"

"No," she said. "I don't want to be responsible for someone else's credit card, especially yours. If I find I can't afford gas, I'll tell you."

At that point, he had wrapped her in his arms and kissed her dizzy. *"In the future, if I'm not allowed to come get you myself, I'm going to start sending a car for you all the time. I worry about you driving up here and back."*

"I don't want a car. I'd rather drive. I drive up here and back all the time."

His head shook, an indication of his frustration. *"You've got my number. If you have any problems, don't hesitate to call me. No matter what I'm doing, I'll stop. I'll take care of you."*

She had found the white knight she had always dreamed of. He cared. No one ever had. Perhaps her parents had at some point, but it was so long ago, she no longer remembered it. Her grandmother cared these days, but where had she been when Shannon was growing up alone with no father and at the mercy of a crazy woman?

Believing that hunky, virile Drake Lockhart cared about her safety and well-being sent profound joy all the way to the farthest walls of her heart and the poor overworked organ had been in a state all the way home.

She went to her real estate office early on Tuesday morning before anyone else arrived and found a message waiting from the Dallas agent. *Bang!* Just that fast, she was back in the real world.

When she returned the agent's call, he told her she had been outbid again and asked if she wanted to up her price. A wave of nausea passed through her stomach. "Thanks," she said. "I'll have to think about it and call you back."

She sat there a few minutes mulling over her bad luck and toying with the Mont Blanc pen Drake had given her for Christmas. What were the odds that in one of the slowest winters she could remember since she had been in the real estate business that she would get into a bidding war over a five-acre parcel in a small town like Camden? She pulled out her file on the five-acres and studied her finances. Her banker had already told her how far he would go in backing her. She had no other place to get money.

She didn't even own anything she could mortgage except the thirty acres, part of which was already mortgaged, and her real estate office, which also was already mortgaged. Even if the bank had been willing to lend her money on some part of the thirty acres, there were the payments to consider. Payments that would bite into her living expenses or her operating expenses and cripple her. She couldn't bid much higher than she already had.

She looked down at the Mont Blanc pen. *Drake.* He might make her a loan. But if he did, their relationship would change forever. She immediately dismissed that idea. They might have connected on a deep emotional level, but that didn't mean she would borrow money from him. She didn't even want to discuss the five acres with him. Thus far, they hadn't intruded into each other's businesses and that was how it should stay.

She brooded for half an hour, put together another bid twenty thousand dollars higher and faxed it to the agent. With that, she was maxed out. Twenty thousand dollars was nothing more than a blip in the commercial real estate world. It probably wouldn't even make the competing buyer blink. In her mind, she began the process of giving up on the five acres.

Everyone in her office knew her anguish. They had experienced the stress associated with waiting for a buyer or seller to make a decision. Terry offered to buy her lunch. Dana, the quieter member of her team, gave her a cute desk ornament with a happy face. All of them joined her in hand wringing.

And while she sat there steeped in disappointment, her cell phone warbled. She checked Caller ID, saw *Unknown Number* and her spirits rose. Drake told her he still had the two tickets he had bought at the

TCCRA auction for premium seats at the Fort Worth Stock Show & Rodeo. "I miss you," he said. "Come up Saturday. We'll do the rodeo, then you spend the night with me."

Shannon hadn't been to the Fort Worth rodeo in years, but she would be more at home at a rodeo than on a golf course. She didn't consider saying no. The Hawaii trip had sealed a bond between them. And anticipating the weekend went a long way to quashing her pain over the five acres.

The next day, Betty waited for Donna at LeFleur, a cozy sandwich shop near Betty's neighborhood. She had chosen a table in the back corner of the small dining room, partially hidden by a Ficus tree. Donna showed up at one o'clock wearing high-heeled boots, beaded and sequined denim that could only be Brazil Roxx and a casual fur jacket. The jeans fit her trim body as if they had been glued on. Her long hair was held in an up-do by a jeweled clip. Her diamond rings and earrings glinted. She looked every inch the heiress she was. Betty would never understand why Drake hadn't hung on to her.

They talked about the cruise, talked about what Donna had been doing. Then Betty did the dirty deed—over a cup of coffee and a steaming bowl of delicious French onion soup topped with baked cheese, she betrayed her son's trust. She gave Shannon Piper's name to Donna, with the agreement that heiress would let her know anything she discovered. Drake might hate her if he ever found out, but in the end, she believed he would understand that she had done it for his own good.

Donna had her own motives, Betty knew. But Betty had news for her. Once Drake made up his mind about anything, wild horses couldn't change it. Nothing his mother could do would rekindle Drake's interest in Donna.

Betty had a motive, too. After having supper with Tammy McMillan the night before leaving on the cruise, Betty knew Tammy had gotten a divorce from her golf pro husband a few months back. Tammy had said in code words that Drake was why she had returned to Texas. And Betty believed her. Otherwise, why would she have contacted Drake's mother? Was restoring the former bond between Tammy and Drake possible?

Despite the friction that sometimes existed between Betty and her son, she knew him. She had long thought that the reason he had never settled down and married was because he had never gotten over Tammy McMillan.

Shannon's period started on Thursday. Now, all she and Drake would be doing on Saturday night was sleeping.

A good test of his character, her ornery alter ego said.

*As if he needed on*e, the persona she feared had fallen in love with him snapped back.

After what had happened in Hawaii, and the week before, she was relieved to see her menses. She and Drake had used no protection at all in Hawaii. She was sure she had been past ovulation and the whole trip had been such an out-of-this-world experience and the passion between them had been so hot, a little thing like safe sex had seemed too ordinary deal with.

If this was going to continue, she had to get to a doctor and get birth control pills or something. Condoms were too unreliable and the rhythm method was too risky.

She drove up to Fort Worth early on Saturday morning, met Drake at his condo and he drove them to the coliseum where the annual rodeo and stock show was held. When she teased him about driving them in his truck, he said, "You've got to have the right vehicle for the right job, Miss Smarty Pants."

They ate junk food and viewed most of the animals on exhibit. He used his phone to take a picture of her with a giant bull that was as gentle as a lamb. When she admired a beautiful bear claw necklace made of green turquoise mounted in silver, Drake pulled out his credit card and bought it for her.

"I just said I liked it," she said. "I didn't mean for you to buy it."

"Turn around and let me put it on you." He turned her around. "It goes with your eyes."

"But just because I said I liked it didn't mean I wanted you to buy it," she repeated.

He hooked the necklace, then turned her back to face him and gave her a quick kiss. "Shh. Don't talk. I'm a control freak, remember."

She looked down and touched the large center stone. Against her black turtleneck, the silver and turquoise piece was truly beautiful. She had nothing like it and would have never spent the money to buy it for herself. She looked up at him. "Can I just say thank you?"

He rested his finger on her lips. "Yes. But that's all."

When evening came and the rodeo began, they did indeed have good seats, right near the action. Just as at the golf tournament, Drake knew many of the performers and stockowners and he introduced her to all of them. She saw yet another world she had never seen before.

When they returned to his condo, he grumbled about no sex, but not seriously. "It's not all about that," he said. "I just want you with me." They settled into his king size bed and he caged her with his long arms and legs. "Next weekend we'll go down to the Gulf and I'll get even with you."

"Promises, promises," she mumbled as she drifted off to sleep in total contentment. The five acres in Camden seemed a million miles away.

Chapter Thirty-Four

THE FOLLOWING MONDAY, Drake's day went to hell early. A weeping phone call came from his construction foreman's wife reporting that he had been severely injured in a grinding collision with an eighteen-wheeler on I-35. Drake dropped everything and rushed to the hospital in Denton to check on Buzz Grayson's condition and offer support to his family. Once there, he learned that Buzz would survive, but he would be out of commission for a long while.

Like it or not, Drake was now the foreman on the construction of his five-hundred-unit apartment complex. He had a multimillion dollar construction loan with interest accruing daily and the deadline for the Phase II inspection had already been missed by weeks. He could afford no more idle time.

The project consisted of multiple multi-story buildings, all still in the framing stage due to inclement weather. Long hours and unknown overtime would be needed to catch up. Bringing a new foreman onto the job would take several days or even a week or two.

Now it was Wednesday and he could see that even with doing it himself, he was still losing money. He knew of only one man who could get the job going again and bring it back on schedule. He called an old friend who now lived in West Texas, Terry Ledger.

Terry had bought a West Texas ghost town on eBay and replaced it with a senior citizen community. Everyone had thought he had gone off his rocker, but he had turned the project into a roaring success. The foreman who had handled that construction job for him was a wizard named Chick Featherston. Terry told him how to get in touch with Chick.

Pic had left a message on his voice mail, but Drake's next call was to Shannon. He explained the situation and postponed the upcoming trip to the coast. She understood his dilemma, which was something few, if any, of the women he had known would have. His mother didn't even understand.

After he disconnected, his thoughts lingered on Shannon and how much he enjoyed her. He liked just hearing her voice. He could barely wait to see her again. He had to do something about her. But what?

Back in his office, he asked Debra to pick up some lunch for him at the deli downstairs. While he ate, he ran through the list of messages and calls he had put off or ignored all morning. As soon as he finished his sandwich, he keyed in his brother's cell number.

"Hey, Bro," Pic said. "Where you been?"

"Up in Southlake. I've got a construction job falling apart up there and I lost my foreman."

"What happened?"

"Truck wreck. A bad one. Looks like I'm it until I can find somebody else."

"Ouch," Pic said. "Hope he's gonna be okay."

"Touch and go, but the guy's tough. We're all saying a prayer. How's Dad? Is he behaving himself?

"He hasn't been lost anywhere, if that's what you mean. Wish you could come down here. Blake and his partner came over and Dad and I had a long talk with them. They've got a new theory about Kate's barn. They think the motive could be revenge."

Nonplussed, Drake left his chair, walked to the window overlooking downtown. "Revenge? What the hell has Kate done that would trigger somebody's revenge?"

"It's not just Kate. He thinks somebody's got it in for the whole family."

"The hell," Drake said, astonished.

"Remember that little bunch of calves that got shot last year? We thought it was teenage vandals, you know? Blake says maybe not.

Drake's memory spun backward to when a dozen six-month old calves had been shot with a .22 and left to bloat in an outpost pasture.

"And you know all the rustling that's been going on."

"Those statistics are up all over the state. That could be coincidental."

"True, but there's more. Remember that time when the brake line on my truck got cut when I went up to Fort Worth to the cattle sale? And there's been other stuff. Anyway, Blake thinks he sees a pattern."

Drake had forgotten about Pic's brake line, but a cut brake line couldn't be a coincidence. "The hell," he said again.

"Blake wants us to get together and talk about things that have happened to us. Things that have done us harm or cost us money. He wants to know if you've had anything happen up there on your end."

Drake's thoughts swerved to Buzz Grayson's accident. Buzz could have been killed. As it was, he could possibly be injured for life. A little flutter began in Drake's stomach. For someone to have nearly killed his foreman out of revenge against the Lockhart family was too diabolical to accept until he knew more facts. "I don't know, Pic. But I'll give it some thought."

"Tom Gilmore arrested a kid named Billy Barrett for Kate's barn. I didn't mention it to you because I don't think it's going anywhere."

"Who is he?"

"Just a kid who got acquainted with Kate and Troy up at the futurity. I suspect they'll have to cut him loose pretty quick. You know Tom. He's just showing off, trying to look like he knows what he's doing. What's the insurance company saying? When are they gonna pay Kate's claim?"

"They're not saying much of anything. They're still investigating. Kate and Troy are still on their persons of interest list. I've turned it over to the lawyers. You and Dad should put up a pole barn for her until we figure out something else. She can't keep boarding her horses over at Will's place forever. That stresses his pasture as well as his facilities and his pocketbook."

"We're paying him boarding fees," Pic said. "He's glad to help Kate out. Wish to hell she would take an interest in him instead of some of these other losers she comes up with."

"Well, you know our little sister. She might be a sweetheart, but she doesn't always exercise the best judgment."

"Don't I know it. She's liable to drag home another Jordan Palmer."

Shannon's week had begun busy. Monday and Tuesday had been taken up by closings that would bring nice commissions into the company and she had her own closing on the house she had sold in December. Terry had brought in a new listing on one of the historic bed and breakfast homes near the town square. The new year was starting off right.

On Wednesday, more than a month and a half after Shannon had made her initial offer on the 5.17 acres, she heard from the Dallas broker that the competing buyer for the five acres had upped his bid by a lot and the owner of the property had agreed to the deal. After she hung up, she closed her office door and sat for a long while, fighting back tears and scrabbling for control of her emotions. Finally, she felt composed enough to send a text message to Christa: *I lost the corner.*

A minute later, her desk phone warbled. "Oh, hell," Christa said. "What happened?"

"I got outbid. Probably someone from Dallas. Can you find out who?"

"Only if the sale closes in our office. I'm sure there's a confidentiality agreement."

The sale would close at a location convenient to the seller, Shannon knew. "Maybe they'll do it here in town since the property's here. Keep an eye out for it, will you? It's a cash deal, so it's going to close real soon."

"I'll find out what I can," Christa said. "But what good will it do to know who bought it?"

"You never know what might happen. His deal could fall apart."

"Cash deal? Quick closing? Not likely."

"The thirty acres I already own aren't much good to me without the corner. As soon as I find out who the buyer is, I can contact him and offer to sell him my acres."

Shortly after noon, Betty waited for Donna Schoonover for a second lunch date at LeFleur, the same café where they had met last week.

The blonde swept in late, wearing a full length mink coat over tight jeans and boots. Without saying hello or removing her coat, she slapped a brown mailing envelope onto the corner of the table. "She's nothing but a tramp. And this proves it. I cannot believe he broke off with me for that."

A large diamond ring on Donna's right hand glinted under the indirect lighting. Betty never failed to notice striking jewelry, especially diamonds. She detected a familiar smell—a combination of alcohol and Listerine. She had smelled it often enough on Bill Junior.

Donna shrugged out of her fur coat and threw it across a chair as if it were made of rags, then plopped onto a chair opposite Betty.

"What do you mean, tramp?" Betty asked her.

"White trash. Lived in a dumpy singlewide trailer house her whole life. My God, it wasn't even in a trailer park. It was parked on a bald knob in Camden County. She got pregnant in high school. Got married and divorced before she was twenty-one years old. Slept with a dozen men we know about. And get this." Donna made a snort of disgust. She tapped the brown envelope with a long acrylic nail, her diamond ring throwing off shards of fire. "She had an affair with a married man. She tried to break up his marriage. Drake's new sweetheart doesn't have much to be proud of."

An oft-ignored sense of justice surged within Betty. For a thrice-married, reputedly alcoholic party girl to be criticizing any woman based on the laundry list Donna had just itemized was the pot calling the kettle black. But before Betty could go further with that thought, the waitress came and took their order for two glasses of Chablis and the daily special, chicken salad sandwiches.

"That isn't what it says online," Betty said. "I looked her up."

"Honey, you can't believe anything you read on the Internet. People write just any old thing, whether it's true or not."

Betty wanted to get the goods on Shannon Piper all right, but she also wanted the information to be accurate. If she were going to risk alienating her son, she wanted to do it with the truth. "Where did you learn all of those things?"

"I told you. I have resources."

"But what are they? How do you know they're reliable?"

"I'm good friends with one of daddy's PIs. He does things just for me."

"Oh, my goodness. A private detective?"

"The only way to get good info."

The waitress returned with their lunch. As Betty spread her napkin on her lap, her curiosity scurried in so many directions, she didn't know what question to ask first. She tasted the winc, gathering her thoughts. "Who was the married man? Someone in Camden?"

Donna wrapped her long manicured fingers around her wine glass, gulped half the contents and set the glass back on the table. "Fort Worth. He's a prominent insurance broker. Justin Turnbow's his name. My God. Drake probably knows him. He's one good-looking sonofabitch, I'll say that. Anyway, someone who knows him told me he nearly divorced his wife for her."

Betty searched her memory, couldn't recall ever seeing or hearing the name Justin Turnbow. "She has an ex-husband?"

Donna finished off the wine and signaled the waitress for another glass "He's a mutt. Works at odd jobs. My daddy's friend thinks he's a meth-head. I'll show you."

She pulled a thin sheaf of papers out of the brown envelope, paged through them to a black and white photograph. She slid it across the table. Betty stared down at what looked like a mug shot. A gaunt, hollow-eyed young man with pimples stared back at her, most of his visible skin, except for his face, stippled with tattoos. While his face might not show tattoos, it showed metal jewelry protruding from one brow, his nose and lips. Nausea crawled up Betty's throat. If Shannon Piper had been married to this man, she must be what Donna said she was. Indeed, Drake had taken up with a tramp.

The waitress returned with another glass of wine for Donna. "Just bring the carafe, honey," Donna told her, then turned her attention back to Betty. "So now," she cooed. "I've done this for you. What are *you* going to do for me?"

The compromising position she had put herself in fell onto Betty's shoulders like a boulder. "What do you want me to do?" she asked cautiously.

"Something easy. I want you to fix up a make-up date between Drake and me."

Such a strong sense of relief shot through Betty, she had to check herself before a laugh burst out. Her son had not ended his relationship with Donna because of his new girlfriend. He had simply had enough. Donna's wealth and social standing meant little to him. In her heart of hearts, Betty was proud of him for that, though she wished circumstances were otherwise.

Even if she were able to influence Drake, she wasn't sure she wanted to. "He doesn't necessarily do what I recommend."

"You can tell him this. I've cut way back on my drinking and I've quit smoking. I know he hates both of those. If I could spend some time with him again and just talk to him, I know he'd change his mind about me."

As Donna picked up the full carafe of wine the waitress had just set on the table and refilled her glass, Betty studied her. True, she hadn't smoked in either of their meetings, but seeing how she swallowed glasses of wine as if they were water, Betty doubted her claim about drinking. Donna quitting one, or even two, bad habits would make no difference to Drake.

Betty wasn't about to make promises she couldn't keep or had no intention of trying to keep. "All I can do is mention it to him," she said, hedging. "I've already mentioned you to him often. But I'm sure I don't have to tell you he has a mind of his own."

"I know," Donna said petulantly. "One of the reasons I want to get back together with him is he's got some *cajones*, forchrissake. I get so damn tired of the wimpy snivelers who chase after me. They aren't interested in me. They're interested in what Daddy can do for them."

Donna's blue eyes misted over, spurring sympathy in Betty. Even a spoiled heiress had feelings. She sighed. "Oh, Donna, I can well imagine that you'd have that problem, but I—"

"Drake never expected anything from my daddy," Donna said. "Daddy loves him. Drake's so smart, Daddy would love to get him involved with some of his business deals, but Drake's never showed any interest." She sniffed and touched the corner of her heavily-made-up eye with a fingertip.

Betty had been growing more uncomfortable with this meeting the more it unfolded. Now she could scarcely sit still. Donna had almost emptied the wine carafe. Any one of Betty's neighbors might drop into this neighborhood cafe and she didn't want someone who knew her to see her lunching with a weeping drunk woman, even if that woman *was* Don and Karen Stafford's daughter.

"Well, what can I say?" she said with false cheer. "Drake's his own man. He's been that way since he was a child."

"There's more than that." Donna leaned forward and lowered her voice, which had taken on a slur. "I'll tell you frankly. Your little boy is the best piece I ever had."

Betty's eyes bugged, her face flushed. Donna had a reputation for letting whatever popped into her head fall out of her mouth, especially if she was drinking. Betty glanced left and right to see if anyone she knew was near.

"He just knows what to do with that thing, you know?" Donna drained her glass, then set it on the table with a *clunk* and reached for the carafe again. "And he can go and go. And I've really hated not having that."

Horrified, Betty lowered her chin and cleared her throat. "Donna, you're embarrassing me. Please remember, this is my son we're discussing."

"I meant it as a compliment. Honest." Donna lifted a full glass of wine and took a large swallow. "Haven't you ever lost a big ding-dong that you just hated doing without?"

For absolutely no reason, an image of Bill Junior in his naked glory flashed in Betty's mind and she felt a tingle down low. As he had warned, he had come to her house before daylight last Thursday morning and they had stayed in her bed all day. Late in the afternoon he had headed to the Stock Show for the bull sale, leaving her worn out and well-sated. As usual.

As those erotic memories danced in her head, she looked up and stared at Donna. Not because of what the woman had said about Drake, but because Betty was appalled at realizing the one thing she and Donna Schoonover had in common after all. She knew exactly how it felt to miss and do without a big ding-dong. A flush crawled all over her body. Good God, she had to change the subject.

She grabbed her napkin off her lap, dabbed at her brow and upper lip. "Please excuse me. I'm having a hot flash."

An hour later, Betty returned to her home, vowing never to socialize with Donna Schoonover again. But their lunch date really hadn't been social, had it? Donna had given her the brown envelope of printed material and photographs.

Betty carried it to her study. In the quiet and calming atmosphere of the small room, she thoroughly perused the PI's report. Shannon Piper had lived in Fort Worth nine years. During that time, she'd had half a dozen jobs—store clerk, maid in a nursing home, waitress, cocktail waitress. Good Lord, it appeared the only tacky job the woman had avoided was lap dancer. No wonder she had chased after a successful insurance broker without regard to the fact that he was married. And now she was chasing after Betty Lockhart's son.

Betty sat back in her chair, looking out into her manicured back yard, letting part of her brain flit to how beautiful her roses would be if spring ever came. At least Shannon Piper doesn't appear to be a criminal, another part mused. There was *that* to be grateful for.

Betty was sure Drake didn't know all that she now knew. What woman would reveal such damning personal information to a man she wanted to capture?

But she couldn't give this file to him. She couldn't even tell him about it. He would want to know where she had gotten it. He might be annoyed that she had the information, but if he knew where it had come from, he would be enraged—not as his trampy girlfriend, but at his mother. He might never speak to her again.

After a few minutes, she thought of a subtler and even more desirable solution to the problem. She went to her purse, found her cell phone and keyed in Tammy McMillan's number.

Chapter Thirty-Five

DRAKE HAD BEEN in a dead run all week. He awoke on Friday reminding himself that he had one day left to accomplish what he should have gotten done through the week. He left his condo before daylight for his office.

On his walk to and from his office every day, he passed the jewelry store where he had bought the pen he had given to Shannon for Christmas. The small store's black marble front stood out in a slot of space between a dress shop and an office supply store.

He paid its window little attention usually, but with the morning still dark, its lighted display of a snow-white porcelain hand slowly turning on a pedestal caught his eye. He stopped and looked. Among other wares that glinted under the focused lighting, the white hand's left ring finger wore an impressive bauble made of diamonds and emeralds. Though he had rarely bought jewelry in his life and knew little about the fine points, he recognized a wedding ring when he saw it.

He stood there staring at it, trying to sort his emotions, trying to think why suddenly looking at a wedding ring seemed like the natural thing to do. Since Tammy McMillan, he had never again considered getting married, even once.

Hot sex has fried your brain, hoss, a part of him said.

Who're you kidding, buddy? another part said. *You're the one who told her you wanted something more. So, you got it. Now what are you going to do with it?*

He still hadn't digested all that was going on between him and Shannon.

He forced his gaze to something less unsettling. And less binding. Like the heart-shaped diamond pendant to the left of the ring. After a pause of seconds, he expelled a great breath of frustration. "Fuck it," he mumbled and resumed his trek to his office.

He hadn't even started the day before his assistant poked her head through the doorway. "Your mother's on the phone."

He picked up his desk receiver. "Hey, Mom."

"Drake, I'm so glad I caught you before you run off somewhere. I'm having dinner tonight with an old family friend. I want you to join us."

"Who is it?"

"It's a surprise. We're eating at Cattlemen's. You can make it, can't you?"

"I guess so. I've got a crazy day ahead, so I'll probably be fried, but—"

"We'll be there around six-thirty. And wear a tie."

Oh, shit. Mom was fixing him up again. "Mom, you know I hate wearing ties. I'm not in the mood to impress anybody. I've had a long week."

"Well, maybe not a tie. Just make sure you look nice. Not that you don't always look nice, but just take some extra pains."

"Mom, don't do—"

"Now don't argue with me. This is someone you'll want to see. Just say you'll be there at six-thirty."

She hung up before he could protest more. He sat for a few seconds running through a list in his head of people he and his mother both knew that he would want to see. No one jumped out at him. He was tempted to call her back and cancel, but he felt guilty because he hadn't seen her since before her trip with Barron Wilkes. He sighed. Why argue? He had to eat somewhere.

When daylight broke, he left his office for the apartment complex construction site thirty miles away. Not quite ready to turn the job over to his new construction boss, he stayed there until he was satisfied that Chick needed no further handholding. He was back in his office by two, making phone calls and doing busy work.

At five, he started back to the condo to dress for dinner with his mother and her mystery guest. He stopped again at the jewelry store's display window and looked at the diamond and emerald ring. It looked flashy. Like something his mother would wear. Shannon would probably have a smart-ass comment about the cost of it. He smiled inwardly.

At home, he tapped out a quick text to her: *Hi. Busy. Thinking of you.*

Then he showered and shaved and pulled fresh clothing from his closet. He put on a dress shirt, but left off the tie.

He checked his phone again for a message from Shannon and it was there: *Looking forward to Lubbock.*

At the Cattlemen's Steak House, he handed his coat to a valet and the host led him to his mother's table. And there before his eyes sat a woman he never expected to see again in his life. His stomach rose and fell and for a second he grew dizzy.

Eyes the color of a Texas summer sky looked up at him from a face familiar from long ago. Long honey-blond hair fell like strands of gold over one bare shoulder.

She put out her right hand. “Hello, Drake. How are you?”

Like a robot, he took her hand. “I’m—I’m fine, Tammy. How are you?”

His mother gestured toward an empty chair on one side of the table for four. “Son, don’t just stand there gawking. Sit down.”

Like a stone tossed into a lake, Drake dropped to the chair seat, trying to slow his racing pulse and unable to take his eyes off the woman who had once meant everything to him.

“Tammy’s living in Fort Worth now,” his mother said. “Out on the west side, aren’t you, dear?”

“Yes,” she said to Drake, smiling faintly.

Where had she come from? What was she doing here? “Uh…good part of town.”

She laughed, which must have come from nerves because no one had said anything funny. He used to think her laugh had a musical quality. Hearing it now flooded him with memories.

“I know this is a shock,” she said. “I told your mom we shouldn’t surprise you.”

No shit. He angled a narrow-lidded look at his mother. “No problem. I’ll get over it in a minute.”

The cocktail waitress came. They all ordered drinks. A blue margarita with a name a mile long for Tammy, Maker’s Mark with a splash of water for his mother. For himself, he ordered the same, neat, and wondered if he should have asked for a double. Why the hell was seeing her affecting him like this? He was over her. And had been for years.

Hadn’t he?

The drinks came, followed by the wine steward. They ordered wine. Their waiter came. They selected steaks. Tammy chose the same thing she used to—filet mignon, medium rare. All of it felt surreal.

Drake looked at her, really looked at her for the first time. She was wearing a strapless thing, shiny and pale blue. The fabric stretched like a second skin across her breasts. An impression of her nipples showed. “You left Arizona? What are you doing here?”

She shrugged her tanned shoulders. “I don’t know if you remember, but my uncle—my mother’s brother—is an attorney here. I’m working for him.”

Drake had forgotten that fact, had no reason to remember it.

“Tammy’s a free woman now,” Mom said.

Something squiggled through Drake’s midsection. Tammy turned her head away and he could tell his mother’s bluntness had embarrassed her. A part of him felt sorry for her. Another part wanted to ask about a thousand questions, but he wouldn’t give her the satisfaction.

The wine steward delivered the wine and poured. Drake disciplined himself not to gulp it. Soon the waiter brought the steaks. As they ate, they talked about golf, ranching, Tammy’s parents, life in

Arizona, and a dozen other things, all of it hollow small talk. He couldn't keep his eyes off her fine features, her thick blond hair, the deep cleavage at the top of the strapless dress.

"I'm really not feeling well," his mother said all at once.

Drake swung his gaze to her. "What is it, Mom?"

"I don't know. I ate something on that cruise that didn't agree with me and I've never totally gotten over it."

She didn't look sick, but Drake placed his napkin on the table and started to rise from his chair. "I'll drive you home."

She waved away his effort. "No, no. I do think I'll go, though. But I'll take a cab."

Now he was standing. He picked up her purse. "No. I'll drive you."

"No," she said sharply and yanked her purse away from him. "You probably came in that sports car. Riding in that thing will only make me sicker. I'd rather take a cab. I'm going to ask them to call one for me." She summoned the waiter and gave him that instruction, getting to her feet. "I'm going up to the front door and wait."

As Drake pulled her chair back for her, she looked up at him. "Tammy rode with me. You can see that she gets home, can't you?"

Drake mentally swore. Now he didn't believe for a minute that his mother was sick. "Sure, but—"

"Thank you, darling." She turned to Tammy. "I'm so sorry to abandon you, but as I'm sure you'll remember, you're in good hands with Drake. I'm just going to go home and take something."

Tammy, too, was standing, "I'm so sorry you aren't feeling well, Betty."

Mom made her way to the front of the restaurant. Drake glared after her, a litany of cusswords scrolling through his mind.

"Do you think she's okay?"

Tammy's question took his attention back to her. Her brow was furrowed with concern. Apparently she had fallen for his mother's ruse. Or was she in on it? He studied her face for a few beats. "Yeah," he said at last and walked over and held her chair for her. He reclaimed his own chair, picked up his napkin and spread it on his lap. "I'm pretty sure he's just fine."

"This is awkward. I hope you don't think—"

"I don't think anything. Let's just finish eating."

Minutes passed and Drake found no more words. If one wanted steak, the Cattlemen's Steak House was one of the better places to eat it, but he scarcely tasted his rib-eye. The silence grew heavier.

Tammy finally spoke. "Betty told me you're in the real estate investment business. She said you're very successful. I always knew you would be."

He shrugged. "I've had some luck. You're a free woman? Does that mean you're divorced or what?"

Her eyes lowered to her plate. She nodded, smoothing her napkin on her lap. "It's been final about four months." She looked up at him then, her gaze clouded, her eyes almost teary. "He found someone else," she said in a small voice.

And you wanted that fucker so goddamn much. Drake flashed back on the havoc their broken engagement and wedding cancellation had caused, not just in his own life, but in the lives of other people. Since Tammy had immediately hightailed it to Arizona after the breakup, she didn't personally experience the repercussions. He drew in a deep breath. "Seems to be hard to keep a marriage together these days." After a pause and another bite of meat, he came up with the next logical question. "Kids?"

She nodded. "Two boys. Twelve and nine."

Hearing that affected Drake oddly. Once he had planned for Tammy to be the mother of *his* children and it struck him that since her, he hadn't met another woman with whom he had felt that desire.

After a few beats, she added, "He got custody."

A surprise. Drake knew few men who had gotten custody of their kids in a divorce. Judges favored mothers unless there was a damn good reason not to. Was the woman he had once expected to be the mother of his children a bad parent or what? He stopped cutting his steak and looked at her. "How'd that happen?"

She shook her head and avoided his eyes. "I agreed to it. I haven't even settled on a place to live. My life's torn up. I have to start over. He—we…"—her shoulders lifted and fell—"thought it would be better for the kids if he kept them."

She reached for her wineglass and took a large swallow. "They'll visit me. Or I'll visit them. My folks are still in Sedona and they'll see them." She placed her long fingers on the stem of her glass and turned it, then drank again. Drake noticed her manicure and long nails. Plastic, like most of the women he knew. Except for Shannon.

Tammy obviously wasn't happy about her circumstances. Drake saw her vulnerability, but he didn't want to probe it, didn't want to make her think he cared. Now, if only he could figure out whether he did.

She looked up at him from an unsmiling face. "You never got married?"

He shook his head. "No time for it."

She nodded again and returned her attention to her food, moved it around on her plate. "I've, uh…I want you to know that I've thought a lot about all those years ago, Drake. After what I just told you, you're probably thinking what goes around comes around. And I don't blame you." She looked up at him again. "I—I hope we can let bygones be bygones."

Meaning what? Needing to distance himself, he sat back in his chair. "I don't know. Are you willing to let bygones be bygones with what's-his-name?"

She stiffened, a stricken look in her eyes.

A little pinch tightened his gut. That remark had been unnecessarily cruel. Of course he remembered Ian Harper's name, probably would never forget it. "Sorry," he said, returning to his food. "I'm not trying to be a shit. I honestly don't have a chip on my shoulder if you might be thinking that."

She relaxed and smiled. "I'm glad. Of all the people I wouldn't want to hate me, one of them would be you. All of my memories of you…of us…are good ones."

Drake rarely dredged up the past or tried to analyze it, particularly the part that included Tammy. He was still puzzled why he had shared a little of it with Shannon in Hawaii. He cleared his throat. "Forget it, Tammy. It's water over the dam."

"Would it matter if I said that with Ian, it was never like it was between you and me? That most of the time Ian and I were married, I missed what we used to have?"

What the hell did she mean by "It?" Sex? There had been no dearth of that with Tammy. They had screwed like rabbits whenever and wherever they could find a place. Thinking back now, he remembered that lust for her had thrummed within him day and night. Sating it was the most all-consuming pleasure he had ever known up to that point in his young life. Even better than football.

He had been a virgin when they first started really dating in high school, but that wasn't true of her. Though she was a year younger than he, she had been more experienced, was already on the pill. She'd had to show him how to make her come. The barrage of memories was starting to make his butt want to squirm in his chair. He did not want to be reminded of how weak he had been during those years with this woman.

"We were kids," he said. "Things are different when you're a kid."

"But that doesn't mean heartfelt feelings change. What would you think if I said I came back to Fort Worth because *you're* here?

He reached for his wineglass and gulped, cleared his throat and dabbed his mouth with his napkin. As uncomfortable as he was, he had to admit he was curious. She had left Texas a newlywed while he was a college student in Dallas and still living part time in Drinkwell. How or why would she have kept up with him? "How did you know I'm living in Fort Worth?"

"My folks still talk to your dad occasionally." Her shoulders lifted in a shrug and the corners of her mouth tipped in a wan smile. "They miss you, too."

"Things change, Tammy. People move on."

She nodded. "I know," she said softly.

They finished their food in uncomfortable silence. When the waiter came with the dessert menu, Drake declined and asked for the check. To Tammy, he said, "I'd just as soon go. I've had a helluva week and I'm exhausted."

"That's fine. I'm tired, too. I don't need the calories anyway."

Minutes later, they left the dining room, with him walking behind her, which gave him a back view of the blue dress. The *little* blue dress. It covered less than half her back, barely covered her ass and clung like plastic wrap. Her extremely high heels gave her hips a sexy sway. Nothing had been wrong with her body when they were kids. He used to look at her naked and tell himself what a lucky sonofabitch he was. Now she had filled out and giving birth to two kids had damn sure done her no harm. She was all woman, from the silky blond hair to the soles of her high-heeled shoes.

To his dismay, the dragon in his drawers hadn't forgotten her either. It had perked right up.

He paid the bill, they collected their coats in the vestibule and left the restaurant. He took her elbow as they crossed the street and walked to his car, all without talking. He stopped her at the Virage's passenger door and opened it for her.

"Nice car," she said, giving him a sidelong look from beneath hooded eyes. She folded her long limbs into the small space. Her short skirt rode up to the tops of her thighs and he wanted to howl. He reached the driver's door with a boner pressed against his fly. Luckily, he was wearing an overcoat.

"This is a step up from a Corvette," she said when he ducked behind the wheel. "I'm not surprised you're driving a sports car. I remember that Corvette your dad bought you that time and how upset you were when Betty took it back."

Inside the Virage's close quarters, her scent filled the space. Something sexy and womanly. Old habits rose up and he had to will himself not to place his hand on her thigh as he once did.

"Do you remember what we used to do when I was wearing a dress?" she asked softly.

From the corner of his eye, he saw her knees slightly parted. He was positive she was talking about how he used to slide his hand under her skirt and tease her. She would open her legs and without even taking off her panties, let him play with her until she climaxed. Those memories did nothing to quell the action in his shorts.

"I don't have much memory of what went on that far back," he lied.

She shifted in the seat. "We're in a dark place. Better than sitting at a traffic light like we used to."

Jesus Christ! He kept his hands to himself and asked her where she lived.

Her address was a stylish luxury apartment complex he knew about. He was acquainted with the architect who had designed it.

"Betty said Lockhart Tower is a fabulous place," she said as he eased into traffic.

Fabulous. There was that Donna Schoonover word he hated. He winced.

"I considered buying there when I first got back here. A Realtor I contacted told me one of the smaller units was for sale, but I decided I'd be better off renting."

He never passed up an opportunity to boast about Lockhart Tower. "It's a great place to live."

"Your mom said you live there yourself. That the building has this fantastic pool that's like this private tropical garden."

Fantastic. What was it with women and these friggin' empty words? "That was the designer's concept," he said. "I rarely use it myself. I'm not a swimmer."

She laughed. "I remember that. When we were kids in Drinkwell, if you weren't part of the swim team, there weren't a lot of places for us to swim."

"For sure."

"Betty said the school has a new fancy pool now and a winning swim team. That's nice. I got used to having my own pool in Sedona. I love swimming. I'd love to see your pool. Actually, I'd like to see the whole building."

"Come by anytime. We don't do tours, but I'm always happy to show it off." He merged onto the freeway. "What made you leave Arizona? If your folks and your kids are there, why didn't you stay?"

"Sedona just isn't big enough for me and Ian and his new wife. But I might go back…if things don't work out here. That's why I'm only renting."

Drake didn't miss the implication in what she said. He also recognized the symptoms of a woman lost and confused and searching for something. God knew, he had encountered that circumstance before, usually in women newly divorced and looking to replace something or somebody, a scary situation for a single man.

Once they were on the freeway, they could see the Fort Worth cityscape from the overpass. She looked out at it. "My uncle's practice is downtown, down by the courthouse. That makes it easy for me to drop by your condo after work. Maybe we can renew old acquaintances."

A huskiness in her voice revealed how she intended for them to renew old acquaintances. The hair raised on the back of Drake's neck. A late-day visit from her was the last thing he wanted. But like a fool, he said, "You're welcome anytime." Then he covered himself by adding, "I'm often gone, but even if I am, the concierge can show you around. You're welcome to use the pool. Or the gym. I can add your name to our guest list."

"Would you? I'm going to do that then. Go swimming, I mean."

When they reached her apartment complex, Drake walked her to her front door, weaving through a maze of buildings and landscape features.

"Do you want to come in?" she asked as she plugged her key into her front door lock. "I brew a mean cup of coffee."

He didn't dare step into that trap. He shoved his hands into his coat pockets. "Can't. Early day tomorrow. I've been out of my office most of this week. I'm still trying to catch up."

"Do you still like sports?"

As kids, they had both been into sports. In a town as small as Drinkwell, school sports events had been at the heart of their social activities. Then, after he left for college and tried to play football, college football had become important to them. She had kept up with all the statistics and could readily quote them. His friends at the time had thought she was cool.

"Sure," he answered, setting back on his heels.

"TCU is playing the Aggies tomorrow afternoon. Home game. I've got an extra ticket. Wanna go?"

"Basketball?" He snorted, vapor spewing from his lips into the cold air. "I can't remember the last time I went to a basketball game."

"As an alum, I get super seats. It's supposed to be an exciting game. You know how it is when anyone plays A&M."

He chuckled. "I don't follow college sports these days."

"Come on. Be my guest. For old times' sake. The tip-off's at two o'clock. TCU is expected to win. There'll be lots of spirit. You'll enjoy it."

Okay, he had been a grouch all evening. He forced a smile. "I've got to run up to Southlake tomorrow morning and check on my project, but I guess I could be back in time."

She smiled back at him. "I like it when you smile. You were such a good-looking boy. Now you're a handsome man. What about food?"

"I probably won't finish up there until after eleven. I'll just—"

"That's great. There's a little breakfast place in that shopping center just up University Drive from the gym. They specialize in gourmet pancakes and omelets. It's called Benjamin's for Breakfast. I'll buy."

Located near the TCU complex, Benjamin's was a popular spot for the college crowd. "I'm familiar with it," he said. "Okay, I guess I can meet you there."

He left her at her front door and was home by eleven.

But at midnight he was wide awake and sitting in his living room, lit only by lights from outside, thinking about the past. And Tammy McMillan. Amazing how easily he had slipped back into what had once been routine—dining with her and his mother, sharing inside jokes and a camaraderie of familiarity that was no longer a part of his life except when he returned to the Double-Barrel.

He missed it, he now acknowledged, though seeing his former fiancé again caused him more stress and *dis*tress than anything he could remember. He tilted back his head and rested his neck against the sofa back, closed his eyes and let memory carry him back to his senior year at SMU...

He was twenty-two, going on twenty-three. Too damn young to get married, but he hadn't known that then. With both sets of parents pushing, the die was cast. The wedding was to take place in June.

Spring break. He had gone back to the ranch to spend the off time. Tammy was home from TCU. He picked her up for a date and in the front seat of his truck, she returned his ring. Just like that. No quarrel, no previous discussion. She confessed that she had been seeing Ian Harper, a pro golfer from England who was in the States playing on the pro circuit. Drake and she both had met him at a golf tournament. She hadn't said she was already sleeping with him, but even as dumb about women as he had been as a kid, Drake hadn't had to be slapped in the face with a wet towel.

He took the ring home and gave it to his mother. To this day he didn't know where it was. Probably locked away in his mother's safe deposit box. He had paid thousands for it with money from the trust fund gifted to him by his grandfather.

In the days that followed, he increasingly couldn't abide his surroundings, felt as if ants were crawling under his skin. He couldn't stand the looks of sympathy from his friends and family, didn't want to share his pain with his prying mother. He didn't even wait for the end of spring break to leave the ranch. He pulled himself together and went back to his apartment in Dallas.

He sleepwalked through the rest of the semester. Still, he somehow graduated with a 4.0. Even with a broken heart, he was too responsible to betray his parents by fucking up the education the ranch had paid for.

When summer came, he returned to the Double-Barrel with a chip on his shoulder the size and weight of a bowling ball. He moved into the bunkhouse where the unmarried ranch hands lived and gave himself over to learning to be a cowboy from Silas Morgan.

To a man, the hands looked at him with a jaundiced eye, but with steely resolve, he endured their resentment and worked with them seven days a week. He ate and slept with them. They gave him no mercy. Eventually he proved himself and they accepted him as a peer. In time, they even invited him when they went to town on Saturday nights.

He scarcely entered the ranch house, had little contact with his parents or his siblings. Later, Pic had told him his dad had stopped his mother when she wanted to intervene, saying, "Leave him alone. He's growing up." Back then, his mother had still listened to what her husband said.

Drake had done more than grow up. He had worked harder than he had ever worked before or since. Even when he had previously cowboyed for his dad, he hadn't born the full brunt of the job of being a cowboy. That tumultuous summer after graduation, he learned that he and his brothers and sister had mostly been seen as the boss's namby-pamby spoiled kids and were barely tolerated by the real cowboys. He hated that.

He had never been inclined to fight, but a deep-seated anger festered inside him. His temper flared at the slightest provocation. On the face of every man he tangled with, he saw the visage of Ian Harper. He rarely lost a fight.

His salvation came when he met a woman fifteen years older in a bar in a neighboring town. She offered something more appealing than fighting in bars. He started spending his free time in her bed engaged in vine-swinging sex that pushed what had gone on between him and Tammy McMillan far back in his imagination.

College might have taught him discipline and critical thinking, but real work and the real world toughened his hide and hardened his body. He learned the meaning of responsibility and self-reliance and how to make decisions on the fly. He had begun that summer as a boy, but had emerged from the eighteen-month experience as a man, annealed and ready for life.

He had gone back to SMU's renowned Cox Business School and earned his MBA in record time. Armed with that and what was left of his trust fund, he had jumped into the pulsating world of high-stakes real estate in the Metroplex. He could have lost all of it, but he hadn't. Instead, he had made his own fortune.

By dumping him and moving on, Tammy McMillan had done him a favor.

He opened his eyes and glanced at his watch. *Shit.* He had to get to bed.

Chapter Thirty-Six

THE NEXT MORNING, Drake was up and driving to Southlake early, arguing with himself the whole distance. He should break the date he had made with Tammy, but he didn't have her phone number. He could just not show up, but how rude would that be? He would feel like a coward who had no discipline and he would never hear the end of it from Mom.

How would Shannon react if she knew what he had done last night or what he planned to do today? He should call her. But in the next instant, he decided against it. If he couldn't explain to himself why he was going to a ballgame with his former fiancé, how could he explain it to his lover? If she asked what he had been doing, he didn't know what he would tell her. He didn't want to lie to her, so when he reached his job site, he sent her a text: *Just saying hi. Busy*.

After lining out his crew, he returned to Fort Worth and met Tammy at Benjamin's as planned. She looked fresh and beautiful. Tanned and fit, a slightly older version of how she had looked when she was twenty. She was wearing a purple TCU booster sweatshirt and the color set off her blond good looks.

Over a western omelet, they talked about sports, but didn't mention golf or her ex-husband. Then they rode together in her BMW to the TCU gymnasium.

TCU lost the game, which might have surprised some, but not Drake. The Aggies had come to play, as they always did. That much hadn't changed since his own days as a college athlete. He had enjoyed the basketball game and wasn't sorry he attended. He and Tammy had cheered and clapped and sung and done the college thing. They'd had fun. But it was all unrealistic and a part of him thought it silly. He had outgrown it.

He had left his construction crew in Southlake with instructions to work all weekend and call him if necessary, so back in the car, he switched on his phone and checked for messages.

"Expecting a call?" Tammy asked.

"Always," Drake answered, and that was the truth.

As he started to return the phone to his belt, it bleated and he checked caller ID. *Mom.* He swore mentally, but keyed into the call. She started talking at once. "I want you to bring Tammy and come to my house for supper. I've been cooking all day. Everything's ready and waiting. My old recipe for beef stew and fresh cornbread like I used to make it at the ranch when you two were kids. And I made a chocolate fudge cake, the one I won a ribbon with at the Treadway County Fair."

Drake wanted to go home and unwind. He needed some private time to regain his equilibrium. "How you feeling, Mom? Still got a stomach ache?"

"I'm just fine. I came home and took some Pepto Bismol. Now I'm better."

Giving up resistance, he turned to Tammy. "Mom's cooked supper. Are you up for it?"

"I'd love it. Your mom's a great cook."

"We're on our way," he told his mother.

He started to hook the phone back onto his belt again, but Tammy held out her hand and said, "Could I?"

"What, the phone?"

"Uh-huh."

He handed it over, she dug her own phone out of her purse and pressed numbers into both of them. She handed his back with a smile. "There. Now we've exchanged phone numbers."

He didn't want her phone number, didn't want her to have his. But he said, "Okay, fine."

The home-cooked meal was delicious, as it always was when his mother prepared it, reminding him of happier times at the ranch. The conversation turned out to be a stroll down memory lane even more detailed than it had been last night. Pleasant enough, enjoyable even, he admittedly grudgingly. He had found it easy—too easy—to fall into the comfort of familiar company and shared past experiences, though those experiences had nothing to do with his present lifestyle.

Tammy had driven her own car to his mother's house, so he didn't have to take her home, a relief. They said goodnight with no future plan.

Driving home, he couldn't stop thinking about the weekend's dizzying turn of events. And Tammy. When he was eighteen, sex with her had drawn him like a spider to its web. He hadn't been able to get enough. Was that same powerful lure in play again? How else could he explain having half a hard-on last night and all day today? But was the arousal anything more than how a man reacted when he saw any beautiful woman who made no secret that she was ready and willing?

The day and the evening had triggered even more memories. Tammy had always been a toucher. At the ballgame, when she had put her hand on his arm when she talked to him, he had almost covered the top of her hand with his, as he used to, but he had stopped himself just in time.

She used to have a way of looking at him with eyes that held an invitation to something naughty and fun. She still had that about her and today at the ballgame, he had found himself looking back with anticipation, just like fifteen years ago. Back then, they would have left the ballgame, found some out of the way spot and got it on in the backseat of his crewcab truck.

Maybe he and Tammy shared too much to ignore—history, family, common interests. He had spent more time with her than with any other woman. They knew each other. How could he not remember that they had touched each other in every way, that she had been his first teacher for one his greatest pleasures. A guy would have to be unconscious not to find her attractive. It would be easy to pick up where they left off.

No way, buddy, his wiser inner voice said. *She fucked you over once. She'd do it again.*

Thank God for that inner voice. It had saved him more than once.

Drake awoke on Sunday morning tired. His mind and emotions had stewed all night. He couldn't wipe away the feeling that somehow he was cheating on Shannon. She was the woman with whom he felt a bond of souls, something he couldn't even have recognized as a kid when he had been with Tammy.

He had an overwhelming urge to hear Shannon's voice, but he stopped himself from calling her. He was unsettled and he wore a cape of guilt. He didn't know what to say to her, feared saying the wrong thing. He couldn't call her until he figured out what was going on inside himself.

His mother called before he got up. "Wasn't yesterday fun? Like old times, wasn't it? You and Tammy—"

"What are you doing, Mom?" Annoyed, he swung his feet to the floor and sat up. "You know I'm seeing someone."

"Yes, I do know it," she snapped. "And it's high time you took a hard look at that someone. I know who she is. And I know more about her than you think. She isn't good enough for you, Son. In fact, I don't know who would be a good partner for someone like her. Why, she's nothing but white trash. She was married to white trash. Maybe she still is. I'll bet she hasn't told you that."

That speech stopped him. Where the hell had she gotten such specious information? He couldn't remember ever telling her or anyone in his family Shannon's name, much less anything else. Annoyance turned to anger. "Cut it out, Mom. You don't know what you're talking about."

Her breath hitched, then she quickly went on. "What I do know is that you and Tammy were the perfect couple. You still could be."

"Forget that. You know what she did. You think that's okay?"

"People forgive people, Drake. It happens all the time." He heard anxiety, even panic in her words "Look at the Andersons. My God, Kathy had an affair. Al divorced her and she married another man. Then she came back and asked Al to forgive her. He took her back. And now they're remarried and happy as can be. They've even had another child."

Drake had gone to high school with the couple. His mind zipped to another example of reconciliation he knew of. His new construction boss, Chick Featherston who had gone through a bitter divorce from his ex-wife Amy. Later for the sake of their son, they had remarried. Big mistake. Now they were separated and headed for a second divorce.

"Look in the mirror, Mom. You're not exactly the one to be telling me about how I should conduct myself with any woman."

They argued for another few minutes, then disconnected. Now he was awake and couldn't go back to sleep. He got up and headed for the shower.

On Sunday evening, he called Shannon to discuss the Lubbock trip. Besides that, he wanted to hear her voice, wanted her to set him straight. He had spent more than twenty-four hours mixed up between the past the present and mentally battling the question of the "right thing."

As Betty Lockhart readied for bed Sunday night, she was beside herself with disappointment and frustration. She had awakened this morning so delighted with how well last night's dinner had gone, she couldn't wait to hear that Drake felt the same. But after this morning's argument, she'd had a headache all day.

She turned off her bedside light and stared into the dark night. What could she do about the woman Drake appeared to be so taken with? Then an idea came to her. She could get the file Donna Schoonover had given her into his hands anonymously. All she had to do was mail it. Simple.

The next morning, she dressed and drove to Kinko's first thing, made copies of every document in the file. Then she bought a plain white envelope, had Drake's office address typed on it and stuffed the documents inside. She dropped it in the mailbox outside the door, calculating he would receive it by Tuesday or Wednesday at the latest. In the end, when it saved him from making a terrible mistake, he would appreciate getting the information.

As the week passed, Shannon's loss of the five-acre parcel became like a dull ache instead of a sharp pain. Grammy Evelyn's frayed old saying about windows closing and doors opening came back and guided her. She would find a better investment and start over. She was only thirty-three. She had plenty of time to build her retirement. But knowing and accepting those facts did little to keep a pall of gloom from settling over her.

She had received messages from Drake here and there and had sent a few to him. That they were both busy was just as well. Hawaii had been emotional in a way Shannon had never experienced. Time apart gave both of them a chance to step back and look at where they were going. For the first time in a month, she forced all of her energy and time onto her business.

The date for the Lubbock trip loomed just a few days ahead. In a phone call to discuss the arrangements, Drake had again offered to hire someone to stay with Grammy Evelyn, but Shannon declined. The idea seemed absurd when Colleen lived twenty minutes away.

She should tell her sister who she was seeing. Perhaps sharing personal information would make Colleen more cooperative in the future. She drove out to Colleen and Gavin's house on Saturday to discuss it.

She found her sister in the kitchen baking. Colleen invited her in and offered her a seat at the white breakfast counter and a cup of coffee. Perhaps the positive vibes from Christmas had carried over. While Shannon shrugged out of her coat and laid it on a neighboring stool, Colleen took a cup and saucer from the cupboard and poured the coffee. The sound of a football game came from the TV in the family room.

Shannon sipped at the coffee. "That's good coffee, Colleen."

"It's a special blend I got at one of those stores downtown on the square." Colleen opened a drawer and pulled out hot pads. "What's up?"

Shannon sighed. "Colleen, can't we just—"

"Just what? I know you didn't come out because you enjoy my company."

"Okay, fine. I'm going out of town again."

"I don't get it. Don't you and your boyfriend ever do anything in town?"

"He lives in Fort Worth. His work requires him to travel sometimes."

"Humph. A traveling salesman. I'm not surprised." Colleen turned her back and opened the oven door.

Irked by the conversation, Shannon said to her back, "You know something, Colleen? I haven't told you his name because I don't want a big deal made of it. It's Drake Lockhart I'm dating. I'm sure I don't have to add that he's got projects going on all over the place."

Colleen closed the oven door, tossed her hot pads onto the counter and planted a skinny fist on her hip. "Is that a name that's supposed to mean something?"

Shannon sighed again, not surprised that Colleen hadn't heard of Drake. Her world was as small and as confined as a turtle's.

But Gavin was a different story and he was standing in the kitchen doorway, a newspaper dangling from one hand. "You expect us to believe you're shacking up with Drake Lockhart? In your dreams. What a bunch of BS."

A shot of rage zinged up Shannon's spine and she sprang to her feet. "I'm not shacking up, Gavin, and I wasn't talking to you." She turned to her sister. "Colleen, all I want you to do is keep an eye on Grammy Evelyn for a few days just like you did before. Can't you do that? Stop in and check to see that she's okay or if she needs anything? It would give you a chance to spend some time with her. You hardly ever see her."

"That's not true," Colleen replied indignantly. "We take her to church."

"Every two or three months? Big deal. Drake offered to hire someone to look after her, but I thought that was unnecessary when she has a granddaughter a short drive away."

"You're really going off on a trip with Drake Lockhart," Gavin said. "You're not kidding." Statements, not questions, as if he finally believed it.

Colleen glowered at her husband. "Well, my Lord. Who is Drake Lockhart?"

Shannon suddenly felt as if a hammer pounded an anvil between her temples. She picked up her coat. "You know what? This is ridiculous. Just forget it. Drake and I'll pay for someone."

Gavin came over, tossed his newspaper onto the counter and thrust his face at her. His lawyer mode. Shannon had been on the receiving end of that look before, when she had confronted him about lifting the lien on Grammy Evelyn's home.

"How'd you meet somebody like him?" Gavin demanded.

Roasting him with a glare, Shannon zipped up her coat, picked up her purse and started for the door.

"We didn't say we wouldn't do it," Gavin said, following her.

"Yes, you did," Shannon replied. "I can't count on my family for one damn thing. And neither can Grammy Evelyn."

She reached for the doorknob, but Gavin had already grasped it. He had a silly grin on his face. "That's cool that you're dating somebody like that. Really cool, man. Your taste is getting better, little sister. Hell, he's a rock star. I read about him all the time."

Shannon glared at him. "Move your hand, Gavin. I need to go."

Colleen had come up behind them. "Will someone please tell me *who* is Drake Lockhart?"

Ignoring his wife, Gavin said, "I'd like to meet him. You know, maybe get a good word from him, know what I mean? 'Course a guy like him's probably a Republican."

Now her brother-in-law was more like a Toy Poodle than a Rottweiler. Shannon knew what was going through his mind. Now that he had decided to run for something, he was suddenly interested in begging for an endorsement from someone like Drake. Exactly what she had expected if and when Gavin and Colleen learned about Drake. "You and many others, Gavin. Open the door. I need to go."

"You think you might introduce him to your family?"

"We're a long way from that."

"But, hey, if you decide you want to, we can have y'all out to dinner sometime. Your grandmother, too. Make it a family affair."

"We're only shacking up, Gavin. I don't think that calls for a family dinner."

Sighing, he straightened. At least he had the civility to back off. "Well, anyway, we'll keep an eye on Grammy Evelyn, won't we Colleen? Don't worry about it, okay."

"Thank you," Shannon said. "Now will you please let go of the doorknob?"

Shannon's anger cooled the closer she got to town and she started to think about the position Drake was in every day of his life. Someone must always want something from him. She was glad now that she had considered asking him for a loan for no more than a nanosecond. She would never ask him for anything.

Chapter Thirty-Seven

SHANNON DROVE TO Fort Worth Monday afternoon, packed and prepared to travel to Lubbock the next morning. The sky was gray and bleak and the temperature had dropped into the twenties, but thank God, there was no moisture to freeze on the highway. At Lockhart Tower, Drake didn't meet her in the lobby. Instead, the doorman told her he had just arrived and was waiting for her in his residence. She knew he always walked to and from his office above the deli.

When she reached the condo, his cheeks were rosy from the cold and he was still wearing his overcoat. He looked handsome and dashing.

That he was glad to see her showed in his eyes. Between covering her face and mouth with kisses, he helped her peel off her coat. "I haven't had time to order supper," he said, grabbing her around the waist. He swept her tightly against him and planted a lush long kiss on her lips. "God, I want you. How long has it been? Six months?"

She giggled as a thrill zipped through her. She had anticipated just such a welcome for the whole forty-five-mile trip from Camden. She, too, had been counting days since they had last been together. "Since before the rodeo."

"That makes it almost three weeks," he said, pushing her sweater up and pulling it over her head. She shoved his overcoat panels back and slid her hands up his chest, unhooking buttons. He whipped off the overcoat, stepped into the living room and tossed it across a chair back.

"C'mon." he grabbed her hand and started toward the bedroom, but stopped, pulled her against him and they kissed again, stumbling across the dining room into the hallway as he unhooked her bra, bumping the wall as he peeled it off her and tossed it aside, turning and bumping the opposite wall. He half carried her through the bedroom doorway, but she wrestled free of him and continued unbuttoning his shirt. Still, he kissed her.

"Stop," she said, her breath coming in gasps, his unrestrained passion fueling her own. "Let me un-do this shirt."

He scraped back the duvet that covered the bed and they fell onto the mattress. She toed off her shoes. He peeled off her jeans and panties, parted from her long enough to sit up on the edge of the bed and pry off his boots and socks. He stood and stripped off his jeans and shorts all in one motion. He was as aroused as she had ever seen him. He was beautiful. His impressive erection almost had a life of its own. She still marveled that the long, thick thing fit inside her and just thinking about it had her sex already wet and clenching for him.

He caught her staring. His eyes, dark with lust, locked onto hers and he took his jutting penis in hand and stroked himself up and down. "Like what you see? he asked huskily.

"I love it," she answered breathlessly.

"You can have it. All of it."

She scuttled backward on the bed and he moved over her, kneeing her legs apart. "I love my skin against yours. Tell me it's okay to fuck you without a rubber."

Indeed, the Hawaii trip had spoiled him. Her, too. "Bad idea," she said breathily.

Swearing, he stood on his knees between her legs, reached for the bedside table drawer and groped for a condom inside it. She watched, fascinated as much as excited as he rolled on the latex with trembling fingers. "Hurry."

He leaned over her, bracing himself on one hand. Her eyes locked on his. "Pull your knees up," he said roughly. She did as she was told and he placed the hot, smooth head of his penis at her entrance. He slowly eased into her.

She drew a shaky shallow breach, relishing how good he felt, stretching her, filling her. "Oooh, Drake…"

He stayed a few seconds, then pulled out just as slowly, the luscious drag drawing a keening whimper from her.

"God, you're wet," he breathed, his jaw clenched. Then, he slammed into her so hard, a gasp burst from her throat.

"Okay?" he said raggedly. "I'll make it up to you later. I promise."

"'Sokay," she said, not even missing their usual foreplay. Flames of passion licked within her, all around her, threatened to consume her. Her insides already felt as if they had melted.

He heaved a sigh and held himself still for a few seconds, the pressure of him deep inside her and motionless both delicious and maddening. Then he slid his arms underneath her and tightly hugged her to him. "I feel so much better."

"Are you all right? What's wrong?"

"Nothing. Now." His fists gripped her hair and he began kissing her and kissing her, burying his tongue deeply in her mouth, suckling her lips declaring between kisses how must he had missed her and what erotic things he intended to do to her.

But you've hardly called me, she wanted to say, but at this moment, filled by his hot, rock-hard thickness, the lack of a phone call was a non-issue. What was more appealing was wrapping her legs around his buttocks and gliding her hands all over his smooth shoulders and back, touching all of him at once. He kept kissing her, clutching her head, not letting her turn away even once from his ravaging mouth.

"I've nearly gone nuts," he said, raising his upper body and pinning her wrists beside her head.

Her blood pounded through her veins. "Drake. You have to move. I'm going crazy."

Drawing a hiss through clenched teeth, he slowly pulled out of her and just as slowly came back in. "Like that?"

"Uh-huh"

"I want to do you so hard..."

"Just do it...:.I want you to."

He began to move. She found his rhythm—in and in and in, fast, steady and unrelenting, each stroke rasping every inch of her vaginal walls with mind-numbing friction.

She closed her eyes, giving in to the heat blazing through her.

"Don't close your eyes," he commanded.

Her eyes popped open and locked with his.

"I want to see the look in your eyes while we fuck," he said gruffly.

She was far more focused on the pressure low in her belly and the tiny core of her sex screaming to be sated. "Drake," she panted. "I'm so hot. I need you to—"

"This?" He moved up, high above her, pressing the root of him against her clitoris with each hard, rocking stroke.

"Yes," she gasped, flexing her hips and meeting his rapid thrusts. She was poised so explode. "Yes...That's it..."

He stopped, his jaw tight. He drew a great breath through his nose and pulled out again.

"Oh, no!" she cried. "Drake, I'm going crazy."

He crouched between her knees, his hands still pinned her wrists beside her head. His eyes burned into hers. "That's good..." His head ducked and his warm open mouth moved over her breasts, licking and teasing her nipples with his tongue, nipping and sucking first one, then the other madly. Sensation echoed in her clitoris.

"I want you crazy..."

She lifted her hips to him. "Drake, please..."

"...Crazy for me...every time...we do it."

"Oh, Drake," she whimpered, her nipple tingling.

He pressed the eager bud against the roof of his mouth and sucked hard. "Your nipples are delicious," he murmured as he moved to her other breast and applied the same treatment. She moaned and gasped.

He released her wrists, his hands gripped her hips and his warm mouth raced down. "Wanna kiss you everywhere," he mumbled against her belly, licking and biting and sucking.

And she wanted no less. She arched her back and let her thighs fall wide, making a convenient offering of the tiny magical spot that pushed and strained for his attention. In her mind, it had become the size of a baseball. "Yes, yes....Do..."

He scooted down her body. She lifted her knees. Then his mouth was there and his fingers were parting her labia and his tongue was laving and swirling. Two fingers slid inside her and he sucked her demanding little clit full into the flaming wetness of his mouth. Need spiraled through her. Deep muscles convulsed inside her sex...Animalistic sobs escaped her throat as she came again and again.

But it wasn't enough. A desperate longing for him back inside consumed her, burned her. She pulled him up by the hair, panting his name. "Drake....Drake....Come back...up here."

His mouth and tongue and teeth trailed back up her body and he slammed his hard penis into her again, hooked his forearms behind her knees and pushed them high and wide, pinning her. to the mattress. He hammered into her as he never had before, each plunging thrust lifting her buttocks off the mattress, punishing her, thrilling her, the root of him pressuring and rasping her clitoris. The need exploded within her again. A kaleidoscope of colors darted behind her eyes. She dug her fingers into his back, bit into his shoulder to keep from screaming as her deepest muscles convulsed around him.

He came hard, stiffening and grunting and growling and puffing. She hung onto him, wrapping him tightly in her arms. He seemed to be in such a state, it was the least she could do for him.

When it was over, he eased his weight down on top of her, his chest heaving. He was shaking and drenched with sweat. So was she. "That damn near killed me," he rasped, clasping her hands beside her head and interlocking their fingers again.

She had never felt so thoroughly possessed. Something was wrong.

When she had recovered enough to speak, she said, "Oh, my God, Drake. That was so scary."

"No. It was good," he mumbled against her neck.

"I know. Scary good. I love it when you want me that much. What's wrong with us? With me, that you can do that to me?"

"It's been too long since I had you."

But there was more to it than that. She just didn't know what. "Was that just sex or are we calling it something else?"

"Sex. Down and dirty." He freed her hands and turned to his side, hauling her with him. "I wanted it to be dirtier. I wanted a repeat of Hawaii. I wanted to make you come a dozen times in a dozen ways. But everything caught up with me and I couldn't fool around. I had to get to the point."

Something was definitely wrong.

But all she could think of was how much she adored him. She smiled and traced his lip with her fingertip. "You certainly made your point, cowboy." She giggled and stretched her smooth front against his hairy one. "Wanna do it again?"

"Later. The sweet stuff comes next. Valentina bought a can of whipped cream."

Shannon laughed. "You are so awful. After the mess we made with that chocolate mousse, I'm surprised your housekeeper didn't quit. I don't think—"

"What, you don't like whipped cream?"

She traced the bow of his brown brow with her fingertip. "I love whipped cream, especially in all the right places."

He kissed her, hard and quick. "And I know the places. Don't worry about Valentina. She isn't going to quit. She's well paid."

And for a fleeting moment, Shannon wondered how much Valentina must know about Drake and his women. And how many times a week she had washed his sheets after a night of wild sex. She had never met Valentina, wondered if she would be able to look her in the eye if she ever did.

"Lets get up and eat," he said. "We need our strength. I've got some canned soup around here somewhere and some crackers."

They heated chicken noodle soup and ate in front of TV. Soon afterward, they returned to bed. After playing games with the whipped cream and exhausting each other a second time, they drifted to sleep with him spooned behind her and her tangled in a web of his hairy arms and legs and thick bedding. She had never felt more sated or been more comfortable. Or been happier.

She awoke in the night, cold and dreaming and whimpering. About what, she didn't know. Only half-conscious, she felt him pull her closer. She pressed her cheek against his arm, her back and bottom against the source of heat, felt him push her hair away from her neck, felt his warm lips near her ear. "You're okay. I'm here."

"Cold," she mumbled.

He pulled the covers over her and she slid back into the dark blue, floating in semi-consciousness, aware of nothing but warmth and caressing and fingertips lightly fondling her down there. She distantly felt him push her top leg up, felt his fingers stroking her opening. "Drake?" she said drowsily.

"Hm?"

She felt him shift, then he was inside her, thick and hard and hot and filling her flesh to flesh and she felt more than warm. She felt complete. She sighed.

His hand pressed against her belly holding her against him and he began to move inside her. Slowly, rhythmically. Instinctively, she moved with him, her body in tune with his so exquisitely it became a part of her dreamlike state. Soon, his knowing fingertips were stroking her where her opening stretched around his penis. *Lust! Need!* Heat so intense she could barely stand her skin. Yet, she shivered. "Drake?..."

"Shhh," he breathed against her ear, holding her still. His fingertips found her clit and with a soft sigh, she came.

Then he stiffened and pulled her even more tightly against him. She barely heard him grunt, but knew he had found his climax, too.

"Stay inside me," she mumbled. "Don't leave me.

"I won't. Ever."

They drifted back to sleep.

Daylight came. He was no longer inside her, but they were still closely bonded. Something was different. She had thought sex couldn't get more intense, more passionate than it had been in Hawaii, but the only word she could think of that applied to last night was the word "desperate."

"Morning," he said softly, looking into her eyes.

With his morning stubble, rumpled hair and sleepy eyes, he looked sexy and male. She smiled and stretched against him. "Morning."

"Last night was a little rough. Did I make you sore?"

She smiled into his eyes. "A little, but I'll get over it."

"I can never get enough of you," he said softly. "I want you even in my sleep. But I don't like making you sore."

She continued to smile like a loon. "Did you hear me complain? It was wonderful. *You're* wonderful."

"We should get up. The plane will be ready to fly at ten." He made no move to let her go.

"Phooey," she said, still smiling.

"C'mon. Let's go."

"Nag, nag, nag," she said and kissed him long and sweetly.

They hit the shower and stood front to front in a tight embrace as warm water poured over them from the overhead shower fixture. Steam fogged around them. His heart pounded against hers. Emotion hung between them. He didn't say what was on his mind, but she sensed the weight of it. Her own chest couldn't have felt heavier if a boulder had lodged in it. It felt almost like sadness, a lot like surrender.

She had read somewhere that women were usually the first to say "I love you." She had never said those three words to any man since her marriage to Kevin Barton, couldn't recall if she had said them to him. This morning, they were on her tongue, but she feared the result of forcing them out of her mouth. How many times had Drake said them? He must have at least once. He had been engaged for a long time.

As he drove them to the airport in his pickup, he keyed into his BlackBerry and told someone to pick up a fast breakfast for two and put it on the plane. By his clipped orders, she could tell he was strung as tautly as a banjo string. He usually didn't speak so sharply. Was he worried about his deal in Lubbock? Or was it something else?

She thought back to how anxious he had been yesterday, too, even before what had happened in bed last night. Something was going on with him. Was that why they'd had such powerful sex? She cautioned herself to be open-minded. He would surely make himself clear soon.

When they boarded the immaculately clean plane, she saw a big McDonald's sack sitting on one of the seats. No gourmet breakfast this morning and no steward to serve it. He scowled at the sack and mumbled an oath.

She was famished. After nothing but soup and crackers for supper, she didn't care if it was cardboard. "It's fine," she said. "There's nothing wrong with McDonald's."

Then they were airborne and bright morning sun streamed through the porthole windows. He let down the Formica-clad table between their chairs and began unpacking the sack of food. He handed her a breakfast sandwich and a cup of coffee. "Breakfast of champions," he said.

"Egg and sausage on a biscuit. What's wrong with that?"

They ate in silence. After they finished, he folded the table back into place and moved to the seat beside her. He held her hand, but he stared out the window.

The flight was short. Just before they landed, he told her his plans. He would inspect windmills already under construction on his family's land and sign leases for more. Then he would meet with the Lubbock company that wanted him to invest in wind turbine engine construction. He wanted her to see the wind farm, wanted to know what she thought.

After the smoothest flight in her limited experience, they stepped out of the plane into chilled air, bright sunshine and a brilliant blue sky. An upbeat attitude fought through the doldrums. Looking across the landscape toward the distant horizon, she had never seen land so flat. Or so treeless. "Hunh. That must be why they call this part of Texas the high plains." She smiled up at him.

He gave her a quick kiss on the temple. "You're too smart."

"I know. I get it from hanging out with you."

The murky mood of earlier seemed to have brightened.

A white SUV rental awaited them. As they left the airport and started away from Lubbock, the windmills that heretofore she had seen only in pictures became the view. Tall columns topped by three giant turning blades. For as far as the eye could see, they filled the landscape and the skyscape, marching off into the horizon. "Wow," she said. "There must be hundreds. I can't even count them. I had no idea."

He seemed to be as fascinated as she. "Amazing, isn't it?"

He drove them miles out of Lubbock, passing vast flat and barren fields, marred only by more windmills.

"This is it," he said, driving off the highway onto a dirt road. "The Lockhart cotton farms. What do you think?"

In front of her lay more unplanted fields of red earth and a closer view of the windmills. He behaved as if he sincerely wanted her opinion. And she didn't have one. She kicked her brain into gear. "Can you still grow cotton with all of these things here?"

He nodded. "We'll soon be planting. The windmills won't interfere."

The windmills' white sleek minimalist profiles presented an ethereal beauty against the brilliant blue of the winter sky. Some of the blades turned lazily, while others spun at a pace. The capriciousness of the wind? "What if the wind doesn't blow?"

"The wind always blows here. Only a major shift in the jet stream would change it. Too much wind is the more likely problem. Either way, the energy company that's doing this says they've got it handled."

She had now been around him enough to recognize skepticism. "You don't think this is going to work, do you?"

"I don't know. We started leasing the land about seven years ago. The first phase is finished and the leases are paying off. But I can't keep from thinking of the facts. They've been doing this wind and solar shit for thirty years. Spent billions. And they're no closer to making it work on a grand scale than they've ever been. I'm afraid it's kind of like hunting unicorns."

"They don't make electricity?"

"That's not the issue. Nobody seems to have an organized plan. There's no support system. No practical way to consistently deliver the energy they produce. A universal collector and transmission system is so expensive to construct, it might not be possible, even for the government."

"So the answer to my question is you don't believe in it."

"I haven't seen any data that makes me think we're even close to replacing oil and gas or coal with wind and solar energy. My dad keeps reminding me that there's no green energy that will get a seven-forty-seven off the ground. And he's right."

"But that isn't true. Grammy and I watched a TV show about a thing in space that's entirely solar-powered. It's up there now."

He gave her a smirk. "That may be, but I'm pretty sure it didn't get up there on green energy."

She smiled, hoping to add some humor to the mood. "The stuff you hear about green energy is that it's all good."

He shook his head. "All I know is that even with government help, these wind and solar companies are going broke every day. My dad also keeps reminding me that it's all political. He calls it a money-laundering scheme for politicians. They have to talk it up to the public. Otherwise, the bastards might get lynched for how they're misappropriating taxpayer money."

"But aren't they putting people to work? Isn't that one of the goals?"

He shook his head again. "Compared to oil and gas companies, the number of people employed by green energy companies would fill a teacup. And the payrolls don't come close to oil and gas. These turbines you're looking at right here?" He made a sweeping gesture that encompassed the horizon. "Pennington Engineering stood up the windmills, but the turbines were made in China. No American worker earned a dime."

He looked at her directly, the crease between his brows a deep dark line. "And this is what I'm here to make a decision about. When Pennington first approached me for seed money, the plan was for the turbines to be made in the USA and employ hundreds of locals. Somewhere along the way, that changed. So now I have to decide if I want to put my family's money into a venture that might go broke next year and a company that employs damn few Americans in America. My family has strong feelings about that."

"I've never heard about the turbines being made in China," she said.

"As far as I'm concerned, it's one of the biggest holes in Pennington's plan. I was on board with him two years ago. Now I'm not sure where I am. The decision has been pestering me for months. I've thought about it so much my perspective is screwed up."

She hadn't expected to ever see him unsure of anything. Was a lack of confidence the source of his anxiety? The longer he talked, the less certain she was how to respond. "How many windmills are they going to build?" she finally asked.

"Good question. Are they going to cover the whole Texas Panhandle with a forest of windmills? If so, I'm not thrilled about that either. I'd rather see the blue sky without looking through steel columns."

"Are they fireproof? They have wildfires out here. It's on the news all the time. Thousands of acres at a time. What happens then?"

"Nothing's fireproof."

"You're upset over so many things," she said. "Yet you and your family are leasing your land for the windmills to be built on. I don't get it."

"Cattle ranching is fraught with hazards from all directions. Lockharts haven't survived for a century without being pragmatic. Or opportunistic. The windmill leases have given the Double-Barrel badly needed cash. These green energy people are zealots. They're going to build these friggin' things no matter what and they have to lease land to put them on. If not from Lockhart Farms, then from somebody else. My family and I figure it might as well be from us. Fortunately for us, in Texas, private land is where the wind blows."

She made a little huff of sarcasm. "Aren't you the cynic."

He gave her a wink. "Have you found a part of the real estate business that's not cynical?"

She had no answer for the question. She, too, had given up many ideals, even before she got into home sales where her hard work often became victim to silly squabbles between buyers and sellers over dumb things like toilet seats and towel bars, where hard-earned deals and commissions got wiped out in a few second by unscrupulous mortgage bankers or arrogant lawyers. "I know what you mean," she told him.

"I know you do," he said. "That's why I want your opinion."

"Why? And about what? I don't know anything about all of this."

"I want to benefit from your gut instincts."

Shannon's stomach jumped. He had never asked her opinion about his work and for sure, not something that involved his family. Did this mean they were a team? The idea left her dizzy.

She hesitated, grasping for a reply. Finally, she found the frank honesty that had served her well in the past. "Well…if it were left up to me, I wouldn't put a bunch of money behind something I wasn't a hundred percent sold on. And if your family objects to the turbines being made in China, why get involved? It isn't like there's no other place to invest money."

He looked at her a few beats, then smiled and gazed out at the horizon. She wanted to say, *a penny for your thoughts*, but she had already said enough.

Chapter Thirty-Eight

WHEN SHANNON AWOKE the next morning, the room was dark and she was alone. Drake had an early meeting with the company that wanted to build more turbines. In China.

She switched on the lamp and found a note on his pillow: *Order room service for breakfast. Back by noon. D*

After showering and styling her hair, she examined her body in the vanity mirror. Her nipples were brighter than usual and tender from Drake's attention. She placed her hand over her breast, feeling her nipple against her palm and wondering how it felt to him when he had it in his mouth.

A purple hickey showed on her belly and another where her thigh joined her torso. They had made love again last night. He had been gentle, concerned that she was still sore. She was, but she didn't care. She had taken him eagerly and they had made love no less fervently than the night before in his condo in Fort Worth. Afterward, he had lain between her thighs, his head on her belly, his arms around her hips and she had combed her fingers through his hair for a long while.

And today, in spite of little sleep, she felt glorious. She opened the draperies and let bright sunlight drench their room. She ate breakfast listening to TV news and wondering what was going on in her office back in Camden. She took her time with her makeup, then put on a black sweater and jeans so she could wear the turquoise bear claw necklace Drake had bought her at the rodeo a couple of weeks back. He returned, picked her up and they ate a delicious barbecue lunch in a place someone had recommended to him.

"Palo Duro Canyon is up the road from here," he said. "Ever been there?"

She laughed. "You know me. I've never been anywhere."

"Let's drive up there. I need to think."

They motored up to Amarillo and Palo Duro Canyon, another spectacular landscape. They spent the afternoon like every other tourist. As they clung to each other's hands, moving from one exhibit to another, he wore a grim expression. She could almost see gears grinding in his head. His mind was somewhere else and decisions of some kind were being made.

That evening, dinner with Robert Pennington was scheduled at Mr. Pennington's private club. Shannon put on an outfit she would wear to work—black slacks, a white top splashed with a few crystal beads and a lavender blazer. Lavender was one of her best colors. As she added crystal earrings to her earlobes, Drake came behind her, slid his arms around her waist and kissed her neck. "You look beautiful," he said softly.

And his attention made her feel beautiful. She turned in his arms, rose to her tiptoes and kissed his lips. "Thank you, kind sir."

At the dinner table, Robert Pennington announced that his daughter would be joining them. "I hope you don't mind," he said to Drake. "She's taken on more responsibility in the company."

An expression Shannon could only define as worried flitted across Drake's face, but he said, "Not at all."

Uh-oh. Shannon was sure Drake hadn't expected the daughter's presence.

Shannon had heard Heather Pennington's name and knew she was an engineer like her father, but she was unprepared for the glamorous woman who entered the dining room alone and took the fourth seat at the table.

Structural engineering might be viewed as a man's field, but there was nothing mannish about Heather. Like Donna Schoonover, she was tanned and long and lean, with the look of hours spent in a gym. She had startlingly blue eyes. Her hair—dark brown, waist-length and straight-as-a-string—draped over her shoulder like a shiny silk shawl. Bangs just covered her brows. Tonight she looked stunning in sexy plain-but-clingy black. Other than being roughly the same age, Shannon and she had zero physical features in common.

Shannon strained discreetly to check Heather's left hand, but saw no wedding ring. Anxiety seized her. Now she knew the reason for the odd expression on Drake's face when Mr. Pennington announced that his daughter would be joining them for dinner. That Heather was a woman on the hunt was obvious. And the man that Shannon was beginning to think of as hers was the prey.

The woman's high regard for Drake was as glaring as the nose on her face. She talked only to him, looking into his eyes as if no one else were present. She even openly flirted with him. Her remarks held a teasing intimacy and her behavior toward him revealed that they had shared more than a business acquaintance. When Drake tried to bring Shannon into the conversation, Heather shut her out by changing the subject or mentioning something familiar only to her and Drake.

As for Drake, he kept his cool-dude persona, behaving as if he didn't notice Heather's wheedling. Either he truly did not or he was a damn good actor.

He might be an expert at reading people, but Shannon knew a little about human behavior herself. No man could be as unconscious of a striking female's attention as Drake appeared to be. He was working at it.

Sitting at the table with him and a woman Shannon was sure had the same carnal knowledge of him as she did was as paralyzing as a straitjacket. In her mind's eye, an image formed of him between Heather's long legs, naked and hovering above her, uttering the same words of intimacy that he had said to her, Shannon.

Their conversation veered to school days and football games. Heather had much in common with Drake. She was a graduate of A&M, with a masters in engineering. Like her father, she mentioned once. She and Drake traded college rivalry jokes. Shannon had never attended a college football game, had no particular loyalty to any school. The evening became ever more tense and uncomfortable, heaping on more insecurities.

Time dragged on. The dining room's walls began to close in and Shannon wondered if she could last through dinner.

She did last and at the end of the meal, over coffee and brandy, Drake declined to partner with Pennington Engineering on the wind turbine manufacturing project. Shannon was aghast. Though she had seen his skepticism, she hadn't heard him say he would tack in that direction.

She had gleaned from scattered conversation that the Penningtons expected—and needed—a large amount of money. Their disappointment at not getting it from Drake was palpable. Robert Pennington rose at once and left the table. Snatching up her evening bag and rising, Heather leaned down and spoke near Drake's ear, telling him she wanted to speak to him privately later.

"I'll be back in my office on Monday," Drake said to her. "Or call me on my cell."

His last sentence struck Shannon like a slap. His BlackBerry was his business phone; his "cell" was his personal phone. Heather Pennington had Drake's private cell phone number, the one always labeled *Unknown Number* when a call came from it to Shannon.

"I'll be in touch," Heather said and strode after her father.

Drake summoned their waiter and asked for the check. The waiter tried to explain that dinner would be added to Mr. Pennington's account, but Drake insisted the bill be brought to him. After the waiter agreed and hurried away, Drake looked at her. "I don't expect a guy to buy dinner after I cut him off at the knees."

Her mind a blank, Shannon nodded robotically. "I understand."

As Drake drove them back to the hotel, Shannon couldn't keep from wondering exactly how much Heather had to do with Drake even considering investing in wind turbine manufacturing in the first place. From the first time he mentioned it, Shannon had thought that particular venture was out of his realm.

She thought the reason he had backed out of the deal was because of the turbines being manufactured in China, but she didn't know that with certainty. She thought he would talk to her about it as well as what he had to discuss in private with Heather, but he remained quiet.

In the silence inside the SUV, Shannon sought refuge in her own thoughts. *...call me on my cell....call me on my cell....call me on my cell....* The echo wouldn't stop.

Nor would her next question: *How many other women have his private cell number?*

Staring into the black night, like an arrow shot to her heart, a hard truth struck Shannon. The conversation in Hawaii about trust notwithstanding, he was a thirty-five-year-old rich, good-looking, unmarried guy who had been single all of his life and he hadn't lived like a monk. Besides being a highly-sexed man, he was a very experienced lover and he hadn't learned that in church.

She pictured a parade of women who had passed through his life—the Donna Schoonovers, the Heather Penningtons, the Tammy McMillans. How many others were there, ranging from buckle bunnies to career women?

Something he had said during dinner at the Rio Brazos Steakhouse came back to her: *...I won't tell you I've never been involved in a one-time deal with a woman...*

Even if the *Texas Monthly*'s "Most Eligible Bachelor" title had been purchased in a PR campaign, eligible was what he was. And sexy and desirable. On a list of ideals women sought in a dream man, he conformed to most of them. No matter where she and he went together publicly, there would always be a woman or women who either wanted him or, like Heather Pennington, had already had him.

Shannon had battled low self-esteem and feeling unwanted her entire life. She had only attained a satisfactory level of self-confidence after she became successful in real estate sales. But that achievement had done little for her self-assurance as a woman. The plain truth was, she had too little self-confidence to deal with all that Drake brought to the table.

For the first time in a while, her alter ego piped up: *You might be happy as lark right now, girlfriend, but in time, you'll be miserable.*

A low-grade anger began to build within Shannon, at herself as well as at him. Him because he had convinced her that he wanted more than just sex from their affair. Herself because she had cast off her own resolve and followed along like the country mouse behind Pied Piper.

By the time they reached the hotel, they hadn't said a dozen words since leaving Mr. Pennington's club. Even in their room as they undressed for bed, neither of them seemed to be able to get around a giant black cloud that had mushroomed between them. She knew what contributed to her own discontent, but she couldn't guess what had him so disgruntled. For the first time, when they went to bed, they went to sleep.

The next morning, they had quickie sex that truly was just sex, ate breakfast, then flew back to Fort Worth. They said a brief good-bye in the parking garage and she drove away.

On her way back to Camden, Shannon tried to sort out all that had happened since Tuesday—the desperate, possessive sex on Tuesday night that had convinced her that something wasn't right. She still wondered about it. But she had dismissed the question after they had two great days afterward. Then Heather Pennington showed up at dinner and he had changed again. Besides being a damn tomcat, he was a chameleon.

After Hawaii, like a silly ninny floating in the clouds, she had switched just sex to lovemaking. Now she had to reverse that classification in her mind. If she couldn't, she had no business continuing to fool around with Drake. Only a naïve and foolish woman would cleave to a relationship with someone she could see that other women constantly pursued. It wasn't that she had no faith—or trust—in Drake, but he was only human. And after all, they had made no firm commitment to each other.

And into that boiling pot dropped two new observations. Though he had always been charming, generous, affectionate and gentle with her, seeing him on this trip showed her a ruthless and deadly serious side of him. With her own eyes, she had seen him look Robert Pennington in the eye and demolish the man's plans and perhaps his dreams.

Her cranky alter ego stepped up again: *He didn't get where he is because he isn't a slick guy who's too namby-pamby to make the tough calls.*

Indeed. He had the same edgy killer instinct, that same play-to-win-at-all-costs attitude she had observed in a few other competitive and successful people. So far, she had seen the latter applied only to his business or issues related to money, but did it eventually carry over into his personal associations? If it was a part of his makeup, how could it not?

She feared she knew the answer. If he became tired of her or decided she was in his way, he wouldn't agonize thirty seconds over dumping her. He would approach her in the same cold-steel way he handled his business. She could be the next Donna Schoonover. But at least Donna had the benefits of a fortune to fall back on. Shannon Piper would have nothing but a broken heart and a business that had gone to hell because she had ignored it. But for Drake, some new—or old—female would be, would always be, waiting in the wings.

As he had asked her to do, as soon as she reached Camden, before leaving her car, she sent him a text: *Home safe.*

As she unloaded her bags from the Sorento, a text from him came back: *K.*

Sometimes K stood for "Kisses." Sometimes it simply meant "Okay." Today, she didn't know which.

&

Drake shoved his phone into his pants pocket, glad to know Shannon was home safe. He had never liked her driving to and from Fort Worth alone to be with him. He preferred going down to Camden and picking her up himself, but she still didn't want him to. Nor did she want him to send a car for her. She didn't understand that the expense of sending a car was no big deal. They were going to have to handle the transportation issue. It was becoming oppressive.

He was tired. The trip to Lubbock had taken a toll on him. He hadn't enjoyed the decision he'd had to make about investing in Pennington Engineering's project. He flopped into a reclining chair in front of TV, pondering all that had gone wrong with the turbine manufacturing deal.

The fuck-ups had begun years back when he had violated his one cardinal rule and let himself get too up-close-and-personal with Heather Pennington. He still wondered how much that relationship had contributed to his ambiguity over the turbine manufacturing project.

His thoughts settled on Heather showing up unexpectedly at dinner. Had she done that for spite? Had she known a woman was with him? Shannon was too smart not to have picked up that he and Heather had had a fling. Once, a long time ago, it had been almost serious between them. He had ended their affair because she had a willful streak and he couldn't abide a woman attempting to exact what he had been unwilling to give.

He hoped not to hear from her. No point in rubbing salt into her and her dad's wounds. But he knew her well enough to know that she would call. She would try to make him change his mind because that was the way she was. But nothing she could say would cause him to invest family money into something his dad and brother didn't like and in which he himself had lost more faith every day.

If it were left up to me, I wouldn't spend a bunch of money on something I wasn't a hundred percent sold on. Shannon's words. And she was right. That blunt, one-sentence opinion had helped him clear his head. Good natural instincts were just one more thing he admired about her.

He picked up the remote and channel-surfed. He was rarely home during the day on a weekday, so he didn't know what came on. TV programming didn't matter because he couldn't concentrate. Shannon kept popping in and out of his thoughts. She had become his focus much of the time—where he could take her, the things he could show her and do with her, what he could do *for* her. He loved being with her, loved bantering back and forth with her. She was so open he never had to guess what she was about. They thought alike. He had even started to listen to her ideas and opinions and be influenced by them.

He no longer questioned how he felt about her. Things had been a little out of sync in Lubbock, which he chalked up to the tension caused by Tammy's sudden reappearance in his life, followed by Heather's appearance at dinner. Women. They drove him crazy. Then there was the stress of dealing with the Pennington deal. He would smooth it over the next time he and Shannon saw each other.

As all of those thoughts tumbled through his mind, his phone warbled and he keyed into his brother's call. "Hey, Pic. What's up?"

"How'd it go in Lubbock?"

Drake grunted. "Tell Dad that deal's off. The wind turbine leases with TXE aren't affected, but I backed out of the manufacturing deal."

"He'll be glad to hear that. He was worried you were gonna plow ahead with it."

"He knows better than that. He knows I won't risk the family fortune. Or go against family opinions."

"That's not why I called. Remember me mentioning that kid Billy Barrett?"

"Vaguely."

"They arrested him for Kate's fire. But he didn't stay in jail long. Some wealthy woman in Dallas put up his bond money."

"Hunh," Drake said, confused.

"I don't know what they're thinking. They're looking into his connections now and even into the idea that he might be involved somehow in harassing our whole family. Did you get a chance to make a list of incidents like Blake asked?"

"I haven't had time."

"Take time, will you? Blake really wants it. He wants us all to sit down together."

"I'll make a list tonight and get back to you tomorrow."

After more short conversation, they disconnected. Drake sat back in his chair. Now his musing took a different turn. He searched his memory for the name Billy Barrett, but came up blank. He thought back to his various projects over the past few years, trying to target things that had happened that had caused him unplanned expense.

Reconstruction of the Millennium Bank building had taken more than two years. During that project, an elevator had fallen five floors. The one passenger, an electrician, had been seriously injured, but survived. The insurance company had been satisfied the fall was an accident and had settled. Other incidents and accidents had occurred on that job, but none that struck him as unusual. Hazards were inherent in rebuilding an old skyscraper.

Soon after Lockhart Tower had opened, he had bought the old six-story Sears building just a block from the city center. He had gutted it and just begun reconstruction to turn it into condominiums when a fire had broken out on the third floor and threatened the whole building. The Fort Worth cops had investigated along with the fire department and the insurance company. The incident was declared an accident although no one ever established conclusively how the fire had started. Then there was Buzz's truck accident.

Could all of those incidents have been planned?

He called Pic back. When his brother answered, he said, "Is Rafferty going to be around tomorrow?"

"Probably," Pic answered.

"See if you can round him up. If his theory is legit, we need to get to the bottom of it. I'm going to fly down there. Pick me up at the airport in a couple of hours."

He got to his feet, called the airport and requested the plane be readied to fly. Then he re-packed his duffle and headed out.

Shannon was back in her office mid-afternoon. All but Chelsea were out in the field, hopefully getting listings or making sales or at least trying to do both. She chatted briefly with Chelsea, then closed herself into her office. She sat at her desk, preoccupied with all that was going on in her personal life. At the top of the list was Heather Pennington. Drake had probably heard from her by now.

She stared at the calendar. The end of the workweek. Symbolic, she thought, of her affair with Drake. She didn't know when, or if, she would hear from him again. No dates were planned and so far, he hadn't been one to call up and idly chat. She was so distressed over the Lubbock trip she didn't know if she cared whether he called.

On Saturday, she fell back into her routine, played catch-up in her office all day. She took Grammy Evelyn to church on Sunday morning and worked in her office on the files in the afternoon. The only extraordinary occurrence was getting a call from Colleen wanting to know about the trip. Now she wished she had never told Colleen and Gavin about Drake. No telling what they would do with that information.

Chapter Thirty-Nine

DRAKE STAYED AT the Double-Barrel five days, during which he rode with Pic and Dad and helped with their various chores around the ranch. They had talked extensively about who could be out to inflict revenge on the family, but had come to no conclusions.

He had been sobered by the meetings with Texas Ranger Blake Rafferty and his partner, Jack Dawson. They had convinced him of the revenge angle. What had been an isolated, arson-caused barn fire had morphed into something bigger and more insidious. So far, damage had been done only to livestock and property. But were any of the family members in personal danger? If the weather hadn't been cold, wet and lousy most of December and January, Drake might be persuaded that the mysterious villain rather than the weather was responsible for his problems with Lone Star Commons.

Who hated the Lockharts so much? The cops didn't know. But Drake knew that with the family's history, the list could be long. Through the years one Lockhart or another had stepped on many toes.

From Drinkwell, he had arranged to beef up security on everything he had anything to do with and Dad and Pic now had ranch hands patrolling the pastures at night, hoping to prevent harm to the cattle herd. Drake and Pic had personally moved some of Kate's horses back to Will's secure barn and some to the Double-Barrel's horse barn, where someone would be watching twenty-four/seven.

He pondered what to do about Shannon. By association with him, was she in danger? Should he warn her?

The threat of incoming bad weather and more possible delays on the Lone Star Commons project recaptured his attention. Just when he was considering it was time for him to return to Fort Worth, a call from his assistant came on his BlackBerry.

"Are you coming back soon?"

"I'm thinking about flying back today before the bad weather moves in. What's up?"

"Mail you should take a look at, I think. It's personal."

His BlackBerry had numerous security features. For Debra to call him on it about something personal, the reason had to be highly confidential, thus important. And it was likely something he didn't want to discuss in the presence of his brother and father. "I'm finished here. I'll definitely be up there later today."

By the time Drake reached Fort Worth, the rain had started and he was in his office. His assistant sat patiently across from him while he perused a thin sheaf of papers that included a young man's picture that looked like a mug shot.

The report in his hands was a summary of an investigation conducted by Pruett Security Services. He hadn't used the company himself, but he knew someone who used it regularly—Don Stafford. Neither the security company nor Stafford would have sent this information anonymously. The more Drake read, the angrier he became. A few bits of information jumped out at him as being similar to what his mother had said on the phone a few days ago.

"This came yesterday?" he asked Debra. "But you don't know where it came from?"

"No idea."

"You've read it. What do you think of what's in it?"

His assistant shrugged a shoulder. "This is the woman who went to Hawaii with you?"

"Yes."

"Honest opinion? I don't see anything damning in there. Who hasn't done dumb things as a kid?"

Thinking of his own younger days, Drake couldn't disagree. "What concerns me more than what's in it is who's responsible for it."

"Someone's trying to raise a stink," Debra said. "No doubt about it."

Mom? But how would she get to know one of the top corporate spy organizations in the Metroplex? Some of her friends at Riverside Country Club where she played golf? Had she indiscreetly discussed him and his activities with people who might not have his best interests at heart? The possibility only contributed to his simmering anger.

Then, there was a darker possibility than his mother. He had lost count of number of times Donna had called him since the night of the TCCRA party. He had never returned her calls. She was spoiled and determined to have her way. She was also scheming and small-minded enough to do something like this. He couldn't believe she and his own mother would be in cahoots, but the evidence glared back at him. And how had they learned who Shannon was? He thought he had been cautious about keeping her name from everybody.

He turned to the last page and slid it across the desk to Debra. "See that small logo on the bottom left corner? That's the name of the security company this came from. See if you can find out who ordered this."

"Will do, bossman."

After Debra left his office, he picked up the picture of Shannon's former husband and studied it more thoroughly. Based on what Shannon had told him, nothing about it was shocking or even surprising.

He checked his watch, then picked up his desk phone. His mother answered after only a couple of burrs. "Drake. I'm so glad to hear from you. Are you back from the Double-Barrel?"

Drake's jaw tightened. She and Dad had been talking. Otherwise, how would she know he had been at the ranch. "I'm in my office. How's it going today, Mom?"

"Not well. I had a golf date, but just look at the weather."

"Say, Mom, have you ever heard of Pruett Security Service?"

Silence. Then, "Uh…I'm not sure. What is it?"

The hair on the back of Drake's prickled. Oh, yeah. She knew the company. But Drake resisted believing she was complicit in a scheme to damage Shannon. "Remember seeing Shannon Piper's picture on that billboard outside Camden?"

More Silence. Then finally, "Drake, what's this about?"

Rage Drake had rarely felt coursed through his system. He checked himself to keep from shouting. "It's about a report I got in the mail, Mom. Sent anonymously. Your fingerprints wouldn't be on it, would they?"

"Drake, I tried to discuss this with you," she said rapidly. "But you cut me off and—"

"This is a smear-job. And it's despicable. Please tell me you haven't had personal contact with Shannon Piper."

"Don't be ridiculous. Why would I do that?"

"I don't know. I've never known why you try to get into the middle of what I'm doing. I just want the answer to one question. Is Donna Schoonover a part of this?"

Silence. Then, "She—she was kind enough to, uh—"

"Kind, my ass. I wonder if you even know what you've done."

"You will not speak to me like this, William Drake Lockhart. What I've done is try to save you from yourself."

"I don't need saving. You've exposed somebody I care about and her small business to a viper who's liable to do anything to cause trouble. And what's worse, I don't know how either you or I can un-do it. This is it, Mom. The last straw. No more of your meddling bullshit." He slammed the receiver back into its cradle.

His pulse pounded in his temples. He willed himself to calm down. He got to his feet and walked over to the windows, looked out onto the streets below. He had to protect Shannon. But how? He had no control over what Donna did or might do. And apparently he had no control over what a member of his own family might do.

Just then, Debra tapped on his door and stuck her head into his office. "Come in," he told her.

"Wasn't hard to find out. I called on an old friend. Apparently that investigation was done for the one and only Donna Schoonover."

Drake closed his eyes and shook his head. "Thanks, Debra."

All at once, all he could think of was going home. Chick had met him in the parking garage at Lockhart Tower and driven them to Lone Star Commons. The rain started before they reached the site, shut down the job and sent the workers home. Then Chick had delivered him back to his office. To get to his condo, he either had to walk or take a cab. The traffic snarl below him would be at least half an hour straightening itself out. He stepped out of his office and asked Debra if there was an umbrella in the office and she promptly produced one.

On his way home, he stopped again in front of the jewelry store display window. Through the veil of a steady rain, his gaze volleyed between the diamond and emerald wedding ring and the diamond encrusted heart necklace. One was a nice gift that meant one thing; the other meant something infinitely more profound. Then it dawned on him. There was one way to protect Shannon for damn sure. He walked inside.

Thirty minutes later, he walked out with a simple ring in his pocket, a style more suited to Shannon's personality than the splashy emerald-diamond style. When he reached the condo and checked with the concierge, he was told a guest, Tammy Harper, had come several times to swim. Drake was glad he had missed her.

At home, he set his crazy family out of his thoughts and placed the ring on the granite island in his kitchen. He studied it, perched and glittering in its black velvet box. He had told the jeweler he wanted the ring to let the recipient know how much she meant to him, yet be unpretentious.

The center stone that the jeweler had called a princess cut was a certified natural yellow diamond. Two lines of smaller white diamonds flanked the larger one in the middle. An investment piece, the jeweler had called it. Drake was no expert on jewelry, but he had to admit, it was as good-looking as any piece of jewelry he had ever seen. For sure, he could have bought something bigger and flashier, but Shannon might not like wearing it.

Now he had to decide the perfect way to present it to her. Thinking about the mischievous things he could do made him smile. He called her and got her voice mail. Instead of leaving a message, he sent her a text: *Busy week. Sorry not to call. Come up for the weekend.*

A couple of hours later, he received an answering text: *Can't. Sorry.*

What was that about? He re-read her text message. Was this a repeat of an old story—him waiting, her sending unclear signals and text messages? The last time, he had weakened and called her. This time, he would not. He was in no frame of mind for bullshit. If she wanted to talk to him, she would have to call. He walked back to the kitchen island and snapped the lid on the ring box shut.

Just then, the person who did call was Pic. He sounded breathless. "Drake, I just talked to Blake. Well, to tell the truth, it wasn't a conversation. It was an interrogation. They're adding a new name to their list of persons of interest."

"Who is it? You sound like it's you."

"That's not funny. It's Troy, Drake."

That news came like a punch. Drake's butt sank to the edge of the counter. "Are you shitting me? Why?"

"He doesn't have an alibi for that night. He's lied to them twice, so now they don't believe anything he says."

Drake's pulse began to thrum in his ears. "What kind of lies?"

"He first told them he was with a date in Fort Worth, but they couldn't locate the woman. So he gave them a different name. They couldn't find her either. Then he told them everything he had already said to them was wrong information and that he was really at a woman's house in Dallas. But he refused to give them her name or an address."

"Why?" Drake asked again, growing more disbelieving with every second.

"Well…if that's where he really was, she's married, Drake. He said he didn't want to damage her reputation."

Drake couldn't hold back a huff of impatience. "Is her reputation worth his ass?"

"That's exactly what I said to him. After I threatened to kick the shit out of him, he finally told me her name. Her husband's a politician. A *well-known* politician. You remember Duncan Fisk?"

The faint thrum in Drake's ears became a drumbeat as the fight or flight instinct spiked inside him. Fisk was a six-term congressman who sat on half a dozen powerful committees in Washington. He was no friend to agriculture and no friend of the Lockharts. Dad had locked horns with him many times over water and fences and more recently, permits for new gas wells. The family had actively opposed him in every election. His wife continued to live in Dallas most of the time.

Drake gave himself a few seconds to pick up his jaw. Finally, he asked, "Why am I just now hearing about this?"

"Calm down now. I'm just now finding out about it myself."

"Like hell. You told me Troy was with a woman in Dallas back when Kate's fire happened."

"I knew he was fucking around with somebody up there, but I didn't know her name. I thought it was probably some cute chick he met at a horse show."

"That description fits Dorinda Fisk. Except she's about ten or twelve years older than Troy."

"You know her?" Pic asked. Drake heard the incredulity in his brother's tone.

"She's a satellite friend of Donna Schoonover's. She's a cougar. Makes a hobby of collecting young guys. She puts pictures on Facebook."

"Jee-sus Christ. That sure is a set-up a horny kid like Troy might fall into."

"Does Dad know what Troy's doing?"

"I don't know how he would. I haven't mentioned it and Troy ain't talking to nobody."

Drake sighed for a third time.

"Troy said they asked him for permission to search his house and garage, but he refused to let them," Pic said.

"Goddammit, Pic—"

"It's no big deal, Drake.

"When the cops want to search your house, Pic, it's a big damn deal. Kate's fire took place back in December. It seems a little late after the fact to be searching somebody's house. Do you have any idea what they're looking for?"

"Nope. Troy said his conversation with Blake was casual. He said he told them he was gonna be gone and didn't want them in the house when he wasn't there."

"Where is he?"

"He and Kate pulled out for San Antone a little while ago. They're going to a horse show. What else is new?"

"That casual attitude on Blake's part is a ruse, Pic. They want to throw Troy off guard. If they decide to get a search warrant, they won't give a damn if he's there or not. In fact, they'd probably like it if he *wasn't* there."

"Guess being friends with Blake doesn't mean much," Pic said.

"You can't be that naïve, Brother. Rafferty's a cop first and always will be. Listen, we need to get on top of this. Get in touch with Blake and invite him and his partner to go through Troy's house. Set up a definite time. We'll go with them if they'll let us. I'm guessing they won't find anything, but if they do, we all need to know about it.

"Okay," Pic replied, his doubt traveling through the phone line. "You're coming back down here?"

"I'm on my way. Pick me up at the airport in a couple of hours."

"There's one more thing, Drake. You know the wealthy woman who went on Billy Barret's bond? It was Dorinda Fisk."

Possibilities flew at Drake like a bee swarm. "Well, fuck."

On his way to the airport, Drake's mind zig-zagged through all that had happened. Dorinda's putting up bail for Billy Barrett added a layer of conspiracy. But it probably didn't begin with Dorinda. She had impressed Drake as not being smart enough to put together a conspiracy to accomplish even something simple. Somebody had to be behind her pulling strings. He doubted it was her husband, but who could it be?

He thought about the cast of characters and what he knew about them. The cutting horse world was a vortex of money, booze, drugs and loose relationships. Both Donna Schoonover and Dorinda Fisk were part of a cutting horse investment syndicate. Dorinda was the ultimate, if aged, buckle bunny. What owning a cutting horse meant to her was an opportunity to meet young guys on the make. Like Troy. And even like he, himself, had been once. The recollection that he had been like that made his cheeks warm with embarrassment, even in the privacy of his truck cab.

There had been no love lost between the Lockharts and the Fisks for years and he already had a taste of just how pissed off Donna was. Had she and Dorinda conspired to somehow get even with him and the Lockharts by luring Troy into Dorinda's web and instigating mischief through him? Though Troy's last name was Rattigan, everybody knew he was Bill Lockhart's son.

Before boarding the plane, Drake sent a text to Troy: *You got trouble, hoss. Get your ass home. See you at the ranch.*

The search of Troy's house occurred the next morning with Troy still in San Antonio. Drake and Pic had been allowed to hang around outside. Neither of them knew what the cops were looking for, but as far as Drake could tell, nothing incriminating was found. Still, Troy's name was not removed from their persons of interest list. Nor was Kate's because of her close association with Troy. It was time to hire a lawyer to represent Troy and Kate both. A *criminal* lawyer.

Troy showed up late Friday. Knowing he could be in deep shit, he loudly proclaimed his innocence. Drake and Pic believed their little brother when he said he didn't know what was going on. The family circled the wagons and stood with him, but nobody could doubt that his association with Dorinda Fisk had something to do with something.

Troy said he had never heard of Billy Barrett, but it was obvious now to everybody that both Barrett and Troy were Dorinda's "boys."

In Troy's favor, incidents against the Lockharts had occurred before he met Dorinda, so was she a pawn or a player? More questions than answers had surfaced.

Unfortunately, now, Dorinda's husband had stepped in and the cops couldn't even talk to her. An appointment for an interview had been arranged for later. With the powerful friends Duncan Fisk had in Dallas, nobody could guess how much later.

"This ought to teach you to be cautious where you dip you wick, you little fart," Drake told Troy when he, Troy and Pic convened in the ranch house den.

Troy looked sheepish. His typical cockiness had disappeared.

Pic came to Troy's defense, confronting Drake. "Who're you to talk? Do you run a test before you put the moves on some chick? There used to be a time when you couldn't even name all the women you screwed."

"I grew up, Pic. It took a while, but I grew up. And it's time Troy did too. He's twenty-nine years old, forgodsake."

Another weekend came and went and Shannon heard nothing from Drake. No doubt the abrupt text she had sent him a week back had ended their affair. She had expected that. Drake wasn't a man a woman, or anyone, could toy with. She couldn't imagine that he would ever dive off a cliff over losing a lover.

A part of her wanted to wail, but a more sensible part believed it was better to have it over with than suffer a thousand tiny cuts. Reliving multiple moments like the one at dinner with the Penningtons in Lubbock would be too demoralizing.

Her alter ego must be pleased because it remained silent.

She blamed her blue mood partly on the time of the month. She went to bed Monday night expecting her period by morning. But on waking, she felt no telling cramps, no heaviness low in her belly. Tuesday was the same.

At her office, bouquets started showing up for her team members from their respective husbands and boyfriends and she realized it was Valentine's Day. She hadn't even noticed, hadn't even thought about sending a card to Drake. A traitorous part of her dared to sneak in and hope for something from him, but nothing came.

Her alter ego came to life. *What did you expect? It's over. He got the message. Get up, dust off your backside and get on with your life.*

"Amen," Shannon muttered to the air.

Thursday brought no sign of her menses either, nor did Friday. Panic set in. She had all she could do to get through breakfast with Grammy Evelyn. Once at her office, she closed herself inside her office and studied her calendar. Dismayed by what she learned, she called Christa on her cell phone.

Christa came on the line with, "Hey, what did Drake send you for Valentine's Day?"

"Christa, my period is four days late."

Silence on the other end. Then, "Jeez, Shannon. That could be a gift that keeps on giving."

"I'm never late. If anything, most of the time I'm early.

"Is there a reason for the problem?"

Shannon's forehead tugged into a frown and she winced. "I don't know. We weren't careful in Hawaii, but I've had a period since then. Every other time we've been together, we've used condoms."

But even as she said that, she couldn't keep from thinking about how careless they had been the night before they left for Lubbock.

"You should've gotten birth control pills, Shannon. Why didn't you?"

"I don't know. I just never took the time. Don't fuss at me. I can't take it today."

"I'm not, I'm not. But I'm sure I don't have to tell you that condoms aren't all that safe."

"Birth control pills aren't a hundred percent either."

"They're a hell of a lot more reliable than rubbers, girlfriend. But don't panic."

Shannon rolled her eyes. "Are you crazy? I'm about to jump out of my skin."

"Just go to the drugstore and get a test. I think they've got them now that can tell as early as a few days after you've missed a period."

Recognizing that reality waited as close as a shelf in the drugstore, Shannon began to tremble inside. "Oh, my God, I can't believe this."

As soon as she disconnected, she reached for her calendar and studied the months of January and February again. Lubbock. The time was right. That evening in his condo, when they'd had desperate sex and he had pulled out, then...she closed her eyes and shuddered. No telling what had been going on with the condom through all of that. And then later that same night, when they were both half asleep...

Dear God!

She was so distracted, she couldn't work. She left the office and drove out the highway toward the town to the south. No way could she walk into Walgreen's in Camden, where she personally knew most of the employees and buy a pregnancy test. Nor could she do it at Walmart, even at self-check. Someone who knew her might see what she was buying, might even strike up conversation about it.

She had never paid attention to the home pregnancy tests on store shelves. For more than two years, that particular condition hadn't been a concern. Now, as she stood in an out-of-town Walgreen's in front of the aisle where half a dozen brands of pregnancy tests resided, she realized just how much of a stress inhibitor the absence of that worry had been.

She set her jaw and chose the one that flaunted "early detection" and "99% accuracy," then, for good measure, she tossed three different brands into her shopping basket. At the cash register, she didn't use her credit card, wanted no traceable evidence. She sheepishly paid the $55.00, plus change, in cash. The bored teenage cashier gave no indication that she noticed that the neatly dressed professional woman handing over the money was on the verge of a hair-tearing, chest-beating fit.

That evening, after supper with Grammy Evelyn, she claimed fatigue and went to her room early. Twenty minutes later, she knew one thing she hadn't known this morning. She was pregnant. And she had no one to blame but herself. She was no teenage virgin. She knew plenty about sex.

She slept little through the night, trying to figure out what to do next. Between bouts of wakefulness, she made some decisions.

The next morning, she called Christa again and made a date for lunch. She needed the support of a friend. As they sat in a booth in Chili's and munched on southwest egg rolls, she told Christa her latest news.

"Oh. My. God, Shannon," Christa said. "You've got so much at stake. Maybe you should try another test. It's awfully early."

Shannon shook her head. "Christa, I spent over fifty dollars on tests. Three out of four were positive. For your information, there's one brand that claims it's accurate even before you've missed a period." She sat back against the booth's back and looked out the window. Gray clouds threatened. Appropriate. She sighed. "Looks like rain. No one will be looking at houses today."

"How does he feel about kids?" Christa asked.

Shannon turned back to the lunch for which she had no appetite. "We haven't talked about kids. We haven't been into future-planning. He's said his mother wants grandchildren, but I haven't heard him say he wants to be the supplier."

"Well, whatever. Even if he hates kids, he'll support you. I know he will. You said he's a decent guy."

Shannon nodded, remembering his remark after he had refused to partner with Robert Pennington. "He is. But hell, Christa, this is the screwiest fling I've ever had. I think we've broken up, but I'm not sure. I don't know if or when I'll hear from him again." She signaled the waitress. "I've got to get back to the office. I've been gone so much. I'm still trying to catch up."

The waitress hurried over with the check. "My treat," Shannon said, digging into her purse. She handed the waitress a credit card. "You know what's funny? The last time he asked me to come up to his condo, I said no. I didn't hear from him for almost two weeks. Then all of a sudden, I get a two-sentence text from him. All he wants is sex."

"But Shannon. A few weeks ago, that's what you wanted. You made a deal with him."

"Don't remind me. I still don't know why I did that."

"Yes, you do. You wanted to be with him, but you thought you could just have an affair and not get involved. That just doesn't work."

Shannon winced and sighed.

"I think this is the point where the heroine's friend says the phone lines run both ways," Christa said.

Shannon shook her head. "I don't want to discuss it with him on the phone. I couldn't have a casual conversation without blurting it out. Or breaking down."

The waitress returned with Shannon's credit card and a ticket to sign.

"You know where he lives," Christa said. "Just drive up there. Talk to him in person."

"I'm thinking about it." Shannon signed the check and handed it back to the waitress. "But I don't want to talk to him at all until I've made up my mind what to do. And until I've decided what to say. He's so persuasive. I want to have my own decisions already made and firmly in my mind.

They left the restaurant and ambled toward the parking lot. "You wouldn't be thinking about doing something drastic, would you?" Christa said.

Shannon shook her head. "I couldn't live with myself."

"Maybe you should go to the doctor. Make sure before you say anything to him." Christa reached into her purse and pulled out her iPhone, started scrolling with her finger. "I'll give you my OB's office number."

"No! I can't go to your doctor. My office sold him and his wife a house."

"You have to, Shannon. There aren't that many OBs in Camden. You can't be pregnant and not go to the doctor."

As another dose of reality slapped her, Shannon heaved a great breath. "Maybe I won't tell him, period. Maybe I'll just wait and see what happens."

They reached Christa's car and she unlocked the door with a bleep. "Kid-raising is hard, girlfriend. And doing it alone is even harder."

"You do it every day," Shannon said.

"Yes, but the boys' daddies are around. I get a little child support and a little moral support. I'm pissed off at one or the other of them most of the time, but they do help out.

"My life's always been hard, Christa. And I've always been alone. I'm not afraid of it."

Christa looped her arm around her and hugged her. "Oh, Shanny, I'm so sorry this has happened to you. You deserve better."

"I'm not sure I'm sorry," Shannon said. "I mean, look at my life. I'm thirty-three years old and I have no one but Grammy Evelyn. I've never had anyone. I can't even count on my sister. A little kid to love and love me back might be nice."

"You're brave, Shanny. And strong. I've always admired that about you."

Shannon huffed. "Thanks, Christa, but right now I don't feel brave and strong. Right now, I feel mostly dumb."

Christa's eyes misted over and she dabbed at them.

"Christa, don't cry," Shannon said, wiping away a tear herself. "If you cry, I'll cry." She managed a weak little laugh. "If anyone who knows us sees us, they'll wonder what's wrong. Then we'll have a bunch of explaining to do."

"Life's just so damned unfair," Christa said, sniffing back her tears. "Whatever you do, Shannon, it's going to be okay. Things have a way of working out. Both times I got pregnant, I thought the world would end. But I got through it and now, I wouldn't take anything for those kids. They make my life worthwhile. I rant about their daddies all the time, but I can't really hate those jerks. Without a few passionate nights with them, I wouldn't have the kids."

"That is what sex is supposed to be about, you know," Shannon said. "It isn't supposed to be fun and games. It's supposed to propagate the species."

Christa rolled her eyes. "Good grief, you're quoting the Discovery channel at a time like this?" She made a little nervous laugh. "But I'll say this. Looking at it strictly from an anthropological perspective, could you find a more perfect specimen to father your kid than Drake Lockhart? Even if you went to one of those sperm banks and prowled through their catalogs?"

They both laughed and Shannon felt better. "Listen, I've got to go. We didn't even talk about my five acres. What have you found out? The deal should be about ready to close by now."

"I've checked our log every day. But it's been a fruitless effort since we don't know the name of the buyer."

"Please keep looking," Shannon said. "I need something to go my way."

Drake returned to his office in Fort Worth on Sunday morning. He couldn't afford to spend more time at the Double-Barrel. He had already lost two weeks and problems and undone tasks were piling up in Lockhart Concepts.

Shannon still hadn't called him back. Though she was on his mind day and night, his pride wouldn't let him call her again. Their affair, or whatever it was, now seemed distant. And even done with. The very thought of that gave him a constriction in his throat.

He put coffee on to brew. The box that held the wedding ring still sat on the cooking island. Every time he saw it, he felt a pinch in his chest. He didn't open it. His next thought was did jewelry stores accept the return of diamond rings?

The coffeemaker pinged. He poured a mug, sat down in front of TV and turned on the golf tournament, debating if he should just drive down to Camden and see what the hell was wrong with Shannon. If she was already pissed off, what difference did it make if his showing up in Camden made her madder? He had lived by Silas Morgan's philosophy too long to give up easily on something he wanted. He wasn't ready to give up on Shannon. Not yet.

He knew she took her grandmother to church, so he could time a trip to where he would arrive early afternoon.

In the end, he decided to send a text. He had just pressed SEND when his landline warbled. When he picked up, the concierge told him a Miss McMillan was on her way up.

What the fuck? His grip tightened on his mug handle. He had put her name on the guest list so she could have access to the pool and the gym. Why the hell was she coming up to his condo? "Thanks. Tell her I'll meet her at the elevator."

He trekked up the hall toward the elevator and the glass entry door in the hallway where she waited for entrance. As he approached, the door glided open.

"Hi," she said, a wide smile showing snow-white, perfect teeth. *Good dentistry* was his first thought.

Today her long hair was tied back in a ponytail like she had often worn it when they were kids. "Hey," he said.

She stepped into the hallway before he could reply. "I came to go swimming." She walked through the doorway even before he invited her. "But I've got a few minutes. I'll let you show me your condo first. After the way your mom described it, I'm really excited to see it. Love the pool, by the way."

Mom. He might never get over being pissed off at her. He still hadn't come to grips with her and Donna Schoonover's sudden new alliance.

Before he could reply, Tammy started up the hall as if she knew where she was going and he had no choice but to follow alongside her. Mentally, he swore. Where the hell was his willpower? Why couldn't he make himself just tell her he didn't have time for this?

She angled a look up at him. "I think you're taller than you used to be.

He couldn't remember how tall he used to be. He said nothing.

She bumped his arm with her shoulder. "As I remember it, we were almost eye-to-eye. But now, I think I'd have to stand on my tippy-toes to kiss you."

Not taking the bait or flirting back, he ventured sideways, putting a foot of space between them.

"Love the posterwork," she said taking in the murals on both sides of the hallway's walls.

"It's not posterwork," he said, cranky-voiced. "It's original art. Painted by a local artist."

"Ooh. Impressive."

They reached his front door and he pressed in the combination that unlocked it. Once inside the condo, while slipping off her coat, she made the usual oohhs and aahhs that everyone made about the view.

It was colder than a witch's tit outside, but she had on a white top that looked sort of like a bra, sort of like a bathing suit top. Instantly, the male animal in him saw that it hooked in back and tied around her neck. One pull on the right string and it would be gone. She had on low-cut jeans that showcased a glittery object in her navel.

She handed him her coat and walked over to the window wall, giving him a view of her back and plenty of opportunity to admire her firm ass in skintight jeans. One of those tribal-looking tattoos peeked up from the edge of her glittery belt.

She looked to be tanned all over with no sign of bathing suit lines. Living in Arizona, she probably had not gotten that uniform tan in a salon. Her attire, or lack of it, and a visual of her tanning nude beside a pool set off a stir inside his shorts. More than two weeks had passed since he had last been with Shannon. Little stimulation was required for him to get hard. He diverted his attention to hanging her coat in the entry closet.

She walked around the living room/dining room, looking around, the heels of her high-style cowboy boots clacking against the hardwood floors. She strolled into the kitchen and he followed. "Nice," she said, running her fingers along the granite island.

Her top barely covered her nipples and didn't cover her breasts entirely. *Too round and too perfect to be real.*

He must have been staring because she stopped, ducked her chin and gave him an old familiar inviting look. "Yes, Drake. I had a boob job. Don't you remember how I used to complain about my flat chest?"

True, she hadn't been that chesty when they were kids. His face warmed. "Guess I forgot that."

Unsmiling, her eyes locked on his. "I had a very good plastic surgeon. Would you like to see?" She raised her arms, placed her hands behind her neck as if to untie the strap.

"No," he blurted. "Not necessary."

She shrugged, then frowned. "The only thing I hate is that my nipples are kind of numb. Don't you remember how much I liked it when you played with my nipples?"

Heat began to crawl up his neck. He said nothing.

She turned and walked over to the window wall again. "Is this all of it? Where do you sleep?" She made an abrupt turn and started back to the hallway, on her way to his two guest bedrooms where guests, if he had them, slept.

His composure a wreck, he gave himself a few seconds, then followed her and caught up with her in the largest guest room that also had a spectacular view.

"Who sleeps here?" she asked.

"Family sometimes."

She walked out of the room and back up the hall, then stopped and peeked back at him from around the corner. "I want to see where *you* sleep."

She ambled off in the opposite direction where she would find the master suite if she kept going. He followed. She circled the room, exclaiming about the view. When she wandered to the bathroom, he followed her there, too, and stood in the doorway, his back against the doorjamb, his arms crossed over his chest. At least the bathroom wasn't humid from his shower. He had showered and shaved before leaving the ranch this morning.

"On, my gosh, this is some shower," she said looking it over. She came toward him and passed through the doorway in front of him, her bare shoulder brushing his forearm. She gave him another inviting smile. "Looks like fun." She walked toward the bedroom door "Are you going to join me in a swim?"

His mouth had already gone dry; now his brow broke into a sweat. He swallowed. "I'm going to work pretty soon."

She stopped in the middle of the bedroom and faced him. "Are you still hot?"

His brow squeezed into a frown so tight it was painful. "What?"

"Hot. That's one of the things I remember about you. How good you were, even as a kid. You had so much…um, energy."

His whole head, face and body grew warm. "I don't know what you're talking about, Tammy."

She came to him and looked up at him with those inviting eyes. "Yes, you do," she said softly. "In man-talk, I think they call it stamina. And you used to have a lot of it."

Now he was embarrassed. "C'mon, Tammy. Cut it out."

She ran a manicured finger down his chest. "Remember that first time you went down on me? After we watched that porno movie when Mom and Dad were gone that time? How we tried all that naughty stuff? You blew my teeny little mind."

He caught her wrist and moved her hand away from his chest. "Tammy, I'm seeing someone," he choked out, even though he wasn't sure if things with Shannon were going to work out. But he had to believe they would get past this bump.

"I know. Betty told me." Her eyes traveled down and landed knowingly on the bulge at his fly.

"But see?" she said. "Here you are all excited and she isn't here. And *I* am."

He shook his head, grasped Tammy's arm and urged her toward the bedroom doorway.

"Okay, Okay. I get the message." She lifted her arm from his hand, stopped and looked up at him. "But if you change your mind, just call. I've been fixed, so there's nothing to worry about that way."

On the way back in the kitchen, her attention swung to the golf tournament on the living room TV. "Oh, I forgot about the golf tournament today. Is Tiger playing?"

He didn't believe she had forgotten about the golf tournament. She had been married to a pro golfer for chrissake. She probably knew the circuit by heart. And she had always been a wizard at sports statistics. She would know the day and time of every tournament everywhere and probably the players. "Not today. I was just going to get some coffee. Do you want some?"

"No, thanks."

Whether she wanted coffee or not, he did. As he refilled his mug, she picked up the ring box that still sat on the cooking island, opened it, then closed it. After a pause, she looked up at him, a crestfallen expression on her face.

Please, no tears, he prayed.

"The one you bought for me was bigger." She cleared her throat and set the box back on the counter. "Your mom said she thought you had never gotten married because…Anyway, I thought we might have a chance to—"

"Tammy, don't." He shook his head. "I'm going in another direction. And it has nothing to do with you."

She ducked her chin and toyed with a fingernail. "I see that." She looked up at him again, a glister of moisture in her eyes. "Going back to old times just for fun wouldn't be too much for me to handle, but I can see it's too much for you. You always did have this honorable streak."

Then just like that, she smiled brightly. "You don't mind if I watch a little of the golf tournament, do you?"

Chapter Forty

AS SHANNON AND her grandmother left church, the subject of today's sermon stayed in her mind—engaging in positive acts to garner positive results—had struck a harmonious note inside her and persuaded her to act rather than react to her circumstances.

She still hadn't made up her mind to rush up to Fort Worth and tell Drake he was soon to be a father. Then, after church, she found a text message on her phone: *I know you're mad at me, but I don't know why. I miss you. Please let me come down to Camden. Or come up here and tell me what I've done.*

That message and today's sermon made her decide it was time to drive up to his condo and tell him the news in person. Not to tell a man who had been your lover that he was to be a father was meaner than she could be. Who knew? He might be happy. Surely he had considered the possibility that she could get pregnant.

Sunday was the only down time he had in his fast-paced life. He used it to think and refill his energy well, so he would be home today. After she and Grammy ate lunch, she changed her clothes, putting on her best-fitting jeans and a thick green sweater that flattered her figure and enhanced her hair and eye color. They might have no future together, but she still cared about how she looked when he saw her.

She would tell him she didn't expect him to marry her, she mused, while she took extra pains re-doing her hair and makeup. They had known each other only two and a half months, which hardly seemed enough time to make a decision about the rest of your life. But in her heart, even unmarried, she hoped he would want to be a part of their baby's life.

Soon she was motoring toward Fort Worth with an unusual joy filling her heart. Now, for some reason, she could hardly wait to tell him.

When she arrived in Lockhart Tower's parking garage, she saw that both his pickup and his Virage were parked. She had been a guest here often enough for the concierge not to question her or call Drake and announce her arrival. She waved at him as she boarded the elevator. A case of nerves struck her as she zoomed to the twenty-eighth floor. She couldn't even guess what to expect when she told him the news.

She pressed in the code at the glass doorway, then quickstepped to 28C. Before she could press his door bell, the door opened and there stood a blond woman who must surely be a movie star. And her upper torso was practically bare. Shannon did a double-take, thinking at first she was at the wrong unit. "Hi," the blonde said.

Then Drake walked up behind the blonde, his eyes round as saucers. "Shannon!"

Shannon stared. For a moment, she stopped breathing. Finally, adrenaline took control of her brain and body. She turned and ran down the hallway toward the glass doorway.

When she reached the glass door, it glided open on cue and at the same time the elevator doors slid open. Drake's voice called behind her, but she didn't stop. She stepped into the elevator car and it whisked her away. Minutes later, she was in the parking garage and inside her car. As she exited the garage onto the street, through her rearview mirror, she saw Drake step out of the elevator into the garage.

Tears rushed to her eyes, but she continued blindly toward the highway that would take her home. Before she reached it, she began to sob. Hyperventilating, she turned off the road into a Red Lobster parking lot. After long minutes of weeping and self-flagellation, she composed herself, wiped her eyes dry and blew her nose. What was wrong with her? She couldn't sit in a parking lot and bawl. She had to get home.

As she pulled out onto the street, her brain finally engaged. That woman in his condo had a familiar face, like...Brittany Spears! His former fiancé, Tammy McMillan.

"Oh, my God," Shannon mumbled. "Oh. My. God." And he had told her he wasn't in touch with his former financé, had no idea what she was doing. He had lied to her, used her until something else he wanted more came along. Grammy Evelyn's words came down on her like a hammer: *...You must be careful. Those Lockharts, they're takers....They think the world belongs to them...*

How could she have been so naïve? How had she let him talk her into trusting him? He had spellbound her with sex. He was what she had feared in the beginning. She had seen plenty of evidence, but she had let herself be blind to it. Anger replaced grief.

She avoided the highway and headed for a seldom-traveled back road that took her south. Her phone bleated from inside her purse. She dug it out, saw *Unknown Number* on the tiny screen. She threw it back into her purse, hating him as much as she hated herself. A few minutes later it bleated again. And again. After half a dozen times, she pressed it to OFF.

Back in Camden, she couldn't go home, couldn't face her grandmother. Her face was red and swollen form crying. She made her way to Christa's house.

"Come on into the kitchen," Christa said. "I'm cooking. Ronald took both boys to the movies, so I'm baking him a pie. And I'm babysitting my sister's baby."

Ronald was Christa's first husband and the father of her oldest son. Christa's beautiful little niece, Victoria, just under a year old, sat on the floor playing with a plastic toy. Shannon had always thought she looked like a Gerber baby.

Babies suddenly engaged a block of Shannon's attention. She thought back to when she had gone to see Victoria at the hospital as a newborn. She picked her up and had an overwhelming urge to bury her nose against the soft little cheek. "Hiya, Vic."

She took a seat at the kitchen table and sat Victoria on her on her lap. "How old is Victoria now?"

"Eight months," Christa said, resuming her pie-making. "Can you believe it? She's such a good baby. Nothing like my rowdy boys."

The baby laughed and gurgled and touched Shannon's face. And from out of nowhere, tears rushed to Shannon's eyes and she began to sob. Victoria screeched. Christa rushed over and picked up the baby. "Shanny, what's wrong?"

"I'm so sorry," Shannon said. "I didn't mean to upset her." She grabbed a baby wipe from a box on the table and dabbed at her eyes. "I just got back from Fort Worth."

"What happened?"

"He was with a woman. His fiancé from years ago. I suspected there was a reason he took so long to call me and now I know why."

The baby calmed when handed a cookie. Christa returned her to the floor to play. Then she pulled her chair close and listened while Shannon told her the whole story between bouts of weeping and nose-blowing.

"You don't know why she was there," Christa said.

"She was half-naked."

"Maybe there's a logical explanation."

Shannon gave her a flat look.

"Okay, maybe not. But it doesn't matter. If he doesn't know about the baby, you can't presume he doesn't want it or that he doesn't want you," Christa said.

"He's a womanizer, Christa," Shannon said with finality, her speech thick from the crying jag. "I'd never be able to trust him. I shouldn't have trusted him already. Even if he wanted to do something crazy, like marry me, I couldn't. My God, in the two months I've been with him, I already know of three different women he's slept with. I've been face-to-face with two of them. Who knows how many there are?"

Christa gave a huge sigh. "Men can change, Shanny. Maybe it wasn't what it seemed. You need to give him a chance to explain. If you're going to have his baby, you can't just shut him out without giving him a chance."

Shannon rolled her eyes. Calmer now, she got to her feet. "I'm going to go, Christa. I don't want to be here when Ronald brings your kids back and have him see me crying."

They walked to the front door together. "No matter what happens, I'll be here for you," Christa said.

Shannon gave her a wan smile. "Thanks, Christa. You're the best friend I have. Meanwhile, I have to stop bawling. Every time I turn around I'm breaking into tears."

"It's hormones. Your hormones are all screwed up. Being pregnant does that."

Shannon at last went home. Her grandmother made no comment about her swollen eyes and red face, for which Shannon was grateful. While they ate supper, Grammy Evelyn chattered away about Arthur and church and making cupcakes for the children at church. She was making an effort at being nonchalant.

Instead of watching TV with Grammy Evelyn, Shannon went to bed. She had never been so tired in her life. Solitude and sleep were what she needed now. And intestinal fortitude. At some point, she had to tell her grandmother about her condition.

Shannon set out the next morning determined to have a normal day without tears. She had many blessings for which to be thankful. She was healthy. She had loyal friends and associates. Her business was doing better than most of the real estate offices in Camden.

Her team members went out early, leaving her alone with the receptionist. After a busy morning, she was thinking about lunch when the front door chimed and she could tell from Chelsea's conversation something had been delivered. She left her office at the end of the hall and walked up to the reception room. There she saw Chelsea holding a tall vase with a beautiful bouquet of blood-red roses.

Drake! They were too elegant and looked too expensive to be a gift from a team member's husband.

"Oh, my Lord," Chelsea said with an ear-to-ear grin. "There's two dozen of them And they're for you." She plucked a card from the ribbon and handed it over.

Shannon took the card, but said to Chelsea, "Just put those somewhere out here in the reception room."

Inside her office, she slid the card out of its small envelope and read the familiar printing: *DRAKE.*

One word. Typical of his ego. She tore it in half and dropped it in the trash can.

When the workday ended, Chelsea put on her coat to go home. Shannon gave her the roses, telling her she didn't want them to be a topic of conversation in the office.

The next day, at about the same time, the same florist brought two dozen white roses tied with a red ribbon and another card: *LET ME EXPLAIN.*

This time, her team members all giggled and teased her, but she didn't share the message with them. Knowing Chelsea lived near the hospital, Shannon asked her to take the flowers to Mrs. Bates, one of their customers who'd had surgery.

On Wednesday, a padded envelope arrived in the mail. Inside, Shannon found a small gold heart pendant and yet another card: *DAMMIT, PICK UP YOUR VOICE MAIL.*

Indeed, she had ignored his calls, hadn't even listened to his messages. She wasn't taking orders or even suggestions from him anymore. Flustered, she stuffed the heart back into the envelope, took it and one of Drake's business cards out to Chelsea and instructed her to mail it to Drake's office address.

The week and weekend passed. The middle of Monday morning, Christa called. "Are you sitting down?"

Her tone had an ominous ring. "What's happened?"

"Your five acres closed at Star Title in Dallas. I've got a friend who works there and she called me. The buyer is Lockhart Concepts, LLC. That wouldn't be Drake's company, would it?"

For a moment, Shannon thought she had suffered a lung collapse. She couldn't breathe. She dropped to her desk chair. "Do you—do you have the address"

A pause, then Christa came back on the line. "It's a downtown Fort Worth address."

An adrenaline rush like she had never known blasted through Shannon's system. She began to shake. She had never experienced blind rage, but this must be it.

Her thoughts collided as she put together all that had happened. He must have known weeks ago that she owned the adjacent thirty acres. Five acres wasn't large enough for most commercial projects. Discovering the owner of surrounding land would be the first thing any land investor and speculator would do so he could try to buy it. Yet Drake had said nothing to her. He had betrayed her in the most ruthless way he could have and he hadn't even had the guts to say anything to her face. No wonder she hadn't heard much from him after the Lubbock trip.

"Shannon, are you there?" Christa asked.

"I need to hang up, Christa," she said in a steely voice she almost didn't recognize.

Shannon stared at the phone as another painful reality slowly sank in. A wave of nausea threatened to send her racing to the bathroom, but she swallowed a few sips of water and managed to keep down breakfast. She was as exhausted as if she had run two miles. She left her office, went home and threw up in her bathroom.

Grammy Evelyn fussed over her and tried to nurse her, but all Shannon wanted to do was lie down. She sat down on her bed, toed off her high heels and did just that. She drifted to sleep, but awoke an hour later still tired and hungry. She padded to the kitchen and pulled a container of yogurt from the refrigerator and joined Grammy Evelyn in front of the TV.

Her grandmother questioned her, but she explained she must have caught a bug. She had never discussed the five acres with Grammy Evelyn, didn't want to do it now. A heart-to-heart with her grandmother would come soon enough.

Monday. The gold necklace Drake had sent to Shannon had arrived back in his office. No note, no message. After Shannon had run into Tammy and raced away from his condo, he had driven like a madman to Camden, but she was neither at her office nor at home. He had even parked at the end of the block down from her grandmother's house and waited for a time for her SUV to appear. When it hadn't, he had driven back to Fort Worth in a more depressed state than he had ever been.

He had sent flowers, he had called and texted and left messages, but gotten no response to anything he had done.

Life's events did turn on a dime. He couldn't believe how quickly and how easily the fragile trust he had worked so hard building with Shannon had been shattered.

At a loss, he had finally done the thing that cured most of his ills—he immersed himself in work, determined to keep himself too busy to think about Shannon Piper. Or Tammy McMillan. Women brought more chaos and disorder into his existence than anything else he could think of.

He couldn't accept that she no longer cared until he heard it from her mouth. Today was the day. No matter what else happened, he intended to see her today and explain Tammy being in his condo.

He was signing documents, catching up before leaving his office when Gabe's head popped through the doorway. "Hey, boss."

"Come in, Gabe."

"I've been trying to catch up with you for a couple of weeks. You know that little piece of land on the highway down in Camden County? The one we picked up for the company? The one another buyer kept bidding up?"

In a different compartment of his brain, Drake recalled that Gabe had told him someone was bidding against him on the five-acre parcel and he kept having to up the ante. "The five acres?" Drake asked, preoccupied with the paragraph he was reading. "What about it?"

"I got distracted by nailing down those leases in Dallas, but now I've gotten back to the five acres. I've been doing some research on the surrounding properties. I think there's a sweet deal to be had. Remember me telling you that one lady, all by herself, owns the thirty acres all around it? Add the five acres, and you've got a perfect five-acre square on the corner of a major highway and a county road. Perfect location for a big box or a super C-store. Even a truck stop."

Now Gabe had Drake's interest. Lots of little old ladies sat on valuable undeveloped real estate in small towns. He willed his thoughts away from his emotional turmoil and set aside his papers. "Sounds good. Who's the owner?"

"Lady named Shannon Piper."

A surge of adrenaline shot straight to Drake's brain. "Who?"

"Shannon Marie Piper is her name. It's three different parcels, including the one that's got that old vacant house on it. Probably ought to be torn down."

All of his instincts told Drake something was wrong with the scenario Gabe had just presented to him. He just didn't quite know what. That same instinct told him he had better find out. "Leave the information with me," he told Gabe. "I'll take care of it."

"If we list all of it, I'll get both ends of the commissions, right?"

"No problem." Drake's mind locked on Shannon and Camden. "Listen, Gabe, I need to finish up what I'm doing. Shut the door when you leave, okay?"

"But Drake—"

"We'll talk tomorrow," Drake said, pulling his desk drawer open and rummaging for Shannon's business card. He had avoided calling her at her office, knowing she didn't want her personal life aired inside her business. At the moment, he didn't care. He had to talk to her. He pressed in her office number.

When she came on the line, he said, "Shannon, don't hang up. This is Drake."

"I know who it is." Her voice came across the line brittle as glass.

"Don't hang up," he said again.

"Do not send me flowers. Do not send me gifts. Do not ever call me again." *Click!*

Frustration didn't describe the flash that ignited within Drake. "Goddammit!"

He marched out of his office, stalked home and got in the Virage. Forty-five minutes later, he was parked in front of Piper Real Estate Company in Camden.

Inside, he came face to face with a young receptionist. He asked for Shannon.

Recognizing Drake's voice, Shannon left her desk chair and strode up the hallway to the reception room, saw him in front of Chelsea's desk. "What are you doing here?"

He looked as he typically looked for work. Boots, starched and ironed jeans and a beautiful lavender button-down shirt.

"Shannon, I—"

Thunk! Chelsea knocked over a mug of coffee. It spilled across her desktop. "Oh, damn," she said. "Please excuse me." She sprang to her feet and dodged Shannon, bumping her shoulder, on her way to the bathroom. Shannon followed her. Together, they returned with a roll of paper towels.

A wave of nausea gripped Shannon. Her hands shook so badly, she knocked over a pencil holder, splaying pencils and pens all through the puddle of coffee. "See what you've done," she said to Drake, on the verge of breaking into tears.

"Let me," Drake said, and took the paper towel roll from her.

Chelsea stepped out of the way and he calmly sopped up the coffee and returned the pens and pencils to their holder. Afterward, he stood wiping his hands and looking into Shannon's eyes. "Can we talk?"

Her team members had come into the reception room and began scurrying around, helping Chelsea put her desk back together.

"You can come into my office," she said coldly. He followed her and she shut the door behind him. "Make it quick. I'm busy."

"I appreciate that. So am I....Look, I'm sorry to just show up. But you weren't communicating and—"

"There's nothing to communicate. I've already gotten the message. And by now, you should have, too."

"Can't you just sit down and listen to what I have to say?"

Shannon was in no shape for this. She was clammy and sweating, her head was spinning and she struggled not to throw up. She sank into her desk chair, barely managing to glare up at him. "You've got five minutes."

"That woman in my condo? That was Tammy McMillan. We used to be engaged. I told you about her when we were in Hawaii. We were watching a golf tournament."

"She was half naked. And I don't care who she was."

"She came to swim."

"In your living room?" She shook her head then and raised both palms. "I don't care who you screw."

"Don't say that. You have to care. She came to go swimming and that's it." He sliced the air with a flattened hand for emphasis. "The golf tournament was on TV and she sat down to watch it a minute."

Shannon huffed. "I don't believe you." She dropped her damp forehead into her hand.

Drake had never been so frustrated. He shoved his fingers through his hair. "Shannon, forchrissake. You've got to believe me. Because it's the truth."

"I know you," she said shakily. "And I know your reputation. You're nothing but a…a…a taker!"

He gave her a squinty look. "A what?"

"You steamroll everyone. You take everything in your path. What you can't take, you buy. Then when you finish with it, you just throw it aside and move on."

"My God, is that the kind of man you think I am?"

She got to her feet and looked him in the eye. "I don't know what kind of man you are, or who you are, really. I thought I did. I believed you. I was starting to believe in us. Now all I know is I can't trust you. It really was just sex." Sobs broke from her throat.

Drake's heart wrenched. She was the last person he ever wanted to make cry.

"You—you took my land," she said. "My land that I needed. It was my future….I've been trying to buy it for two years and you overwhelmed the seller with your money and…and God knows what you did to seal the deal."

His eyes bugged as facts became clear. "You were the other bidder?"

She glowered up at him.

Deep regret squeezed his heart again. He should have paid more attention to what Gabe was doing, especially knowing he was dealing with land in Camden. "My God, you were."

Now her lower lip trembled, which did another number on his heart. "Shannon, I didn't know. I wasn't the one doing the deal. It was one of my associates. If I'd known, I would've—"

"It doesn't matter now," she said bitterly. "I blame myself. I knew I shouldn't have trusted you. I let you pull the wool over my eyes. And now you've shown me who you really are." She got to her feet, sobbing and babbling. "I went up to Fort Worth to talk to you….To make some plans…so you could be a part of the baby's life. But now, I—"

His stomach lurched. His eyes felt as if they might jump out of their sockets. "Baby? What baby?"

"*Our* baby!"

"You're pregnant? But how…"

He stepped back and wilted to the wicker love seat across from her desk. She was pregnant? He was going to be a father? White noise roared inside his head. He was having trouble breathing. He couldn't have been in worse shape if somebody had whacked him across the knees with a ball bat.

Her voice became as distant as an echo. "…don't want you around us. No way would I want the influence of a charlatan on my child….It's bad enough she'll have your genes. We'll get by without you….Go back to Fort Worth. Leave me alone."

"No," he said, finding his voice. He leapt to his feet. "No. You don't mean that. You don't get to do that."

"I do mean it."

Suddenly, she sank to her chair seat, grabbed her trash can and wretched into it.

Stunned, Drake rounded the end of her desk, snatched tissues from a box on the corner of her desk and tried to help her wipe her mouth. "Shannon, my God, what's wrong? Do you need a doctor?" He straightened and yelled for the receptionist, who appeared in the office doorway. "She's sick," Drake told her.

The receptionist dashed away. Other women came from somewhere and appeared in the doorway, all of them looking at him with a jaundiced eye. The receptionist returned with damp paper towels.

"I'm okay, Chelsea," Shannon said, dabbing at her forehead and mouth. "Honest. I'm okay now."

"Are you sure?" Chelsea asked. "Do you want some water. Some Seven-Up?"

"I'm fine, y'all," Shannon told them. "Please. Just go back to work."

To Drake's relief, they faded away. He placed his hands on her shoulders. "Look at me," he said softly. "Shannon, you're it for me. I'll do anything to be with you. I'd do anything *for* you. Don't you get that?"

She shoved a wad of tissues against her nose. "I want you out of my life."

He pulled her up and against him, wrapped his arms around her. He squeezed his eyes shut as emotion almost overwhelmed him. "Shannon, I—I've fought it. I know I've been clumsy, stumbling around, but I—"

She wasn't responding, he realized then. She was standing still as a statue. Rigid, even. He set her away. The fire in her eyes roasted him. "Get out of my office," she said.

He stepped back, staggered by the ice in her voice. He stared at her for a few beats, but her expression remained unchanged. Wounded and at a loss for words, he walked out.

Chapter Forty-One

DRAKE SLUMPED OVER his desk, unable to concentrate on the document in front of him. He had never been so lost. His heart had never hurt so much. He still hadn't recovered from the initial shock of learning Shannon was pregnant. He thought they had been careful, but he would try to figure out when and how it had happened later.

At the moment, he had to figure out how to solve the problem at hand, which was rejection by the woman he now realized he loved.

He had been taught—and believed—that success came as a result of problem solving. He couldn't think of when he had faced a dilemma he couldn't resolve, rarely failed to persuade someone to agree with him.

He had intended to propose before he learned she was pregnant. If the latter new development hadn't occurred, he believed she would have accepted. Now that she was going to have his baby, she wouldn't speak to him. The irony of that would be almost humorous if his heart wasn't affected.

Outside, rain poured. He paced more. He had to make her understand there was nothing between him and Tammy, that none of the women he had ever known had been important since he met her. That was a tall enough mountain to climb, but equally important to Shannon, he had to make her understand that he had not schemed against her in a business deal. But how? What could he say?

His assistant came in with a steaming mug of coffee. "You okay in here?"

He accepted the coffee. "Just trying to understand women," he said with a bitter laugh.

"Good luck," Debra said. "I don't think you're the first man who's ever tried to hurdle that fence."

She turned and started for the door, but he stopped her. "Tell me something. If a woman won't talk to you, how do you get through?"

She shrugged. "You need something irresistible."

"Like a diamond ring?"

"Lord, no. Something that's soft and sweet and helpless. Like a kitten or a puppy."

He frowned. "An animal?"

"All girls are suckers for kittens and puppies. Don't you know that?"

He had never had a kitten, but he liked puppies himself. "A puppy?"

His assistant shrugged. "It's one of those nurturing things. I know you're dense about relationships, bossman, but you surely must know women need something to love and take care of."

He thought about Shannon's grandmother's cat. He had never heard her say she hated pets. "I guess I have been a little dense in that area."

"You need to narrow your focus. Think about this. I just happen to know that the city pound has one of those adopt-a-pet programs going on right now. All week on TV, they've been showing the ones that are about to be put down. I just hate to see that."

"You're trying to tell me something."

She shrugged. "I'm just saying…"

Shannon was a strong woman with a formidable will, but she had a soft heart. The idea was worth a shot. "Where's the pound?"

"Over on the east side, by the Loop."

He walked over to the coat closet and pulled out his coat. "I'm leaving for the day," he said.

Her lips tipped into a huge smile. "Remember. Something little and cute and helpless."

"I'm not little and cute, but in this situation, I'm damn sure helpless."

He trekked back to his condo, shoved the diamond ring he had bought in his pocket and headed for the pound.

He reached Camden mid-afternoon. In his backseat, he had a dog-collar, a dog sweater, a doggie bed, doggie toys, a bag of Puppy Chow and a big red bow. In a fiberglass pet carrier, the cutest female half-grown puppy he had ever seen slept. He had found her at the pound, in line for euthanasia. The keeper at the pound said her name was Prissy and he believed her to be a purebred Bichon Frise. She was the last of a whole litter an owner had brought in.

Drake hadn't hesitated. From there, he'd had her checked out by a veterinary friend and paid extra to have her moved to the head of the line to be groomed at a pet grooming shop. Now she was clean, fluffy, snow-white and perfect. She looked like a stuffed toy. He stopped in a gas station outside the city limits of Camden, tied the bow around Prissy's neck and attached the velvet pouch that contained the ring box.

At Shannon's office, he was told by Chelsea that she had gone home. The girl had been reluctant to give him directions to Shannon's grandmother's house, but when he showed her the puppy and told her his intent, she cooperated.

He parked out front of the Victorian mansion, gray with white gingerbread trim, a white picket fence and a trellis that probably had roses growing over it in the summertime. Maybe even yellow roses. He gathered the loot and his will power and made his way to the front door.

Shannon answered the door and stood there with a blank expression on her face. She eyed him up and down. “What’s this?”

“Please. Let me come in.”

Her eyes misted. “Please don’t do this. I don’t want to be upset. It’ll worry my grandmother if she sees me upset. She still doesn’t know what’s going on.”

“Please, Shannon. A business meeting. No upset.”

Her chest rose and fell with a huge sigh, but she invited him in and led him to a formal parlor that looked like something out of an old western movie. She was still dressed for work in a sharp green suit and high heels. She looked beautiful, but she would be even more beautiful if he could just put a smile on her face. He set his packages on the floor.

“What is this?” she demanded, looking at them. Just then, Prissy barked. “Is that a dog?”

He opened the pet carrier and lifted Prissy out. She began to fidget and lick with her little pink tongue and strain toward Shannon. In spite of the tension, Drake smiled. “Look, Shannon, she already loves you.” He stepped nearer, putting Prissy within Shannon’s reach and capturing her eyes. “As do I. Honest to God, I do.”

His profession of affection went ignored, but she didn’t ignore Prissy. She hesitated, then reached out and rubbed Prissy’s head with two fingers.

Drake took advantage of the moment. “Her name’s Prissy.” He placed the dog in her arms. He could see her open up, could see that maybe, just maybe, he had hit a homerun. Prissy played it to the hilt, snuggling and licking and squirming.

Shannon fingered the pouch tied to Prissy’s collar. “What’s this on her neck? I said I didn’t want you to bring me a present.”

“It isn’t a present. Just look at it.”

“I don’t need gifts,” she said, but she untied the pouch and peeked inside. She looked up at him, not fooled. A jeweler’s ring box was hard to disguise.

“Just open it. Just look at it,” he said. “See what you think. I’ve had it for a few weeks.”

Without letting go of Prissy, she eased down to the edge of a fancy little red sofa’s cushion. He wanted to sit down beside her, but the sofa looked so fragile, he feared it wouldn’t hold his added weight. He took a seat across from her a few feet away. Her breath caught when she opened the box. She looked at him. Prissy looked at him, too and gave a puppy bark.

"We can make it, Shannon," he said softly, trying to hold her eyes with his.

She started to say something, but he raised his palms, stopping her. "I know what you're going to say. You're going to say we haven't known each other long enough, but how long is long enough? If I didn't believe we belong together, I wouldn't be here now. Shannon, I've always believed it, from the first time I saw you."

She sniffled. "I have a hard time dealing with the surprises you keep throwing at me. I told you I don't want to be hurt. And our arrangement was no sharing."

He sighed. "It was a goofy agreement designed to fail. I knew that, but it was what you wanted and I was willing to try it just to be with you. I haven't been sharing, Shannon. I swear to you, I haven't."

"You seem to have an awfully long list of admirers."

"I can't erase the past. Neither can you. I promise you, there hasn't been anybody but you since the minute I saw you at that TCCRA party. You're all I think about, Shannon. I want to grab onto the future we can have together. I've never felt that way about any other woman."

Prissy let out a snore that belied her size and changed the tenor of the conversation. She had snuggled on Shannon's lap and gone sound asleep.

"This is a house dog," Shannon said. "I don't know if I can have it. You know my grandmother has a spoiled cat."

"If it doesn't work out, I'll take her to live with me."

She nodded. "I'll see." Then she got to her feet, tucked Prissy under her arm and handed the ring back to him. His heart sank.

He stood up, too, only a foot away from her. Every part of him wanted to take her in his arms. He stepped close to a small table beside a chair, opened the ring box and placed it on the table. "I'm going to leave this right here. When you get time, maybe you'd like to take a look at it. Maybe even try it on. It's a size seven."

She looked down at her hands. "I don't have any rings. I don't know what size I wear."

Hope inched forward within his chest. Maybe she was tempted. "Not a problem. If it doesn't fit, we can have it fixed. I love you, Shannon. And I'm excited about the baby. What do I have to do to show you?"

"I don't know right now. I'm still trying to come to terms with it myself. I guess I can let you know."

Training Prissy and Arthur to live together took much of Shannon's time the next few days. Prissy was enthusiastic; Arthur was sarcastic. Drake called every day just to chat, something he had never done.

Shannon was a wreck. She was also insane. What sane woman would have turned down a marriage proposal from Drake Lockhart? And a big diamond ring that was now tucked into her lingerie drawer?

One who was terrified, that's who.

*...I love you, Shannon. And I'm excited about the baby....*The words played over and over in her mind. She had never expected to hear them fall from Drake's mouth.

...I can't erase the past. Neither can you. I want to grab onto the future we can have together....

Had he somehow learned about her past, the part she had so carefully guarded? She wouldn't be surprised. She had to admit that her past was probably just as worthy of question as his. Yet, he had never questioned her. He had taken her as she was on blind faith. Why couldn't she make herself be equally open-hearted?

Because she knew how real estate brokers worked, she might be convinced that he didn't know about her thirty acres, but believing he had no feelings for his former fiancé was harder. The woman was beautiful and she had been in his condo. Shannon knew, because Drake had told her, that few women ever were ever invited to his condo. And she was pretty sure the ones who had been there had slept with him. The thought was as painful as a stab.

But he had sworn he had been faithful. And he had never lied to her, something she couldn't say about herself.

She missed him. She liked him. Adored the time she had spent with him. She had already admitted, at least to herself, that she loved him.

And now Christa's words pestered her: *....You need to give him a chance to explain. If you're going to have his baby, you can't just shut him out without giving him a chance....*

And while all of that swirled inside her head, he called. "Hey," he said. "How you doing today?"

"I'm good," she said and couldn't keep from smiling.

"Are you sick or anything?"

"Only when I brush my teeth. There's something about toothpaste."

"Really?" he asked, sounding interested and concerned. "Is that unusual?"

"I don't know," she answered.

"How's it going with Prissy and your grandmother today?"

"She's won Grammy over. Arthur's coming around. I don't see them ever becoming close friends though."

"I was thinking about coming down to visit her today."

"Prissy?"

"Sure. I'm her savior."

"I suppose that's okay. Grammy Evelyn's at home all day."

"You won't be there?"

She hesitated. She was gripping the phone as if it might spring out of her hand if she let go. “I, uh…I guess I could be.”

“Would you? It’s important.”

“What time are you coming?”

“I can be there by five.”

And he was. Shannon stood behind the front door and watched as he strode up the brick sidewalk to the wide front porch. Holding Prissy under her arm, she opened the door and met him. He tickled the puppy’s head with his finger. “I’d call this a lucky dog,” he said, grinning his cute half grin. She loved his grin.

His expression turned serious. “Can we sit down and talk? Maybe in the parlor like we did before?”

Her pulse rate accelerated. No doubt this visit was about the baby. She led him into the parlor and took a seat on the sofa as she had before and he sat down in the chair across from her. He pulled a blue-backed document out of his coat’s inner pocket. She stiffened. She was right. He was about to hand her some kind of legal document related to her baby.

“I figured out what you were trying to do with that five acres,” he said.

She lowered her eyes and stared at the dog. Okay, not the baby. He was going to try to buy the whole thirty acres from her. A payoff.

“I know why you needed it.” He offered the blue-backed document to her. “This is the deed. It’s yours. To do whatever you want to with it.”

She stared at him, “But I can’t take that. I won’t take it. Your agent, he’s owed a commission. You said—”

“Gabe will get his commissions.”

She blinked in confusion.

“This deed has a condition attached to it, Shannon.”

Of course it did. Wasn’t he the master negotiator? “I should’ve known.”

“It’s a wedding present.”

“But—”

“We can make it, Shannon. I know you’re scared. I’m a little scared, too, but I love you. I believe you love me. We can make it. We just have to take that step.”

He got to his feet and went over to her, grasped her shoulders and drew her to her feet. “I need you. My life’s been a mess this past couple of weeks. One thing I’ve learned is I can’t be happy if I don’t have you with me or near me. I’ve never had these feelings before. I want to take care of you. And I want to make a home for the baby, where he’ll grow up secure and happy. Do you think I’d let my son run around the world without me to guide him?”

Now she was really a wreck. Her knees wobbled. “But—but…we’ve…we’ve…Oh, God, I’m stuttering.”

He smiled. “You can’t say the words? Just the words. That’s all you need to say.”

But the words seemed to be stuck in her throat.

She knew only one thing. She could no longer fight this battle. She didn’t know what lay ahead, but she had to take the risk. She broke into tears and pressed her face against his shoulder. “I do love you, dammit. I didn’t plan to, but…”

He rubbed her back, kissed her temple. “I know, baby, I know. It was just sex. We’ll get it all sorted out.”

She sniffled. “I promise you, if you ever cheat on me, I’ll stab you in your sleep.”

Drake squeezed his eyes shut, fighting back tears of his own as he stroked her back, caressed her neck. She had saved him.

He had cleaned up his act in short order. After seeing that he had bought a ring, Tammy had given up. He had told Heather he planned on getting married and they would have no further contact. He had told Donna that if she did one more thing to harm Shannon, he would tell her father that she had used his security company for a nefarious purpose, something that would incense Don Stafford who placed high value on his reputation as an ethical businessman.

Just then, his cell bleated and he recognized Pic’s ringtone. Pic always called at inopportune times, but with Troy’s future hanging, Drake didn’t dare ignore the call. “That’s my brother,” he said. “Something’s going on at the ranch. Is it okay if I take it?”

She nodded.

Still hanging onto her with one arm and pressing her against his side, he keyed into the call. “Hey, Pic.”

“Drake, they’ve re-arrested Billy Barrett,” Pic said. “And he’s talking.”

ABOUT THE AUTHOR

Anna Jeffrey is an award-winning author of mainstream romance novels as well as romantic comedy/mystery. She has written six romance novels under the pseudonym of Anna Jeffrey and two as Sadie Callahan. She and her sister have co-written seven comedy/mystery novels as USA Today Bestselling Author, Dixie Cash. She is a member of Romance Writers of America and several of its chapters. She enjoys many hobbies—reading, painting and drawing, crafting, needlework and beading among others. She and her husband live outside a small town in North Central Texas.

You can keep up with her on her website: www.annajeffrey.com
On her blog, www.annajeffreyauthor.wordpress.com
On her Facebook page at Anna Jeffrey Books
On Twitter, annajeffrey@annajeffrey and on LinkedIn.

Or you can write to her at annajeffrey22@yahoo.com

If you enjoyed THE TYCOON, please recommend it to friends, readers' groups and discussion boards.

CPSIA information can be obtained
at www.ICGtesting.com
Printed in the USA
LVHW03s1553150818
587067LV00016B/1716/P

9 781481 887250